BEFORE THE BATTLE

In the night, Mangus Coloradas peered at the flickering lights of the White Eyes encampment, and then, farther south, at the fires of the Mexicans. Never had he viewed so many enemies. He raised his fist into the air as he spoke to his men. "The People have been given this land by Yusn, and the White Eyes are not greater than He. If the White Eyes refuse to let us live here, we will make them pay for every valley with their blood and bones."

In the American camp, Lieutenant Nathanial Barrington listened to a veteran sergeant. "Lieutenant, I been in a few scrapes afore, and the only thing to do is just go all-out and fight like a son of a bitch. Don't ask for no quarter, don't give one."

And a thousand miles away in New Mexico, young and beautiful Maria Dolores Carbajal wondered what would happen to her family and her if the Apaches chose this time to attack, or if the Yankee invaders reached her home on the Santa Fe Trail.

The battle the next day would not end the struggle for any of them ... but only mark the beginning of a tidal wave of conflict that would sweep up them all. ...

DESERT HAWKS

←————————→

Volume One of
The Apache Wars Saga

by

Frank Burleson

𝒪
A SIGNET BOOK

SIGNET
Published by the Penguin Group
Penguin Books USA Inc., 375 Hudson Street,
New York, New York 10014, U.S.A.
Penguin Books Ltd, 27 Wrights Lane,
London W8 5TZ, England
Penguin Books Australia Ltd, Ringwood,
Victoria, Australia
Penguin Books Canada Ltd, 10 Alcorn Avenue,
Toronto, Ontario, Canada M4V 3B2
Penguin Books (N.Z.) Ltd, 182–190 Wairau Road,
Auckland 10, New Zealand

Penguin Books Ltd, Registered Offices:
Harmondsworth, Middlesex, England

First published by Signet,
an imprint of Dutton Signet,
a division of Penguin Books USA Inc.

First Printing, December, 1994
10 9 8 7 6 5 4 3 2 1

 REGISTERED TRADEMARK—MARCA REGISTRADA

Printed in the United States of America

To Deborah

ONE

U.S. Army tents lined the grassy swales of South Texas, unit flags undulated in the breeze, and firepits provided light for soldiers preparing for war. It was May 7, 1846, and the Mexican Army was straight ahead on the road to Matamoros.

American President James Knox Polk had ordered General Zachary Taylor's Army of Observation to the Rio Grande, because the Mexican government refused to negotiate over Texas. Then Mexican President Mariano Paredes had dispatched General Jose Mariano Arista and his Army of the North to drive them back. Cannons, musketoons, and bayonets had become the ultimate diplomatic gestures, with mass carnage scheduled for early tomorrow morn.

The smack of a flintlock hammer could be heard in the 3rd Infantry Regiment, while somebody laughed at an off-color joke in the command post tent of the Second Dragoons. Letters were written home, Bibles consulted, and hidden quantities of food consumed, because dead men have no appetites.

On picket lines soldiers tended nervous horses dancing in the small spaces allotted them, for the smell of gunpowder was in the air. Other soldiers swabbed out the bores of cannon in Major Sam Ringgold's Flying Artillery Battalions, confident that their new quick deployment tactics would demolish the Mexicans.

Soldiers without duties tried unsuccessfully to sleep, while the Texas Rangers, a hell-raising bunch that served as the army's scouts, played seven-card stud beside a campfire. No one hated Mexicans more than the Texas Rangers, because all had lost friends and family members in the War for Texas Independence.

On the eve of bloody confrontation, one lone U.S. Army staff officer strolled along at the edge of the encampment, hands clasped behind his back, as he gazed at endless expanses of mosquito-infested gulf plains. The insects had left his exposed skin covered with welts, but his most important concern was whether he'd be alive tomorrow night.

Lieutenant Nathanial Barrington was six feet two inches tall, wide of shoulder, with a thick blond beard and mustache. Recently graduated from West Point, he'd been posted to the traveling circus known as General Taylor's staff, becoming an errand boy with gold shoulder straps.

Nathanial Barrington had read the Federalist Papers, Ben Franklin's autobiography, and the works of Thomas Paine, but he knew the Mexicans had their own traditions, ideals, and blood sacrifices. They wouldn't surrender Texas without a fight, and tomorrow General Taylor would rip right into them.

Nathanial couldn't help reflecting that General Arista purportedly possessed the best cavalry in the world and outnumbered the Americans. He narrowed his blue eyes and peered south from whence the slaughter would come.

It troubled him to know that not all of America backed the Army of Observation on that perilous night. According to newspaper reports, many citizens considered President Polk's policy nothing more than unconstitutional land theft, while others viewed it as America's manifest destiny. Ralph Waldo Emerson, the intellectual light of New England, had denounced the war in an uncharacteristically passionate speech on Faneuil Square, while William Allen of Ohio, chairman of the Senate Foreign Relations Committee, had stood on the floor of that chamber and argued

that Texas was part of America and must be defended
at any cost.

Some claimed Mexico City was too far away to administer Texas efficiently, and eighty percent of the
population were Americans anyway. Others said the
Mexican Army hadn't been able to defend Texans
against Indian depredations, so they'd forfeited rights
to the land. Nathanial was a native New Yorker, but
whenever he consulted a map, it seemed obvious that
California, Texas, and Oregon—and everything in between—should be part of one great nation, the United
States of America.

If the stew had bitter flavors, it was because successful annexation of Texas would create a new slave
state, upsetting the delicate balance in the Senate, and
possibly leading to civil insurrection. America had
been convulsed since the Missouri Compromise of
1820 over the slavery issue, and now it intruded into
every cranny of national life, including Nathanial's
possible funeral.

Nathanial saw his ancestors staring at him from the
skies above Texas, and swore to do his duty despite
doubt, fear, and the slavery issue. He visualized a
lump of jagged metal slicing him in half, and wanted
to run for the hills, but instead, to distract himself
from the doubtless horror of tomorrow, reached into
the pocket of his blue tunic and withdrew a small daguerreotype of a tall slim blond woman with a half-
amused smile, gazing into the camera.

Her name was Layne Satterfield and she now wore
his engagement ring. They'd had the picture taken one
night during a walk down Broadway. They'd been
early for the theater, so out of curiosity stopped at
one of the new picture galleries near Chambers Street.

Nathanial reflected upon the threads of fate that
delivered him to Texas on that night of nights. Once
he'd wanted to become an Episcopalian priest, and
during another period had considered working for his
uncle Jasper, a stockbroker. Another uncle, Caleb,

owned ships, and Nathanial could've gone to sea, but didn't appreciate small enclosed places with unwashed men for two years. Instead, he might end in a cold dank Texas grave.

Nathanial swallowed a lump in his throat, as he contemplated the termination of his existence. He wished he'd lived a more responsible life, but he'd never turned down a glass of liquor, and had visited houses of ill fame when the mood struck him.

He still believed in what the Bible said, but life had become complex as he'd grown older. He'd studied all the great philosophers, but not one had shown how to die at an early age. Judgment Day has arrived, he told himself, smiling grimly. He clasped his hands together and closed his eyes. "My God—please help me." He felt alone, afraid, and prayed that he wouldn't show the white feather before his fellow officers.

He heard the advancing footsteps of Timothy Reardon, a Texas Ranger with a long brown beard, green canvas shirt, deerskin trousers, and a Colt Paterson pistol in his hand-tooled leather holster, slung low and tied down. "What'cha doin', Lieutenant?"

"I was wondering what time we'd run into the Mexicans," lied Nathanial.

The Texas Ranger scratched beneath his armpit, where a louse had taken residence. "The sooner the better, I'd say. Let's git this damned mess over with." Reardon peered at Nathanial suspiciously. "You ain't skeered, are you?"

"You're damned right I am," Nathanial replied honestly.

Reardon grinned, then slapped Nathanial's haunchlike shoulder. "So'm I. Be a fool not to." He yanked his Colt, aimed it between Nathanial's eyes, and smiled cruelly. "This is the only thing a greaser understands. Give 'em a-plenty tomorrow, and they won't stay around long."

"Would you mind pointing that in some other direction?"

Reardon persisted in his aim, as if trying to communicate a seminar on gun and knife work. "They won't know what hit 'em once we open fire. Lissen, Lieutenant, I been in a few scrapes afore, and the only thing to do is jest go all-out and fight like a son of a bitch. Don't ask fer no quarter, don't give none, and if a cannonball comes with yer name on it, jest a-swaller it down and keep on a-fightin'."

It didn't occur to Nathanial that people other than Americans and Mexicans might reside in the vicinity. But examining Nathanial and the Texas Ranger at that very moment was an Apache chief named Mangus Coloradas, lying among juniper and stunted mesquite trees on a nearby mountain, trying to understand the incredible encampment sprawled before him.

Mangus Coloradas had heard reports of the *Pindahlickoyee,* the White Eyes, invading his ancestral homeland, and he'd ridden south to see with his own sharp eyes. Fifty-three years old, surrounded by subchiefs and warriors, Mangus Coloradas focused on stacked rifles and rows of bronze cannon gleaming evilly in the moonlight. He estimated that the White Eyes and *Nakai-yes* Mexicans had more warriors in the vicinity than the entire population of the People!

Mangus Coloradas presented a staunch facade for his warriors, but was staggered by what he saw. He knew that both sides would clash tomorrow, and the desert would be drenched with blood. Maybe they'll kill each other and leave the People alone, hoped Mangus Coloradas.

The fighting chief knew that the land was immense, and the People could always escape the Mexicans, but now the White Eyes were coming in great numbers, and he wondered how many would follow. He gazed at the White Eyes' encampment, and its size obliterated the walls of his mind. The White Eyes are like

ants covering the face of the earth, he thought. How
can we avoid conflict with them?

Approximately one thousand miles to the north-
west, a sweaty horse and vaquero rider galloped down
the main street of Las Vegas, New Mexico. "The
Americanos have invaded!" he hollered. "It's war!"

He rode past the church, where choir practice ended
abruptly. A young woman in the front row, Maria Dolores Carbajal, looked up from her hymn book, her
heart beating wildly. War?

Twenty years old, Maria Dolores had auburn hair,
brown eyes, and a shapely body. Taller than the other
women, she followed Father Juan and the rest of the
choir out of church. The rider headed toward the
headquarters of the military governor, General Manual Armijo, and Maria was swept along by the crowd
as she experienced terrible premonitions. The Americanos possessed a powerful army that had twice defeated England, the world's greatest power. When the
Americanos wanted land, they merely took it under
any pretext.

The crowd coalesced as the rider climbed down
from his stained saddle. The front door of the building
opened, and General Armijo stepped outside, followed by his wife, family, aides, and guards. The courier bowed low. "Sir, the gringo army has crossed the
Nueces River, and General Arista is organizing the
defense of the nation."

Maria Dolores became apprehensive as she fingered
the rosary beads suspended from her neck. She'd seen
Americanos pass through Las Vegas on their way to
Santa Fe, and they'd all seemed to despise Mexicans.
Sometimes the Americanos made lewd suggestions as
she collected money at her father's store, but she'd
learned to smile and pretend she hadn't understood
their English.

Consternation verging on panic swept across the
crowd as the courier completed his report. There were

rumors that the Americanos intended to enslave Mexicans as they had the Negritos, and Maria Dolores contemplated picking cotton or growing rice for gringos, with a whip across her backside whenever she slowed down.

General Armijo faced the crowd, placed his fists on his hips, and declared, "Townspeople—do not be afraid. No exertion will be spared to protect you, and I will send today for reinforcements from the south. There is no need to panic—the Americano Army is not in this vicinity, but if they come, we will be ready for them."

Maria Dolores didn't believe General Armijo, for her father had said he was a liar and conniver for whom bribery was a way of life. His method of dealing with Indians was brutal repression, which had only made matters worse. Many of Maria Dolores's relatives had been killed by Indians, and the Apaches had driven her father out of the family ranching business.

Maria Dolores turned toward the east, from whence the Americanos would come, and there was no question that General Armijo couldn't stop anybody. We must get out of here, she concluded, but where can we go? She felt trapped, doomed, and destined for an early grave, but Jesus had taught that glory awaited she who had faith to move mountains.

Las Vegas was an important stop along the Santa Fe Trail, and the American Army would come eventually. What will they do to us? wondered Maria Dolores. Will they really make *me* a slave?

General Zachary Taylor, known as Old Rough and Ready to the men, sat at the collapsible desk in his command post tent, studying a map. Sixty-one years old, he was short, heavyset, with caterpillar eyebrows and a large nose. He'd been a farmer's son raised on the Kentucky frontier, and his great-grandfather had served as a lieutenant colonel in the Continental Army.

General Taylor wore loose-fitting blue jeans, a long tan linen duster, and his old floppy-brimmed straw hat hung on a peg extending from a tent pole. Unlike General Winfield Scott, dubbed Old Fuss and Feathers, General Taylor preferred comfortable civilian clothes, informal manners, and the occasional chaw of tobacco. He looked up from the map and spit a long, thin stream of brown juice into a polished brass cuspidor engraved with a scene from the Black Hawk War, in which then-Colonel Zachary Taylor himself had captured the rebellious Chief Black Hawk.

General Taylor's command comprised three thousand men, more than half the Regular U.S. Army, and the fate of the nation lay in his callused hands as he perused terrain features on which the upcoming battle would be fought. He knew that large-scale military operations depended on many complex factors, and Lady Luck was always throwing her loaded dice onto the table. Old Rough and Ready was no philosopher of war like Napoleon Bonaparte, or a master technician such as Lord Wellington, yet his aggressive take-it-to-'em style had won battle after battle, usually against superior odds.

All generals travel with retinues of aides, factotums, and orderlies, and General Taylor was no exception. He turned to one of his young staff officers near the front of his tent. "Lieutenant Barrington," Taylor said. "I'd like to have a word with you."

The officer appeared surprised, as if someone had awakened him from a dream. He threw back his shoulders, came to attention, and replied, "Yes, sir?"

General Taylor inspected the officer carefully. Lieutenant Barrington was physically everything the general wanted to be: young and tall, instead of a rotund gentleman of a certain age. Moreover, Barrington was a West Point graduate, whereas General Taylor had risen through the ranks during the expansion of the army prior to the War of 1812.

"You should get some sleep, Lieutenant Barrington. I'll need you to be alert tomorrow."

"I was on the way to my tent when you called, sir."

"Tomorrow should be an interesting day. Remember your training, follow your orders, and you'll be just fine." General Taylor leaned back in his chair and spit another stream into the cuspidor. "The worst part of war is the goddamned noise. Well, good night, Lieutenant Barrington. See you in the morning."

Lieutenant Barrington snapped a West Point salute, performed a smart about-face, and marched out of the command post tent. Like most of the junior officers in the camp, he considered General Taylor a great combat commander, but Old Rough and Ready had many critics, some of whom considered him a crass and vulgar fool. Nathanial knew from personal observation that the general combined many qualities in varying proportions, as did everyone else, and character was no simple subtraction lesson.

He passed a campfire of Negro slaves singing softly in a strange lilting beat. They were owned by Southern officers, and he could've bought one for a thousand dollars in the New Orleans slave market, but had hired a creole orderly instead.

Nathanial considered slavery a clear-cut evil, though he did not pretend to carry the solution in his back pocket. He approached his tent, where a candle burned inside its dirty white canvas walls. Pushing the flap aside, he saw his two tentmates sitting on the ground. One was Lieutenant Beauregard Hargreaves of Charleston, South Carolina, and the other, Comte Philippe de Marsay, an observer from the French Army. Lamplight washed their bearded faces, studded with mosquito bites, as they smoked cigars and passed a silver flask of cheap local whiskey back and forth.

"Have a seat," said De Marsay, making a grand gesture, as if in his parents' castle in Burgundy.

Barrington joined them, and Beau threw him the flask. "Have a drink."

Nathanial knew he should keep his mind clear, but one swig might help him sleep. He raised the flask and took a gulp, which scorched his innards all the way down. He wanted to say something clever or droll, but the prospect of real battle rendered everything inconsequential by comparison.

De Marsay tapped him on the shoulder. "Do not take it so hard, *mon ami*. Five hundred years from now, no one will know that we were here, and if you mentioned Frederick the Great or even Napoleon, people would ask who they were. After all, life is just a passing shadow, as your Shakespeare said."

The comte was tall, rangy, light blond, and wore a cynical smirk. He could be living in luxury in France, with pretty servant girls bringing him any delicacy he desired, but instead was a student of war.

Lieutenant Hargreaves, a West Point classmate of Nathanial's, would also face his baptism of fire on the morrow. He had dark brown hair, was shorter than Nathanial, and had a husky build. "How are you feeling, Beau?" Nathanial asked.

"I'm going to kill some Mexicans," the South Carolinian replied, raising his Colt Paterson. "That's all I know."

Why can't I be a regular fellow like these two, Nathanial asked himself. If I die—so what? But I want to marry Layne Satterfield, I miss the Hudson River in summertime, and I do not want to return to New York in a pine box.

"Hey," Beau said, "don't get serious on me, soldier."

Nathanial forced himself to smile. The flask came around again, and he took another swallow. He wiped his mouth with the back of his hand and said, "I just had a talk with the general. He said to get ready for the noise."

"You cannot hear yourself think on a battlefield," agreed the Comte de Marsay, "but who needs to think? In war, it is best to act. That is why I admire your General Taylor. He is not one to sit in a hotel behind the lines and wait for something to happen. Audacity is everything in battle. I have complete confidence in him."

"So do I," agreed Beau. "And the men are spoiling for a fight with the Mexicans. They remember the Alamo and Goliad, and they're going to give 'em hell tomorrow."

Nathanial wanted to make a ringing declaration, but felt strangely dispirited. The rotgut whiskey simmered his brain, and he imagined himself decapitated by a random cannonball. Layne would probably marry somebody else. She was too beautiful to remain single for long.

He wanted to look at the picture of her, but not in front of his friends. Yet, in the glow of cheap whiskey, he could evoke her flawless cheekbones easily. Many men had pursued golden-tressed Layne Satterfield, but she'd selected him, Nathanial Barrington, out of the pack of hounds. Sometimes he felt like the most fortunate man in the world, but occasionally suspected something wrong with her judgment, for she could have done far better, in his opinion.

The Frenchman broke out a half loaf of brown bread that he'd bought from a vendor who'd set up his wagon at the edge of camp. "Is it not strange," he declared, "that whenever I contemplate fundamental questions, I am forced to the conclusion that my happiest times have been with women? I revere God, of course, for He has made us all, but I'd rather have a *jeune fille* beside me than all the rosaries, crucifixes, and theology in the world."

Lieutenant Hargreaves agreed. "I met a gal in Charleston once. Her father owned a restaurant that I frequented, and she was working as a waitress. I took one look at her and, boys, I'd do anything she told me."

The Frenchman twirled his mustache. "Surely you are not going to end there. Did you ... ah ..."

"It required considerable expenditures of time and money, but yes, I'm pleased to say we did. I'd always believed that if I ever achieved that dream, it could never match my expectations, but to my surprise, our hours together far exceeded them. Whenever I become unhappy, I think of fair Melanie."

The French aristocrat and Southern cavalier turned toward the New Yorker, to hear his confession regarding females. "I think of Miss Satterfield constantly," he admitted. Now he had an excuse to take out her picture again. "She has ennobled my life, and if I die tomorrow, I will not have lived in vain."

The Frenchman burst into laughter, spilling a few drops of precious whiskey. "Let us not become too extravagant in our praise, for we all know the little darlings can be quite awful at times. They are called the delicate sex only because you do not feel anything as they slice off your balls. It is only much later that you realize you have been defeated by an expert yet again."

Beau accepted the bottle, threw back his head, and his Adam's apple bobbed up and down. He grunted and wiped his mouth with his sleeve. "Just when they tell you they love you, and will do anything for you, that's when they're planning to leave. If you really want to be honest, and cut out the poetry, you can't trust any of them. As for the nagging, it was Shakespeare himself who said, *What do they want?*"

"If I did not need them so badly," added De Marsay, "I would not have anything whatever to do with them."

Again, they were curious to receive Nathanial's point of view on the fair sex, but he didn't consider tender moments with Layne Satterfield a topic for campfire conversation. "Miss Satterfield is an exemplary person, and I don't believe she has ever lied to me."

"At least not that you are aware of," replied the

worldly Comte de Marsay. "The little angels believe their 'harmless' fabrications are facts."

"But they're so delicious," said Beau, whose eyes were becoming glassy. "The only thing that bothers me about death is no more women."

"How do you know?" asked the comte. "Perhaps there are wonderful orgies taking place amid the flames of hell. But let us not become morbid, *mes amis*. Tomorrow brings battle, and we must set the right example for the men."

Nathanial gazed at the candle sitting on the ground, and saw naked men and women writhing amid the flames. The rotgut had gone to his head, and he imagined himself decomposing, with worms and bugs nibbling his putrescent flesh. My mother, father, and brother will give me a funeral with full military honors, but I'd rather be alive.

His mother would probably faint when the missive arrived with news of his death, while dear father would behave normally, because that officer was careful never to betray human emotions, while young Jeffrey had never known his big brother well, and probably would carry exaggerated memories. Thus I'll pass into eternity, Nathanial reflected philosophically.

"Let's get some sleep," said De Marsay. "It's going to be a rough day tomorrow."

He blew out the candle, and its acrid odor wafted through the open flap, along with squadrons of mosquitoes on the prowl. The officers lay on their blankets, swatted insects, and listened to the sounds of the encampment around them as coyotes howled in distant caves and a red-tailed hawk flew across the face of the moon.

Mangus Coloradas selected a campsite surrounded by piñon and willow trees. He ordered the horses picketed, and then the remaining warriors sat in a circle on the ground and waited for their leader to speak. The great chief Mangus Coloradas peered through the night at the flickering lights of the White Eyes' encampment, and then, farther south, he could see the fires of the Mexicans. Never had he viewed so many enemies, and his imagination was overwhelmed.

He couldn't comprehend a chief who gathered his warriors in one spot, and then threw them at the guns of their enemies. Mangus Coloradas's brow wrinkled as he pondered the riddle. The People never fought unless assured of victory. They specialized in hit and run attacks and cleverly concealed ambushes. To stand before your enemy and offer yourselves as targets seemed the pinnacle of madness to the chieftain.

Yet the White Eyes possessed powerful medicine, and Mangus Coloradas wondered why Yusn the Lifegiver had awarded them such gifts? Mangus Coloradas was deeply shaken, as were all his warriors. They witnessed a spectacle that their minds struggled to digest.

"Perhaps they will not stay long," said Mangus Coloradas. "Or better yet, perhaps the Mexicans and White Eyes will destroy each other."

The words of Mangus Coloradas sank into their hearts, then the warrior and subchief Cuchillo Negro spoke. "What if they don't leave?"

"Then we will have to fight them."

"But how could we defeat them?"

Mangus Coloradas turned toward Cuchillo Negro. "We are few in number, but there are many ways to kill a man's spirit." The chief balled his fist and raised it into the air. "The People have been given this land by Yusn, and the White Eyes are not greater than He. If the White Eyes refuse to let us live here, we will make them pay for every valley with their blood and bones."

Nathanial opened his eyes in the middle of the night, and at first didn't know where he was. For a moment he assumed he was back at Corpus Christi, but then remembered that General Arista was over the next rise, preparing for war.

His companions snored softly, but he couldn't get comfortable on his blankets. Again, he found himself contemplating the upcoming battle from which there was no escape, and he knew that even generals occasionally were killed by stray projectiles.

He was no foreigner to death, for disease had run rampant at Corpus Christi, and he'd attended many funerals. Yet he'd never suffered so much as a cough, and his vitality was high as ever.

He decided to get some air and pulled on his boots. It was the dead of night, a horse neighed on the picket line, and the sky was splattered with brilliant swirling constellations. He headed for the edge of the encampment.

"Halt!" shouted a voice. "Who goes there!"

"Lieutenant Barrington."

"Advance, sir, to be recognized."

Nathanial stepped forward, and the sentry appeared in the moonlight, aiming his rifle at the officer's heart. "Sorry, sir," apologized the soldier, whom Nathanial knew as Kramer, one of the many German immigrants in the unit. Private Kramer brought his rifle to present arms and saluted the West Pointer.

Nathanial saluted back. "Quiet night so far, I hope?"

"Yes, sir, except for the mosquitoes."

"Carry on."

Nathanial ambled away, staring at distant mountain calligraphy bathed in moonlight. What's Kramer fighting for? he wondered. Did he enlist so he could get a free trip west, or is he looking for his own farm, something he couldn't afford in Germany?

The wealth of the Barringtons couldn't extricate Nathanial from the Mexican War, and only memories were available to help him through the final hours before battle. He withdrew the daguerreotype of Layne Satterfield and feasted his eyes upon those gently curving lips. Oh, my dearest, if only I could be in your arms right now.

They hadn't been formerly introduced by family or mutual friends, but instead, he'd spotted her by chance one day while walking on Bond Street. He'd thought her the woman of his dreams, tall, blond, with finely chiseled features and a bright manner. He'd lacked the courage to approach a total stranger, so they'd passed like ships in the night, and he wondered if he'd ever see her again.

A few weeks later, at a birthday party on Fifth Avenue, he'd been surprised to see the same woman across the parlor, surrounded by admirers. He engineered an introduction through the good offices of his mother, the most perfect social animal in the world, and finally met the nymph of Bond Street, Miss Layne Satterfield, niece of a banker who had done business with his uncles, because everyone in Nathanial's social milieu was connected to everyone else by dollars and cents.

And thus had begun their great love. He'd even told her, after they'd become good friends, about seeing her on Bond Street. They decided that they'd been destined to meet, like Romeo and Juliet, Tristan and Isolde, and so on.

Can love conquer death? he questioned as he gazed at her picture. If not, her blond hair will contrast dramatically with her black satin dress as she weeps over my grave.

He saw himself getting shot out of the saddle, and shuddered in the morning breeze. What am I doing here? he asked himself. Why in the hell did I ever become a soldier? He grit his teeth and struggled to settle himself down. I've got to be a man, he admonished himself. The soldiers shouldn't see their officers frightened.

His meditations and prayers were disturbed by the bugler blowing reveille. A soldier cursed in a nearby tent, the camp awakened. The day had finally arrived. Nathanial saw the first faint reddening of dawn on the horizon.

All he could do was march back to his tent. I will be a West Point officer to the end, he swore. He walked with his stomach in, chest out, chin in, and shoulders squared, while men spilled out of tents all around him. The star-spangled American flag fluttered in the morning breeze as Nathanial placed his hand on the silver and gold handle of his sword. My loyal friend, you may travel back to New York with my corpse, but today we will fight for Texas, Old Glory, and the officers' corps.

TWO

"Where the hell've you been?" asked the Comte de Marsay, gazing at Nathanial suspiciously.

"Checking the picket line," lied the frightened West Pointer, but he walked sturdily and confidently.

Lieutenant Beau Hargreaves looked to him skeptically, then shrugged.

Beau's slave and the orderlies of Nathanial and Philippe arrived with three buckets of water which they lined in a rank in front of the tent. The officers stripped to their waists and washed themselves, then brushed out their hair and beards. Each understood the importance of appearance, because leadership was twenty-five percent theater, twenty-five percent intelligence under fire, and fifty percent chance.

Nathanial's blue tunic fit his muscled form perfectly, thanks to his Spring Street tailor. He wore a gold braided collar, gold shoulder straps, highly polished brass buttons, a white belt, and a white leather strap diagonally across his chest and back. He set his blue forage cap low over his eyes, the gold star of America gleaming in front. On his right side, snug in its holster, was suspended his Paterson Colt, purchased from a Texas Ranger, and far superior to one-shot flintlock pistols then in general use. On his left, the scabbard contained his saber, a graduation gift from his parents, its handle shaped into the head of a hawk searching for prey.

The slaves and orderlies struck the officers' tent, then loaded personal belongings onto a wagon. Comte de Marsay pulled on his gauntlets, then set his tall black shako at a rakish angle. He also wore a red and green vest, tight black riding pants, and high-topped boots, the uniform of the 15th Legion Hussars.

"Well, gentlemen," he said, "it appears that it is time to go. Good luck to both of you, and I look forward to our usual whiskey before retiring tonight."

They shook hands and smiled bravely, because each knew that his whiskey days might be gone forever. The comte, as an observer, wouldn't participate in the battle directly, but that didn't mean he couldn't get killed. Nathanial and Beauregard, on the other hand, would be in the thick of it.

"I am reminded," said the comte, "of the 1834 revolt in Paris. It was my first experience of actual combat, and I was, I confess, concerned about my skin. But I soon learned, during the course of that rather hectic time, that if it is your time to die, then all any of us can do, really, is go down like officers."

Beau nodded in agreement. "Do you think we might have one last little sip of that whiskey, in case the flask happens to get lost."

The comte reached into his back pocket. "How rude of me to forget, but even I, who have been a target on many occasions, am a little tense, I confess." He peered down the road to Matamoros, made sure no Mexicans were approaching, then screwed off the cap and passed the flask to Beau.

The son of Charleston threw his head back and took a long deep swallow, securing as much whiskey as decently possible. Then he straightened, turned purple, and passed the flask to Nathanial, who said, "A coffin or a promotion—what the hell," and proceeded to guzzle the volcanic amber liquid.

Last to drink was the comte, and he realized with dismay that there wasn't much left, so he polished it off, rescrewed the lid, and said in an odd voice, "You have been fine companions, and I look forward to entertaining the both of you in France someday."

Staff officers were gathering in front of General Taylor's tent, and no one wanted to be late. Side by side, the three musketeers strolled among soldiers dismantling the campsite as tension and anxiety crackled the air. Nathanial examined the faces of the men, and all seemed resolute, like himself.

A crowd of officers was milling in front of General Taylor's command post, but Old Rough and Ready had not yet emerged. Orderlies set up a table, and a cook placed platters of biscuits and bacon upon it, with a pot of coffee and tin cups.

The officers breakfasted quickly, and Nathanial observed the old veterans carefully, for his guide to behavior. They appeared bluff, confident, discussing dispositions, tactics, strategy, and the sorry state of the Mexican soldier.

"You know how the Mexicans recruit their men?" asked Captain Charles A. May of the Second Dragoons. "They send a detachment to the nearest village, pick out the best men, and march them away under the gun. I'm sure you can appreciate that soldiers like that will not have the highest morale."

What about the famous Mexican lancers? wondered Nathanial, but he kept his mouth shut. This wasn't the time for reality, but for pumping up each other's confidence.

"The Mexican Army," said Captain Seth B. Thornton, also of the Second Dragoons, "doesn't know what a real war is. All they've ever done is put down the rebellions of hungry peons. They won't be able to stand up to us, and by the way, their weapons are the discarded junk of Europe. Isn't that right, Marsay?"

"Yes, sir," replied the attaché. "They have old Prussian muskets, much slower than your new percussion models, and much less reliable. You also have superior cannon. I do not see how you can lose, if you want my professional opinion."

The tent flap was pushed aside, and General Taylor appeared with his wide-brimmed straw hat perched firmly on his head. He looked like an old Kentucky dirt farmer as he sat at the head of the table and munched biscuits calmly, apparently unconcerned about the Mexican Army.

Men will live or die today according to the decisions of that old man over there, thought Nathanial. I wonder how history will document this battle, and whether my name will be mentioned. Despite his fear, Nathanial wished he were leading his own company of dragoons, instead of being a fancy messenger boy.

A horse and rider approached as the meal was coming to an end. It was Timothy Reardon of the Texas Rangers, with patches of sweat on his dirty canvas shirt. He climbed down from his horse, marched toward General Taylor, threw a ridiculous unmilitary salute, and said breathlessly, "The greasers are set up and a-waitin' about eight miles down the road, sir."

"How many would you say?" asked General Taylor.

"Five, six thousand, sir. Maybe more, 'cause some is hidin' in the woods. They calls the place Palo Alto 'cause there's tall timber in the area."

General Taylor finished his cup of coffee calmly. "Time to move out, gentlemen."

Orderlies waited with horses as the officers mounted up. General Taylor sat upon his favorite, Old Whitey, a most uninspiring nag, in Nathanial's opinion. The army coalesced on the road like a huge lumbering beast as the sun rose in the sky. Officers rode up and down the line, shouting orders, as the men sweated and cursed.

Nathanial noted that General Taylor wasn't very impressive in the saddle, for he tended to slouch like an old man. The general and his staff rode to the head of the column, and all the soldiers gazed upon their commanding general and his aides, orderlies, foreign observers, military historians, and sketch artists. Nathanial rode behind the senior staff officers and ate their dust as he peered into the faces of the soldiers forming on the road. Some appeared exhausted before they started, others were frightened and uncertain, while the old veterans were prepared to follow Old Rough and Ready into the maws of hell.

The great man took his position at the front of the column and raised his stubby arm in the air. Orders were shouted, bugles blown, whips fell onto the haunches of oxen, and the Army of Observation fell in behind him like a huge arthritic snake. They passed expanses of gray-green coastal grass, the sun drew higher in the sky, and wagon wheels squeaked in protest as the soldiers of manifest destiny advanced toward their appointment with the Mexican Army.

General Mariano Arista deployed his troops across a plain dotted with small muddy lakes and bordered with chaparral. His plan was to wait and see what the Americans would do, then counterattack as opportunities presented themselves.

He understood his enemy well, or so he thought, for he'd lived in Cincinnati, Ohio, during an unfortunate period when he'd fallen out of favor with the government of Santa Anna. There he had studied English and agriculture until Santa Anna was deposed, and then returned to Mexico.

Forty-three-year-old General Arista was an unusual Mexican, because he had red hair and freckles. He owned substantial land in northern Mexico and wasn't about to give it up to the gringos. It infuriated him to think that the brazen clowns would actually invade Mexico.

Many of his soldiers were conscripts and convicts, but he also had been blessed with experienced units such as the redoubtable Tampico Veterans, the 2nd Light Infantry, the 4th and 10th Regular Infantry, and sixteen hundred well-mounted lancers under General Anastasio Torrejon.

His left, consisting of General Torrejon's lancers, was anchored on the Point Isabel Road beside an expanse of chaparral. To his right rode a light cavalry regiment on an elevated wooded plain. His center was held by the Tampico veterans, and in between were artillery and infantry regiments, perspiring impatiently and anxious to annihilate the Yankee invader.

General Arista sat upon his horse and surveyed his perfect textbook deployment. We Mexicans are hospitable people, he thought with a wry smile. When the Americanos come down this road, we will give them a welcome they'll never forget.

High in the Palo Alto Mountains, the People watched in shocked disbelief as the White Eyes drew closer to the Mexicans. The warriors had heard tales of Mexican and White Eyes absurdity, but it was another matter to actually see it. The Mexicans sat like dogs and waited to be attacked, while the White Eyes appeared intent on blundering into them. Evidently each side was resigned to huge casualties, and whoever was left standing at the end—that was the winner.

Mangus Coloradas was getting a headache thinking about it, for it was difficult to conceive how a chief could be so profligate with the lives of his warriors. He knew each of his men personally, and was related to many through family and clan. The death of a warrior was a terrible loss to the People, and a war chief could be stripped of rank if too many warriors were lost on his raids.

Mangus Coloradas believed he knew how to fight the White Eyes. The People had no smelly towns to defend, so they'd vanish into the mountains and strike at remote outposts, supply trains, and scouting detachments. The People had killed many Mexicans with such tactics, and Mangus Coloradas had no reason to believe the same wouldn't be true with the White Eyes.

He stared in befuddlement at the White Eyes army closing with the Mexicans. They must be in the spell of sorcerers, the war chief speculated, for no one *wishes* to die.

*   *   *

Nathanial's horse danced skittishly, perhaps from the smell of the Mexican Army ahead. Nathanial held the reins tightly as he said, "Settle down, boy. This is no time for second thoughts."

I don't want to be here, the horse seemed to say as he shook his massive head from side to side. He'd been wild not long ago, and sold to the army by Mexican vaqueros. Nathanial had named him Duke because the animal had a certain regal flair.

Nathanial raised himself in the saddle and looked behind him. Most of the men had become obscured behind churning clouds of dust, but he could hear the thud of hoofbeats, clank of metal, and whip cracks across the backs of oxen. He faced front again and glanced at Old Rough and Ready astride Old Whitey. What's going through his head right now? wondered Nathanial.

"Here comes a ranger," said Lieutenant Ulysses S. Grant, one of General Taylor's quartermaster officers and a former West Point upperclassman of Nathanial's.

Galloping down the road came a bearded rider on a black stallion. This time it was Sam Walker, leader of the Texas Rangers, waving his hat in the air. He pulled in front of General Taylor and said, "They're about two miles straight ahead, sir!"

"What're they doing?"

"Looks like they're just a-waitin' on us, sir."

"Well, we shan't disappoint them." General Taylor turned to the side. "Lieutenant Blake—please ride ahead and made a reconnaissance."

"Yes, sir!" replied Lieutenant Jacob E. Blake of the Topographical Engineers as he threw a salute to the old soldier.

The ranger changed horses and trotted off with Lieutenant Blake. General Taylor betrayed no emotion now that the enemy had been spotted. Neither did he strike historic poses nor pretend to be a successor to Napoleon. Looks like he's on his way to the cotton fields, thought Nathanial.

"There they are," said Beau, who was riding beside Nathanial.

Nathanial saw a long dark line in the distance. He might've mistaken it for a strip of dark grass, or a long shadow, but then he detected the glint of bayonets through the hot, hazy air.

The American Army rolled inexorably toward the Mexican positions, and Nathanial could see battle flags, pennants, and brightly colored Mexican uniforms. He began to feel dispirited, but his back was ramrod straight, with his elbows tucked close to his sides.

His stomach tied in knots, and his mouth went dry. He wanted to wheel his horse and ride the hell out of there, but he'd be ridiculed and spat upon for the rest of his life, and Layne Satterfield would never talk to him again.

He was tempted to look at her picture, when he heard General Taylor call his name. Lieutenant Barrington urged his horse forward and came abreast of the great man himself.

"How are you managing, Lieutenant?" the general asked.

"Fine, sir," lied Nathanial.

"Would you ride ahead and tell Lieutenant Blake that I'm anxious to hear his report?"

"Yes, sir." Nathanial saluted, pulled his reins to the side, and separated himself from the main column. Then he touched his spurs to Duke's withers, but the animal raised his two front hooves in protest.

"Something wrong with your horse, Lieutenant?" inquired the general mildly.

"Nothing I can't handle, sir," replied Nathanial, flashing his most confident smile and hiding the anger he felt toward his horse, which was embarrassing him before the entire army.

Nathanial fought Duke's erratic movements, and the

bit was too much for the animal's sensitive lips. Duke surrendered, his great lungs heaving, and all he could do was trot forward.

Nathanial rocked easily in the saddle as he pulled ahead of the column. I wonder why the general selected me? he wondered. Nathanial's restless mind analyzed and quantified everything, even though he could make out Mexican cannon in the distance. Old Rough and Ready must trust me, Nathanial surmised. Now there's evidence that his mind is gone.

Duke increased his speed, because it felt good to work the tension out of his muscles. Nathanial bent over his shimmering black mane as he neared Lieutenant Blake.

Nathanial couldn't understand why the Mexicans weren't firing at Blake, because he was within cannon range. Then Nathanial realized with a start he was within cannon range too! He took a deep swallow and wondered if a Mexican soldier held him in his sights. He felt vulnerable and terrified, but again maintained his West Point composure as he pulled his horse to a halt beside Lieutenant Blake, who was sketching on his pad. "General Taylor wants to know what's taking so long?"

"The Mexicans aren't disturbing me, so I thought I'd make a detailed drawing of their positions. If you're quiet, you can hear somebody over there making a speech."

Nathanial listened to the wind carrying the faint voice of a man talking excitedly in Spanish. The Mexicans were so close, Nathanial could determine the difference between infantry, artillery, and cavalry, the latter with pennants fluttering from the ends of their lances.

General Arista galloped across the front of his line, making final adjustments in the positions of individual units and trying to inspire his men for the battle that lay ahead.

"All Mexico is watching you!" he shouted as his horse pranced before glittering battalions. "Today is a gift for soldiers, because we are offered an opportunity for glory! Your countrymen will remember your names forever, for the brave deeds you perform on this field today! You *will* stop the American Army, because you *must* defend your nation from a *degenerate* breed that would steal your land and *enslave* your mothers and sisters! *Viva la Republica!*"

General Zachary Taylor sat on the ground and studied Lieutenant Blake's map. A straightforward soldier of the old school, General Taylor decided to mass on his right and send a bayonet charge to roll up the Mexican flank, after softening them first with a bit of grape.

He ordered Colonel Twigg's brigade to the right of the road, supported by Lieutenant Colonel James S. McIntosh's 5th Infantry and Major Ringgold's Flying Artillery. His center would be held by two 18-pound cannons commanded by Lieutenant William H. Churchill, and covered by Captain Lewis N. Morris's 3rd Infantry augmented by Captain George W. Allen's 4th Infantry. Protecting the weakened flank against sudden attack would be Captain May's dragoons.

Lieutenant Barrington rode from unit to unit, delivering messages from General Taylor. The soldiers were taking a brief rest and drinking from their canteens. On the way to Captain William Montgomery's 8th Regiment, Nathanial heard the first cannon open fire on the Mexican side. The sudden sound, in the summer afternoon, made him jump two inches off his saddle.

More booms echoed across the open plain. "Here they come!" shouted an officer in the 8th Regiment. "Hold steady, men!"

Nathanial narrowed his eyes at round black objects flying through the sky. They landed in front of the American soldiers, bounced, and the men easily

dodged out of the way. Meanwhile, Nathanial rode
back to the spot where General Taylor had established
his command post. Old Rough and Ready sat sidesad-
dle atop Old Whitey, his left leg hooked over the pom-
mel, and he was using his knee as a desk as he wrote
orders on his notepad, providing a tempting target for
Mexican sharpshooters. Nathaniel reined Duke in
front of the general, saluted, and reported successful
completion of his latest errand.

"Stay nearby, in case I need you," said the general.

Nathanial saluted again, then moved away from the
general, but not too far. He was amazed at how calm
the general appeared, in view of his exposed position.
Nathanial drank from his canteen and tried to be calm,
as the inaccurate enemy barrage continued. The men
returned to their positions after eluding bouncing cannonballs, then slapped mosquitoes and awaited orders
to attack.

At two-thirty in the afternoon, General Taylor
turned to his adjutant, Captain William "Perfect"
Bliss, and said calmly, "Direct the artillery to commence the barrage."

Captain Bliss was considered the most promising
junior officer in the U.S. Army. He saluted smartly,
then performed a West Point about-face and passed
the order to the sergeant-at-arms. Finally the command devolved to the bugler, who raised his polished
brass instrument and blew stirring notes soon overwhelmed by deafening roars as the American artillery
batteries opened fire.

Nathanial sat atop his nervously prancing horse and
realized he finally was seeing the culmination of all
those years marching and saluting by the numbers.
But he yearned to know what kind of officer he really
was, instead of carrying pieces of paper around.

Thundering explosions made him sick to his stomach as he wondered *why* he felt the need to participate
in an activity that could get him killed or maimed.
Strangely energized, oddly depressed, and extremely

apprehensive, he watched Mexican cannonballs rolling through the American position as in a Broadway bowling alley.

The Mexican artillery was short, while Major Ringgold's well-trained artillery batteries functioned like oiled machinery, wreaking havoc on the Mexican left. Nathanial peered through his brass spyglass and saw men torn to bits by explosions, the color red predominating in the field of fire. Nathanial's mind reeled at the slaughter, but all he could do was sit erectly in the saddle and portray an officer surveying the tactical situation.

Immense holes were blown through the Mexican line, and Nathanial couldn't understand why the Mexicans didn't either attack or retreat, but instead they stood at attention while being bombarded. His spyglass fell on Major Ringgold's Flying Artillery reloading and firing continuously. Nathanial had studied the latest textbooks and manuals of war, and understood well the scene before him. He was confident, in his youthful ignorance, that he could direct the battle himself, should that become necessary.

He focused on Major Ringgold riding among his cannoneers, shouting orders, offering suggestions, and exhorting them to greater effort. Now that's a fine example of an officer, calculated Nathanial. He's right in the middle of it, calm and fearless, deftly commanding the situation, and how splendid he looks. If only Rembrandt were here to paint this scene.

Then Major Ringgold slumped in his saddle, leaned to the side, and fell toward the ground. Aides rushed toward him, as blood poured out his legs, while his horse lay nearby, struggling feebly. Both had been hit by Mexican grapeshot.

Nathanial felt ill as he set his lips in a grim line. Shells burst before him as ranks of infantry awaited for the order to attack. Nathanial had never felt so alive, vital, mentally acute, and anxious to take command of something beside the next message. He real-

ized that war was a duel of generals and understood
why officers endured military bureaucracy to get those
stars on their collars.

A general is like God, he surmised, and they can
alter the course of history. He realized that it was
better to have a calm steady general like Zachary Taylor than a peacock strutting about pretending to be
Lord Wellington.

A fire had broken out on the battlefield, soldiers
couldn't see what they were aiming at, and a lull came
over the fighting. Nathanial was learning lessons that
don't come in books, and could only be understood
in the roar and shriek of battle itself.

"Here they come!" shouted a voice to his right.

Nathanial turned in that direction and refocused his
spyglass. It was the famed Mexican lancers charging
across the plain, sunlight glinting on their brass hel-
mets covered with mortarboards and plumes of feathers. They held their lances parallel with the ground,
shouting encouragement to each other and insults at
the gringos. Their hoofbeats like rolling thunder, their
brilliant red and black uniforms visible through the
smoke, they seemed unstoppable.

Dust rose around them as their horses sped toward
the American 5th Regiment. The lancers' mission was
to turn the American flank, and then break through
to the rear, where they'd destroy supply wagons and
maybe kill a few high-ranking officers such as Old
Rough and Ready himself.

General Taylor appeared unruffled as the well-
trained Regular Army 5th Regiment formed into
fighting squares, with eight-pounder cannon at the corners. Then the front rank dropped to one knee, locked
and loaded, while the second rank prepared to deliver
the next volley. Meanwhile, American cannon took
deadly aim at the charging lancers. Nathanial watched
enthralled as the Mexican cavalry galloped toward the
rigid formation. Can we hold? wondered Nathanial. It

was the timeless riddle: the irresistible force against an unmovable object.

"Lieutenant Barrington?"

General Taylor called his name, rousing Nathanial out of his intellectualizing. He angled his horse toward General Taylor and saluted. "Yes, sir."

General Taylor made a friendly smile, as if they were meeting on a Louisville street corner. "Please relay my compliments to Lieutenant Ker, and direct him to pursue."

"Pursue who, sir?"

"Why, the enemy cavalry, Lieutenant. Who else?"

Cannon and rifle fire echoed across the battlefield, as the 5th Regiment squares opened withering fire on the Mexican lancers at a distance of one hundred feet. Lancers were blasted off their horses, while others charged onward, and the first rank of Americans stepped back to load. The second rank dropped to one knee and fired on command.

Lancers and horses vanished in swirling clouds of smoke, while meanwhile, to the far right, Ranger Sam Walker and about twenty of his men poured lead into the lancer left flank. It appeared that the Mexican cavalry had met their match, and Nathanial realized with a flash that the American Army of Observation was winning the battle!

Exhilarated, Nathanial galloped toward Lieutenant Ker's dragoons. For the first time, he was truly part of the action. He pulled Duke to a halt, saluted Lieutenant Ker, and said, "General Taylor sends his compliments, sir, and would like you to pursue the Mexican lancers."

Lieutenant Ker passed along the order to his sergeant major. His men were already formed in a long skirmish line and awaiting the final push. Then, suddenly, the American artillery stopped firing, and Nathanial's ears rang like a hundred liberty bells. The battlefield was relatively silent for a few brief moments, then Lieutenant Ker drew his sword and raised

it high in the air. "Charge!" he screamed at the top
of his lungs.

He spurred his horse, and without looking backward, the gallant young officer raced after the retreating Mexican lancers. His men followed en masse,
and Nathanial watched them in confusion, for once
again he was a spectator while the real men were
doing the fighting.

Nathanial found himself at the crossroads of his
young life. In years to come, when people asked what
he did in the war, he didn't want to say he was a
messenger boy. The first battle of the Mexican War
was nearly over, and he had yet to fire a shot.

All the conflicts and confusion of his young life
came together in his turbulent consciousness, and the
only thing to do was draw his gift sword. Sunlight
glinted on the blade as he waved it in the air and
wheeled Duke around. That frightened creature was
so spooked, he'd go anywhere, and before he knew what
was happening, he was carrying Nathanial toward the
retreating Mexicans.

Nathanial bounced in the saddle and brandished his
sword murderously over his head. All those years of
studying and marching had formed a white-hot point
in his mind, and he had to know whether he was made
of silver or dross. It didn't take long to catch up with
the charging dragoons, and they made way, letting him
pass. "Cut them down!" he hollered as he whipped
the sword through the air.

Ahead were Mexican lancers fleeing for their lives,
while Mexican infantry advanced to meet the new
threat. Nathanial found himself in the midst of hoofbeats, battle cries, and the sound of sabers whistling
through the air.

Lieutenant Ker was far in front, and Nathanial
urged Duke to catch up with him. Nathanial finally
felt part of the unstoppable force, he exulted with
weird terrified joy, and it was more thrilling than any-

thing he'd ever known. "Onward!" he cried. "Don't let them get away!"

The Mexican lines lay straight ahead, and the lancers turned around to meet the approaching threat. Nathanial realized soon he'd be killing, and never had he known such intensity could exist for human beings on the planet Earth.

The drama for which West Point had trained him for was rapidly approaching in the form of a young Mexican cavalry officer also brandishing a long gleaming saber. Lady Death giggled above the thunder of cannon as Nathanial and the Mexican officer careened toward each other, then their sabers crashed together, sparks flew into the air, and they drew back for another swipe.

Nathanial took note of the Mexican's fine riding posture, his long flowing brown mustache, and the glitter of war madness in his eyes, as he swung his saber at Nathanial's very skull. But Nathanial had served on the West Point fencing team, and carefully practiced techniques clicked on automatically. He raised his saber, blocked the blow, and guided the point toward the Mexican's chest. The Mexican recovered quickly, but his block only diverted Nathanial's thrust. Nathanial watched with morbid fascination as his saber buried itself five inches into the Mexican's lower abdomen. The dashing young caballero's brown eyes rolled up into his head, he coughed violently, and fell to the side, as Duke bounded away, totally out of control.

Nathanial struggled to remain in the saddle, horrified by what he'd done. *Thou shalt not kill,* said the voice of the Lord in his right ear, while his left ear tingled with the exhortations of Lieutenant Ker, who was literally slicing his way through the Mexican Army. "Follow me, boys! We're almost there!"

West Point training took over once more, as Nathanial saw the color sergeant go down, victim of a bullet from a Mexican sergeant's rifle. The sergeant struggled to reload, as Nathanial bore down on him.

The fencing champion raised his sword in the air, to lop off the sergeant's head, as the sergeant primed his cartridge for fire.

Nathanial was ready to deal the death blow, when he realized that the sergeant might be a husband or father. What does it profit a man if he wins a battle but loses his soul? Nathanial asked himself, but then saw the American flag fluttering in the distance, along with the Second Dragoon colors. Nathanial became aware, in that elastic moment, that he was a soldier, and a soldier must carry on. Once again West Point conquered the young philosopher, and he took his swing at the Mexican's head.

Unfortunately, his moment of abstract reflection had produced serious consequences. The sergeant pulled the trigger before Nathanial had completed his swing, and Nathanial's pupils dilated as a lead slug rammed into his ribs. It felt as if he'd been struck by the Baltimore and Ohio Railroad, and then the battlefield became quite confused as unimaginable pain sent him into shock.

His eyes glazed over as he dropped from the saddle. His head slammed into the ground, knocking him cold, and he rolled into the path of charging horses. They tried to swerve out of his way, but one stomped Nathanial by mistake as he rampaged onward.

The Mexican flank fell back, leaving killed and wounded from both sides in their bloody tattered wake. Among them lay a motionless young staff officer, sword still clutched tightly in his hand, his blood irrigating the Texas soil.

The People watched from their perches in the distant hills as dusk fell over the battlefield. The Mexicans had withdrawn, while the White Eyes were setting up camp on the ground they'd just won. Many dead and wounded littered the landscape, and Mangus Coloradas pondered the amazing spectacle that he'd just witnessed.

In his opinion, the White Eyes had used their weapons to better advantage than the Mexicans, and utilized more effective tactics. Mangus Coloradas still didn't know whether courage or madness inspired a man to charge cannon, for no sane warrior would ever do such a thing.

Mangus Coloradas felt disoriented, because something indefinable was telling him that his holy life-way was coming to an end. It wouldn't be tomorrow or the next day, but he envisioned a time when the powerful White Eyes would come in such numbers that the Apaches could never stop them. Darkness fell on Palo Alto as the warriors rode north to the Mogollon Mountains, their hearts filled with darkness.

THREE

Nathanial couldn't move, see, or think. His existence was pain too great to bear, so he lapsed into coma. In weeks to come, he lay in the valley of the shadow of death as his body fought infection and destruction. Occasionally he'd open his eyes, but never for long. He didn't know where he was, couldn't take nourishment, and flesh vanished from his mangled bones.

Then, gradually, he became aware that he lay in a large walled tent with other wounded men, and their screams frequently pierced his dreams. At first he thought he'd died and been condemned to purgatory. Sometimes the screams he heard were his own, and that terrified him most of all.

The doctors tried to talk with him, but he couldn't make words. He was certain that death would bear him away, but somehow managed to breathe. "This officer has an amazing will to live," a doctor declared one day while making his rounds.

Nathanial wanted to laugh, but his mouth wouldn't move. Muddled though he might be, his will had nothing to do with it. No, something else was keeping him alive, perhaps his youth or the Barrington blood that remained in his flaccid veins.

They gave him laudanum, and he experienced dreams that seemed more real than the tent in which he lay. Sometimes he sat with his family in their home on Washington Square, or rode horseback on the Bloomingdale Road north of New York City. Occasionally he found himself alone with Layne Satterfield, performing acts no decent person would attempt even within the institution of marriage.

"I think he's about ready to take nourishment," said a doctor one day.

"A miracle he wasn't killed," replied the orderly.

The next thing Nathanial knew, someone was trying to spoon hot broth down his throat. Around that time he realized that he was indeed Lieutenant Nathanial Barrington, U.S. Army, wounded in action at Palo Alto, and evidently convalescing at Corpus Christi.

Pain diminished, strength returned in small increments, and soon he was able to reconstruct the events that had laid him low. He had volunteered for a cavalry charge, of all things, and his path of glory had led to the leaky hospital tent.

Next time the doctor came around, Nathanial managed to ask in a raspy voice: "Do I have my arms and legs?"

"He just spoke," declared Dr. Eames.

"Amazing recovery," replied Dr. Herkimer. "A man can rarely lose this much blood and live."

The doctors prattled on as Nathanial struggled to introject himself into the conversation. "Do I . . . have my . . . arms . . ."

Dr. Eames gripped his shoulder warmly. "You haven't lost anything that we're aware of, and if you ever wanted to get married, I'm sure you could give a full account of yourself."

Relieved, Nathanial sank back onto his canvas cot. He dreamed about his mother, goddess of his life, and wished she were there to care for him. The Barrington mansion on Washington Square ran as efficiently as Major Ringgold's Flying Artillery, but Mother also was Old Army, for her father had fought in the Battle of Saratoga, while her brother had assaulted Fort George during the War of 1812. Nathanial smiled as he remembered his dear mother. How upset she'd be when she learned he'd been wounded in action. She was as sentimental as a child, yet possessed a temper that never failed to intimidate him. He'd contemplated resigning during his plebe year at West Point, but she'd told him icily that she didn't want to be mother to a quitter, and that had ended his last longing for civilian life.

As weeks passed, he began to feel almost normal, except for the pain in his chest and gut. He realized that he'd let himself get shot due to sheer stupidity in the face of the enemy, and wondered what had been wrong with him. War was kill or be killed, not a chess game or philosophical theorem.

He remembered stabbing the Mexican officer in the abdomen, and didn't know whether to be proud or ashamed. He'd seen suffering in the officer's eyes, but Nathanial didn't order the officer to appear on the road to Matamoros. The Mexican believed in his cause, I believed in mine, and I prevailed.

And then he realized that he had not yet thanked God for saving his miserable worthless life. Too weak to clasp his hands together, he could only close his eyes and whisper faintly, "I was not worthy, but you spared my life, O Lord. From now on, I shall try to live according to your Commandments, with no more irresponsible habits, such as the patronage of whorehouses. I don't understand why you have saved me, but from now on I will live by Your Holy Gospel, like the Knights Templar of the Middle Ages, so help me God."

And even as he said it, he knew he was lying yet again.

In Las Vegas, New Mexico, Maria Dolores Carbajal and her father Diego sat apprehensively in the parlor of their home. The American Army was expected to arrive within the hour, and they wondered if they'd be tortured, massacred, enslaved, and so on.

General Armijo had sworn to defend Las Vegas to the last Mexican soldier, but he and they had fled as soon as the Americans came into view. Now the inhabitants of the town waited for the conqueror to lay down his terms.

They knew the bad news from farther south, where the Americans had defeated the Mexican Army at Palo Alto, Resaca de la Palma, Matamoros, and Camargo. President Parades had been deposed, and Santa Anna was on his way back from exile in Cuba, to become virtual dictator of Mexico. The advancing Americans had killed civilians indiscriminately and raped countless women, according to reports. No one had been enslaved yet, but Maria Dolores fully expected to be wearing a ball and chain before the week was out.

Her mother had died of consumption ten years ago, and her only relative in Las Vegas was her beloved father. That gentleman shopkeeper appeared on the verge of apoplexy, but tried to be brave, although he might become a slave too. Tears came to Maria Dolores's eyes as she recalled their vast hacienda with its many airy rooms, a far cry from their tiny residence in Las Vegas. Her father, who had loved to ride the range with his vaqueros, was forced to sell beans and bacon to travelers, thanks to Apache marauders.

"Here they come!" somebody shouted.

Maria Dolores and her father glanced at each other nervously. They lived on a side street, but could hear massed hoofbeats and shouts of American officers and sergeants. A cloud of dust drifted past the windows, and through openings in the buildings, they could see blue uniforms accompanied by oxen pulling massive cannon into their town square.

"Just be calm," said her father. "Perhaps they will be friendly."

"I think it would be better for us to pray." Maria Dolores took out her rosary, and she led with "Hail Mary, full of grace, the Lord is with thee. Blessed art thou among women and blessed is the fruit of thy womb Jesus."

They could hear American soldiers spreading

through town. A shot was fired, and they wondered if anybody had been killed. A loud knock on the door brought them to their feet. They looked at each other anxiously, then the man of the house said, "I will get it."

He stood, his belly protruding over his hand-tooled black leather belt, then he strode toward the door and pulled it open. An American officer in a dusty blue uniform stood there, pistol in hand, glancing inside the room suspiciously. When satisfied that no Mexican soldiers were lurking about, he said in halting Spanish, *"El Generale quiere hablar contigo. Venga."*

There could be no quarrel with loaded guns, so Maria Dolores and her father followed the soldiers outside, where other civilians were being herded toward the square. Maria Dolores wondered if they were going to be massacred, or if the conquering soldiers simply intended to commandeer their homes.

"Courage, daughter," said her father. "If we die, we shall go with the Virgin's name on our lips."

Other Mexican Catholic residents prayed also as Protestant American soldiers peered at them unsympathetically, because Catholics and Protestants had been killing each other without letup since Martin Luther had nailed the 95 Theses to the door of the Wittenberg church.

A group of officers were gathered in front of the alcalde's office, and that worthy was speaking earnestly with a tall American general who wore long brown side-whiskers and a blue uniform with gold shoulder straps. The general pointed to the flat roof of a nearby building and said, "I want to go up there with you."

The alcalde called for a ladder, one was brought on the run and angled against the building. The American general invited the alcalde to climb up first, then followed him.

Maria Dolores had to admit that the gringo general looked imposing in his neat uniform, and his every motion betokened courteous manners. She thought him a decent man, but often experienced strange impulses with no basis in logic.

The general stood at the edge of the roof, and declared, "Mr. Alcalde, I am Brigadier General Stephen Kearny, commander of the Army of the West. I am here by the orders of my government to take possession of your country and extend over it the laws of the United States. But we come as friends—not enemies or conquerors. Henceforth I absolve you from allegiance to the Mexican government and obedience to General Armijo. Until further notice, I am your governor. Those who remain peaceably at home, attending to their crops and herds, shall be protected by me. Not a pepper or an onion shall be disturbed or taken by my troops without pay and the consent of the owner. But listen well, citizens of Las Vegas. He who promises to be peaceful, and is found taking up arms against me—him I will hang!"

A wave of consternation swept over the crowd, when this last line was translated by the alcalde. But General Kearny was playing the old game of carrot and stick. The conqueror of New Mexico raised his finger in the air and intoned loudly, "You owe nothing to the Mexican government, because they have never given you protection. For generations the Apaches have come down from the mountains and carried off your sheep, goods, and even your women. I swear from this day onward: my government will keep off the Apaches and protect you in your persons and property."

The citizens glanced at each other knowingly and laughed up their sleeves, for who had ever controlled the Apaches? The Mexicans believed that the Americanos wouldn't be any more effective against the red devils than they, and General Kearny had made a promise he couldn't keep.

"My army stands before you today," the general continued, "but you see only a small portion of it.

There are many more coming, and all resistance is
useless. Mr. Alcalde, if you and your captains of mili-
tia will take the oath of allegiance to the United
States, I will continue you in office and support your
authority."

And thus, on August 15, 1846, a representative of
the U.S. Government accepted official responsibility
for the most ferocious Indians in North America.

Unsteady and requiring use of a cane, Nathanial
was sent home on convalescent leave. His stomach
and chest ache never ceased as he rode a stagecoach
to New Orleans, boarded a riverboat, and played
poker all the way to St. Louis, losing fifty dollars to
cardsharps, and distracting himself from the pain with
the aid of whiskey. Then he caught another stagecoach, sat by the window, and glared gloomily at the
peaceful Allegheny landscape passing in an endless
blur.

Everywhere he went, folks discussed the great war.
Santa Anna was on his way to San Luis Potosi to stop
General Taylor's advance, while General John Wool's
army had captured Monclova. American casualties
had been kept low, and Old Rough and Ready had
become a hero to those who supported the war, while
an increasingly vocal minority of war protesters considered him guilty of crimes against a sovereign nation.

Vast expanses of forest and farmland passed Nathanial's half-closed eyes as he sat wrapped in his
army greatcoat. At moments of repose, his thoughts
often turned to Palo Alto, for no longer was he a
happy-go-lucky overgrown boy beset with minor
confusions.

Now Nathanial appreciated the full import of the
prophecy: *There will always be war and talk of war.* If
a nation didn't protect its interests, it would be picked
apart by the Santa Annas of the world.

Nathanial hated Santa Anna, because the despot
had massacred American prisoners of war at Goliad

and the Alamo during the Texan War of Independence. There could be no peaceful coexistence with
such as he, and Nathanial believed that despite his
wounds and the rancor of his fellow Americans, his
decision to enter West Point had been correct, even
his mother had known it, and that's why she'd insisted
that he follow the course.

He felt at peace with himself, for he'd stared into
the face of Death, and not been a coward under fire.
His one mistake had been a spate of highly unproduc-
tive speculation, but he resolved in the future to follow
his soldierly instincts and stop analyzing everything to
the nth degree.

In a Pittsburg hotel he fell in with a bunch of officers heading for the front, and he'd got so drunk they
had to carry him to his room. In Philadelphia he'd
gone to church, but departed during the sermon because the minister had railed against the war.

He wore a one-inch scar on his left cheek, and
couldn't get about without the cane. His stomach frequently doubled him up, his strength had not yet fully
returned, and sometimes he suffered blinding headaches. He spent most nights in ramshackle roadhouses,
lying on his greatcoat in a bed with two or three other
men. But in just a few more days, he'd see Layne
Satterfield again.

He rode the final leg of his trip with ardent anticipation, and tears filled his eyes when the New York
skyline became visible from the Jersey shore. He could
make out the spire of Trinity Church as the ferry
glided across the Hudson, and Manhattan Island
looked like a magic world gleaming in the night.

The ferry docked at Battery Park, and Nathanial
carried his leather satchel ashore, steadying himself
with his cane. He passed lovers strolling in the dim
lamplight beneath stately oak and maple trees, while
circular Castle Garden sat at the end of the promon-
tory, a former fort now used for concert and theatrical
presentations. At the curb, a row of carriages were

lined. A driver helped him in and said, "Where you want to go, sir?"

"Ten Washington Square."

The driver hopped into his seat, flicked the reins, and the carriage rolled up Broadway. The streets were crowded with pedestrians, store windows blazed with expensive merchandise imported from all over the globe, and crowds gathered in front of brightly lit restaurants, theaters, and taverns. They passed Trinity Church, where Nathanial's grandfather had been a vestryman, and soon came the renowned Astor Hotel, owned by the richest man in New York, John Jacob Astor. Across the way sat City Hall, whose new gold cupola glowed in the light of the moon.

Nathanial gazed at elegant ladies strolling the sidewalks, and wondered where Layne Satterfield was spending the evening. He was tempted to visit her first, but his mother would never forgive him. Neither did he dare stop for a drink at one of his old haunts, but there'd be plenty of time for that later.

He noticed prostitutes hovering in alleys near Canal Street, as a group of urchins prowled along, searching for something to filch. Private homes still occupied this stretch of Broadway, but the port of New York was growing every day, increasing the need for office buildings, hotels, restaurants, and other commercial establishments. For a decade, wealthy citizens had been relocating to Fifth Avenue, Gramercy Park, Murray Hill, and Washington Square.

The carriage turned left on Waverly Place, and the driver said over his shoulder, "Was you wounded in Mexico?"

"How'd you guess?" replied Nathanial.

"I was in the army onc't meself, and I knows an officer when I sees one, sir. But I don't know about this war with the Mexicans. We used to fight fer the flag and the republic, but now soldiers die so's some son of a bitch in Texas can git some free land."

Nathanial could recognize the validity of what the

carriage driver had said. All the man wanted was a good meal followed by a roof over his head, and he didn't care about manifest destiny.

The carriage came to Washington Square, formerly a hanging ground, now a public park and parade ground surrounded by elegant homes. His parents had moved here in 1842, shortly after Nathanial departed for West Point. His mother had preferred the quiet neighborhood to stuffy Fifth Avenue, while Nathanial's father, a colonel in the War Department, lived in Washington, D.C. Nathanial's parents had been separated for several years, for reasons Nathanial didn't fully understand, although the family still got together for holidays and pretended that everything was normal.

The carriage stopped in front of a three-story red brick residence facing south on Washington Square. "Can I help you, sir?"

"I can make it on my own, thanks."

Nathanial nearly fell out of the carriage, then hobbled up the steps. He stopped at the top and peered east at a building that looked like a many towered white castle that had mated with a church, the University of the City of New York, and next to it sat the Reformed Dutch Church, which possessed only two towers. Across the park were another row of Grecian Revival and Italianate mansions. I'm home, he thought happily.

There was a light in the parlor, and he wondered if his mother had gone to bed. He rapped on the door, which was opened by a short dumpy red-faced woman with rust-colored hair and a black uniform. Shirley Rooney stared at Nathanial in shocked disbelief, then touched her fingers to her cheeks and said, "Lord have mercy."

Nathanial kissed her forehead. "Is my mother home?"

Shirley Rooney seemed struck by paralysis. Her eyes touched his scar, cane, and the awkward way in which he stood. Then, at the rear of the corridor, a spare but erect figure appeared, wearing a crown of gray-blond hair. "Nathanial!" cried his mother, rushing toward him.

He held her tightly, and she appeared smaller, her hair grayer, and deep lines were etched around her mouth. This was the woman who had carried him in her belly, and he'd always felt as if an invisible umbilical cord still bound him to her.

She touched his lips to his scar. "My poor little boy," she whispered, although he was a head taller than she.

"How're you feeling, Mother?" he inquired, trying to sound cheerful.

"I've been so worried about you."

"Where's my brother?"

"Asleep, and if you wake him, he won't go back to bed. He's been fighting again, and you can speak with him in the morning."

She led Nathanial into the parlor, and he dropped heavily into his father's old easy chair. On the wall above the fireplace hung a painting of Joshua Barrington, Nathanial's grandfather, painted by Gilbert Stuart, who'd also done portraits of George Washington, Thomas Jefferson, and other patriots of the American Revolution. The room contained additional likenesses of Nathanial's ancestors in military uniforms, and they seemed to be saying, "Good work, Nathanial. You have not embarrassed the family name."

His mother stared at him intently, and he wondered if she could see his inner changes. In the golden effulgence of gaslight, he could discern the beautiful woman she'd been, and he felt honored to have such an exceptional woman for a mother, but now she was the tragic muse of Washington Square. Colonel Stephen Barrington had deserted her, and now she was alone with twelve-year-old Jeffrey and the servants. Nathanial wondered what his mother would think if she saw him sticking his saber into that Mexican officer.

"No," she said as she looked him up and down. "You're not my little boy anymore. I wondered how war would affect you."

Nathanial just shrugged and smiled. "I'm a soldier, and we don't even think of these things."

Tears came to her eyes. "You've been hurt very badly—I can see it in your every move."

"Not at all," he replied. "One moment I was riding my horse, and when I opened my eyes again, I was in the hospital tent."

Shirley arrived with a pot of coffee and a silver platter covered with sandwiches, which she placed on the low hand-carved table before him. "Can I get you anything else, sir?"

"Is there something to drink?"

Shirley glanced at her mistress, who nodded slightly. "We have your father's whiskey and brandy, sir. Also some port and claret."

"Whiskey," said Nathanial.

Shirley departed the room, and Mrs. Barrington gazed at her son with new interest. "I think I liked you better the other way."

"Have you seen Layne lately?"

Amalia Barrington tried to smile. "I'm afraid I have bad news for you, Nathanial. Are you ready?" She paused. "Miss Satterfield has become engaged to somebody else."

The stalwart young officer thought perhaps his wounds had affected his hearing. "That's funny, because I thought you said she'd become engaged to somebody else."

"That's exactly what I said."

A pain more excruciating than a lead ball struck him in the gut, his lungs deflated, and he developed a nagging pain in the middle of his brain. "What happened?"

"No one wanted to tell you, because you were at

war. I've never said this before, because God knows, I try to keep my place. But I never really liked Layne Satterfield. She had something of the schemer about her. No, I've always thought you could do much better."

Nathanial knew that his mother was lying, because she'd doted on Layne Satterfield, but would say anything to ease her son's grief. Her eyelashes fluttered, and her lips parted. "There are many interesting young women in town these days, and I'm sure they'd love to meet you. After all, as your dear old grandfather used to say: 'There's more than one mackerel in the ocean.'"

Nathanial felt crushed as his last remaining dream evaporated. Now, in addition to everything else, he'd have to find another woman to marry, a long difficult process fraught with pitfalls. "I don't understand," he said in a choked voice, "how a person can say she loves you today, and then marry somebody else tomorrow?"

"You can't rely on shallow people, because they change their allegiances whenever it suits their pleasure."

She was referring to Layne Satterfield, but the subtext included her husband, Nathanial's father. It was rumored that Colonel Stephen Barrington kept a mistress in Washington, D.C., and had left his family for her.

"Who is he?" Nathanial asked.

"One of the Astors, a distant relation from Germany named Franz."

"Not a bad match," Nathanial had to admit.

"The girl has a cash box where her heart was supposed to be."

Nathanial bantered on although his heart was splitting down the middle. "For all she knew, I might never come back from Mexico. But an Astor is a joy forever."

His mother smiled bitterly. "The Astors don't go to war. They just make more money."

"The world needs landlords as well as soldiers, I suppose," he chattered, although he felt like crying. "Perhaps there's a blessing in all this, because we'll be able to spend more time together now that I'm single again. Next time I'll let you pick my wife, since you seem to know so much about it." He tried to smile, but it came out lopsided.

"It's important to marry someone who shares your values," she counseled. "Perhaps your father can introduce you to such a person when you visit him in Washington."

"What do you think I should say if I ever run into Layne Satterfield."

"You must congratulate her, and pretend that her little act of treachery is of no concern to you. On the other hand, it would give her great satisfaction to know that you're wasting away because of her. You won't, will you?"

"Not a chance," replied the devil-may-care officer, but Nathanial suspected his mother could see right through him.

Shirley arrived with a bottle of whiskey. "How much should I pour, sir?"

"About half a glass. No water please."

She blanched, glanced at Mrs. Barrington, but that great lady pretended that nothing was amiss. Shirley filled the glass as ordered, then passed it to Nathanial. "Sir."

It went down like silk, so different from the fermented garbage he'd imbibed in Texas and Mexico. Palo Alto seemed far from Washington Square as he conversed with his mother and the maid. He stopped at Jeffrey's room on the way to bed, and peered inside at the lad sleeping on his stomach, lips parted slightly, a ray of light illuminating his golden curls, and he looked like a cherub sleeping innocently. We'll have

fun together, thought Nathanial. It's time he learned
about the world that men live in.

While preparing for bed, Nathanial gazed at the daguerreotype of Layne Satterfield for a long time, and
wondered if he should throw it away. He could send
it back to her, but that would be an admission of
something, he wasn't sure quite what.

He dropped the picture into the wastebasket, then
undressed in front of the mirror, comparing his scarred
battered body with the physical specimen that he used
to be. After a hot bath, he retired to his familiar old
bed, with the same cozy sag in the middle. Exhausted
by his journey and undermined by bad news, he
dreamed of Mexican lancers pursuing him through the
dark Matamoros night.

Twenty-five hundred miles to the southwest, the
great chief Mangus Coloradas crossed the border into
Mexico, along with fifteen of his best warriors. They
wore loincloths, buckskin shirts, their hair in bandannas, and ochre stripes painted across their cheeks and
noses. Their most important accoutrements were their
izze-kloths, or Killer of Enemies Bandoliers, a loosely
braided sash of hide strings twisted about each other,
draped across their chests from right shoulders to left
sides, carrying bags of sacred pollen. Only a *di-yin*
medicine man could make a Killer of Enemies Bando-
lier, which possessed power to be called upon only in
dire emergencies.

The People weren't in Mexico as tourists or geolo-
gists, but on a raid where they expected no opposition,
because Mexicans were too busy fighting the White
Eyes. Mangus Coloradas believed that no peace was
possible with the Mexicans, because nine harvests ago
he'd been present at the Santa Rita Copper Mines,
the bloodiest hour in Apache history. With his own
eyes, he'd seen Mexican fiends slaughter women and
children, for the sake of bounties on the scalps of
the People.

Mangus Coloradas could neither forgive nor forget the massacre at the Santa Rita Copper Mines. The Mexicans and a few White Eyes had invited the People to a feast, but cannon were concealed in the chaparral. At the height of the celebration, the hosts had opened fire at close range. Even Chief Juan José had been killed, but miraculously Mangus Coloradas had managed to escape.

The desire for revenge burned hot in the chief's veins as he led his warriors deeper into Mexico. There had been other atrocities too numerous to mention, but the Santa Rita massacre had hardened the chieftain's heart for all time. In addition, the People depended on raids for economic sustenance, because the People could not let themselves be starved. The People harvested the Mexicans—cattle, horses, and other property—as the Mexicans harvested deer and antelope belonging to the People.

Rifles, ammunition, and food were the main objectives of the raid, but too many Apache heads had been chopped off by bounty hunters, and the debt must be paid in kind. This was the foreign policy of Mangus Coloradas, chief of the People.

Nathanial opened his eyes in the middle of the night, and at first thought he was in the hospital tent. But the smell wasn't rotting flesh and the latrine in back. Calm down, soldier, he said to himself as he sniffed fresh sheets.

He was covered with sweat, for he'd been dreaming about Palo Alto again. Nearly every night he evoked that gore-bedecked plain, and the vision of hell in a Mexican officer's eyes. Nathanial knew he'd be fighting Palo Alto for the rest of his life.

He lit the lamp, illuminating a painting by William Sidney Mount showing hunting dogs pointing at pheasants on Long Island. Nathanial's old West Point fencing foil was suspended on two pegs, and he took it down. He flexed the blade, then executed a parry, but his timing was off, and his left leg gave out. I've got a long road to travel, he cautioned himself as he replaced the foil on its stand. His old West Point uniform hung in the closet, along with his finely tailored suits.

He gazed out the window at Washington Square. Only a few blocks away, Broadway was thronged with beautiful prostitutes, and all he had to do was put on his clothes. The best way to forget one woman is sleep with another, he'd learned. He wondered if he'd made a too-hasty bargain with God at Palo Alto, or was the devil tempting him again?

Nathanial preferred clear-cut issues, but they became scarcer as his age increased. He reached for the bottle of whiskey, and swallowed without benefit of a glass, then reclined once more and closed his eyes. I've got to get well, he lectured himself. This is no time to be chasing jezebels.

Pedrito sat with his back to an adobe hut, flintlock musket in his hands, struggling to stay alert. Every able-bodied man in the village rotated guard duty, due to the Apache menace. He was barely five feet tall, but had good aim and no fear where Indians were concerned.

I've rested long enough, he said to himself. So he arose, adjusted his sombrero, slung the musket over his shoulder, and proceeded to walk around the perimeter of the village. Another guard, Ricardo, was also on duty. Windows were dark, everyone sleeping, and Pedrito wished he could be cuddling his lovely wife, Elena.

He turned toward the open desert and observed trees, bushes, and clumps of cactus. Nothing moved, the scene was serene and beautiful, but then he heard a sound like the twang of an Apache bow. Next thing he knew, an arrow pierced his gullet and pinned him against the wall of a building. He tried to scream, but a hand closed over his mouth, and his jugular was sliced open. Blood gushed out as the warrior named Lucero lowered the Mexican gently to the ground.

The other warriors advanced out of the night, led by the great chief Mangus Coloradas, who had shot the first arrow. The guard was dead, his partner had been dispatched previously, and now the town was wide open. Without a word, the warriors readied their bows, lances, war clubs, and knives. Then they spread out and silently melted into the shadows.

Mangus Coloradas crept through a window, slithered to a door, turned the latch slowly, and saw two figures lying in bed. He arose beside them, recalled the massacre at the Santa Rita mine, and plunged the iron point of his lance into the heart of the sleeping Mexican man.

The victim didn't know what hit him, but his wife awoke with a start. She was old, toothless, shrieking at the top of her lungs, and Mangus Coloradas finished her without a moment's hesitation. A rifle leaned against the wall next to the bed, and Mangus Coloradas picked it up. He was surprised to see that it was a new model, like the American soldiers carried.

Mangus Coloradas didn't know how to load it, but slung it barrel down over his shoulder, padded to the door, and looked down the corridor. Screaming, shots, and tumultuous panic could be heard from other parts of town. He peered out a window and saw a villager with a rifle tiptoeing down an alley. Mangus Coloradas raised his bow, pulled the deer sinew string, and the arrow pierced the Mexican's chest, shot out his back, and the Mexican dropped before he could utter a sound.

It didn't take long for the People to silence the adult males and older females. Then they herded terrorized children, one young woman, and a roly-poly medicine padre in a brown robe into the tiny square in front of the church.

The medicine padre dropped to his knees before Mangus Coloradas, bowed his head, and clasped his hands together. "I cannot prevent you from killing me, but please, for the sake of whatever god you believe in, spare the children."

Mangus Coloradas had picked up some Spanish words due to his relations with the Mexicans over the years. "If your god is so powerful, Brown Robe, why does not *he* save the children?"

"Because only you can make that decision, great chief. If you kill them, their blood will be on your hands, and your soul will be in mortal danger."

Mangus Coloradas cast a significant glance at his warriors, and two of them grabbed the medicine padre by his arms. They dragged him to a cottonwood tree, then a warrior tore off the brown robe, revealing folds of fat and no underwear. Another warrior threw a rope over a branch, while a third tied the end of the rope to the priest's ankles. The priest didn't struggle, his eyes closed, and his lips moving frantically in prayer as they strung him up head down.

The children begged for their padre's life as the warriors gathered twigs and branches beneath the padre's shaved head. Victorio brought a match, scratched it on the rock, and made the fire.

"No!" shrieked the woman captive—her name was Elena Galindez—but a warrior batted her in the mouth, knocking her cold. Crazed with horror, the children screamed at the tops of their lungs as the padre struggled frantically, for the flames were licking his shiny pate.

The corner of Mangus Coloradas's mouth turned down as he watched the padre's head turn purple. The chief comprehended the cruelty of his act, but it was no worse than the massacre at the Santa Rita Copper Mines, which had come first, only to be followed by countless other outrages against the People.

The medicine padre became still as the sickening odor of charred flesh filled the air. Meanwhile, the warriors loaded weapons, clothes, jewelry, utensils, and firewater onto wagons, while other herded to-

gether horses and cattle. The red ball of sun cleared
the horizon as the warriors torched the town. Singing
victory songs, they climbed onto their mounts, carrying their blubbering captives with them.

Riding solo, the great chief Mangus Coloradas led
his warriors onto the open sage as flames enveloped
the town and the medicine padre swung in the light
evening breeze.

FOUR

"Breakfast is served, sir."

Shirley Rooney's footsteps padded down the hall as Nathanial gazed at himself in the mirror. He wore a dark blue vested suit, white shirt, and dark green cravat. It felt good to be home, instead of living in a tent with lice and fleas. Yet, in the mirror, he saw a scarred young man with haunted eyes. Gripping his cane, he headed for the dining room, with needles of pain shooting through his left leg.

He descended the spiral staircase laboriously, made his way across the parlor, and entered the dining room. Jeffrey jumped to his feet as soon as he saw his big brother, but then paused at the sight of the cane, scar, and halting step. The color drained from Jeffrey's cheeks, and the boy didn't know what to say.

Nathanial ran his fingers through his brother's hair. "I hear you've been fighting at school."

"I didn't start it," Jeffrey said defiantly.

It gave Nathanial satisfaction to know that his brother was a fighter. "The main thing is that you finished it."

His mother became livid. "How can you say such a thing to the boy? You're just encouraging his worst instincts!"

"A man has to defend himself, although I haven't been doing such a good job for myself lately."

He sat and served himself from the platter of fried eggs, sausages, and biscuits. Shirley filled his cup with coffee, and he savored the aroma, so different from the muck they'd drunk in the field. Meanwhile, Jeffrey stared at him with unalloyed hero worship.

Nathanial could perceive how impressive the fighting officer would appear to a young male, but Nathanial felt like an imposter, because he'd only been in one brief action and hadn't really lasted that long.

"Does it hurt much?" Jeffrey asked.

"No," lied Nathanial. "What are your plans this afternoon?"

Jeffrey made a face. "I'm going to a birthday party, but perhaps I can say I'm sick."

"You shouldn't tell lies," Nathanial admonished him, "because a man's word should be his bond."

"But everybody else lies," replied Jeffrey with a pout.

"If everybody jumped off Battery Park, does that mean you have to?"

"But even Mother lies!"

Mrs. Barrington stiffened in her chair. "That's not true," she said. "It's just that I have my own version."

"Perhaps Jeffrey and I could take a walk after breakfast," said Nathanial. "I'm sure that we two men have a lot to talk about."

Jeffrey appeared speechless, but his mother said, "Just remember that he's still a boy."

"Don't worry, Mother. I won't bring him to a tavern or any place like that."

"Children grow up too fast these days," she complained. "They know about things that I never heard of until I was married. New York was a wonderful city, but now it's filled with the scum of the world. The sights one sees every day on the streets of this city almost beggar the imagination."

"You should see the New Orleans slave market, Mother, and some of those frontier towns make New York look like Athens during the Age of Pericles."

Jeffrey had stopped eating and was watching his brother's every movement with adoration. "Have you ever seen any Indians?"

"They see you, but you generally never see them."

"What were they like—the ones that you saw?"

"They were in forts, and were either educated or corrupted by civilization, depending upon your point of view. The ones who live in the wilderness are the real Indians, but I never met any of them. They're supposed to be very brave, especially the Apaches."

"Who are they?" asked Jeffrey.

"They live in the New Mexico Territory, and no one has ever been able to make peace with them. They don't farm or hold jobs, and evidently prefer to steal what they want. Even other Indian tribes are afraid of the Apaches, and I imagine the army'll probably have to fight them after we finish with the Mexicans."

"Will *you* have to fight them, Nathanial?"

"Depends on the War Department."

"It must be wonderful to live free like the Indians," Jeffrey said haltingly. "Go hunting every day, instead of to school."

"Don't romanticize Indians," warned Nathanial. "Who is really free, the man who lives on Washington Square, near docks unloading food from all across the world, or the one who has to chase rabbits and deer for his dinner?"

"The one who chases rabbits and deer."

"I'm not surprised to hear you say that, since I've been told that you're behaving like an Apache in school."

Their mother said, "He always claims the big boys push him around, but why do they choose him, out of all the children?"

Jeffrey seemed genuinely puzzled. "I don't know."

She continued, "I hope you're not being overly sensitive to remarks of the other boys. If you don't like what they're saying, just ignore them."

"What if they hit me when I don't do what they say?"

Nathanial said, "I think it's time I spoke with your schoolmaster."

"No, *I'll* speak with him," said Amalia Barrington.

"I'll go with you," volunteered Nathanial.

"I don't need help with schoolmasters, thank you."

Maria Dolores could see that the Americano soldier was drunk as soon as his shadow appeared in the doorway. His forage cap was crooked, his eyes half closed, gait unsteady. He took one look around and saw a lone big-busted young Mexican woman behind the counter of the store, for her father had gone to a meeting with the alcalde.

She'd learned some English, and knew how to smile even when frightened. "I can help you, sir?"

The soldier was a Missouri volunteer, and the judge had told him to join the army or go to jail for robbery, burglary, and several other charges including attempted murder. His name was Toomey and sometimes he wished he'd gone to jail, because one thousand miles had been hell on his feet. He slouched to the counter, looked around, and said, "Bottle of mescal."

His breath nearly took the skin from her nasal passages. She reached underneath the counter, withdrew a bottle of fermented maguey, told him the price, and he dropped American coins on the counter. She counted them carefully, not yet completely familiar with American currency, as he pulled the cork, leaned back, and took a long swig.

He leaned at an impossible angle, and Maria Dolores felt certain that he'd fall on his head. Then, as her eyes widened with surprise, he lost his balance, his cranium crashed into the floor, and he lay still as death. She ran around the counter, took his head in her arms, and a wave of incredible body odor nearly knocked her over. But she swallowed it down, tapped the man's cheeks, and said, "Are you all right?"

He opened one eye. "Who the hell're you?"

His eye was only inches from her breast, at which he leered. She recoiled, letting his head drop to the floor. He rolled around and arose to his knees as she returned behind the counter, placing her long strong fingers on the flintlock pistol on the shelf.

The gringo soldier ascended unsteadily to his feet, then leaned toward her. "You ain't bad-lookin' fer a greaser woman. How much?"

"For what?" she replied.

"You."

"I am not for sale, sir."

He shrugged. "I don't want to buy yer li'l ass. I jest want to rent it fer a while." He slogged toward the counter and pulled out some coins. "This enough?"

"Not all Mexican girls are prostitutes," she told him coolly.

"You must be the first who ain't."

"Perhaps you are too drunk to notice."

The crooked smile vanished from his face. "You think yer too good fer an American soldier?"

She pulled the gun from beneath the counter, pointed it between his eyes, and said, "Start walking out the door."

He appeared stupefied by the sudden turnaround, angled dumbly away, but then his hand darted up out of nowhere and grabbed her wrist, while his other hand clasped her throat and pinned her to the wall. "You'll have to git up pretty early in the mornin' to fool old Jed Toomey," he spat into her face. "Yer just another Mexican whore and now it's time to show me what you got." He reached into the collar of her dress and was about to tear it off when a voice came from the door. "What the hell's going on in here!"

A fearful expression came over Toomey's face as he drew himself to attention. An American officer with gold shoulder straps and white belt entered the store, his scowl framed by dark brown side-whiskers. "Are you all right, senorita?"

She rubbed her sore neck. "I think so."

The officer spun around and punched Toomey in the mouth. The force of the blow lifted the errant soldier off his feet and propelled him across the room, where he crashed into the wall, slid down, and lay in a heap on the floor.

The officer removed his forage cap and bowed slightly. "I am Lieutenant Beauregard Hargreaves, First Dragoons, and I apologize for the behavior of that pig lying over there."

Maria Dolores noticed the officer's tanned complexion and cordial smile. "Thank you," she stuttered. "If you had not arrived, I do not know what might have happened."

"I do, and we would've had to hang him. Unfortunately, ma'am, armies don't always attract the best people, but even *I* draw the line somewhere."

The soldier lay still as death, his lips pulped. The officer pushed back the brim of his hat, leaned his elbow on the bar, and said, "I'm looking for a pair of boots, because the ones I'm wearing are all beat to hell. What've you got?"

"Boots are handmade, sir. I will have to take your measure. Will you sit?"

Beau dropped onto a chair and laboriously pulled off his knee-high cavalry boots, while she fetched pencil and paper. He'd been dispatched north with a message for General Kearny, then managed to get himself transferred. Now he commanded a company of dragoons, instead of being an aide-de-camp.

She knelt in front of him, he placed his left foot on the paper, and she traced his pattern, feeling his man's eyes upon her. He seemed a different species compared to the other one lying out cold on the floor.

"I guess it's not easy for you to live in your own conquered country," he said softly.

"That is *corriente*."

"If I were you, I'd move to Santa Fe. It's much safer than this little place. We're setting up a perma-

nent camp there, and the Apaches would never dare
attack it. That's where I'm headed."

"My father has often spoken of moving there," she
replied. "We used to have a ranch, but Apaches took
the land."

"We'll take care of those savages—don't worry. A
lot of soldiers are coming to New Mexico, and soon
you'll be able to go home again."

She raised a skeptical eye. "For nearly three hundred years the Conquistadors and then the Mexican
Army have tried to 'take care' of the Apaches, as you
say. But the Apaches are still here."

"They haven't faced the U.S. dragoons yet."

A tall man with gray mustaches appeared in the
doorway. He looked first at the soldier stirring on the
floor, then the American officer, and finally his daughter. "What has happened?" asked Diego Carbajal.

"One of my men was bothering this woman, but I
took care of him. I apologize on behalf of the United
States Government."

Diego was clearly embarrassed. "I should not have
left her alone."

Toomey picked himself up off the floor, tried to
speak, but his jaw was broken. Beau darted forward
and kicked the soldier through the door. "Wait for
me at my tent—*Private* Toomey!"

The soldier stumbled away as Beau turned toward
Diego. They were about the same height, but Beau
had more massive shoulders, a barrel chest, and more
muscle, not to mention youth. Diego knew that the
Americano could defeat him in a fight, and the notion
dispirited him. "Thank you for helping my daughter,"
he said coolly.

"Anytime."

Maria Dolores tried to hate the officer as he headed
for the door. He represented the arrogance of
America, and the belief that they could accomplish
anything. But he'd probably saved her life, and if that
wasn't enough, he was a customer.

"I detest them," Diego hissed when the officer was out of earshot. "I wish I never had to look at another Americano."

"He said he is going to get rid of the Apaches."

They looked seriously at each other, then burst into laughter and hugged in the middle of the floor. "The gringos are funny," he said, "because they do not know how stupid they are."

"He said we should move to Santa Fe, because the army is going to build a camp there."

"So I have heard. Would you like to go to Santa Fe, my dear?"

"Well, Las Vegas is not much of a place."

"You deserve better than this, my dearest child." He touched her cheek tenderly. "That man did not hurt you, did he?"

"Scared me more than anything else, and it is a good thing the officer came along. But it will never happen again." She raised the gun and aimed at the wall. "There is no point in having one of these if you are afraid to use it."

Nathanial limped past tall masted ships lined up on the East River docks. The scents of brine and pitch filled the air. Wagons delivered stores or carried away cargoes, sailors shouted from the rigging of ships, and sidewalk vendors hawked their wares as the inevitable gangs of urchins lurked about.

It was ten o'clock in the morning at America's busiest port, and Nathanial stopped to rest before a sturdy four-story brick building. The sign above the door said:

BARRINGTON SHIPPING
No Cargo Too Large or Too Small

Nathanial climbed the stairs and entered an office full of male clerks working at desks. "I'd like to see my uncle," he said.

They recognized the returning war hero, and a clerk led him to a back office, where he knocked on the door. A voice inside bade them enter, and a chubby man in a white beard arose behind the desk, holding out his one remaining arm, for he'd lost the other in the Battle for Queenston Heights during the War of 1812. "My boy," he said, clasping his nephew to his bosom. "Your mother sent me word that you were home, and I'm so glad to see you."

"Many times I thought of you, Uncle Caleb. It's good to be home."

Uncle Caleb helped Nathanial to an upholstered green leather chair, then took his seat at the desk. Behind him, through the window, a sailor furled a canvas sail on the topmast of a ship.

"They didn't kill you," observed Uncle Caleb, "but it sure looks like they tried."

"It must be the good Barrington blood in my veins that saved me."

Caleb smiled gently. "I'm proud of you, Nathanial. You always were a fine lad. How long will you be with us?"

"The doctors say it might take a year before I'm back to normal."

"I know how you feel, because I've stopped some lead in my day too," allowed Uncle Caleb, moving the stub of his left arm. "So have all the Barrington men, and some never came back."

Nathanial's Uncle Robert had been killed at Cowper's Farm, and the earlier generation had lost Barringtons in the Revolutionary War. "I thought I was coming home to get married," said Nathanial. "But it appears that my dearly beloved is engaged to another gentleman."

"We must maintain marriage in proper perspective, my boy. Flowers and poetry are lovely, but money buys homes on Murray Hill."

"You may think me ridiculous, but I believe love is more important than Murray Hill."

Uncle Caleb nearly laughed in his face, but this was his nephew, and he wanted to be helpful. "You've always been a conundrum to me, Nathanial. On one hand, you've been a hell-raiser practically from the time you could walk, and I know from personal observation that your father had to chastise you on numerous occasions. But you also had an easy side, like a poet or a dreamer, or one of those Boston Transcendentalists who go around sniffing leaves and saying how wonderful everything is, while their parents foot the bill." Uncle Caleb referred to one of his own sons, Christopher Barrington, who had removed to Boston and become a follower of Ralph Waldo Emerson.

"But the world would be boring without philosophers and priests," replied Nathanial. "As the Bible says: *In my father's house there are many mansions.*"

Uncle Caleb examined Nathanial carefully. "Perhaps you should've been a priest, but I could use a smart young fellow like you here, and your salary would far exceed what you earn now. You don't have to answer at this moment—think it over—and by the way, what are you doing tonight? I happen to have two tickets to the New York Philharmonic, and I'd intended to take your aunt, but she's not feeling well and you can have them if you like. Perhaps you might want to invite your mother or Jeffrey. It's an all-Beethoven program, and some consider music good for the health."

Nathanial's next stop was Wall Street, where gentlemen in stovepipe hats rushed about carrying satchels filled with paper, while the Trinity Church steeple greeted the morning light. Carriages roared down the middle of the street, everyone rushing madly, and from the perspective of a frontier soldier, the brokers and clerks appeared totally deluded. How can people live like this? wondered Nathanial.

He entered a sedate stone building and climbed to the second floor. At the end of the corridor sat a clerk with spectacles on the tip of his nose. "Nathanial Barrington—am I correct?"

"You have a good memory."

"I've been seeing you here since you were a boy, sir. Let me tell Mr. Rutherford that you've arrived."

Nathanial dropped to one of the purple velvet chairs, while on the far wall hung a portrait of his mother's great-grandfather in a powdered wig. Michael Rutherford had founded the investment firm of Rutherford & Rutherford in the era when America was a colony of England. The uncle whom Nathanial was about to visit had inherited the business, and was the richest member of his mother's family.

"Right this way, sir," said the clerk.

He led Nathanial to a bald gnome with an impish smile seated behind a desk in an austere wood-paneled office. The old man's skin appeared translucent, with veins and white bones showing through, for he'd spent most of his life in offices, studying numbers as if they were keys to mastery of the universe.

"When did you arrive, my boy? My God, have you been wounded?"

Nathanial supplied basic information about travel arrangements and battle experience, omitting certain embarrassing details, such as his hesitation over killing a certain Mexican sergeant.

"I don't mind telling you, Nathanial," his uncle declared, "that I am thrilled to see you. Although you carry the Barrington name, you'll always be a Rutherford as far as I'm concerned, and if there's ever anything you need, don't hesitate to ask. Your mother has had a very trying time lately. I don't know if anybody's told you yet, but your father's carrying on more or less openly with a widow half his age in Washington."

For the first time, Nathanial heard the true version. He recalled his mother's melancholy the previous night. "I've heard intimations."

"People don't talk about such things, especially people like your mother, but you're a man, you've fought in a war, and you might as well know the sordid details. It's not the first time your father has been unfaithful to her, but at least he was discreet before. If I were young and reckless, I'd challenge him to a duel, and he'd blow my head off. By the way, what are you doing tonight?"

Nathanial's face betrayed not one iota of emotion, but he was disturbed by what he'd learned about his father, as if it were a reflection on him. But he recovered quickly and said, "Uncle Caleb gave me tickets to the Philharmonic, and I thought I'd take Mother."

"When the concert is over, why don't you come to my home? It's your aunt's birthday, and I'm throwing a little party. I've invited your mother, but she turned me down. Scandal isn't one of the necklaces that she cares to wear in public, but maybe you can change her mind. Everyone will be there, including many people you know. There might even be a general or two."

Nathanial couldn't help smiling, because Uncle Jasper knew how to get along in the world. Ostensibly it was a birthday party for his wife, but actually business as usual. "Have you invited the Astors, by any chance?"

"But of course," replied Uncle Jasper. "I suspect your real question concerns a certain soon-to-be member of the Astor family, am I right? Yes, Layne Satterfield will be there, but I hope she doesn't scare you away. If you could stand up to the Mexican Army, I'm sure you can manage an old flame. Don't be angry at her, Nathanial. How many of us could walk away from the biggest fortune in America?"

Nathanial smiled. "Do people sometimes act for reasons unrelated to money in New York?"

"Whatever made you think such a ridiculous thing?" Uncle Jasper laughed sarcastically at his own joke. "There are always exceptions, like your father, but I've never been able to understand the affection some feel for the military. I only put on a uniform to fight for my country, and when it was over, I returned to my profession. But if you want to impress silly young girls, I suppose it's helpful to wear a uniform with gold braid or other gewgaws. I hope you don't think I'm being disrespectful to the army, but I notice that you're wearing civilian clothes, unlike your father, who's always dressed for the next Fourth of July parade."

"Somebody might throw a loose cobblestone at me, if I wore my uniform. A lot of civilians are opposed to the war, I understand."

"Only the usual maniacs. You might want to wear it tonight, because many marriageable ladies will be available for your perusal. You still intend to marry, I hope?"

"As soon as I can find the right woman, sir."

"Men who don't marry end as drunkards and wastrels with certain diseases of the flesh. And then of course there are some like your father, who marry on the surface but behave as if they're still single. I hope you won't be annoyed by my uncomplimentary remarks concerning your father, but he's broken my sister's heart and I'll never forgive him. I think he's weak, selfish, and idiotic—and you may tell him that I said so."

Nathanial wouldn't argue with the wealthiest member of his family, but had to be fair. "I should hear his side of the story before I pass judgment, sir."

"He'll probably tell you that he's found true love, and I'm certain he means it, but he's already got a wife, and what about his much vaunted soldier's honor? I suppose you think I'm an old crank, ranting and raving about family obligations when all I care about is money, but my word is my bond, that's how this business has been built, and that's how life should be conducted. I have no respect for those who break solemn vows, but the highest aspiration of most people is to indulge themselves in as many shabby love affairs as possible. However, I'm sure you have more important tasks than listening to me discuss your father. I look forward to seeing you tonight, but now, if you'll pardon me—I have important work to do."

Horses and carriages crowded in front of the Apollo Rooms, at 410 Broadway between Walker and Canal Streets, prior to the beginning of the evening's performance. The blazing marquee illuminated begowned and bejeweled laughing ladies stepping to the curb, assisted by dark-suited escorts, as crowds of concert-goers milled about.

There were oohs and aahs as friends greeted each other, and everyone noticed what everyone else was wearing, appearance being extremely significant in Calcutta on the Hudson. Politicians, actors, journalists, and other celebrities jostled each other on the sidewalk, while urbane sophisticates pretended not to gawk. These were the New Yorkers who appreciated art, culture, and all the other fine accoutrements that civilized people supposedly require.

There were old men with young women, middle-aged husbands and wives in silent feuds, old women with young men, and groups of gentlemen rovers with saturnine eyes and red noses from excessive alcoholic intake. Beggars hovered on the periphery of the crowd, holding out grimy palms.

In shadows next to a poster stood a young man with a scarred cheek, pale features, and a black cape, leaning on his cane. Nathanial had acquired a haircut and shave, his mustache neatly trimmed, and beneath the cape wore a black suit with the jacket cut trim to his waist and flared over his hips. A white shirt and black tie completed his uniform, and he puffed a cheroot, not certain whether to be amused or disgusted by what passed before his eyes.

It was a gaudy and silly charade, compared to what he'd seen at Palo Alto. He couldn't help feeling contempt for them, because these people enjoyed the fruits of America, while others bled on far-off battle-

fields. Nathanial wanted to step forward like an Old
Testament prophet and lecture on the vanity of vani-
ties, but perhaps he was the vain one, for he saw glory
in what some might call butchery. He flashed on blood
staining the grass at Palo Alto, then opened his eyes.
One would hardly guess that these people had blood
in their veins, for they looked like puppets in the
gaslight.

He'd been unsuccessful in convincing his mother to
leave her sitting room, and Jeffrey had caught a sniffle
at the birthday party, requiring hot towels and bedrest,
according to Shirley Rooney. So Nathanial had come
to the Apollo alone, with an extra ticket in his back
pocket. His sturdy and reliable cane would enjoy the
concert with a seat of its own.

A delicate young man in a black usher's uniform
made his way through the crowd, tingling a bell. "The
performance begins in ten minutes!" he declared in a
mellifluous voice.

Nathanial took a few last puffs on his cigar as the
others streamed inside. He waited until the path to
the door was clear, so no one would bump him, then
placed the cane before him and was taking an uncertain step when a small filthy figure appeared in front
of him, hand outstretched. It was a child, and it appeared that he'd spent his life in a coal bin. "Kin yer
spare a coin, sir, fer sumpin' ter eat?"

Nathanial stared at the child in grim fascination and
thought, This is the face of truth. He reached into
his pocket and dropped five dollars into the fragile
little palm.

The boy stared at the coin in disbelief. "Thank
you, sir."

"What's your name?"

"Tobey."

"Where do you live?"

"Nowheres, sir. You look like you been hurt. Git
runned over by a horse? It happened to me onc't, but
I moved so fast, he didn't hurt me much."

Nathanial had read about New York's armies of homeless children, but if he invited the boy to his mother's home, she'd collapse, Jeffrey would become jealous, and the urchin might advise the worst thieves and cutthroats in Five Points regarding the value of certain gold and silver items lying around.

The child had a bony undernourished face and skinny legs. Nathanial simply couldn't walk away from him. "How'd you like to have a job?" he asked.

"A job, sir? Me?" The lad became suspicious, because he'd been propositioned for "jobs" before. "What yer want me to do?"

"Help me until I can take better care of myself. You'll be my manservant, except you're not a man."

"I don't do none of that funny stuff, sir."

"Neither do I, but I haven't time to talk now. Meet me at noon tomorrow at the Winkin' Pup Tavern on Nassau Street, right off Printery Square."

The boy stood wide-eyed on the curb, the five-dollar coin in his hand, and his jaw hanging open. But before Nathanial could enter the Apollo, a carriage came to a halt at the curb.

"Don't start the show without me!" slurred a man in a stovepipe hat, who stepped unsteadily to the sidewalk. The carriage rolled away, the man reached into his back pocket, withdrew a silver flask, took a swallow, and returned it to his pocket. Then he leaned to the right and left, as he tried to focus glassy eyes on the entrance.

"Good evening, Reginald," said Nathanial. "If you're looking for the Apollo, it's straight ahead."

Reginald Van Zweinan blinked uncertainly at a man with a cane. "My God—it's Nathanial Barrington."

The West Pointer bowed stiffly. "At your service, sir."

"I believe someone told me that you got shot up in the war. Are you going to the concert?"

Nathanial withdrew his tickets. "I have two seats in the pit. Want one?"

"The pit? No friend of Reginald Van Zweinan's sits in the *pit*. You'll come to my box, of course."

Nathanial helped Reginald across the lobby and up the stairs, although Nathanial appeared in need of assistance himself. Reginald had been reading law at Columbia College when the West Pointer had been in town last. As boys, they'd attended the Pembroke School together, and known each other since the early grades. Reginald was scion of a distinguished old Dutch family, far more distinguished than the Barringtons, but Reginald had been drinking heavily since his midteens and appeared as if he'd never walked away from a plate of food.

They came to the Van Zweinan box, and the corpulent Reginald collapsed into a chair. The audience stretched beneath them, with the stage to the right. Nathanial lowered himself into his seat, enchanted by the spectacle of a New York concert. He saw beautiful ladies in the latest flounced gowns, elegant gentlemen with enormous stomachs just like Reginald's, plus the usual scattering of those with more money than sense when it came to clothes. Occasionally a sallow fellow in tattered coat could be seen, probably an out-of-work musician or composer with a free ticket, and there were certain women of such elegance and splendor that they could only be expensive prostitutes.

Nathanial raised his eyes to the boxes on the far side of the concert hall, and the veteran of Palo Alto saw jewels gleaming on the pale necks of women trained from birth to be beautiful and gracious. He could even recognize some of the ladies, for New York was a small town in many ways, and he'd attended their birthday parties just as they'd come to his.

His box partner burped. "You don't happen to have a pencil, old man?" asked Reginald.

Nathanial reached inside his jacket pocket. "Have you just received inspiration for a poem?"

"I've become a critic for the *Post*," replied Reginald, "and I've got to write a review."

"But you're practically out on your feet, Reginald. Can you see the stage?"

"Music is not about seeing, you Philistine. It is about listening to the harmony of the human soul." The pencil fell from Reginald's hand as he hunched in his seat, out cold. His tie was askew, and a bit of drool escaped from the corner of his mouth. The audience burst into applause as the conductor approached the podium. Nathanial turned toward the stage, but a certain blond lady caught his eye on the opposite tier.

His heart stumbled, and he felt the pressure of blood against his cheeks. The house lights dimmed, but he couldn't remove his eyes from Miss Layne Satterfield. Nathanial didn't know whether to leave the Apollo at once, or commit suicide in spectacular fashion by diving headfirst onto the stage, or walk to her box and break his cane over her head.

He heard the first strains of the Eroica Symphony as his heart thrashed wildly in his chest. He'd given her his love, but she'd spurned him for another while he'd been fighting a war. Her treachery was almost beyond comprehension, and he thought again of jumping off the balcony, but he'd probably land inside a tuba, and his death would provide a laugh for her.

He wondered what flaws she'd noticed in him, or if it was just a matter of filthy lucre. She'd always seemed a sensible woman with solid moral inclinations, and that's why he'd wanted to marry her. He feared that she perceived something inside him that he didn't know about, and money had nothing to do with it. She probably thinks I'm shallow and simpleminded because I chose the army instead of a legitimate profession, and maybe she's right.

All eyes were riveted to the orchestra, but Nathanial continued to peer at Layne Satterfield. Next to her sat a short, balding gentleman with muttonchop whiskers and spectacles, the man with whom she'd sleep every night. Nathanial nearly gagged on the anguish arising in his throat.

He wanted to leave the box immediately, but his limbs couldn't move swiftly, and then he noticed, through the gold mists separating them, that she was looking not at the orchestra pumping out Beethoven's hymn to Napoleon, but at *him,* Lieutenant Nathanial Barrington.

He couldn't help remembering the time he'd placed his right hand on her left breast, although she'd been wearing a dress at the time. That's as far as he'd ever gone with Miss Layne Satterfield, but the gentleman sitting beside her, the one who looked like Humpty-Dumpty in evening clothes, would soon caress her naked body every night, while Lieutenant Barrington had only his mattress.

Nathanial smiled malevolently, because he'd charged the Mexican lancers at Palo Alto, and brave Major Ringgold had given his life for the flag, while the Astors, Vanderbilts, and others attended concerts and gala parties.

But my family profits from the war too, Nathanial admitted. He could understand why some preferred to fight with a pen, but he'd assumed that Layne Satterfield knew the difference between profit and glory. His biased opinion was that she'd made the wrong choice.

Powerful chemicals trickled into his bloodstream as he gazed at Layne Satterfield across the concert hall. In the darkness it appeared that she was looking back at him.

Nathanial wasn't hallucinating, for Layne Satterfield was studying him carefully at that very moment. She wondered if he'd noticed her, but it was difficult to see clearly in the darkened auditorium. She'd heard that Nathanial Barrington was in town, but was shocked to see him limp into the box with Reginald Van Zweinan. How he must hate me, she brooded.

She knew the gossip, because she'd heard the same story about other women. *She married him for the money, and is no better than a common prostitute.* And the apple hadn't fallen far from the tree, because she knew, deep in her heart, that she would never in a million years become engaged to Franz Astor if he'd been poor.

Her family's secret was that the Satterfield fortune had shrunk considerably due to decades of unwise investments and extravagant spending habits. They'd managed to keep up appearances just barely, and her original plan was to marry Nathanial and subtract one expense from her father's headaches, but then she'd met Franz, who had clearly been smitten with her, and she'd seen an opportunity to save not only herself but every member of her family. So she and Franz had made a business arrangement that they'd never formally signed or even negotiated overtly, but each knew the terms full well. She'd possess great wealth for the rest of her life, in exchange for certain boring interludes best not discussed in public.

Nobody dared say anything to her face, because the Astors had the power of financial ruination. So everyone was courteous to Layne, and she was eager to become an Astor, surrounded by opulence, with no more worries about her father's possible prosecution for embezzlement. As for the "interludes," she'd get through them somehow. One man is as good as another, she had lectured herself.

But now her first true love sat on the other side of the concert hall, and the Astors naturally had been invited to the Rutherford party that night. Nathanial probably would be there, and she knew that invariably they would meet, everyone would be watching, and she might faint dead away.

Layne Satterfield suffered from shame, pride, and confusion, despite her comely exterior. She'd committed indiscretions with Nathanial that no decent woman would permit, but she'd loved him deeply, or so she'd thought at the time.

There's a time to be romantic and a time to be mature, she lectured herself. Whatever happens, I'll

hold my head high. If he says something awful, I'll
pretend that I haven't heard. She wiped away a tear
that was rolling down her cheek.

"Anything wrong, dear?" asked Franz Astor, leaning closer to her.

"Beethoven is so beautiful," she whispered.

Deep in the Mogollon Mountains, atop a craggy eminence, the People danced around a bonfire burning
furiously into the night. The *di-yin* medicine men wore
fantastic headdresses made of sticks and painted
stretched animal skins, while performing ancient steps
taught their ancestors by the mountain spirits. Firelight flashed on the naked breasts of prancing *bi-zahn*
women, who were widowed, divorced, and unmarried
nonvirgins with no men to care for them.

The sacramental property dance celebrated the ac-
quisition of new wealth into the clan, but also was a
special night for the *bi-zahn* women. At this time only,
they were permitted to sleep with married or unmarried warriors, in return for a share of the treasure.
Firelight illuminated their rosy buttocks as they em-
ployed every strategy to attract the warriors. The
mountain spirits had ordained that they should enjoy
passion and receive prizes, while the bravest warriors
fornicated themselves into unconsciousness.

The Mexican captives sat huddled nearby, whispering prayers to Jesus, Mary, and the saints. Drums
pounded their ears as they watched warriors escort
women to the darkness at the edge of the campsite.
The captives were all children except for thin but wiry
Elena Galindez, twenty-five-year old widow of Pedrito, the guard whose throat had been sliced at dawn.
Trembling with hysteria, she was determined to fight
any warrior who tried to rape her in the course of the
evening's festivities.

She saw warriors asleep from excessive drink, and
wanted to steal a knife. The chief of the Apaches and
other warriors cast leers in her direction, and she knew

what they wanted. She'd feared Apaches all her life, and now they'd finally caught her. Warriors walked past, jabbering their strange language. She wondered if they were planning to chop off her head.

The Apache camp was worse than any hell she'd imagined, and not even Father Alfonso's sermons on purgatory had described anything like it. Elena couldn't understand how God could let such a thing happen, and doubted for the first time whether He truly existed.

She gawked at women shaking their hips convulsively, even picking up their skirts and displaying themselves. Elena's heart throbbed in time to the drums, stars twinkled in the heavens, and someone fired a gun, causing her to jump three inches off the ground.

She was afraid they'd tear her limb from limb and cook her in the fire. Imagining one torture after another, she prayed for rapid death. More than ever, she could understand bounties for Apache scalps. I'll take one with me, if I ever steal a knife, she swore.

A black-shellacked carriage rolled past gaslit Union Square, and in the cab Nathanial and Reginald Van Zweinan gazed at a neighborhood of taverns, billiard halls, oyster cellars, and bowling alleys. The streets were crowded with men in varying stages of inebriation, enticed by bright lights and prostitutes, some fairly pretty, others faded flowers soon to be viewed in the Five Points slum, on the Peyster Street docks, or other less salubrious locales.

"I'm curious about the war," said Reginald as he passed the flask to Nathanial. "Most of what I hear is third and fourth hand, but you were actually there. What were your impressions?"

"Never saw so many mosquitoes in my life."

"What do the soldiers think of the war?"

"You're not writing all this down, are you?"

"You don't expect me to make up the news, do you?"

"But you slept through the concert!"

"I was listening carefully to every modulation."

"You were snoring so loud, the people around us were looking at you."

"The concert put me to sleep, and that's what I'll say in my review."

"It was my impression that you fell asleep because you were drunk."

"If the concert had been more fascinating, I would've been more attentive. Why won't you give me a straight answer about the war?"

"I was only a lieutenant and don't know that much about it."

"Did you ever meet Old Rough and Ready?"

"I was one of his aides, and he's a great general."

"Some say he's an ignorant, backcountry tobacco-chewing buffoon who wants to be president."

"He'll get my vote anyday."

The carriage turned uptown on Fifth Avenue, lined with stately stone mansions illuminated by flickering gaslight emanating from lamps on wrought-iron poles. This was Manhattan's gold coast, and Nathanial could perceive heads behind draperied windows, where residents drank fine Madeira and enjoyed opulent living.

"There's something I've always wondered about," said Reginald. "Could you tell me, in your own words, what it's like to get shot at."

"Exactly what you'd imagine."

"Can't you be more specific?"

"No."

"People are curious about such things."

"Let them join the army and find out for themselves. Now it's time for me to ask a question. Why are you working as a reporter when your father is rich?"

"Father has cut my allowance and thrown me out, because he claims I'm disgracing the family escutcheon, which of course is true. So I called Bill Bryant at the *Post,* and he gave me a job. The pay's not bad, and I can indulge my natural tendency to be curious under official auspices. What do you say to critics of the war who claim it's just a crime against another sovereign nation?"

"Maybe it is."

"Meet any Indians?"

"Saw a few at a distance."

"What do you think they'd say if they saw Fifth Avenue."

"Is this an interview?"

"All my conversations are interviews."

"You're not going to use my real name, I hope."

"Do you have something to hide?"

"Don't tell me you've become a sneaky double-dealing journalist like all the rest of the so-called fourth estate?"

Reginald smiled affably. "But of course."

They approached a white Georgian mansion just past Eighteenth Street. Other carriages were crowded at the curb, their drivers gathered beneath a gaslight, smoking cigarettes and telling jokes about their employers. They lowered their voices discreetly as Nathanial and Reginald climbed down from the cab.

The front door was opened by a uniformed manservant, who recognized both of the new guests immediately. "Good evening, Mr. Van Zweinan, and it's so good to see you again, Lieutenant Barrington. This way, please."

The vestibule's walls were covered with hand-painted Chinese wallpaper depicting pagodas, herons, trees, and crags. A crystal chandelier provided bright illumination for a painting of Nathanial's grandmother Frances as a somber young girl.

A uniformed Negro maid led them to the parlor, where expensively attired men and women stood or sat, with tobacco smoke thick in the air, while a gen-

tleman with a violin performed a Telemann sonata in
the corner.

"Nathanial!" The spry Jasper Rutherford held out
his hand. "So glad you could come."

They embraced, then Nathanial turned toward Aunt
Mildred and kissed her cheek. "Happy birthday."

Her eyes widened at the scar on his cheek. "Oh,
Nathanial . . ." She kissed the scar gently. "You've
done your part in the war, and now we need you
here."

Nathanial opened his mouth to reply, but was
swamped by cousins, distant relatives, old friends, old
enemies, and even his uncle's cocker spaniel remembered him. Bathed in love, covered with honor, Nathanial felt like a charlatan. *I nearly got myself killed,
but these people think I'm a hero.*

He made his way through well-wishers, including
people he didn't even know. Splendid women were
everywhere, bursting with life, looking him up and
down. *So this is what it's like to be Caesar,* he reflected as he removed a glass of champagne from a
handworked silver tray held by a Negro waiter.

Uncle Jasper maneuvered in front of Nathanial. "I
was afraid you wouldn't come."

"I'd like to sit down, if you don't mind."

A maid placed a chair beneath him as he lowered
himself beside a raven-tressed beauty approximately
sixteen years old. "May I present Donna Wilbourne,"
said his uncle graciously.

He took her proffered hand. Her skin was creamy,
her nose aquiline, and cleverness gleamed out of her
eyes. "I've heard so much about you," she said. "Your
uncle's been talking about you all evening."

Uncle Jasper puffed out his chest. "It's men like this
who've made America the great country that it is!"

A cheer went up from the crowd, and Nathanial
wanted to comment caustically on his performance at
Palo Alto, but decided not to spoil their pleasure. His
uncle sidestepped toward a nearby group of investors,

while women gathered on the far side of the room. A few couples sat beneath a crystal chandelier, and everyone was distorted in the reflection of the curved girandole gilt-framed mirror above the mantel.

The wallpaper showed monuments of Paris, and the furniture was dark mahogany with blue silk cushions. Nathanial's military aesthetic found it too ostentatiously luxurious, as if every possession said, "I have wonderful taste," instead of "this is a comfortable place to live."

"Excuse me, Lieutenant Barrington," said Miss Wilbourne. "I do believe you've spilled something on your pants."

Nathanial realized that the night of drinking had begun to take it toll. "I'd better swallow it all down, before I spill more."

He leaned back his head and swallowed the dregs of the glass, then placed it on the tray of a passing maid, and selected another full one.

Miss Wilbourne watched with an amused but skeptical smile. "They say that army officers are fond of spirits, and you evidently are upholding that fine old tradition."

"It's always the best way to handle it," Nathanial replied. "I don't believe I've ever seen you before."

"I'm from Maine, and I'm visiting with my mama." She gave *mama* the French pronunciation.

Nathanial cynically calculated her game. There weren't many eligible men in Maine, so her parents trundled her to New York in search of a husband. She appeared intelligent, well bred, and comely, in Nathanial's estimation. "Where are you staying?"

"With relatives."

Nathanial wanted to invite her into a broom closet, but in New York society, he'd have to court her for a year, and then be engaged for a year, but unfortunately he couldn't wait that long. What other choice do I have? he asked himself. Maybe I should take advantage of this opportunity while I've got the chance.

"Are you *sure* you're all right, Lieutenant?"

"Perfectly fine," he replied, sipping the top off his beverage. "Have you ever thought of getting married, Miss Wilbourne?"

She appeared surprised by his question. "Of course."

"Please try to keep an open mind about what I'm going to say. You and I are approximately the same age, and we're both single. I think you're beautiful, and I myself am not lacking certain charms. I realize this is sudden, but why don't we cut all the folderol and get married as soon as humanly possible?"

"Do you mean elope?"

"Why not?"

She smiled indulgently, then tapped the back of his hand. "Lieutenant, I don't mean to be presumptuous, but I really think you shouldn't drink so much."

There was a swirl of skirts, then she was gone. Nathanial blinked as he found himself alone with the glass of champagne in his hand. It occurred to him that he'd behaved boorishly, but it wasn't his fault that civilians couldn't manage direct communication. *Maybe I was around Old Rough and Ready too long,* Nathanial concluded.

He noticed an empty seat in a dark corner near a shelf of books. Limping in that direction, he collapsed onto the chair, took another drink, and surveyed the scene before him.

All the men were trying to impress each other, while selling this or that bill of goods. He turned his attention to the women and undressed the pretty ones with his lonely eyes. He knew he was being disgusting, but it was better than meditating upon the decline and fall of American values. *I can't manage loneliness anymore,* Nathanial admitted to himself. *If God wants to hurl a lightning bolt at me, it can't be worse than this.* A Negro maid passed, carrying a tray of little

sandwiches. Nathanial selected one, and his eyes met
hers. Another stab of passion upset his equilibrium,
because she looked like a Nubian princess, or what he
imagined a Nubian princess to be.

The Negress walked away, and his eyes followed.
She was big and strong, with a carriage as erect as
any army officer, but more graceful, with a certain
jungle charm. He couldn't take his eyes off her, and
wondered what it was like to make love with a
Negress.

He wanted to entice her into the cellar, and gently
remove her uniform, but she was out of bounds. There
seemed no way to satisfy his aching desire, so he decided to ask Reginald for whorehouse recommendations. Glancing toward the ceiling, he thought,
Evidently I made a promise I can't keep, but at least
I tried.

Guests appeared to be talking about him. He realized that he was part of the decor, a melancholy and
poetic hero home from the war, entertainment for
tastes jaded by fashionable pastimes.

Then he saw Layne Satterfield arrive, and his heart
stuttered in his chest. Their eyes met, and he was out
of his chair in an instant. Leaning on his cane, he
made his way into a corridor, opened the door to the
kitchen, hobbled past cooks at the stove, and landed
in the backyard, where the half-moon floated over the
rooftops of Manhattan.

The yard was cramped compared to expanses he'd
seen in the West. A few trees had been planted, with
wood furniture placed in strategic spots, but even a
rich man couldn't afford much room on the island
of Manhattan.

He entered the barn, where his uncle's three horses
were sequestered. Mixed fragrances of hay and manure reminded Nathanial of the army as he approached the nearest horse. The animal's intelligent
eyes studied him, as Nathanial patted its head, won-

dering what happened to his Duke, his warhorse at Palo Alto.

Then Nathanial sat on a barrel, lit a fresh cigar, and wondered if he could escape without seeing Layne Satterfield. It frightened him to know that she was only a few feet away, and he'd rather face a squadron of Mexican lancers.

I've made my appearance, and maybe I should just get the hell out of here. He sipped champagne and wondered if he could climb the back fence, but decided he might break his skull. He returned to the kitchen, peeked into the corridor, made sure the coast was clear, and followed his cane toward the parlor, wondering how to reconnoiter without appearing odd. Nothing came to mind, so he squared his shoulders, gripped his cane firmly, and advanced into enemy territory.

He saw Layne Satterfield immediately at the far side of the room, their eyes met, and then he turned toward Reginald Van Zweinan, who was standing near the fireplace with a group of investors. One of them declaimed, "This nation cannot continue to admit so many foreigners and expect to maintain its integrity!"

Reginald noticed Nathanial winking at him, and excused himself from the group. "Something wrong with your eye, old man?"

Nathanial furtively glanced at Layne Satterfield on the other side of the room. "I've been away a long time, Reginald, and was wondering if you could ... ah ... recommend a decent ... house of ill fame."

Reginald raised his eyebrows. "There are many good ones. What are you interested in?"

"The prettiest women in the safest surroundings."

"I don't suppose you want to whip them or have them whip you?"

Nathanial stared at him icily. "I am not the Marquis de Sade."

"Try Miss Nell's on Twelfth Street, right off Broadway."

Nathanial headed for the door, while keeping as much parlor as possible between Layne Satterfield and his person. He entered the vestibule, and the pretty Negro maid was there, looking at him expectantly.

"My coat, please."

She pulled it out of the closet, and he couldn't help admiring her form. But there was no place to meet her, and he didn't know what to say anyway. She had large breasts and was looking at him apprehensively. "Are you all right, sir?"

"Do I look sick?"

"You sure seem as if somethin's wrong."

"What's your name?"

"Elizabeth."

"Are you married?"

"Yes."

"Your husband is a lucky man."

She helped him with his cape, he placed his top hat on his head, turned to the door, and Layne Satterfield was standing there, an uncertain smile on her face.

He was taken aback, but had the good sense to remove his hat. "Good evening, Miss Satterfield."

She couldn't look him in the eye. "Do you think we can talk for a moment?"

"I really don't have much time."

Her eyes became watery. "How you must hate me."

"You can't help being what you are."

She stiffened, and stern resolution appeared on her face. "I will always love you, Nathanial, but I must do what I think is right."

"I feel the same way, and if you'll excuse me, there's a certain whorehouse that I want to go to."

A tear rolled down her cheek, but she stopped it with the knuckle of her hand. He looked at her small left breast, the one he'd cupped in his big right hand, and couldn't help recalling sheer ecstasy. She blushed as if she knew what he was thinking.

"Don't take the easy way out, Nathanial," she said in a quavering voice. "You're too fine for that."

"But not fine enough for you, eh?"

"Far too fine, but love is more complicated than I'd imagined."

He looked her in the eye. "Everything has its price, I suppose."

"Now you're being cruel."

He wanted to enumerate her crimes, but then it struck him that she was as desperate and lost as he. *Let he who is without sin cast the first stone.* "I'm sorry," he stuttered, becoming confused. "I had no right ..."

She removed a handkerchief from her purse. "I deserve every mean thing you say, but I truly did love you, and you know it."

It was her turn to stare him down, but he couldn't disagree. "I wish I were rich," he whispered.

"But you're not."

A short man with a bald head, eyeglasses, and pointed jaw strolled into the room. "Are you all right, Layne?" asked Franz Astor.

"I have a cinder in my eye," she replied. "This filthy city will be the death of me yet. By the way, do you know Lieutenant Nathanial Barrington. He's just returned from Mexico."

Franz Astor looked up at Lieutenant Barrington. "Oh, I believe I haf heard somebody speak about you. You were wounded in the war?"

Nathanial didn't know what to say, but a West Point officer must continue advancing, even when he doesn't know his objective. "Congratulations," he said, extending his hand. "Layne Satterfield is an extraordinary person. How I envy you."

"I haf never been so happy in my life," exclaimed the Astor.

The smile faltered on Nathanial's face, and all he could do was turn to Layne. "Best of luck."

They shook hands, and he recalled a hot night when they'd kissed passionately for hours.

"Be careful," she replied.

Nathanial turned toward the door just as a new figure stepped into the vestibule. It was William Backhouse Astor, Franz's uncle twice removed and first heir to the Astor fortune. William Backhouse managed the family holdings, as aged John Jacob purportedly was confined to bed.

"Uncle," said Franz, "do you know Nathanial Barrington?"

"Stephen Barrington's boy," replied William Backhouse Astor. "I've been hearing good things about you, Nathanial. Are you leaving? Can I give you a lift somewhere?"

"I'm on my way to Twelfth Street, sir."

"There's something I'd like to discuss with you."

Nathanial couldn't imagine what it was as William Backhouse ushered him to a carriage parked at the curb. A footman opened the door, and the Astor heir followed Nathanial inside. "Stop at Twelfth Street," William Backhouse told the driver.

The carriage rolled away from the curb, made a U-turn on Fifth Avenue, and headed back downtown. William Backhouse sat stolidly on his seat, his stovepipe hat brim low over his eyes as he examined real estate passing his window. "You may not remember me, Nathanial," he began, "but we met when you were a boy. You impressed me because you appeared extremely alert and intelligent, and I'm pleased to see that my observations were correct."

Nathanial couldn't recall meeting him, and didn't know what to make of the declaration. "I'm not sure everybody would agree, but thank you, sir."

"Do you like the army?"

"I can't think of anything I'd rather do."

"Let me give you something to think about. I'm always looking for men who can shoulder responsibility and make the right decision at the critical moment, but it's not always easy to find them. I respect your dedication to the army, but I wonder if you might consider employment with me? I would of course increase your salary substantially. Think it over and let me know your decision."

Nathanial gazed through the shutters of the carriage at the most expensive real estate in New York City. If I accepted the job, I could live on Fifth Avenue or anywhere else that I wanted, he realized. Or I could travel the world like a gentleman, instead of sleeping in tents. "Thank you for the confidence you have shown in me, sir," he replied. "You may be sure I'll give your offer my most serious consideration."

The great chief Mangus Coloradas danced drunkenly around the bonfire, a bottle of mescal in one hand, with a ladies' silk handkerchief in the other. His heart beat rhythmically with the drums, the living desert rushed through his veins, he hopped on one foot, then the other, as *di-yins* in fantastical headdresses whirled about, along with children, dogs, and the seminaked *bi-zahn* women trying to entice the wealthy chief into the wilderness.

Mangus Coloradas could have anyone he wanted, but tonight his taste was for something different. He kept glancing at the pale-skinned Mexican woman sitting near the fire, with straight black hair and wraithlike form. The more he looked at her, the more attractive she became.

He laughed, leapt into the air, and leaned to the side as the power of Yusn smashed him about. He loved firewater because it opened his mind and showed visions of what might be. He imagined himself writhing with the young Mexican nymph and roared like a lion. Everybody watched the great chief execute esoteric dance steps, and just when he appeared ready to fall on his face, somehow he righted himself.

But he couldn't simply rape the captive woman, because that would bring bad luck according to the holy life-way. Mangus Coloradas continued glancing surreptitiously at her for reasons he comprehended all too well. He rocked in time to the music, while wiggling his fingers in the air.

He had to dance the tension away, because the captive woman made him powerful. It frightened him to know that she had such influence over him, but a respected chief couldn't express feelings openly. *I should give her to one of the other warriors, but I want her myself.*

If he selected her as his slave, his present wives would make him miserable. But her skin was without blemish, and she reminded him of White Painted Woman, queen of the universe.

He knew she hated him, for he'd killed her family and the medicine padre. Even if Mangus Coloradas selected her, that didn't mean she'd sleep with him. And after a few years of hard work, she'd look as worn as any of the People. He wondered how it'd feel to place his tongue on that delicious mouth. She appeared fragile, exquisite, drawing him toward her.

He became aware of a *bi-zahn* woman swiveling her hips and trying to catch his attention. Her big, naked breasts bounced up and down, while she worked her hips back and forth. Mangus Coloradas danced in front of her and rotated his body in time to hers. They stood inches apart, staring into each other's eyes, as she licked her lips and the drummers worked themselves into a frenzy.

Luceza the widow had set her cap for the great chief, for he could afford the most fabulous gifts. Thirty harvests old, her husband had been killed on a raid into Mexico, and she had two boys, who themselves were dancing and yipping like puppies, brandishing their little bows and arrows.

Luceza moved closer, and Mangus Coloradas could feel her body heat against his skin. A delicious musky odor arose from her body, and her large breasts flopped before his eyes. He looked over her shoulder at the captive girl, and a rush of mad lust overcame him. *If I can't have the Nakai-yes, I might as well*

enjoy this one, he thought as he caught the shoulder
of the *bi-zahn* woman in his strong hand.

A victorious smile came over her face, for she knew
that she'd won the game. He draped one arm around
her shoulders and eased her onto the range as musicians pounded their drums, the stretched antelope
skins flecked with blood from their numbed fingers.

Nathanial limped down Twelfth Street, leaning on
his cane. The wound in his stomach bothered him
more than usual, his leg hurt, and his mind churned
with tumultuous imaginings.

Shaken by his encounter with Layne Satterfield,
confused by the job offer from William Backhouse
Astor, he decided that Layne Satterfield had become
too tragic to hate, while employment with William
Backhouse could make him a rich man. What do I
like about soldiering? he asked himself. I've done my
duty, and maybe I should make a mature decision for
a change.

The Astor business interests were worldwide, and
the ex-soldier could travel to Cathay, London, Paris,
and all the other exotic spots he'd yearned to see. I
could have a mansion of my own, instead of living
with my mother or in leaky tents filled with bugs. If I
were rich, maybe I could win back Layne Satterfield.

The magic connection between them had been dis-
mantled by money, and maybe they hadn't been so
star-crossed after all. She'd appeared older, careworn,
a fading flower. With a wry smile, he recalled her picture giving him hope before Palo Alto, like a mirage
on the desert.

She didn't deceive me—no—I deceived myself by
investing her with qualities she didn't possess. But he
felt like a discarded old campaign boot, and wished
he could hold Layne Satterfield in his arms.

Absorbed with disappointment, he barely noticed
three figures emerge from the dark alley in front of
him. They were tattered, dirty, and each held a long

knife in his hand. "Let's have yer money," growled their leader. "And don't try nothin', 'cause I'll cut yer damned throat."

Nathanial couldn't run, and was too weak to fight them with his cane. He wished he'd carried his Colt Paterson, but all he could do was reach for his coins. Nathanial dropped his wealth inside the leader's hat, while peering at the long thin nose and curly black hair.

"Don't look at my face," the bandit said.

Nathanial gazed at rooftops across the street. How ironic if I survived Palo Alto, only to be stabbed on the streets of New York. The bandits took his pocket watch, cape, and leather belt.

"Off wit' dem boots, guv'nor, and make it snappy."

Nathanial leaned against the building and removed them laboriously. Then two new figures appeared at the corner of Broadway.

"Here comes somebody," said one of the robbers. "Let's git out here."

The leader turned toward Nathanial. "Start walkin', and if you call the coppers, I'll kill you."

Nathanial hobbled off, wincing as his bare feet touched sharp pebbles, bits of broken glass, tobacco juice, and other vile substances. Behind him he heard the thieves fleeing down the alley. He'd been calm during the robbery, but now trembled uncontrollably. He vowed never to be without his service revolver again.

They'd even taken his flask, and he couldn't visit a whorehouse without money or shoes. Besides, his ardor had cooled as the result of the robbery. Gingerly he continued west on Twelfth Street, heading for Washington Square. "Naturally there are no policemen in the vicinity," he muttered angrily.

Rage and frustration overwhelmed him, and he wanted to tear down a building with his bare hands. His life had taken a turn for the worst beginning with Palo Alto, and he wondered if he'd been cursed by some old Aztec god. Maybe I should go to church instead of a whorehouse, he counseled himself. Am I being punished for my sins?

Maria Dolores folded bolts of cloths behind the counter of her father's store. There were no customers, her father was working in his private office, and then the handsome American lieutenant appeared in the doorway, removing his hat. "My boots ready?"

"Yes, sir," she replied. "Come try them on."

He sat on the bench, and she brought him the black boots. He had moody eyes and grunted like a bear as he pulled on the new footwear. Then he sauntered back and forth in front of her, the sword at his side, his uniform neat and clean. "They feel fine, and by the way, I want to apologize again for the rude behavior of that soldier. To make certain that no one else will bother you again, may I accompany you wherever you're going after you close the store?" He tapped his service revolver in its black leather holster. "You may consider me your personal armed escort."

"I do not think I am in danger, for the church is only a few buildings away, and I have this." She drew the pistol from beneath the counter. "It is loaded, as you can see. All I need do is pull back the hammer and squeeze the trigger."

He admired her Spanish profile in light streaming through the window. "I'm leaving for Santa Fe in a few days, and it's been a pleasure meeting you, Senorita Carbajal. I hope that Fate will bring us together again one day soon."

FIVE

Mangus Coloradas pulled on his boots, buttoned on a blue U.S. Army shirt with shiny buttons, and poked his head outside. It was around noon, and the rancheria was coming to life. His first wife, named Placid, was building the fire, and Mangus Coloradas headed toward her. "You work too hard," said the chief. "Perhaps the captive girl should help you. She looks strong enough."

Placid bowed. "As you wish, my husband."

A mourning dove flew past and landed on the branch of a sumac bush. Mangus Coloradas ambled onto the open desert, sat on his haunches, and watched the bird nibble a beetle, just as he wanted to nibble the captive girl's ears.

He wondered if she was an evil sorceress who'd placed a spell upon him. *I killed her family and she will hate me until the day she dies. If I turn my back to her, she'll plunge in the knife. When an older warrior pursues a young maiden, he only succeeds in making a fool of himself.*

The Winkin' Pup Tavern was a cellar off Printery Square, its entrance down a flight of five stairs. Dark even in the afternoon, it boasted a bar, billiards table, and tables, illuminated by gaslight.

Throughout the day and night it teemed with reporters, editors, and printers. Occasionally sailors wandered in from the docks a short distance away, not to mention the occasional prostitute. Everybody was talking quickly, loudly, and at the same time as Nathanial read an astonishing story in the *Post*.

The story was about him, of all people, written by Reginald Van Zweinan. Reginald had transformed the glorified messenger boy into the single most important factor in the victory at Palo Alto. The story was ninety percent fabrication, and he couldn't help laughing at his wisdom and sheer animal courage in the face of the enemy.

The bartender approached, wiping his hands on a towel. "Hate to bother you, sir, but there's a lad outside who claims he's looking fer you."

"As a matter of fact, he's my manservant."

The bartender raised an eyebrow. "He can't come in here, sir. He stinks to high heaven."

"Then I'll have to go outside."

Nathanial knocked back his whiskey, positioned his cane, and made his way to the door. Tobey sat on a nearby stoop, more ragged and disheveled than last night. He jumped to his feet as Nathanial approached.

"Remember me?" the boy asked nervously.

"Of course. Have you had lunch?"

"No, and I ain't had breakfast neither."

"What happened to the five dollars I gave you?"

"My mum tuck it."

"I thought you didn't have parents."

"I don't see 'em much, so it's not like havin' 'em. They're drunks, sir, and yer a-gonna end up like 'em, if you keep on. Every time I see you, yer half in the bag."

Nathanial felt self-conscious before his manservant, but then decided to ignore the well-intentioned correct advice. He examined the pile of rags before him, shook his head, and said, "I can't take you to a restaurant like that. You'll have to clean up first."

"Where?"

Nathanial couldn't bring him home, because his mother didn't need a smelly little street urchin underfoot. "Is there a bathhouse around here?"

"Over on the Bowery, sir. Only costs a quarter, but you have to watch yer clothes."

"Is there anything safer? I'm not concerned about the cost."

"That's the Constantinople, sir. They don't tolerate no monkey business in there."

"Let's head in that direction, and we should stop at a bakery on the way. I'm sure you know of one?"

"I knows 'em all," replied Tobey.

Nathanial imagined the hungry little boy with his pug nose pressed against the bakery store glass, drooling over cakes and pastries.

"Are you all right, sir? Yer wobblin' an awful lot. You really ought to cut down on the sauce, sir."

"Please don't preach to me, Tobey. I'm a grown man."

Tobey shrugged. "I guess if'n you can afford to be a drunk, it's all right wi' me. But drink done ruined my home, sir."

"I only had a few," replied Nathanial as a wave of dizziness came over him. He reached for support, and the boy caught him. "You'd better set down, sir."

Whiskey, weakness, and constant pain crashed together in Nathanial's turbid skull, and his legs turned to macaroni. My God, he realized, I'm fainting on a New York sidewalk! Then everything went black, he crumpled to the pavement and lay still with his eyes showing white.

The warriors escorted Elena and the captive children to an open space in front of the chief's tent. Nearby, the ground had been strewn with rifles, jewels, coins, and clothing—the spoils of the raid.

They'd taken Elena's rosary, so all she could do was mumble her prayers. She didn't know whether they'd rape her, slit her throat, or hang her upside down and watch her brains broil out of her ears.

She was a simple country girl, an orphan, unlettered, and her only education had been Holy Mother Church.

Her father never married her mother, and no one
knew who he was. Her mother died when she was
four years old, and she'd been raised in a Catholic
orphanage for girls. At the age of fifteen, she'd married Pedrito mainly to get out of the orphanage.

The clan gathered around, talking excitedly, pointing at various articles, and it didn't take Elena long
to figure that they were dividing the booty. Young
warriors looked her up and down thoughtfully, and
she knew what was on their minds. No, they wouldn't
slit her throat immediately. They had other pastimes,
and *then* they'd kill her.

She shivered uncontrollably, tears rolling down her
cheeks, but she saw no mercy on those cold dark faces.
Sinewy rather than frail, she couldn't understand why
God had punished her so, but bowed her head and
continued to pray, when suddenly all conversation
stopped. Opening one eye, she saw the chief emerge
from his wickiup. He was tall, well muscled, half-
naked, and horrifying, but he walked steadily, despite
the liquor he'd drunk the previous night and all the
women he'd dragged into the desert. God forgive me,
thought Elena, but if I had a knife, I would kill that
Apache pig.

The chief and his warriors held a conversation, then
it became quiet as everybody waited expectantly.
Elena realized that the chief was getting first pick of
the ill-gotten gains, and her heart skipped when she
realized that he was walking toward her. It can't be,
she thought as her face drained of color.

The chief made a statement in his guttural language,
then pointed at her. Next he advanced toward the
array of stolen goods and collected a rifle, some ammunition, a few articles of women's clothing, and some
beads. Finally he returned to Elena. "You are mine.
Come with me."

He was bigger than she, so she followed, eyeing the
knife in a sheath at his waist. What if I . . . ? Like a
cat, she dived for the knife, a blur passed her eyes,

she was lifted from the ground, then thrown onto her back. Opening her eyes, she saw his face above her and felt his hand pinning her throat to the ground. "Do not try that again," said the chief. "Because next time, you die. Do you want to die?"

"You'll probably kill me anyway," she said through clenched teeth, but his strength made her feel like a puny little creature.

"You work—you live. But you fight, you die. *Comprende?*"

He let her up off the ground; she rubbed her sore throat and decided that he was too fast for her. She followed him to his wickiup hut, where a stocky, dark Apache woman stood. The chief said something in Apache to the woman, then crawled into the wickiup.

"Get wood," said the Apache woman.

"Where?" asked Elena.

The woman pointed toward the open range. "There."

Nathanial opened his eyes in the darkness of his bedroom. The door was slightly ajar, and he heard his mother's voice. "I don't know what's wrong with him, Doctor, but he's been drinking ever since he came home, and he's always on his way someplace. I shouldn't tell you this, but last night he came home barefoot, half-naked, and drunk as a lord. I don't know what to do— he's a grown man—but do you think you could talk with him?"

"I don't want to wake him, but tomorrow I'll give him the simple facts. He's been severely wounded, and if he doesn't start resting, he's going to die. It's as simple as that, and if he's too thickheaded to understand, there's not much any of us can do."

After obtaining firewood, Elena had been assigned the task of rubbing a smelly sticky substance into antelope skins to make them soft. Her shoulders and arms ached and her belly felt hollow.

She thought of running away, but where? The wil-

derness was home to wildcats, wolves, coyotes, rattlesnakes, poisonous spiders, gila monsters, and other
creatures who could kill a woman.

She'd seen the chief with other warriors during the
day, and evidently he was held in great respect by the
Apaches. He'd looked at her a few times in that man
way, as if he were contemplating eating her alive, but
his interest only frightened her further. She was certain that one night he'd drink too much and rape her.

If he tries, I'll put his eyes out, she swore. *I don't
care if he kills me, but I will never give in to him.*

Nathanial opened his eyes, and his mother was sitting beside the bed, holding his hand. "Are you
awake?" she asked.

"What happened to me?"

"A little boy brought you here. He said you'd
passed out on Nassau Street."

"Where is he now?"

"Downstairs, playing with your brother. We've
cleaned him up and given him some of Jeffrey's
clothes. He'll be staying with us, because after all, he
probably saved your life. I want to tell you something,
Nathanial. If you don't stop drinking, you're not going
to be around much longer. That's what the doctor
said, and I merely pass it along. I know you're a grown
man, and you probably think I'm an old fool, but I
and your brother love you very much, and we'd be
devastated if anything happened to you."

The last word faded away as his mother rushed from
the room, touching a handkerchief to her right eye.
Nathanial felt guilty because he was making his dear
mother unhappy again. The fine old military custom of
continual liquor consumption wasn't appropriate for
Washington Square, he realized.

He went slack on the bed as ravaged arteries
throbbed in his chest. *That sergeant tried to kill me,
and it looks like I'm trying to finish the job. What's
wrong with me?*

He noticed Jeffrey and another little boy standing in the doorway, and it took a few moments for Nathanial to recognize Tobey in his new clothes. They came closer, and Nathanial reached out to the former street urchin, who was scrubbed clean and looked like a sad little angel who knew too much. "Thanks for saving my worthless life, friend."

"I told ya to stop drinkin'," the boy said stubbornly.

"And right you are." Nathanial turned toward Jeffrey. "It appears that I've made a fool of myself, eh, brother?"

"Mother thought you were dead when they carried you through the door," said Jeffrey.

"It won't happen again, I promise." Nathanial tried to smile. "Are you two getting along all right?"

"Oh, yes," Jeffrey said. "Mother is taking us to Barnum's Museum tomorrow."

Shirley arrived, carrying a tray covered with plates. "Be on your way, you two scamps," she said. "The man has got to eat." She lay the tray on a dresser, propped Nathanial on the pillow, then placed the tray on his thighs as the children retreated from the room. She waited until their footsteps could no longer be heard, then said, "You always think you're so smart, Nathanial Barrington, but yer the biggest damned fool in the world. I don't want to lecture you, because yer head's too damned thick anyways, but if yer a-plannin' to kill yer mother, yer a-goin' about it the right way. She's been through a lot, what with yer father's she-nanigans and all, that dirty rotten son of a bitch, ex-cuse my French, but you sure are one selfish son. I guess it's because yer father was never home, and yer mother was too easy on you, but I'm not going to be easy on you. You do this again, and you'll have to deal with me."

Nathanial couldn't help smiling. "What'll you do, Shirley?"

"I'll take down one of them big cast-iron frying pans and beat the livin' shit out of you."

*   *   *

The wagon master turned around in his saddle and waved his hat in the air. "Santa Fe—straight ahead!"

Maria Dolores saw a scattering of squat adobe buildings nestled in the valley below, alongside the Santa Fe River. She sat on the buckboard with her father, the latter gripping reins controlling six oxen. They were part of a wagon train headed to Santa Fe, and it included soldiers, bullwhackers, and cowboys, as well as merchants like her father.

"Thank God," said Maria Dolores, crossing herself. "The Apaches have left us alone."

"I told you," replied her father, "that they never attack a well-armed wagon train, but as usual you did not listen to your father."

They continued the bickering that had become the hallmark of their relationship as the adobe structures of Santa Fe became more distinct through hazy sagebrush mists. Maria Dolores estimated it was at least twenty times larger than Las Vegas, and she looked forward to making new friends, going to church parties, and meeting eligible gentlemen.

Maria Dolores's fondest dream was to have a husband and her own little children to love and rear. Her heart filled with hope as the homes, sheds, outhouses, and pigsties of Santa Fe drew closer.

"You can see it is a growing town," said her father, "but this is only the beginning. If we work hard, we can make a new beginning here."

Maria Dolores wrinkled her nose. "I am not sure I want to begin anything with the Americanos. They hate us, and to tell you the truth, I hate them."

"But, dear," admonished her father, "did not Jesus teach that we are all brothers and sisters?"

"He was not talking about the gringos."

She saw the tall spire of a church, wide thoroughfares, and long rows of adobe homes. She and her father had decided to move their store here, in their search for business success. Santa Fe was one of the oldest cities on the continent, built on the site of an abandoned Indian village, and too big to be attacked by Apaches, she hoped.

Maria Dolores felt excited about living in a real city, and hoped she and her father could turn their failing fortunes around. Something wonderful is going to happen to me here—I just know it, she said to herself.

What she really meant, in the code she used on herself, was *maybe I'll meet my husband here,* for Maria Dolores felt certain needs that only marriage could satisfy. For all I know, she mused, the gentleman is waiting for me in Santa Fe.

SIX

Attended by his mother and Shirley Rooney, Nathanial lay in bed day after day, reading Emerson's *Essays,* Thucydides' *The History of the Peloponnesian War,* and *The Iliad.*

For as long as he could remember, he'd been busy with school, social activities, travel, sports, the army, and so on, but now was free to indulge his curiosity fully. He also read newspapers regularly, as he followed the progress of the war. Old Rough and Ready had taken Monterrey, while General Kearny was regrouping in New Mexico. The bad news was the outnumbered U.S. garrison in Los Angeles had surrendered to the Mexicans.

The war seemed distant, as Nathanial enjoyed his newfound indolence. The philosopher's life appealed to him more every day, and he wondered about the part of himself that had enjoyed strutting about in a uniform.

Sometimes he worried that luxury was making him soft, weak, and unworthy. He thought less about Layne Satterfield, and assumed that she was married. Sometimes he leafed through the Bible, and especially enjoyed Proverbs 5:3.

> *For the lips of a woman drop as a honeycomb
> and her mouth is smoother than oil:
> but her end is bitter as wormwood,
> sharp as a two-edged sword.*

Delicious meals passed beneath his nose, and he heard Jeffrey and Tobey playing downstairs. Tobey had become part of the family, with Nathanial's mother providing a special tutor. The guttersnipe was learning to speak, dress, and behave like an upper-class child.

Nathanial felt strangely content as he lay in bed day after day. His military career seemed absurd, the Mexican War a news story, and he could understand why many New Yorkers disapproved of wasteful military expenditures, for it had nothing to do with them. He'd spent his life running frantically toward this or that goal, but seldom had experienced deep and abiding satisfaction. Perhaps I should become a priest after all, he thought one night as he lay with his head propped up on the pillow, the Bible in his hands. *What does it profit a man if he win a* fortune *but lose his soul?*

Atop a mountain in the San Mateo range, Mangus Coloradas sat stolidly, pondering the future of the People. Before him stretched valleys, mesas, and buttes culminating in the purple and orange horizon. This was the Apache homeland, but for how much longer? he wondered.

He'd seen streams of caravans and military convoys arriving regularly, and felt suffocated by the new immigrants. Game would become more scarce, farms would blanket the landscape, and the Apache life-way would vanish forever.

The great chief Mangus Coloradas needed to formulate important decisions for his people, but didn't know what to recommend. He'd consulted with *diyins,* and they'd offered much high-blown verbiage about Yusn and the mountain spirits, but ultimately they didn't know either.

Some warriors advised attacking Mexicans and Americans at every opportunity. Others suggested an alliance with one side or the other. A vocal minority believed the Mexicans and Americans would team with the Pueblos and Navajos to wipe the People from the face of the earth. Fathomless possibilities lay before the warrior chief, and he had to act soon, for the future of the People depended upon him.

His face was painted bright ochre, and he wore a deerskin vest over his naked chest. He bowed his head low, and murmured, "Oh Yusn—the People have always revered you, but we are threatened as never before. Send me a vision, mighty Yusn. Please help me to save the People.

Nathanial sat on a bench in Washington Square, reading about the Irish potato famine in the *Times*. Evidently, vast numbers of Irish immigrants were pouring into New York City, while in France, factory workers and farmers were threatening revolution against the tyranny of Louis Philippe. Germany was on the brink of civil insurrection, as were the Hapsburg states. Meanwhile, the great domestic slavery debate continued, as angry Southerners threatened secession, while abolitionists demanded justice for poor mistreated slaves.

Nathanial knew that most reasonable people, including many Southerners, agreed slavery was wrong, but there seemed no way to end it equitably. Nathanial had examined all facets of the issue, such as cotton planting wasn't feasible without slave labor, due to competition from Indian cotton, and the wealth of many Southerners was invested totally in slaves. If the so-called "special institution" was forbidden by decree, the economy of the South would collapse, freed Negroes would drive down the cost of labor, and there was fear of economic turmoil, not to mention concerns about ignorant uneducated Negroes winning the vote, and there was always the fearsome specter of miscegenation. Extremists on both sides pushed for violence to accomplish their goals, while citizens in the middle were dragged along by the whirlwind.

Nathanial raised his eyes and contemplated bucolic Washington Square Park. Why can't people live at peace with each other? he asked himself as he watched Jeffrey and Tobey run around the elm trees. We shouldn't be so quick to take offense, and didn't Christ say to turn the other cheek?

He looked back on his military career, and it seemed ridiculous compared to the tranquillity of Washington Square. Let the others wave their flags from now on, because all of Mexico isn't worth one drop of my blood. How could I let myself be drawn into such a mess?

He heard the rustle of skirts and caught a whiff of perfume as two young ladies approached on a dirt path. His eyes roved up and down their clothing, and that old sensation provoked him yet again. He wanted to retire to the nearest secluded bed with both of them, and perform salacious acts for a week or two, but caught his mind before it descended further.

This is my first day outside, and I'm up to my old tricks, he admonished himself. But I can't hide in the bedroom for the rest of my life. It's time for me to make up my mind concerning my future. What should I do with my ridiculous, pointless life?

Elena looked up from grinding corn as the chief emerged from the desert. He'd been gone five days, everybody had been worried about him, but he appeared unharmed, his face immobile, and a distant expression in his eyes. He glanced at her as he approached, then sat beside Placid and held a conversation in front of the wickiup.

Mangus Coloradas then crawled inside the wickiup as Placid roamed the encampment, making a series of announcements. Meanwhile, Elena worked the metate, another constant chore. But she was getting enough to eat, and it appeared the danger of rape and murder was over.

Warriors drifted toward the chief's wickiup from all

across the encampment, some glanced at Elena, one laughed, and she suspected that they were joking about her, but she was under the protection of the chief and at least still alive.

Finally Mangus Coloradas ventured outside and sat at his appointed spot in the circle. Placid walked toward Elena and motioned for her to move away from the warriors. Elena obeyed swiftly, because Placid resorted to kicks and slaps when her orders weren't followed immediately. The Mexican slave wondered what important matter would be discussed by the great chief.

The People waited for their leader to speak, but he appeared deep in meditation. They could see that he'd undergone a transformation, for he was lean, haggard, with eyes glowing like coals. It was silent, and everybody knew that a significant new policy would be announced.

Finally Mangus Coloradas raised his head, paused, and spoke in a calm tone. "We have seen great loss of game," he began. "The White Eyes continue to come, and they will win their war with the Mexicans. What should the People do? I have bared my heart to Yusn, and this is what He told me."

The warriors leaned closer as Mangus Coloradas closed his eyes, lost in thought. Then he raised his eyelids and spoke in a deep clear voice. "No alliance can ever be made with the Mexicans, but the White Eyes are different, and perhaps we can reach an agreement with them. I am not optimistic, but I would not want war without trying peace first.

"Therefore I shall meet with the leader of the White Eyes. If he refuses our peace offer, then Yusn will safeguard the People in the war to come."

The warrior named Coletto Amarillo snorted derisively. "Talk with the White Eyes? But they will kill you on sight."

"I will ride beneath the truce flag, and if they kill me as you say, then you, Coletto Amarillo, together with other brave warriors, will avenge my death. That is what Yusn has told me. *Enjuh.* It is good."

Three days south of Socorro, in the newly liberated New Mexico Territory, General Stephen Watts Kearny led the Army of the West through the foothills of the Magdalena Mountains. He had resumed his journey to San Diego, but California was far away over mountains, deserts, and the most hazardous terrain in the world. To make matters worse, no reliable maps of the route were available.

It was a cool autumn day, and General Kearny was pleased that summer was over. Born and raised in Newark, New Jersey, he found New Mexican heat oppressive, debilitating, and detrimental to the fighting spirit of his men.

His force consisted of the First Dragoons, the Missouri Volunteers, and a detachment of scouts deployed to the front and on the flanks of the main force to warn of sneak attacks by Indians.

General Kearny noticed a cloud of dust in the distance. Someone was riding hard in his direction, and he instinctively reached for his service revolver. But it was one of his scouts, covered with alkali as he slowed his mount in front of the general. "Somebody coming, sir. About ten white men riding hard."

General Kearny raised his spyglass and examined the approaching riders. What're they doing in such a godforsaken spot? he wondered. He didn't expect danger, because ten men would never dare attack the Army of the West.

"It looks like Kit Carson!" cried the scout.

General Kearny refocused his spyglass as the riders drew closer. The leader was a short man with blond mustaches, a wide-brimmed mountain man hat, and a smile. General Kearny had never met Kit Carson, but everybody on the frontier had heard of the renowned trapper, Indian fighter, explorer, and adventurer.

Kit Carson wore a buckskin suit, flintlock pistol in

a holster, and a knife sticking out of his boot. He slowed his horse as he approached General Kearny and threw an unmilitary salute. "And who might you be?" he asked Kearny.

The general told him his name. "Where are you headed?"

"For Washington, with a dispatch for President Polk. We've covered about eight hundred miles in twenty-six days."

General Kearny held out his hand. "Perhaps you'd better let me see that dispatch."

"But I've got orders to give it only to the President, sir."

"Are you in the army, Mr. Carson?"

"I've been commissioned a lieutenant, but I'm really just a scout, sir."

"I've just given you an order for which I will take full responsibility."

Carson thought for a few moments, then reached into his saddlebags and pulled out a packet of documents. General Kearny called the column to a halt, dismounted, and carried the papers to the shade of a nearby bearberry bush. He sat, sipped some water from his canteen, and commenced to read the secret information. He was jolted to discover that the U.S. Navy under Commodore Robert Stockton and a volunteer battalion of soldiers commanded by Colonel John Charles Frémont had conquered California! General Kearny realized that the war had been dramatically altered.

He'd been ordered to occupy California, but no longer needed so many men. General Taylor was still campaigning in Mexico, so Kearny decided to send part of his force south, to aid Old Rough and Ready. "Lieutenant Carson—may I have a word with you?"

Kit Carson was half-starved from his long arduous journey and munched a biscuit as he approached the general. "Sir?"

"I'll need you to guide us to California, so you're

a member of my command as of now. Your dispatches
will travel to Washington with one of my officers."

"But I haven't been home fer a year, sir. I'd wanted
to see my family in Taos."

General Kearny narrowed his eyes. "I'd like to see
my family too, but there's still a war on, and a soldier
can't walk away from it. That is all, Lieutenant Carson. You may continue your meal."

Elena tossed a length of wood into the fire as orange sparks flared into the sky. Mangus Coloradas
watched her out of the corner of his eye as he held a
chunk of roast mule in his hands and tore off a chunk
with his teeth. Her clothes were becoming ragged, per-
mitting views of her bare thigh, breast, and stomach.
He was fascinated by the mystery of her lips and
caught an image of himself sinking his teeth into her
hindquarters.

She's a piece of ripe fruit waiting to be plucked, he
thought. It was her job to tend the fire, and every time
she bent over, he noticed the curves of her body. He
imagined himself placing hands on her naked form.
Anxious with lust, he tried to focus on great tasks
lying ahead for the People.

Tomorrow he and his men would journey toward
the White Eyes' army and ask to speak with their
chief. He knew that the People were depending upon
him, and if a fight broke out, the White Eyes would
try to kill him first. He entertained doubts about the
enterprise, but was hopeful peace could be achieved
with the White Eyes. And if he was lucky, perhaps
the slave girl would permit him to make love with her.

He stared at her hungrily as she sat by the fire, her
chin resting on her knees, eyes gleaming. He wanted
to take her onto his lap and cover her with kisses, but
instead heard the voice of his wife in his ear.

"Why don't you marry her?" asked Placid
sarcastically.

Mangus Coloradas realized that his first wife had

been observing him. He sputtered, "Please do not bother me with your foolishness, because I have many important matters to think about."

"She is your slave—why not just take her and get it over with? I do not care, if that is bothering you. I have seen how she looks at you, and I am sure she would love it."

"Quiet, woman, or I'll shut your mouth."

"Do you really think you are deceiving anybody."

Mangus Coloradas lashed out with his right hand, caught Placid by the throat, and pinned her to the ground, where she wriggled frenziedly, trying to breathe. The chief lowered his head and brought his eyes to within inches of hers. Just as she was about to faint, he turned her loose, picked up his chunk of meat, and resumed his meal.

Nathanial walked along Twelfth Street, his left hand inside his suit jacket, resting on the grip of the Colt Paterson, while his right held his cane. He turned the corner onto two rows of darkened three-story homes, except for one with lights in the windows in the middle of the block. Nathanial climbed the stairs and worked the rapper.

The door opened and a gentleman in a dark suit appeared before him. "Good evening, sir. Right this way, sir. So good to see you again, sir."

Nathanial had never been to Miss Nell's, but the man led him to a murky parlor with thick drapes and the fragrance of sandalwood incense. A bar was to the left, with chairs and sofas to the right, where gentlemen in fashionable suits chatted with attractive women in various stages of undress.

A gaslight chandelier provided faint illumination, and it looked like the bowels of Hades. Behind the bar worked a woman with a fantastic mound of red curls atop her head. "Champagne, sir? You look like you're mad at somebody."

He tried to smile. "What's your name?"

"Dorrie. Why don't you relax, sir. This is a place to have fun."

She was tall, well constructed, with pendulous breasts pressing the front of her chemise, just the brand of merchandise he was seeking.

She leaned against the bar and peered into his eyes. "Are you sure you're all right, sir?"

"Let's go upstairs," he replied.

"You're getting stranger every minute, but I'm game if you are. Wait here a minute."

She refilled his glass, scooted around the end of the bar, and conversed with the madam, a wizened old woman with jet-black dyed hair and a white gown encrusted with rhinestones. The inevitable painting of George Washington hung on the wall, the great Indispensable Man sanctifying everything in America from oyster cellars to whorehouses.

Nathanial scanned round bottoms, fulsome breasts, meaty legs, sloe eyes, and ready smiles. He wanted to dive into the midst of them, and frolic like a satyr. Finally Dorrie returned and said, "Let's go."

He downed his champagne, and they proceeded through a dark corridor, passing other doves and swains returning from *l'amour toujours*. They climbed a flight of stairs, and she went first, with his head level with her rump. Finally they arrived at a room, she closed the door, and he spun her around.

They gazed tenderly into each other's eyes. "You've forgotten something," she reminded him in an alluring voice.

He let her go. "Of course," he said stiffly. "I'd like to stay all night."

"Twenty dollars."

He reached into his pocket, counted the money nervously, and passed it to her.

"I'll be right back."

She left the room, and he reflected that twenty dollars would be about two months salary for a private in the U.S. Army. He sat on the bed and looked around the chamber of love. It featured a mirror affixed to the ceiling above the bed, carved wood furniture, and pots and bottles of cosmetics.

He recalled his solemn battlefield vow, and guilt dripped down his back like a cold snail. He wanted to flee, but the whores would laugh at him, and besides, he believed that he'd die if he didn't have a woman soon.

The door opened, Dorrie swooped inside, turned the latch, reached to her side, unfastened some hooks, and her flimsy gown dropped to the floor.

She stood naked before him, held out her arms, and smiled as if to say: *What're you gonna do about it?* He stared at her transfixed, drinking in her loveliness. She was pretty by any standard, and he wondered what terrible tragedy had forced her to sell her most intimate possession.

Her smile became uncertain. "Is anything wrong?"

He limped toward her, grasped her naked shoulders, and looked into her eyes. "Let's have some fun together and forget our worries, all right?"

She touched her lips to his. "I'll help you with your boots."

He sat on the chair, and she pulled them off. Then she washed her hands in the basin, because no telling what gutter he'd stepped into during the night. Meanwhile, he undressed as quickly as his trembling hands would allow. It was thrilling to be in the same room with a splendidly naked woman, as she took his garments and hung them in the closet along with her costumes. "Where'd you get that scar?" she asked.

"I fell off a horse."

"You look like you've been shot."

Nathanial felt uncomfortable as he stood naked before her. "I was in the war."

An expression of tenderness came over her painted features. "Lie on your back, and I'll make it better."

He followed orders, and she perched on her knees beside him, then bent over and touched her lips lightly to the gash on his chest. He winced, but she whispered, "Relax."

He took a deep breath and closed his eyes as she continued to kiss ever so tenderly. He didn't know whether she possessed therapeutic powers, but sweet thrills ran across his nerve endings. He placed his hand on her caboose, and it was smooth, warm, firm, the best thing to happen since his last trip to a house of ill fame. It excited him to know that she was his, and he could do anything with her that he pleased. She turned her face and looked at him temptingly. "Feel better?"

He took her shoulders in his hands, lowered her to the mauve bedspread, and placed his lips on hers. Her mouth opened, their tongues wrestled, and he didn't even know her last name. But she was luscious, magnificent, in the prime of her career, and still capable of passion, or so it seemed, because a whoremaster can never be sure.

Their bodies became conjoined, they rolled on the bed, and his hands roamed up and down her body. He'd spent most of his life contemplating the very act he now performed, which eclipsed even the war.

"You're like a wild horse," she said breathlessly.

He gripped her buttocks, feasted upon her lips, as the bedsprings creaked. This is all I want to do, he thought happily. Why do I make everything so complicated?

SEVEN

Brigadier General Stephen Watts Kearny rode through cacti, sagebrush, and grama grass as sunlight transformed distant mountains into brushstrokes of colors. He'd sent two thirds of his force south to assist Generals Taylor and Wool, and now wondered whether he'd erred. What if the Mexicans have been resupplied and were threatening the American forces in California?

"Here comes Carson, sir," called one of his aides.

The scout's bay gelding trotted toward the head of the column as wind pushed back the brim of his hat and his blond mustaches trailed in the wind. "Apaches up ahead, sir. They said they want to talk with the soldier father, and I guess that's you, but I wouldn't trust 'em as far as I can throw 'em. About a dozen, and they seemed friendly enough, but they was armed to the teeth."

General Kearny removed his blue forage cap and ran his fingers through his hair. Then he replaced the hat squarely on his head, as stipulated by regulations. "Tell them they're invited to my tent tonight."

Carson was astonished. "But, sir—the might try to kill you. The Apaches ain't like the Sioux, who fight fer more feathers in their caps. If an Apache can git you in the wrong place, he'll take yer head off."

"My hand will never stray far from this," the general tapped his Colt, "and I've seen some blood too, in my day."

Carson saluted the hero of Queenston Heights. "Anything you say, sir."

Kit Carson touched spurs to the ribs of his horse, and the animal quickened his pace. General Kearny felt oddly intimidated by Kit Carson, who wore whatever he pleased, lived off the land, paid no rent, and did as he liked. It was Kit Carson, not the publicity-seeking Captain Frémont, who'd blazed the trail to California.

General Kearny was a methodical man who considered himself too dull for the good of his career. Showy officers like Frémont always attracted the most attention, but Kearny had fought the dirty little wars. He anticipated trouble with Frémont when they met in California, but had more pressing problems in sun-baked New Mexico.

General Kearny didn't have time for fights against Apaches, because America was at war against Mexico. But Apaches weren't farmers like the Pueblos, buffalo hunters like the Sioux, or horse breeders like the Comanches. The Apache nation consisted of thieves, according to what General Kearny had heard.

They've got to understand that they live in America now, he reflected. If they don't obey the laws of the land, the American Army will destroy them.

Nathanial walked across Washington Square Park, twirling his cane merrily. He'd just consumed a tasty meal of chicken, dumplings, and other specialties, plus a bottle of cabernet. Now he was on his way home for the first time in a week.

He knew that his mother had been worried about him, but he'd lived on his own for too long. Maybe I should take my own little room someplace, but she'll be hurt if I move.

Nathanial felt obligated to his mother, but couldn't stop living like an army officer. Some activities are necessary to a man's life, he concluded. He crossed the street, a cigar sticking out of his teeth, his hat tilted rakishly, and his cane beneath his arm. He knocked on the door, and it was opened almost immediately by his mother, who evidently had been watching through the front window for him. Her face appeared strained, as if she'd been crying.

"I'm sorry, Mother," he said, kissing her cheek. "I spent a few days with friends."

She looked him in the eye. "I'm afraid I have bad news, so perhaps you'd better sit down."

Nathanial couldn't imagine what had happened as she led him to the parlor. "Is something wrong with Father?" he asked.

She took a deep breath and recomposed herself. "It concerns ... Layne Satterfield. I'm afraid she's become pregnant, and it appears she's had to marry Mr. Astor earlier than planned. John Jacob has given them a house not far from here, I'm sorry to say."

Nathanial realized that Layne Satterfield was truly lost to him, and no longer could he hope against hope that she'd come back. He imagined the beautiful golden goddess in the arms of Franz Astor, and wanted to rip the carpet off the floor.

His mother said sadly, "It's wrong for a family to place so much responsibility on a woman that age."

Nathanial wanted to cry, but it was against the rules for army officers. So he swallowed down the most foul-tasting lump of his life. "I hope she's very happy, and by the way, is there any of that whiskey left?"

It was night in the army camp as soldiers cleaned mess gear in the light of fires. A light breeze blew, and the sky had become cloudy, affording only occasional glimpses of the half-moon.

General Kearny sat in front of his tent, thinking of his family back at the Jefferson Barracks. He was married to the former Mary Clark, daughter of General William Clark, and a night never passed when he didn't think of her. Beneath his neatly tailored uniform, General Kearny was as homesick and lonely as any soldier in the ranks.

Kit Carson approached his fire. "They're comin',"

he said, an expression of wonder on his face. "And one of 'em is Mangus Coloradas hisself, chief of the Mimbres Apaches."

General Kearny had heard of Mangus Coloradas, the most notorious and bloodthirsty chief the Apaches had. "How many warriors?"

Twenty. Should we disarm them?"

"Of course not."

Kit Carson cocked an eye. "Yer gonna trust an Apache? Have you gone plumb loco on me, sir?"

"We'll treat them with respect as long as they behave."

Kit Carson stalked off into the night, and General Kearny tossed his cigar into the fire. He'd expected to meet a local leader, not the celebrated Mangus Coloradas. General Kearny was prepared to give him the benefit of the doubt, but that didn't mean he'd forget his Colt Paterson.

Footsteps approached, then a crowd of Apaches entered the clearing, led by a tall, fiftyish warrior with a powerful chest, muscular legs, and corded arms. The Apaches were accompanied by Kit Carson and his scouts, while General Kearny's soldiers watched from the sidelines.

The Apaches appeared stiff as they approached the fire. They were keenly aware of the armed White Eyes, but they'd accepted the invitation anyway, trusting the army father to treat them fairly. General Kearny's interpreter was an Apache and Mexican half-breed who also spoke English. "This is Mangus Coloradas, chief of the Mimbres Apaches," he said. "And this is General Stephen Kearny, commander of the Army of the West."

General Kearny peered into the chief's eyes and saw bottomless depths beyond his ken. Perhaps it was his size, but an atmosphere of ferocious energy seemed to emanate out of the chief, despite his earnest smile.

"I am here on behalf of the American government,"

began General Kearny. "We are at war with Mexico, but we have no quarrel with the Apaches. Let us sit and talk together."

The narrator dutifully translated, and Mangus Coloradas dropped to a cross-legged position on the ground. General Kearny sat opposite him, and the other warriors and soldiers followed suit, everyone watching everyone else's hands with extreme clarity of vision.

Mangus Coloradas raised his empty hand in a gesture of friendship. "I have always respected the bravery of the Americans," he declared. "I have fought Americans myself, the trappers and the ones who dig yellow metal in the ground. Also, I have seen Americans fight the Mexicans. We do not look down on the Americans as we do the Mexicans."

"And we admire the courage of the Apaches," replied General Kearny. "But there is a time to be brave, and a time to think of future generations."

"I too think of the future," stated Mangus Coloradas, "and I have seen that the Americans will defeat the Mexicans. We wonder what you plan to do in this land?"

"We plan to bring peace for all."

"Peace is what we want too. We have no disagreement with the American people, as long as we are left alone."

General Kearny looked him in the eye and said very carefully, "If the Apaches want peace, there is only one way to show it. You must stop raiding, stealing, and killing."

The great chief Mangus Coloradas didn't move a muscle as the veiled threat was translated by an increasingly nervous translator. There was mumbling among soldiers and warriors, because General Kearny had drawn the line, and everyone expected Mangus Coloradas to jump over it.

The chief appeared thoughtful as he chose his words carefully. He knew that his younger warriors wanted him to walk away disdainfully, but he had come this far and decided to press on. "Great father," he said, bowing his head slightly, "we have been fighting the Mexicans for many harvests, and the Spanish many more harvests before that. This land was given us by Yusn, and once we were here alone with the animals and birds. Then, when the Spanish came, we tried to make peace with them, but they wanted to enslave us. We have fought back as best we could, and that is the *thieving, stealing, and murdering* that you have mentioned. They have taken our game, so why should we not take their cattle? They kill our children, so why should we not kill theirs? In a tribe farther south, they chopped the left foot off every warrior. So we have fought back, and we have defeated the Spanish *and* the Mexicans."

General Kearny leaned closer and looked him in the eye once more. "But you will not defeat the Americans, because we are many more than the Mexicans and Spanish. This land now belongs to the United States government, and anyone who does not obey American laws will become an enemy of the American people. If you truly want peace, you must stop raiding here, and that includes Mexicans as well as Americans."

Mangus Coloradas appeared confused. "You are killing the Mexicans, but you do not want us to kill them too? Isn't it best to kill as many as possible?"

"We are at war with the Mexican government, but not the people living at peace in this land. They are now Americans."

"But we are neither Mexican nor American!"

"If you violate the laws of the United States of America, you will suffer the consequences."

"If you will not let us live according to our way, we shall have to fight you."

General Kearny didn't bat an eyelash. "If you fight us, you will be annihilated."

A muscle twitched in Mangus Coloradas's cheek, for he'd just heard the death sentence for the People.

A vision of flaming wickiups, decapitated warriors, and women howling in the night came to his mind. So he had to try one last time. "The Americans and the People both hate the Mexicans, and we should be allies. We know Mexico better than you, and we can show you how to strike when they least expect. We stand ready to fight alongside you against the Mexicans, and we offer our lives for you—is that not enough?"

General Kearny could hear the chief's exasperation, but he was only a general in a far-off war. "All residents of this land must abide by the laws of my government, whether they're Mexicans, Americans, or Apaches."

Mangus Coloradas couldn't plead endlessly with a stubborn White Eyes, and suspected that he'd just humiliated himself before his warriors. Without another word or glance at General Kearny, he arose abruptly and stalked away. General Kearny leapt to his feet, to say something conciliatory, but an American general couldn't sell out the Constitution, the Declaration of Independence, and the Articles of War. These Apaches will be a thorn in our side until they're pacified, he realized. You can't negotiate with savages.

EIGHT

Nathanial sat in an eight-wheeled railroad car rolling south toward Washington, D.C. A potbellied stove fought cold drafts blowing in from the Atlantic, and he drew his black cape tighter around his wide shoulders, as he watched misty rain on forested lowlands and daydreamed while sipping from his flask.

He wore a stovepipe hat, white shirt, and red cravat, with a suit of medium gray wool. His feet were protected by new knee-high polished black leather riding boots made to his measurements by an old Jew in Chatham Square.

He took another sip from the flask and told himself, This'll be my last one. He looked around the railroad car at businessmen and politicians on their way to the nation's capital. There was one army officer, but Nathanial didn't feel like talking military. He had more important decisions, such as how to deal with his sire.

It wouldn't be inaccurate to say that Nathanial hated his father profoundly, because his father had destroyed the happy family residing on Washington Square. In the old days, they'd ridden carriages through the winding country paths of Hoboken and, in winter, ice-skated on ponds and lakes in the northern reaches of Manhattan Island. They had been a happy American family dwelling in their cozy mansion on Washington Square, and he could never pinpoint when the disintegration began, but gradually his father had become distant, then requested a transfer to Washington, Mother didn't go with him, and finally one day

Mother had sat Nathanial down and announced tear-
fully that his father had no intention of ever returning
home permanently.

Nathanial had seen the colonel on three torturous
occasions since the big breakup, and had wanted to
punch him in the mouth each time. His vain and selfish
father wanted to be a cavalier forever, instead of the
patriarch of Washington Square. Nathanial couldn't
believe that his formerly sagacious father could be
such an idiot, but sometimes wondered if his youthful
antics had driven his father away, such as his varie-
gated expulsions from the Pembroke School for fighting with other students, absurd pranks, contradicting
his learned teachers, and so on.

But Colonel Stephen Barrington was his father, like
it or not. And the colonel was highly placed in the
War Department, so Nathanial had to step lightly.
He'd rather fight another Palo Alto than see his distinguished old man, but family obligations pressed him
onward, and he couldn't afford to offend a colonel in
the War Department.

Stephen Barrington and all his brothers had enlisted
in the army or navy during the War of 1812. It had
been a one-year contract, and they figured that should
give them sufficient time to kick the stuffing out of the
British. Nathanial's father had distinguished himself
in countless battles, been wounded, won a battlefield
commission, and like Old Rough and Ready had remained in the army after the war ended.

Nathanial considered his father an authentic American hero, as well as a liar and adulterer. This duality
had splintered Nathanial's mind and contributed
greatly to the ambivalence of his nature.

The train huffed and clanged as it approached
Washington, D.C., a jumble of stately official edifices
and monuments surrounded by ugly squat stone or
wood buildings on the drained remains of a former
bog. It gave Nathanial secret pleasure to know that
his father had to live in such a dismal place.

The train pulled into the station, and of course his father wasn't there to greet him, for how could such a distinguished and important officer take time to greet his son just returned wounded from the war. "That son of a bitch," Nathanial muttered as he hailed a porter.

His trunks were loaded onto a carriage, and he set off toward his hotel, the Emory, a gathering hole for army and navy officers passing through Washington, reasonably priced. He carried his Colt Paterson beneath his jacket, for protection only.

The carriage stopped before a brick edifice four stories high, Nathanial strolled into the lobby, where a major was passed out in an overstuffed chair covered with green and gray satin stripes. A team of Negroes carried Nathanial's trunks to his room. As he looked out his window, he realized that if he wanted to see the sky, he had to stick out his head, look up, and hope nobody dropped a cigar butt into his eye.

He sat in the chair and wondered what to do until eight P.M. when he was supposed to meet his father for supper. The lounge downstairs beckoned, but he didn't want to be more inebriated than he was already. It was too stormy for a walk, and he didn't feel like reading.

He descended the stairs and entered the lounge, where gruff men sat about, imbibing, arguing, or staring out the window at the building across the street, which looked like a boardinghouse. Nathanial didn't recognize anyone as he made his way to the bar. "Cup of coffee," he told the man in the apron.

"Yes, sir." The bartender raised a pot from the stove and filled a mug about three-quarters full. "Care for a shot of brandy in there, sir?"

"If you don't mind."

The bartender spiked the coffee and placed it before Nathanial. The fumes made Nathanial dizzy as he raised the concoction and took a swig. A bolt of thunder rocked the building as Nathanial carried the adulterated coffee to a table in a dark corner.

Taking their ease before him were well-tailored blue-uniformed generals, colonels, majors, and captains. Thousands of soldiers in distant wilderness bastions were set in motion by mere strokes of their pens. Nathanial's father preferred the seat of power to front-line command, while his mother had appreciated New York theaters, art galleries, and the Philharmonic Orchestra. *What a strange family we are*, considered Nathanial, *and I've just added the oddest member of all, Tobey.*

A familiar gentleman in a black coat nearly reaching his ankles stumbled toward the bar, positioned himself in front of a chair, missed it on the way down, and landed on his posterior, a perplexed expression on his face.

The bartender headed for the inebriated gentleman, but Nathanial reached him first. "The Comte de Marsay?" asked Nathanial.

The comte fluttered his eyelashes. "Where am I?"

"It's called Washington, D.C., and perhaps you remember me—Nathanial Barrington."

"You ran off with Lieutenant Ker's dragoons, and nearly got yourself killed. What are you doing here, *mon ami*?"

"I'm supposed to meet my father. How about you?"

"On my way back to France. We appear on the verge of another revolution, and my problem is I don't know which side I'm on."

They helped each other to a table in the dark corner and asked the waiter to bring a pot of coffee plus a selection of sandwiches. They gazed drunkenly at each other, bathing in the warm glow of military camaraderie.

"I went to the hospital tent," said the comte, "and found you at death's door. You couldn't speak, your eyes never opened, and the chaplain had given you last rites. Then we left for Resaca de la Palma, and sometime later I heard that you had survived." The comte slapped Nathanial on the bicep. "You look as good as ever."

"Don't you think it's time to stop drinking, at least for a few days, Philippe?"

"Nothing else to do in this city, and I have seen livelier cemeteries. Are you still in the army?"

"I'm on convalescent leave."

"I do not know my own status, and I must choose between the republicans and the royalists, but they're both terrible in different ways, and if I select the wrong side, I may find myself at the southern end of a guillotine."

"Why don't you stay here and become an American citizen?"

"Because my heart is in France, and you know, you really should come to Paris with me. I can introduce you to some truly astounding women."

"We can even be guillotined together, I suppose. Why not come to New York with me? There are literally hundreds of actresses and dancers just dying to meet a real French count of no account such as you."

"A man needs money for actresses and dancers, and that is why I must go to France. Say, how are you fixed?"

"I have some money that my mother gave me. How much do you want?"

"Why don't we go to that whorehouse across the street and pass the afternoon like gentlemen?"

Nathanial gazed through the front window. "I've been wondering about that place. Men keep coming and going."

The comte winked. "Where else would officers live, except across from a whorehouse? You may consider whorehouses vile, due to your puritanical Yankee heritage, but I view them as courts of magic and romance."

"I'd be happy to lend whatever you need. Far be it from me to tell anybody how to live."

"I knew I could rely on an old friend. Have you heard what happened to Beau? General Taylor sent him north with a message for General Kearny, and he never came back. Seems he was transferred to the 1st Dragoons."

"That's Apache country."

"Don't worry about Beau, because he has been endowed with charming qualities, whereas you and I are merely drunkards."

They spent the remainder of the afternoon drinking, eating sandwiches, and discussing the Mexican campaign, women, the state of the world, and the meaning of life itself. Cups and glasses emptied and were filled, the conversation took strange meandering turns, and sometimes Nathanial lost the thread of meaning in the middle of his sentences. The room filled with more officers as afternoon became early evening, and Nathanial realized that he was ready to go to bed.

The comte probed his finger into the air. "It all went to hell when Napoleon began to believe that he was invincible. If he had quit after the Battle of Wagram, he would be the greatest man who ever lived, but he was a greedy little Corsican underneath it all. By the way, could you let me have those few dollars now?"

Nathanial dropped a handful of coins onto the table. Then he tried to count, but the coins kept blurring before his eyes. Finally he said, "Take what you need."

The comte scooped up twenty dollars, when a dark shadow appeared at the edge of the table. He and Nathanial glanced at a tall, gray-haired officer with a stern face and blue cape. "Hello, Nathanial," he said in a disapproving tone.

Nathanial coughed, snorted, and raised himself unsteadily to his feet. "Father, may I present my friend, the Comte Philippe de Marsay."

Philippe bowed. "I am happy to know you, sir, but I was just on my way out of here. Good day."

The comte teetered toward the door, and Nathanial summoned all his courage as he turned to his father. "So happy to see you, sir," he said jerkily, as if English were his secondary language.

"You appear to've been drinking, Nathanial," said the colonel icily.

"I just happened to run into the comte, whom I know from Mexico. We were reminiscing about the war, and I'm afraid I lost track of the brandy."

"You are judged by the company you keep, Nathanial."

Nathanial didn't like his father's accusing manner, particularly since Stephen too was a war veteran, seducer of women, smoker of cigars, and drinker of powerful beverages. "We are also judged by the *women* we keep, Father," he replied.

The colonel stared at him for a few moments, and Nathanial wondered if his old man was carrying a weapon. Then his father said calmly, "Have you eaten yet?"

"No," Nathanial lied, although he felt mildly nauseous.

His father smiled. "Let's get a fresh table."

The colonel raised his hand, and the headwaiter materialized out of the darkness. "Right this way, Colonel Barrington. I have reserved one by the window."

"Overlooking the whorehouse," muttered Nathanial, before he could catch himself.

The headwaiter pulled out the chair, and Nathanial carefully measured the distance, then gently lowered himself. He leaned back, crossed his legs, and lit a cigar as his father examined him with the eyes of a drill sergeant, which in fact he'd been.

"So you've finally seen some real war," said the colonel, "and look what it's done for you. No career can survive being drunk in public too often, my boy." The colonel smiled thinly, and looked like a silver-haired Satan in a blue uniform. "I can recommend the pot roast, and they do fine work with fish."

Nathanial was woozy, in disarray, and nearly incoherent after not seeing his flesh and blood father for nearly two years. "I apologize, Father," he said. "I'll have the pot roast and a cup of coffee, no brandy this time."

The headwaiter took the order, then receded as Colonel Barrington inspected the scar on his son's face. "I know Mexico wasn't a vacation, but you're alive and I hope you've learned something. Give yourself another week of drinking, just to get it out of your system, and then I'd recommend total abstinence, no more smoking, and physical exercise at the War Department gymnasium until you're back on your feet."

"What happens then?"

His father smiled. "I'll find an appropriate assignment for you, and don't you think it's time you started thinking about getting married? The right woman can be a tremendous advantage to an officer, and there are certainly lots around these days, some quite pretty."

There was silence at the table as Nathanial reflected that perhaps his father had just explained the reason he'd married Nathanial's mother, for the sake of his career.

His father blushed, because he comprehended the import of his words. "You're not a child anymore, and I'm aware that I don't set such a good example. I'm sorry, but I'm weak with women."

Nathanial could see panic in the colonel's eyes. "I didn't come to judge you, Father, and I have women problems of my own."

His father sighed, "I've not been a good parent, I admit it readily, but unfortunately your mother and I simply weren't ... well ... compatible."

Nathanial recalled certain women he'd known, and if they'd placed a ring in his nose, he wouldn't have protested. "I understand, Father."

"Find someone who sees the world your way, like the daughter of an officer, and don't get carried away by passion. Please don't think I'm criticizing your mother, because she's a wonderful woman and I'll always love her. Perhaps you consider me shallow, but I only want a bit of happiness before I die, and that's why I'm with . . . Jacqueline."

For the first time, Nathanial heard the name of the witch. "I don't want to meet her, if you don't mind."

"Excellent."

The headwaiter arrived, accompanied by the waiter. Together, they served the pot roast, small boiled potatoes, sliced carrots, warm bread, and fresh butter.

"I think I'll have a beer," his father said.

"I'll join you," replied Nathanial.

Their needs were satisfied swiftly, and Nathanial could see that his father was an esteemed guest, unlike the usual run-of-the-mill officer. "I've always wondered what you actually do, Father?" asked Nathanial as he sliced into soft meat.

"We're planning the army of the future, but citizens expect the army to defend the nation on a pittance. If only it were that easy."

Nathanial placed a forkful of carrots into his mouth. "The future of war is artillery," he said. "I've seen it with my own eyes. The side with the most devastating fire will win."

"But artillery can't go everywhere, and the army will always require the individual soldier with his bayonet. I absolutely believe that an officer in the right spot can turn the tide of a battle. Nathanial, don't fall in with the crowd that's drunk all the time. After a while you won't respect yourself, and then your men won't respect you. I know this sounds offensive, but I wish you'd avail yourself of my experience."

"I realize that I've been overdoing liquor lately, sir, but I was engaged to a woman, and she decided to marry somebody else."

"I'm sure your mother can find somebody appropriate. She's much better at that than I."

Nathanial hesitated, then asked, "What's your new woman like?"

"I'd rather not discuss her, but beware of overly pretty and vivacious females, because they're the most trouble of all."

The waiter cleared away dirty dishes, then the colonel ordered warm apple pie with ice cream, while Nathanial asked for rice pudding. The waiter launched himself toward the kitchen, and the father turned toward his son again.

"Do you intend to stay in the army?"

"Don't know yet."

The colonel narrowed his eyes, and an expression of concern came over his face. "I think you should go to bed. Your eyes are starting to close, and your complexion is turning green."

"I feel perfectly fine," Nathanial said thickly, as beer, pot roast, and rice pudding churned in his stomach. "What do you recommend for my next assignment?"

"If you're planning to stay in the army, perhaps you should put in a stint here at the War Department."

"I'd rather go back to General Taylor, sir."

Colonel Barrington leaned across the table. "I'm going to tell you a secret, so keep it under your hat. A new campaign is being planned against Mexico, and the war will probably end before you're well enough to participate. But first you must pull yourself together, Nathanial. I apologize if I sound overbearing, but I feel responsible for you."

Nathanial decided that he'd tolerated enough of his father's sanctimonious harping. "If you're so damned responsible," he snarled, "I can't help wondering why you left your family."

Colonel Barrington narrowed his eyes. "You're as impossible as your mother."

The waiter refilled the cups, then flitted to the next table. Nathanial stirred his coffee, immediately regretting his accusation. "I'm sorry, Father."

The colonel placed his hand on his son's wrist. "I wasn't much different from you when I was your age, but this room is filled with officers who know me, and now they know that my son is a drunkard."

"And my father is an adulterer," burped Nathanial. He knew he was wrong as soon as the words left his mouth, and bells tinkled faintly in his left ear. Excessive drinking and intemperate habits combined to produce dizziness in his head. He realized that he was losing his balance as he reached for the tablecloth. Then he blacked out, dragging coffee and dessert down with him, and he crashed into the floor, with the unfinished pudding landing upon his head.

Maria Dolores stood on the roof of her adobe home and watched the sun rise over the Sangre de Cristo Mountains. She wore a thick brown wool mackinaw and red kerchief and read her breviary.

Every day brought startling new developments, for Santa Fe was growing rapidly due to increased military and commercial traffic. Unfortunately, she'd met many hostile and cruel Americanos and wanted to return to Spain, home of her illustrious ancestors, or move deeper into Mexico. But travel was hazardous during wartime, and she was stuck living among the gringos.

Her vision turned to the American Army camp at the edge of town, where carpenters hammered constantly, disturbing her prayers. The American promise of protection from Apaches had been false, for the devils were raiding more than ever. The sun rose in the sky, casting gaudy colors on distant sandstone escarpments, as Maria Dolores tried again to pray. "Thank you, Lord God, for the blessings of this day, for the health of my father, and the success of our business. Please safeguard and have mercy upon us, your servants."

"Hello there!" cried a voice from the street.

Maria Dolores saw an Americano in a blue uniform, standing with his hands on his hips in the middle of the street, and she realized that he was the one who'd saved her from the drunkard in Las Vegas. She pulled a strand of hair from her face. *"Buenos dias."*

"What're you doing up there?"

"The view is so beautiful in the morning," she replied, and she could sense his eyes roving her anatomy like the loathsome Americano soldier that he was. "But it is time to open the store." She blushed as she headed for the ladder.

"I'll see you downstairs, because I need some tobacco."

She realized that she was pleased to see him, for she'd been a damsel in distress, and he'd saved her. She unlatched the door, and he was standing before her in his trail-worn uniform. "It appears that fate has brought us together again," he said sagely.

"For the purpose of tobacco," she reminded him, leading him into the store. "How much would you like, sir?"

"A pound."

She weighed the fragrant brown shreds, then poured them into his stained leather pouch. He leaned his elbow on the counter, looked both ways, and asked in a low voice. "Do you think we could take a walk sometime?"

She looked at him askance. "Of course not."

"I meant no insult, senorita, but what could be the harm of a little walk?"

"Much harm can come from a little walk, and you know it as well as I."

"Don't you like men, or is it just me?"

"Do you know what they say about soldiers?"

"There are all types of soldiers, senorita, and I have many interests, some of which may surprise you. Besides, it's only a walk in broad daylight, and the whole town will be your chaperone. I'm from a civilized city called Charleston, and I'm not going to attack you on the streets of Santa Fe, I assure you."

"The only time I take time off is when I go to Mass in the evening. If you care to accompany me . . ."

*   *   *

Nathanial opened his eyes. His father stood above him in the darkness, a marbleized expression on his face. Nathanial lay in a hotel bed, the reproduction of a painting of the Battle of Brandywine on the far wall. Nathanial tried to raise his head, but it felt like chocolate pudding. His heart beat alarmingly slow, and his innards ached.

"I've spoken to the doctor," said the colonel, "and he says you have to rest or else you may well die. You will stay here until you're strong enough to travel, and then you will return to New York, where you will be transferred to the Eastern Department. I cannot begin to tell you how ashamed of you I am, but this is because your mother raised you, not me, and she could never say *no*. If I ever see you drunk again, I will give you the beating of your life. You are a disgrace to your name, and don't expect me to feel sorry for you because of the wounds you've sustained in Mexico. How dare you come drunk to dinner with me! You're a man, and it's time you took a man's punishment. Next time you see me, you'd better be sober, or else!"

Maria Dolores saw him in front of the church, among peasants, beggars, and peddlers selling food and religious articles from pushcarts. The Americano looked out of place and somewhat bewildered as he tipped his hat. "I was hoping that you wouldn't forget Mass, senorita."

"I never forget Mass, but you are a Protestant, are you not?"

"I'll go anywhere to be with you, Maria Dolores."

She led him into a dark smoky room with candles illuminating gaudily painted wooden statues of Jesus, Mary, and the saints. Mexicans and a few American soldiers sat on primitive cane chairs or knelt on the bare floor. It seemed primitive, superstitious, and utterly bizarre to Beau's Methodist eyes.

He followed her into a row of chairs, where she dropped to her knees, crossed herself, kissed her thumb, and began to pray. Beau knelt beside her, sensing her voluptuous body next to his. He glanced at her out of the corner of his eye. Is her piety an act? he wondered as his knees began to ache. He didn't want to rise before her, and thought he should make an attempt to pray.

Beau could trace his forebears to the original settlement at Jamestown, and believed in the way of life that had evolved over the years in the South. Yes, his father owned Negroes, but even the Bible had ordained the correct relations between a master and his slaves. Beau believed that Negroes were inferior to whites, and Maria Dolores's dark complexion disturbed him. He knew that Mexicans had intermarried with Indians, but not with Negroes, yet Maria Dolores didn't look like an Indian. She has proud Spanish beauty, he told himself, and her breastworks are wonders to behold.

She crossed herself, returned to her seat, and he imitated her. He wanted to confess his love and recite poems by Lord Byron, but it appeared that the Mass was about to commence.

A priest and altar boys carried incense and candles to the altar, as sweet-smelling smoke drifted across the congregation. The priest murmured Latin incantations, causing Beau to feel ill at ease, as if he were trapped in an insane asylum. This damned Roman religion has caused much of the mischief in the world, decided Beau, but if this is what I have to do to win her, I'll go to Mass every day.

Beau walked Maria Dolores home after the ceremony. She's only a shopkeeper's daughter, he figured, but she can keep me anyday. Beau thought he understood women well, and it was a matter of breaking through their defenses, like any military campaign.

He loved the chase, and the most exciting quarry of all was beautiful women such as Maria Dolores

Carbajal. He'd learned long ago that the troll who lives beneath the bridge can made love to the empress in the palace if he just has *confidence*. "What was the homily about?" he asked.

"Not judging people harshly."

He didn't want to become embroiled in theology with her, as they walked along the planked sidewalk, passing soldiers, freighters, vaqueros, and other denizens of Santa Fe. "I was wondering if you ever get out at night."

She raised her eyebrows. "What for?"

He lowered his voice to its finest Casanova timbre. "I'd like to be alone with you sometime."

She gazed at him in disbelief, and then laughed. "Beau—you are being foolish."

"Is it foolish to be in love with you?" he inquired. "You're lovely, and surely I'm not the first to tell you. Don't you like me at all?"

"I could never see you without a chaperone, and what would be the point? Beau, please understand that I will never be alone with a man unless I am married to him."

"What about if I bought you a ring?" he asked hopefully.

She shook her head sadly as she came abreast of her home. "I am sorry, but we could never be happy together."

"Why not?"

"You and I are not the same kind of people."

Persistence, thought Beau. "I hope that I can at least see you after Mass tomorrow night."

"You are wasting time that might be better spent with another girl. Good night."

She headed for the door as Beau twisted his black mustache. This one's playing hard to get with the wrong person, he figured. That's the prettiest gal in Santa Fe, and I'm the most dogged man in the world. The only way to stop me is to drive a stake through my heart.

*   *   *

Two weeks later, when he was capable of indepen-
dent movement, Nathanial sat in the lobby of the
Carleton Hotel, waiting for his father's mistress to appear. According to Philippe, his intelligence officer,
she took a walk every morning after breakfast and
another after lunch. She visited friends, all ladies in
the same boat as she, but reserved her evenings for
Colonel Barrington.

Philippe had learned that her name was Jacqueline
Bernays and she was thirty-one years old, widow of
an officer much older than she, who'd died of a heart
attack. Evidently she prefers elderly gentlemen for the
usual pecuniary reasons, surmised Nathanial. The
most unusual tidbit of information was that she was
an octoroon, because one of her great-grandparents
had been Negro. What a strange person she must be,
pondered Nathanial.

Unable to arise for the morning walk, Nathanial had
just arrived for the matinee performance. His father's
love would walk across the lobby within the next hour
or so, and Nathanial wasn't sure how he'd respond.
I'll just sit still and mind my own business, he said to
himself as he scrutinized a couple heading for the
door.

The Carleton was a few cuts above the Emory, but
not the Willard by any means. Thick purple velvet
drapes covered the windows, while a crystal chandelier
glittered overhead. Dark, amorphous, the ideal spot
for foreign intrigue, it was here that his father had
ensconced his octoroon.

Nathanial couldn't wait to see her as he puffed his
cigar. Nearby, a gentleman read a Russian newspaper,
while two Englishmen played cards across the way. A
well-dressed couple in their fifties headed for the door,
speaking French, while two German children chased
each other around the lobby.

At two o'clock he spotted *her* descending the staircase, and there could be no doubt that this was she.

Her skin was that of a healthy woman who'd walked too long in the sun, her nose narrow, and her black hair slightly wavy, like a Mexican. She wore a medium blue dress, and he saw that her posture was good as she walked out the door.

What is a beautiful young woman like that doing with my father? he mused. Why, she's young enough to be his daughter. Before he knew it, he followed her out the door, spotting her headed toward Indiana Avenue. An octoroon? he asked himself, puffing his cigar. I'll bet she's a tigress in bed. How odd.

Nathanial had seen mulattoes before, but this lady was much lighter than that. In fact, if he hadn't known, he might've thought her Italian or French. She glanced back at him, and he lowered his head so his hat brim would shield his face. Then she faced forward and continued her brisk walk, passing three- and four-story hotels and boardinghouses. He continued after her, noticing her strong but graceful movements, her head held high.

She turned a corner, and he quickened his pace, glancing backward to make sure his father wasn't creeping up on him with saber in hand. He hoped she hadn't disappeared into one of the buildings on the next block.

He turned the corner, and she was standing directly in front of him, peering into his eyes, an expression of amusement on her face. "It's not polite to follow a lady," she said softly.

"What makes you think I'm following you?" he countered as he struggled to catch his breath.

Her skin was flawless except for a small mole near her chin, and she had white teeth, while her eyes absolutely devastated him. "You're Nathanial, aren't you?" she asked.

He thought he was going to faint again, but held himself erectly, gulped, and said, "How did you know?"

"Your father described you to me, and told me that you might accost me."

"I'm not accosting you. It's just ordinary curiosity, that's all."

"I'm visiting a friend, and you may accompany me a short distance if you like. We can talk."

He proceeded alongside her, the stately Capitol Building towering in the distance, filled with congressmen and senators speechifying on the great issues of the day, while on the other side of the street a family of pigs foraged garbage in the gutter.

"Your father's very worried about you," she said, as if she were his big sister.

"I can take care of myself, I assure you."

"You have no idea how much your father loves you, but he thinks you're destroying your career." She touched her finger to the tip of his nose, and he felt a jag of electricity. "Just stop drinking, Nathanial. Don't worry about your father, because I'll take good care of him."

As she bussed his cheek, a wave of tropical perfume washed over him. And then she was walking away, headed in the direction of City Hall. He wanted to run after her, but stood immobilized, watching the sway of her hips. There isn't enough room in this city for that woman, my father, and me, thought Nathanial. I think it's time to hit the trail.

He caught a carriage to the railroad station, bought a ticket for the night train to New York City, and then had to eat, so he took another carriage to a ramshackle restaurant near the Potomac River, where his father would never go, and ordered the broiled sea bass washed down with a few pints of beer.

He was feeling like his old rambunctious self again as he rode back to the Emory Hotel. He packed his trunk rapidly as lamplight threw fantastic shadows against the wall. The hotel room was warm, he'd opened the window, but still perspired, his face red and collar too tight.

He gaped into the mirror at white eyeballs traced with red lace, his blond hair mussed, and the ends of his mustache stained by too many cigars. *I look like hell, and that poor woman must've thought I was a madman. He should never have spoken with her.*

There was a knock on his door, and his first reaction was his father had come to visit. Terror shot through him even worse than Palo Alto. "Who is it?" he asked fearfully.

"Open the door," said his father.

Nathanial wondered whether to draw his Colt and shoot himself, or hide beneath the bed. If he refused to open the door, his father would break it down, so he took a deep breath and turned the knob.

Colonel Barrington stormed into the room, his face red as a beet, just like Nathanial's. He closed the door behind him, leaned toward Nathanial, and said through teeth on edge, "Can it be ... is it possible ... is it conceivable ... that I have fathered an imbecile? If you want to be a filthy disheveled drunkard, that's your business, but when you have the god-awful nerve to speak with Miss Bernays, you have finally gone too far. You're packing? Excellent. Superior. At least you haven't lost every shred of honor. I know you're my son, and I'm your father, but it would give me great comfort if I never saw you again. Do I make myself clear?"

Nathanial tried to smile. "I only talked with her for a few minutes, and I think we're both better for it. Why I ..."

His father interrupted him. "Better for it!" he screamed.

Nathanial watched in amazement as his father drew back his fist. There was ample time for the veteran of Palo Alto to attack, get out of the way, or spin his opponent against the wall, but instead he watched the knuckles loom closer and strike him on the mouth. He went flying backward, his head slammed into the wall, and he dropped to his knees, trying to shake his head clear, as his father's boots receded down the hall.

Nathanial collapsed into the nearest chair, touching his fingers to his bloody lips. It was the strangest fight of his life, because he'd been more afraid of winning than losing. At least I haven't killed my father, he evaluated. Jesus, that old son of a bitch has got a punch like the kick of a mule.

It was night in Santa Fe as Maria Dolores sat by her window, gazing at iridescent mountains in the distance. Her rosary beads were wrapped in her hands, and it was time to go to bed.

She removed her robe, revealing a plain white gown. Crawling beneath her covers, she rolled onto her back and looked at the ceiling as her warmth radiated against clean white sheets. O Madre Mio, I feel so lonely and afraid.

Maria Dolores presented a pious face to the world, but often cried at night when she was alone. She had been tempted to run off with the handsome American officer, but knew what happened with other girls who took up with soldiers. Sometimes the girls had become pregnant, then the soldiers moved to their next assignments and forgot all about them. Even if the girls didn't get pregnant, their reputations were ruined forever.

Maria Dolores wanted to be married, but not just to anybody. She believed there lived a special man for her, and she'd meet him one day. Sometimes she considered herself old-fashioned and even absurd, but had faith in romance as much as Jesus Christ, Mary, and the saints.

"Where are you now, my love?" she whispered into the night. "And why are you taking so long to find me?"

It was Ghost Face among the People, the time when snow blankets the land. They had moved to a summit of the Mimbres Mountains, where fuel and game were plentiful, and they could see the approach of enemies far away.

Ghost Face was the People's Sabbath season, for there was no fruit to gather, and not much for warriors to do. So they sat in wickiups or the sweat lodge, talked of great purposes, prayed to Yusn, and plotted new deeds.

They knew the war was going badly for the Mexicans, and the White Eyes would win one day. Thus far, the People had done nothing to antagonize the White Eyes, although they'd been merciless with the Mexicans. It was a happy time for the People.

The women had fewer duties now that they were stationary, so they feathered their nests like mountain eagles, and prayed to the mountain spirits for guidance. Elena spent most of her time collecting and chopping wood for the never-ending fires. Her civilian clothes had become shredded long ago, and now she was dressed like an Apache woman, with a loose-fitting leather blouse and skirt, plus knee-high boots to ward off the scratches of branches and strikes of rattlesnakes. A red bandanna was wrapped around her hair, which fell beneath her shoulders, and she carried a hatchet that Mangus Coloradas had either stolen or purchased.

She was absorbing the spirit of the People, becoming a member of the clan, and feeling healthier every day. The People were kind to her sometimes, and she was confused about her feelings toward them because they weren't merely a band of bandits, although they had massacred her entire town in the most bloody and brutal manner imaginable.

It was difficult to reconcile the friendly men joking around campfires with the fiendish murderers of Padre Alfonso. Elena didn't know what to make of the People, and sometimes thought she was going mad.

She was the personal property of chief Mangus Coloradas, who could do anything with her he liked, but he was always courteous in his dealings with his slave. She'd seen desire in his eyes, and it gave her a sense of power. She had to admit that he was an attractive older man with a flat stomach, unlike the potbellied Pedrito, her former husband.

If the truth be told, Elena had not been that much in love with her husband to begin with. She'd been forced to marry him or fend for herself, and he'd been sweet at the beginning, but then, after they'd been married awhile, hadn't always been the most tender person in the world, and when he drank too much mescal, he'd slapped her around a few times.

She'd known no other man, but sometimes in the dark of night, Elena wondered about a certain tall Apache chieftain.

NINE

The carriage stopped at 10 Washington Square, and Nathanial turned nervously toward Philippe de Marsay. "How do I look?"

Philippe's uncle had been the dandy Alfred Guillaume Gabriel Count D'Orsay, who'd taught that smart appearance results from attention to myriads of details. Unfortunately, Nathanial had lost track of most of them and looked like a blond gorilla in a somewhat too tight but otherwise well-tailored suit of blue wool. "Let me fix your cravat."

The French dandy pulled it tight, Nathanial's eyes popped out, but the main objective was make a favorable impression upon his mother. "I know you're the soul of courtesy, Philippe, but please don't upset her. She's so delicate these days."

"My good fellow," replied the comte, "what kind of pig do you think I am?"

They'd stopped at a tavern on Union Square for a few hot toddies, and now, several hours later, approached their destination. The park was covered with snow, Christmas lights shone in windows, and a carriage rolled past, bells tinkling on the harnesses of horses. It was the Yuletide, Nathanial's favorite time of the year, and he recalled his happy childhood, with peppermint sticks and a fir tree in the living room, in the lost paradise of his youth.

Nathanial knocked on his door, and presently it was opened by Shirley Rooney. "So it's you," she said with distaste as she examined his bruised lips. "Have you been fighting again?"

"I fell down," he lied. "This is my friend, the Comte Philippe de Marsay, who'll be staying with us for a while."

"The what?" asked Shirley.

The lady of the house appeared at the end of the corridor. "Is that you, Nathanial?"

They embraced, and he hoped she couldn't smell the rum from his hot toddies. Then he introduced the comte.

"A friend of my son's is always welcome here," she said congenially. "May we bring you something to eat, or did you have something at the tavern where you stopped on the way home?"

Nathanial tried to smile. "I'm not hungry."

She looked at his lips, decided to keep her peace. "How's your father?"

"Very well, and he sends his best wishes."

The comte was given one of the guest rooms, and Nathanial stored his trunks in his usual bedroom. Since there was nothing to do, the recently arrived duo decided to walk to Broadway, to participate in the holiday festivities.

They were not seen again on Washington Square for several days.

Maria Dolores walked home from choir rehearsal as chords of Bach and Handel reverberated in her heart. Every year she looked forward to Christmas, not so much for the presents she received, but for the hope that the Messiah's birthday brought her. No matter how bad life became, or how lonely she felt, there was always Christmas.

She walked alone, for the gringo army officer no longer accompanied her. Presumably he'd found a more compliant companion, but she was pleased that she'd never surrendered to her baser instincts. Maybe

I'll be an old maid, but I'm not making a fool of myself like some of the other girls.

She filled a pitcher with water, carried it down the corridor of her home, and then a sudden gust of winter wind shook the house, blowing open the door to her father's office. He usually kept it latched, but evidently had forgotten in his haste to relieve her behind the counter. She paused, because she seldom saw the room where her father spent his time adding ledgers, writing letters, and counting money.

She approached his desk and saw sheets of paper covered with numbers. Santa Fe was attracting more merchants, competition had become fierce, but her father preferred to carry high-quality merchandise, when customers wanted the cheapest deal available.

She spotted a tassel hanging out of his desk, and absentmindedly opened the drawer to tuck the wayward tassel back inside. Her eyes widened on a white folded scarf attached to the tassel, a black skullcap, book, and leather boxes with straps. Strange letters were embroidered on one edge of the cloth, and then with a start she realized that they were Hebrew letters! When she'd been small, the priest had been talking about Jews and shown the class what Jewish writing looked like. Flabbergasted, Maria Dolores dropped onto her father's chair. With trembling hands she opened the book on more Hebrew letters.

Maria Dolores was no illiterate country bumpkin, and she knew about the Spanish Inquisition, the sins of the Jews, and the Marranos, who were Jews pretending to be Christian, but worshiped the God of Israel in secrecy. Is my father a Marrano? she wondered, her head spinning.

She tucked the tassel into the drawer, ran to her room, splashed her face with cold water, carried the oil lamp to the mirror, and peered into her eyes. "Good God—am *I* a Jew?"

*   *   *

On the night before Christmas, a carriage dropped Nathanial at 10 Washington Square. He was heavily laden with packages and seriously incapacitated by drink as he climbed the stairs and fumbled for his key.

The door was opened by Jeffrey. "My brother's been home a week, and this is the first time I'm seeing you?" he asked.

"He's drunk," said a serious child whom Nathanial recognized as Tobey.

"It's the Christmas season—what did you expect?" Nathanial replied, barreling past them, balancing the packages, but he tripped over his own feet and went crashing to the floor, throwing gifts in all directions. He rolled over, got to his knees, and saw his mother standing before him like the first captain at West Point. "I want to speak with you alone," she said.

Oh-oh, he thought as he followed to her sitting room. It had a daguerreotype of her husband on the mantel, a large portrait of her father dressed as a whaling captain, bookshelves, the Bible, the Book of Common Prayer, and a semiknit red sweater beside a ball of yarn.

"Sit down."

He dropped to the sofa and said, "Mother, before you begin—I realize that I haven't been very considerate lately, but . . ."

She interrupted him as if his realizations were of no concern. "I've received the full report from your father, and it appears that you've disgraced your family yet again, calling attention to our difficulties and even spying on a certain lady whose name I won't mention in this home. Your behavior has become intolerable, you'll have to move out as soon as feasible. And by the way, where is our house guest?"

"He's moved elsewhere," replied Nathanial, because he couldn't detail the true story, that the comte had taken up with a certain dancer, and a certain second lieutenant was paying for their rent at an out-of-the-way hotel west of the Bowery.

"You may take the remainder of his belongings when you leave, which I hope will be immediately after Christmas. And from now on, whenever beneath my roof, you will present a proper image of an older brother to Jeffrey and Tobey, or else I will smack your face." She raised her hand in the air. "You're not too old for a good beating, and I'm not afraid of you one bit!"

He raised his arm to protect himself, because he feared his mother even more than his father. "I'll do whatever you say, of course."

She lowered her hand. "Your father has told me that he doubts you're his son, because he could not possibly have created such an utter buffoon. It's as if you've lost your rudder, Nathanial. To pass out drunk in public before your father, and then you flirted with his mistress? It's beyond comprehension."

"It's also beyond reality," he replied testily. "I didn't flirt with her in the least. I just wanted to see who this woman was, who destroyed my family."

A sly expression came over his mother's face as she drew back into the shadows. "What was she like?"

"The usual trollop," Nathanial lied. "Nothing special at all."

"That's not the way I heard it. She's supposed to be quite a beautiful octoroon."

"Then why did you ask?"

"I should've known that you wouldn't tell the truth, but we're all beautiful at that age, and even I had many admirers."

"You were ravishing, Mother, and you still are, but unfortunately you married a scoundrel."

He didn't see her hand coming, and caught her palm across his left cheek. His head spun to the side as she arose and walked to the door. In seconds she was gone, leaving him with her perfume, knitting, and sting of disapproval. Not even her husband had received a slap in the face for his many sins, and Nathanial realized that he'd crossed a certain invisible line.

Like a thief he retreated to his room, where he washed, shaved, and put on fresh clothing. Then he slunk to the kitchen, drank a cup of black coffee, and fortified himself with two slices of home-baked bread. Finally he plastered a smile on his face and marched like a soldier to the parlor to celebrate Christmas Eve with his family.

Next day, the great chief Mangus Coloradas was seen walking into the forest, hatchet in hand. He returned around noon with a load of poles on his shoulder and proceeded to build a new wickiup. Warriors and wives all across the rancheria commented on the construction, for it appeared that the chief was planning a new family.

Meanwhile, Elena sat beside the fire and sewed skins together as she made a new coat for one of Mangus Coloradas's many children. The slave girl vaguely perceived what was happening and feared that his wives might try to kill her. She'd seen the expression in the great chief's eyes, and wondered if he'd drag her to the wickiup by her hair or ask like a gentleman. Elena feared the chief, but needed to be touched in that certain way. Although more than twice her age, he was appealing to her lonesome eyes, with his strapping muscles and noble features, unlike her former husband, who'd borne a slight resemblance to a javelina pig.

Mangus Coloradas returned with boughs of trees, which he placed over the poles, and then gathered hides from his other wickiups. Ordinarily he'd trade them for whiskey and bullets, but instead tied his wealth to the outside of the wickiup, to protect its future occupant.

When finished, he walked toward Placid and looked into her eyes. "I want to talk with you ... alone," he intoned.

She cast her eyes down. "I already know what you are going to say, my husband."

She ducked her head and entered their wickiup as he followed and pulled the flap closed behind him. They sat cross-legged on opposite sides of glowing coals in the firepit. "I am sorry, but I must do this," he said, unable to look her in the eye. "Your position will not change in our household, and you will always be my first and most important wife."

She spat into the fire. "I could not stop you, but please do not make it worse with your lies."

"Do not tempt my rage, woman," said Mangus Coloradas. "You will do as you are told, or I will kill you."

Placid lowered her blouse, revealing her throat and the tops of her breasts. "Go ahead, because you have already done everything else to me."

He grabbed her throat and squeezed hard. "If you like."

Her eyes popped out, while her complexion turned greenish-purple. Then he let her go, and she dropped to the ground, gasping. She looked up at him on all fours, like a wildcat. "It shall be as you say, my husband."

"Enjuh," said Mangus Coloradas. "It is good."

He pushed the flap aside and saw the slave girl beside the open fire, working with skins. Mangus Coloradas strolled toward the slave girl as the whole camp watched. "Get up—I want to talk with you."

She arose shakily, half thrilled, partially frightened, uncertain of what was coming.

"The new wickiup is yours," said Mangus Coloradas. "You will sleep there tonight."

"Yes, my lord," she whispered as she bowed her head in obeisance.

In Santa Fe, three priests performed the Christmas Mass, assisted by altar boys, acolytes, and the white-robed choir. All seats were occupied, and the aisles were filled with worshipers dressed in holiday finery as they sang their responses to the liturgy.

In the front row of the choir, Maria Dolores's strong
soprano voice soared through the rafters and balus-
trades of the holy edifice. She loved the ancient
rhythms of the Catholic Church, they'd been bred into
her bones since infancy, although apparently she was
a daughter of those who'd crucified Jesus. She recalled
the line from St. Matthew: *His blood shall be on us
and on our children forever.*

As she sang Christian hymns, the irony wasn't lost
on her. Yet she felt no guilt, for neither she nor her
father had participated in the crucifixion, but the judgment rang on them anyway. The choir leader, a black-
bearded cassocked priest, looked at her and raised
his hand in the air as she held the last note for four
full beats.

The hymn ended, the priest continued the liturgy,
and Maria Dolores gazed at the congregation. They
were all good Catholics, yet people like them had
burned and tortured heretics and Jews. She'd always
considered the Inquisition a minor aberration in the
glorious history of Holy Mother Church, but somehow
it didn't seem so minor when she considered that she
and her father could have been burned alive during
its excesses.

Yet the sacred Catholic mysteries made her feel
pure, clean, and holy. Hadn't Jesus, Mary, and Joseph
been Jews? She felt proud to be descended from the
same people as the Savior, whose birth she was celebrating on the altar of the church.

But who is my father? she wondered as she sat with
the rest of the choir. It was the First Reading, and
the priest spoke the words of the prophet Isaiah, who
foretold the coming of the Prince of Peace. She wondered what stubbornness prevented her father from
truly converting to the Faith. She wanted to talk with
him, but was fearful about his secret practices. What
would these people do if they knew I was a Jewess?
she wondered as she arose for the responsorial psalm.

She knew that the ignorant were easily swayed by

emotional appeals. Would they roast me over an open fire or feed me to the buzzards? she speculated. The priest raised his hand as Maria Dolores sang the words of David, King of the Jews:

> *Thou hast given me the shield of thy salvation:*
> *and thy right hand holdeth me up,*
> *and thy gentleness has made me great*

Nathanial was invited to Christmas dinner by both his uncles, but declined, claiming to be ill, although the real reason was he didn't dare face anyone. He intended to spend the evening alone at home, but became restless around eight P.M.

He lit a cigar, put on his black cape and stovepipe hat, and drifted across Washington Square, passing trees covered with snow. It crunched beneath his boots as families sang Christmas carols in homes all around him, their voices intermingling in his ears.

Nathanial felt disconnected from the celebration, and everything was closed except for a few taverns catering to lonely men such as him. It didn't seem right to spend Christmas with a bunch of drunkards drooling onto the floor, so he crossed Broadway and headed toward the Bowery, where he hoped to find some gaiety, or at least a good German meal of sauerbraten and red cabbage.

He crossed Third Street, his Colt Paterson tucked into his belt, because no respectable New York thief would let himself be stopped by the most important holiday of the year. Nathanial passed private homes and glanced through windows at happy families rejoicing in their parlors, while he was a lone figure lumbering through the darkness.

He imagined himself with a family of his own, carving the Christmas turkey, singing carols, playing with his children. It made him happy to think about such prospects, for family life seemed more appealing than rum-soaked taverns and clubs, with the usual collection of rascals, roués, and fools. He wondered if he'd become a chubby red-faced old bachelor one day, with soup stains on his lapel and his brain rotted by alcohol.

He crossed Fourth Avenue and realized that he wasn't far from Philippe's residence. Philippe had invited him to a Christmas party given by his paramour's theatrical friends, in the very same neighborhood through which Nathanial now walked, and he'd written the address in his notebook. In fact, if the truth be told, Nathanial had known that he'd end up at the party since arising that morning, because how could he ignore an opportunity to meet actresses and dancers?

Nathanial approached the address of the party and heard sounds of laughter within a two-story wooden home. He vaulted up the steps eagerly, hit the knocker, and promised himself that he wouldn't drink excessively, because his mother would kill him, son or no son.

The door was opened by a middle-aged woman with auburn hair and a low-cut neckline of her gown. Nathanial removed his hat and bowed slightly. "I'm a friend of Philippe de Marsay's, and he invited me to this party."

"Are you the soldier from Mexico?"

"I was," he replied.

"The one with whom he shared his tent? According to him, you're the strangest American he's ever seen."

"Perhaps you're confusing me with one of his other friends. I'm quite ordinary, I assure you."

"I hope not, because we don't want ordinary people here. Philippe will have to throw you out."

He followed her into a parlor stuffed with well-dressed people talking loudly and gesticulating extravagantly. The walls were covered with paintings of landscapes, women, gods and goddesses, the air thick with tobacco smoke and whiskey, the revelers illuminated by gaslight, as the brightly decorated Christmas tree stood like a sentinel in the corner and logs sputtered in the fireplace.

"Lay your coat on the bed," said the woman. "Make yourself at home. The drinks are in the kitchen."

"Are you the hostess?"

"I'm just a guest, and I happened to be standing near the door when you knocked."

Nathanial entered the bedroom and saw a huge mound of coats on the bed. Two women stood in front of the mirror, applying cosmetics. "Hello," said one of them. "I'm Doris, and this is Sarah."

"I'm Nathanial," he replied as he removed his coat. "Do you live here?"

"No, do you?"

"I've never been here before in my life."

Doris had long, curly black hair. "Are you an actor?"

"Not professionally. Are you an actress?"

"Yes, but I'm not in a play right now. How about you?"

"I'm in one right now," replied Nathanial as he retreated from the boudoir.

The parlor was so crowded, he could barely make his way to the kitchen, and there was no servant to mix drinks, so Nathanial poured himself a quarter glass of whiskey.

"So here you are!" cried Philippe.

The titled Frenchman pushed his way across the room, dragging a pretty blond woman with a friendly smile. "Merry Christmas," said Philippe, "and this is Constance."

Nathanial bowed to the woman. "How do you do."

"Depends," she replied.

"This is the bravest man I ever saw," Philippe exclaimed. "Or maybe the most insane." He grabbed Nathanial's hand and pulled him through blithering throngs to a long-haired brunette in a low-cut red dress and pearl necklace. "Nancy, may I present Lieutenant Nathanial Barrington."

She turned toward him, and her big brown eyes

examined him carefully. "I've heard so much about you, Lieutenant."

"It was probably all wrong," he replied genially.

Philippe leaned toward the woman. "Take care of him."

"But I'm looking for somebody to take care of me!"

Philippe glanced toward Nathanial. "Take care of her." Then the soon-to-be American citizen staggered away, to be engulfed by the burgeoning crowd.

Nathanial and Nancy looked at each other awkwardly. "Is there someplace quiet where we can sit down?" he asked.

"Not that I know of," she replied. "I've never been here before."

"How'd you get invited?"

"I'm a friend of Constance's."

"Are you an actress?"

"No, a dancer. And you've done something brave, but I can't remember what."

"I've done something foolhardy, but Philippe tends to embroider."

She had a dancer's hard muscular figure, and her face was cute rather than beautiful, with an upturned nose and a few freckles. "Where are you from?" she asked.

"Manhattan. How about you?"

"Peekskill, and the big city isn't quite what I'd bargained for, but I've sure learned a lot about life. One meets so many interesting people. Do you like it here?"

"I miss the West," replied Nathanial. "It's got into my blood, I'm afraid. I'm going back as soon as I can."

"Have you ever seen Indians?"

"A few. They live in their own world."

"You may consider me unduly sentimental, but I feel very sorry about the Indians. They're people just like us, but their land is being stolen by the settlers. It doesn't seem fair."

"The people who care most about Indians live in

New York, Philadelphia, and Boston, and don't have to deal with their depredations."

She raised an eyebrow. "Oh, come now—I'm sure that their depredations are greatly exaggerated."

"Ask Philippe, if you don't believe me."

"It sounds like one of those stories that everybody believes but isn't true. Have you ever seen it happen?"

"Well ... no ..." he replied.

She appeared triumphant, but it would be rude for him to simply walk away. "Are you dancing in a theater?" he asked, trying to change the subject.

"Not at the moment."

He wondered how she maintained herself. Perhaps she had a rich father, or worked as a salesgirl at a Broadway emporium. Many theatrical women were mistresses of wealthy men, semiprostitutes for art.

Sarah threaded through the crowd, took Nancy's hand, and said, "I want to introduce you to someone. Will you excuse us, Nathanial?"

They walked off with arms around each other's waists, and Nathanial receded into the shadows at the corner of the room, where he could reconnoiter New York's artsy folk on Christmas Day. Professionally, they wrote magazine articles, danced on poorly heated stages, played the fiddle in symphony orchestras, and painted the Hudson River in all its luminescent hues. The artistic tastes of the nation were molded by people like them, and they had a carefree exuberance that he found appealing, unlike the stodgy crowd at Uncle Jasper's parties.

But Nathanial felt as if he didn't belong, for he was no scribbler of poems or dabbler in paint. He knew that he could probably seduce half the women there, if he spent enough money, but he didn't want someone who'd slept with another fellow last week, and would sleep with a new one next week.

Nathanial wanted to feel special, not the latest in a long line of ardent swains. Love should be a privilege, reflected he, not just another bodily function, like going to the latrine. Nathanial wished he could enjoy life like other people, but felt confused about his male needs and moral obligations.

A statuesque honey-blonde in a low-cut red dress approached with a glass and an alluring smile. "Why are you hiding in the corner?"

"I was looking at all the beautiful women, such as you."

She fluttered her eyelashes, and appeared to be in her mid-thirties. "Who are you, and what are you doing here?"

"I'm a friend of Philippe's, and by the way, who is the host of this party?"

"Me," she replied.

He blushed. "Excuse me . . ."

"I'm Euphemia White, and this is my home."

"Are you a dancer?"

"A singer. And you?"

"I'm in the army."

"Oh, yes—the friend of Philippe's. He said that you nearly were killed, but you look fine to me." She smiled as she brought her lips close to his ear. "Why don't you remain after the party's over?"

The bright Christmas star that shone over the island of Manhattan also beamed upon the Apache encampment in the Pinos Altos Mountains. In one of the wickiups, the great chief Mangus Coloradas was pulling on his boots, while his first wife pretended to be asleep, her back toward him.

He knew that she was awake, sick to her heart, and he felt like a traitor, but he craved Mexican tortillas. He stuck his head out of his wickiup, but no one was about, thank goodness.

He advanced swiftly toward the new wickiup, his footsteps light on the dirt and rocks, and he suspected everyone in the encampment was listening to him as he created a scandal that would plague him all his days. Yet even that didn't stop him.

He didn't know how the slave girl would respond, and she might even send him away, laughing at his age and aspirations. He wasn't the warrior he'd been ten years ago, or even five years ago, his face was becoming wrinkled like old leather, his muscles no longer tight, but he was Mangus Coloradas, chief of the People, still capable of killing.

This was the moment he'd been dreaming about, and a shiver of fear passed over him, mixed with the hot brand of desire. He barely knew anything about the slave, had murdered her family, friends, and the medicine padre. Upon reflection, Mangus Coloradas was horrified by his acts, but everybody dies eventually, he realized, and *I want this one last pleasure before I go to the shadow land.* He prayed she wouldn't laugh at him as he pushed aside the flap and crawled into the wickiup.

It was dark, and he detected a form in the darkness. He moved toward her, and she rolled over. "I have been waiting for you," she said, reaching toward him.

He sank into her arms as her bare nipples touched his chest. A jolt of female energy shot through him, his hair seemed to thicken on his head, and his muscles throbbed with fresh blood. He touched his lips to hers as they rolled on soft furry animal skins.

No longer was he the aging chieftain whom the young warriors wanted to challenge as he embraced her in the darkness. A coyote howled in a far-off cave as the great chief Mangus Coloradas feasted on her mouth. His heart thundered with victory, and he felt her long delicate legs wrap around him. His body throbbed wildly as he ran his hands along her smooth creamy skin, as she dug her fingernails into the back of his head.

Their tongues licking like dogs, he gripped her haunches in his hands, and she gasped for air. *"Dios mio,"* she whispered into his ear, melting around him, drawing him deeper into her being, and he realized that he wasn't as old as the foolish young warriors thought. He performed the ancient dance as the slave girl writhed beneath him.

Elena fought against screaming as his tongue roved lower and delved into the flower. Then he grabbed her shoulder, threw her roughly onto her stomach, and dived onto her back, sinking his teeth into the back of her neck. She felt like a mountain lion mating in the clouds as he stoked and cajoled, biting her ear and kissing her hair.

On Manhattan Island, a black cat poked his nose out of an alley, looked both ways, and raced across the street, the only creature about in the witching hour. All was still, the only light came from street lamps, and even the great whores were fast asleep, entwined with their jewels, brandy, and erotic dreams.

The moon gleamed across a row of modest wooden homes near the Bowery, and in one of them, on the second floor, Nathanial opened his eyes. His first sensation was that a woman was lying half on top of him, and he smiled inwardly as he luxuriated in the warmth of her body.

The party was over, the revelers had gone home, and he'd made love with Euphemia White in the parlor, on the stairs, and in the very bed where he lay now. She'd been enthusiastic and practiced in the art of passion, and he had to admit he'd had a wonderful time, although she didn't love him, and he didn't love her.

He considered himself fortunate to be selected from the crowd for the august honor of loving her for the night. Some might think her chin too strong, her nose a half inch too long, and she carried too much weight on her hips, but she was an exceptionally beautiful woman by any reasonable standard.

She moaned in her sleep, said something indecipherable, and ground her pelvis into his leg. Maybe I should marry her, thought Nathanial. She'd be the beauty queen of any army post, and it wouldn't hurt my career to have a talented wife. I need someone to keep my bed warm, and maybe, after we live together awhile, we could even fall in love. I'm sure Uncle Jasper would lend me enough to build whatever house she might require.

The more he thought about it, the better it sounded. There is no such thing as star-crossed lovers, he said to himself. That's just Shakespearean fancy, and if I wait too long, I might be alone for the rest of my life. There are probably thousands of women in New York with whom I could be perfectly happy, and true love is just something drunken versifiers have concocted, perhaps the biggest delusion of all.

But do I really want to marry a woman who's slept with scores of men? he asked himself, even though he'd slept with countless women. And if I didn't come to the party tonight, she would've selected somebody else. One man is paying her bills, I'm here tonight, and God only knows what might show up tomorrow. This is a woman with a reputation, and what does this say about me?

Random fornication was counterfeit love, in his opinion, although he never hesitated to participate. We've had fun together, but if I marry her, I won't be available when my own true love comes along. I want a woman who'll teach my children morality, not the rules this woman and I live by. Hell, I need somebody who'll make me better, not worse, and I shouldn't blunder into marriage like my parents. What does it profit a man if he wins a woman but loses his soul?

TEN

In January of 1867, Nathanial donned a neat new uniform and reported for duty at a five-story granite building near Wall Street. He was assigned to the department of weapons procurement, and in association with other officers often traveled to Sam Colt's new factory in New Haven, Connecticut, to evaluate pistol improvements. Sometimes Nathanial was called upon to fire prototypes, and toward the end of the month, one newfangled model blew up in his face, pitting his cheeks with tiny bits of lead. He was given a week's convalescent leave, spent mostly among actresses and dancers in New York's gaslit night world.

In an effort to follow the war, he became a voracious reader of newspapers. The information was always several days stale, but in late February he learned that General Taylor had won a great battle at a place near Saltillo called Buena Vista.

According to the news story, General Taylor's Army of Occupation had been attacked by Santa Anna on the morning of the twenty-third. Old Rough and Ready had been inspecting stores and lines of communication to his rear at the time, but he galloped back to his beleaguered army, found it practically in a route, took command, counterattacked, and defeated Santa Anna after two days of bloody fighting. The Americans reported 272 men killed, 387 wounded, and 6 missing, while Mexican casualties were 591 killed, 1,048 wounded, and 1,894 missing.

During that same period, war correspondents wrote

that General Winfield Scott's army was assembling at Tampico and near the mouth of the Brazos River, his objective secret. Then, according to headquarters scuttlebutt, General Zachary Taylor had been ordered to send him four thousand regulars and five thousand volunteers, and Old Rough and Ready was fit to be tied. About the same time, General Kearny reached his objective at San Diego, and General Alexander Doniphan defeated the Mexicans in the Battle of El Brazito.

On the domestic front, reporters provided daily accounts of abolitionists criticizing the south in the harshest terms, liberally employing words like *demons* and *fiends*. Meanwhile, reports from the other side of the Mason-Dixon Line indicated that increasing numbers of Southerners insisted on their right to transport slaves to conquered territories. There appeared no middle ground, as a woman couldn't be partially pregnant, and sometimes Nathanial feared a note from Euphemia White, stating that she had become great with his child.

At the beginning of March, newspapers reported General Scott poised to assault Vera Cruz, while General Taylor held the Army of Northern Mexico in check. Nathanial sat bored at his desk, while great historical events were occurring all over the world. Often he rested his chin on his hand and gazed out the window at the wall of the office building across the street, full of clerks exactly like himself. They moved paper in one continual swirl, for paper was the lubricant that kept the world rolling along. Do I want to do this for the rest of my life, even if I were paid a huge salary? he asked himself.

Evenings, the deskbound warrior walked home through churning Manhattan crowds, making stops at taverns of his choice. He'd moved into the Alhambra Club on Bethune Street, not far from the Hudson River docks, and no longer need he worry about embarrassing his poor mother.

The Alhambra Club published no principles or lofty goals, and barely was a club at all. A group of friends, associates, and distant acquaintances had conspired with a broker to buy a building, because it would be cheaper than renting hotel rooms, and better than a boardinghouse. Occasionally they held meetings that degenerated into binges accomplishing nothing except breakage of glass, china, and furniture.

"Good evening, sir," said Donald, the aging British butler, who helped Nathanial remove his coat.

"I'll manage," Nathanial replied, hanging up the coat himself. He hated to ask Donald for anything, because the old man seemed ready for the cemetery.

In the parlor, a lawyer named Soames lay unconscious on the sofa, his mouth hanging open. The landscape painting on the far wall was crooked, and a crack showed in the plaster of the ceiling. The Alhambra Club was crumbling around their ears, too many members didn't pay their dues on time, and they all might be tossed into the street next May.

Nathanial climbed the stairs to his second-floor room, withdrew a bottle from the dresser, and sat by the window, where the night sky, obscured by soot and smoke, glowed red like the fires of hell. Cramped and suffocated in the big city, Nathanial found himself longing for the fantastic panorama of the West.

The nation was at war while he, a fairly able-bodied officer, fired Mr. Colt's inventions at paper targets. Occasionally high-ranking officers asked him to research certain facts, which any student could do, or wanted to know his opinions, which they then disregarded.

He missed the camaraderie of the barracks, and always had been attracted to hardship, perhaps because he feared weakness, sloth, and monotony. If I worked for William Backhouse Astor, I'd be another executive clerk sitting behind a desk, not much different from what I am now. My bed would be on Fifth Avenue, but who the hell wants to live there?

Sometimes Nathanial believed himself capable of great achievements, although he couldn't imagine what they were. He continued to socialize with New York's arty folk and enjoyed several meaningless affairs with actresses and dancers, all of whom constantly pestered him for loans that they had no intention of repaying, but anything was better than sleeping alone. He became a regular on the cultural scene, not to mention the fashionable taverns of Broadway.

Every Sunday he dined with his mother, brother Jeffrey, and foster brother Tobey. The boys retired to their study after the meal, and Nathanial would join his mother in the parlor, where they held a civilized conversation about nothing at all.

Just another year approximately, and I can return to the West, he told himself one night as he prepared for bed. Perhaps I'm an imbecile as my dear father claims, but I can't shuffle paper for the rest of my life. New York has its fine points, but I want to feel useful for a change. What the hell—I think I'll go back to the frontier army.

One Sunday, after the morning Mass, Maria Dolores and her father walked home together through the streets of Santa Fe. Most businesses were closed, few pedestrians about, and the sun a silver disk in the bright blue sky. Maria Dolores studied her father, wondering how he could perform the charade so convincingly. No one would ever guess that he was a Jew.

Is he a hypocrite? she wondered. Would people stop patronizing our store if they knew the truth? What's so terrible about being a Jew, and why does my father insist on being one, although he doesn't have to?

These questions had been gnawing her innards since she'd seen the embroidered prayer shawl. She was curious about her father's secret Jewish life, and had decided to ask him that very day, as soon as they returned home.

Her father unlocked the door and departed for his office, where he spent most of his time. Maria Dolores removed her serape, looked at herself in the mirror, and wondered if she was about to commit a major family violation. But curiosity got the better of her, so she walked down the corridor, knocked on the door of her father's office, heard a dresser drawer slam closed, and finally the door opened. He peered cautiously into the corridor.

"It is only me," she said. "I would like to talk with you."

"What is wrong?" he asked. "Are you in love?"

"Do not be so anxious to marry me off, Father." She sat in the chair beside his desk. "There is something I want to ask you, and I hope you will not be upset."

His face blanched. "You are not pregnant . . ."

"How could I get pregnant?"

"Young people always find a way," he said gloomily. "You are a very beautiful woman, whether you realize it or not."

"It has not done me any good, and in fact it has got me into trouble on numerous occasions, but that is not why I am here. A few weeks ago, when I was in the hall, the wind blew your door open. I was curious about this room where you spend so much time, so I came inside. That drawer"—she pointed—"wasn't closed, and I saw a scarf that had Hebrew letters on it, plus a Hebrew book and some other things." She leaned forward and peered into his eyes. "Are we Jewish, Father?"

He laughed falsely. "What a foolish thing to say. Of course we are not Jewish. Whatever makes you think such a thing? You know, sometimes I think you spend too much time in the store. Maybe you should take time off and rest your mind."

"There is nothing wrong with my mind. I bet they are in that drawer right now."

With a victorious smile, he opened it. Inside were

sheets of correspondence, but no scarf or book. "Does that satisfy you, you silly thing? And whatever you do, do not tell anyone your wild dream, especially not the priests, understand? Because if people thought we were Jews, it could have lethal consequences. You have always been an imaginative child, but the objects you saw never existed, and if you don't mind, I never want to discuss this matter with you again."

Nathanial continued to follow the war avidly in newspapers and via Eastern Department office gossip. In mid-March of 1847, he read in the *Times* that General Scott and his sixteen-thousand-man expeditionary force had assaulted Vera Cruz, survived ferocious bombardment, and captured the city. Continuing dispatches told of General Scott's successful attack on Fort Juan de Ulua, and then he set out for Mexico City, 250 miles away over mountains and through jungles. Military experts across the globe wrote that he'd never make it, while reports from Mexico confirmed that Santa Anna was deploying the remains of his army to demolish the threat to his nation's heartland.

The armies collided on April 17 at Cerro Gordo, and the initial phase consisted of artillery and infantry duels, then American soldiers under Colonels Gideon Pillow and William Harney scaled Telegrafo Mountain, defeated the Mexican defenders, exposed Santa Anna's flank, and forced him to retreat.

General Scott occupied Jalapa, Perote, and Puebla during the spring and early summer. One June night, while rustling through the back pages of the *Times*, Nathanial discovered that Mrs. Franz Astor had given birth to a baby girl named Katerina. Nathanial felt saddened, yet strangely remote. That should've been my child, he figured, but what kind of father would I be? He went on a three-day binge, then resumed his perusal of newspapers. On August 20, Old Fuss and Feathers routed Santa Anna and his army of twenty thousand in the Battle of Churubusco. The Mexicans sued for peace, but negotiations broke down and the war continued.

Meanwhile, in the American Congress, politicians debated whether President Polk had the constitutional right to annex territory won in the war. Then the *Times* reported that Senator John C. Calhoun of South Carolina had demanded a unilateral withdrawal to the Rio Grande. "Mexico is to us the forbidden fruit," he'd declared on the floor of the Capitol, "and the penalty of eating it would be to subject our institutions to political death."

Nathanial wasn't surprised to read in *The Liberator* that the famous abolitionist William Lloyd Garrison had stated: "We wish General Scott and his troops no bodily harm, but the most utter defeat and disgrace."

Unmindful of editorials, autumn headlines announced that General William Worth's division had stormed the fortress at Chapultepec on September 13, 1847, and the next day General Scott occupied Mexico City. Santa Anna resigned as President, and was replaced by aging Manual de la Pena y Pena, who reportedly had said prior to the war that armed conflict between Mexico and the United States would be "an abyss without bottom."

News of the victory spread rapidly across America, carrying jubilation to towns large and small. In New York City, crowds cheered, sang, laughed, and kissed in the streets. Paper torn into confetti was thrown out windows at impromptu parades, while every corner featured its own orator.

Nathanial walked home through masses of celebrants, but didn't participate in the rejoicing. His limp gone, hands clasped behind his back, he gazed at the sidewalk and recalled Palo Alto. A stranger slapped him on the back, and a woman he'd never met embraced him, for he was in uniform. But he barely paid attention, he was so moved by the news.

He recalled the death of Major Ringgold, and his own untimely encounter with a Mexican bullet. Many of his friends had been killed in the war, most American towns numbered Mexican War veterans in their cemeteries, and the conflict had created a palpable atmosphere of menace from sea to shining sea.

But now it was over, the air seemed easier to breathe, and America was at peace again. Somebody handed Nathanial a mug of beer, but an army officer couldn't be seen with spirits in his hand. On upper Broadway, Nathanial spotted the delicate Gothic spires of Grace Church, and decided to give thanks to God Almighty. He stepped inside, the edifice was crowded with worshipers, and he stood in a dark corner while studying cornices and columns designed by James Renwick. Some considered Grace Church too ornate and gaudy, but Nathanial found the high ceiling breathtaking. As he was about to pray, he was shocked to see Layne Satterfield enter, attired in a white wool coat, her figure returned to its former glory.

He stared in amazement at the woman who had inspired him at Palo Alto. She looked older and more careworn as she knelt in a pew, and Nathanial's eyes filled with tears as he contemplated what might have been. She was the perfect woman for me, and I'll never find another like her.

He felt the need to make peace with her, as his country was making peace with the Mexicans. She arose from the pew and made her way toward the rear of the church, where he was waiting beside a door. She appeared agitated when she noticed him.

"Hello, Layne," he said with a smile. "Congratulations on the birth of your daughter. I'm leaving for the West soon, and wish you every happiness."

He held out his hand, and she looked at it nervously. Then she took it in hers. They gazed into each other's eyes, recalling passionate kisses and hot embraces in dark corners of carriages not so long ago. "I will always love you, Nathanial," she said softly, "and whenever I'm overcome by the obligations of my life,

I can always take comfort in knowing that once I was courted by the most handsome young gentleman in New York."

"And I'll always cherish the memory of our happy times together, so I suppose our love will never die, will it?"

"Never," she replied, "and perhaps I'd better leave now, before I drag you to the nearest hotel, and do something that I'll never live down."

She leaned forward, embraced him warmly, and he felt the abdomen that had produced Franz Astor's child. They separated, and she headed for the door, engulfed by the crowd, vanishing.

Nathanial returned to the sidewalk as her coat disappeared around the corner of Tenth Street. She was gone forever, with his innocent youth in her purse. He placed his palm on the front of his tunic, which was wet with her tears. I'll never meet another like her, he admitted. I might as well get used to the idea.

He meandered home to the Alhambra Club, changed into civilian clothes, and sat by his window, where he sipped whiskey and listened to victory cannon booming in Battery Park, signaling the end of American's third major war.

Old Fuss and Feathers had captured Mexico City, but it was widely believed that Old Rough and Ready destroyed the Mexican Army at Buena Vista, and he was the true hero of the war. Ailing President Polk had refused a second term, and many thought General Taylor should become the Whig candidate for President of the United States.

When questioned by the press, General Taylor indicated he wouldn't run for the office, but would serve if the people wanted him. "If nominated, I would pledge nothing but a strict adherence to the provisions of the Constitution," declared the old warrior.

On March 29, 1848, the richest man in America died at the age of eighty-four. Suffering from palsy, John

Jacob Astor had spent his final year in bed, suckled at the breast of a wet nurse, and tossed in his sheets every day for exercise, as his rent collectors continued to report to him personally. William Backhouse Astor ascended to the throne, but Nathanial Barrington had made his decision. He didn't like office work, and money wasn't that important to him. His request for a transfer to the frontier was carefully penned and set adrift in the river of paper passing through his office.

In May, 1848, the Democrats nominated Senator Lewis Cass of Michigan on the fourth ballot, over Levi Woodbury, James Buchanan, and James Calhoun. In June, the Whigs convened in Philadelphia and nominated General Taylor also on the fourth ballot, over Henry Clay, General Scott, and Daniel Webster.

Shortly thereafter, Nathanial was promoted to first lieutenant, and finally his orders arrived. He was to proceed to Camp Marcy in the newly liberated New Mexico Territory and report to the commanding officer on or about the first of September.

Nathanial's first stop was Sam Colt's plant, where he purchased a new pistol of the latest so-called "Walker" design, considered stronger and more reliable than the old Paterson model, named after Sam Walker of the Texas Rangers, killed in action at Huamantla.

Then he visited his tailor and bootmaker, made the rounds of taverns and clubs, said farewell to friends, and visited the homes of relatives for the last times. On Sunday morning he caught the ferry to West Point, where he strolled among the castellated towers, recalling his years as a cadet, and reaffirming his commitment to the officers' corps.

As the sun sank on the Palisades, Nathanial stood on Storm King Mountain and beheld the multicolored glory of the Hudson River. No longer was he the giddy youth who'd paraded to Mexico, but a seasoned campaigner in war and boudoirs. "I believe in this great country," he whispered to the river winds, "and I am honored to serve in her army."

Finally he sat for his last supper with his mother, Jeffrey, and Tobey, the latter having become a virtual brother to him. The usual polite conversation ensued, as if the patriarch of the family weren't sleeping with an octoroon in Washington, and Nathanial had not disgraced his family on numerous occasions.

In mid-July, Nathanial rode a train to Philadelphia, first leg of his journey west. As the engine car gathered speed in the marshes and woodlands of New Jersey, he wondered what new destiny awaited him in the wilds of New Mexico. Eager to be a real officer again, he felt confident that he would surmount all obstacles and perhaps become a general someday.

The town had no name and appeared on no maps. It consisted of tents and shacks alongside a southern tributary of the Rio Grande, and its business was stolen goods. Thieves, cutthroats, traders, and desperadoes with prices on their heads had congregated from all across Mexico and American to profit from the turmoil following the war, and they kept their eyes peeled for the arrival of the U.S. dragoons.

One hot day in summer, a contingent of twenty heavily armed Apache warriors appeared on the horizon, led by the great chief Mangus Coloradas. This event caused no special concern, because Indians often came to the settlement, to trade stolen cattle and horses for guns and whiskey.

The People were ready for action as they approached the stench-ridden jacales at the junction of the rivers. Filth and squalor in the streets and alleys disgusted the warriors, not to mention the crude way in which the denizens treated each other. An encampment of the People was an extended family, while the town swarmed with strangers who fought among themselves constantly, with no moral constraint.

Mangus Coloradas led his warriors down the right

side of the main street, littered with garbage, potholes, animal manure, cigarette and cigar butts, and spit. He saw a drunken man sleeping on a dirt sidewalk, and another passed out beside a horse trough. In front of a store, three men sat on a bench and eyed the People suspiciously; Mangus Coloradas watched their hands.

The chieftain angled his horse toward a cantina in the middle of the block, then climbed down from the saddle, gazing calmly at the Mexicans and White Eyes staring at him. Nine of his warriors joined him, the rest sat upon their horses, holding their rifles ready to fire, as the wind fluttered the ends of the bandannas wrapped around their heads. Mangus Coloradas entered the saloon, followed by his warriors. Smoke and the odor of dirty bodies assailed his nostrils violently, but he strode directly to the bar, where two bearded Mexicans made way for him.

Mangus Coloradas looked at the rotund man in the white apron. "Tell the Mustache that I want to speak with him outside."

"Sí, senor!" replied the bartender, who turned and ran toward a corridor in back of the ramshackle building.

Mangus Coloradas returned to the sidewalk, examining the enemies gathering around. Images of the Santa Rita massacre clouded his vision, the cannons opening fire on unarmed warriors, women, and babies. He peered into windows across the street, searching for cannons. If anybody struck a match, he'd be on his way to the ground.

A short obese man with long flowing brown mustaches came outside and placed a sombrero on his head. "*Buenos dias*, Mangus Coloradas," he said with a slight bow. "How good to see you again, senor. You have come to trade?"

Mangus Coloradas pointed in a northerly direction. "We have two hundred very good horses about a half-day ride from here. We trade?"

Mustache rubbed his hands together. "We trade."

Mangus Coloradas pointed at the trader's nose. "This time you pay more, because these are very good horses."

Mustache smiled nervously. "All right—we will meet you at noon tomorrow."

"Enjuh," said Mangus Coloradas. "It is good."

Mangus Coloradas and his warriors climbed onto their horses, wheeled them around, and kicked their ribs. The horses sprang forward and galloped out of town, the Apaches yipping and yelling, brandishing their weapons. In seconds they were disappearing over prickly pear cactus and through groves of palo verde trees, becoming one with the unknowable desert that had spawned them.

ELEVEN

Nathanial arrived at Camp Marcy after a month-long journey across America. The wagon driver unloaded his bags in front of the orderly room, and inside, a sergeant with red side-whiskers and a corncob pipe was seated at the desk. "You must be Lieutenant Barrington," he declared, rising to his feet and saluting smartly.

Nathanial handed over his orders and records. A wooden sign on the desk said FERGUSON.

"Take room eight in the Bachelor Officers' Quarters. Leave your things here, and I'll have someone deliver them to your room. The major will see you later this afternoon."

Nathanial leaned toward the sergeant and narrowed one eye. "What's he like?"

There was silence for a few moments. "He's seen a lot of war."

Nathanial walked outside, the sun hit him full blast, and the sky was dotted with fluffy clouds. In the distance, the sun cast gaudy shadows on the Sangre de Cristo Mountains. Fort Marcy had been constructed alongside the Palace of the Governors on a plateau about seventy-five feet above the central plaza of Santa Fe, and the whole town could fit inside a few blocks of New York City. It was here at the junction of the Santa Fe Trail and the wagon road south to Mexico City that Nathanial would advance his military career.

His room in the Bachelor Officers' Quarters was a

monk's cell with a bed, desk, chair, and closet, all simply constructed and functionally strong, no ornamentation. It appeared drab to the New Yorker's eyes, compared to his bedroom at the Alhambra Club, which itself had come in second to his former bedroom on Washington Square.

Two privates brought his luggage, departed, and he felt desolate and dispirited as the vast empty spaces of the West engulfed him. He wondered why he'd been so eager to leave the bright lights of Broadway for dusty remote Santa Fe. His uniform was covered with alkali, and the army didn't seem quite so heroic close-up, but all he could do was open the nearest trunk and began unpacking. Then someone knocked on the door.

Nathanial expected a message from the commanding officer as he turned the latch, but standing before him at attention was Lieutenant Beauregard Hargreaves, formerly of Palo Alto. They stared at each other for a few seconds, then Nathanial said, "What the hell are you doing here?"

"The same thing you're doing here. Sure is a boring place, and the Apaches are sons of bitches."

Nathanial opened a trunk and took out a silver flask, which he threw to him. "Try some of this. It's the best brandy in New York."

The officers proceeded to regale each other with tales of their excesses since last meeting, while Nathanial put his clothes away and the flask diminished. Finally, some time later, Nathanial asked, "Tell me more about the Apaches."

"They're operating without much restraint throughout the area," explained Beau. "I don't know how much good we're doing, but occasionally we kill a few of them, and they kill a few of us. That's what happened to your predecessor, Captain Dellinger. One thing I can tell you—don't ever turn your back on an Apache."

"What's Major Harding like?"

"It's time he retired, but he's got a pretty daughter."

"Are you sleeping with her?"

"Hell no—I don't want any more trouble with the son of a bitch than I've got already. But you might like her."

"I don't want trouble either. Are there other women around?"

"Whores are everywhere, but decent Mexican girls don't have anything to do with American soldiers. I met one fabulous beauty, as fine as anything you'd see in Charleston or New York, with tits out to here"—he held his hands in front of his chest—"but she was a religious fanatic and will probably end up a nun someday. Whenever we get word of Apache raids," Beau continued, "we try to track them down. But unfortunately we seldom catch them. One of their favorite tricks is to fire on a detachment, then draw them into a bushwhack, which is what happened to poor Dellinger. Apaches love to mutilate their enemies, so if they ever corner you, save the last bullet for yourself. And I'm not joking, because I've seen results of massacres. They're savages, and the only way to deal with them is to exterminate them. The sooner you understand that—the better off you'll be."

The cold black ledger told Diego Carbajal that business was falling off at the store. Although more traffic passed through Santa Fe, many additional businesses competed for the dollars and pesos, and the bigger firms were more successful because they could afford to operate on tighter margins.

I've come to Santa Fe too late, but what if I could find the next important city on the trail to California? wondered Diego. If I set up a business at the right place, I can be the big fellow that the others have to beat.

The sun was going down, time for evening prayers. He made sure his door was locked, because he didn't want Maria Dolores to stumble onto him, not to mention his friends and neighbors who'd string him up by his heels if they knew he was Jewish.

His grandmother had told him about the Inquisition, when Jews had been burned alive for refusing to convert to Christianity. They were the brave ones—the old-timers who'd held the line and died for the faith of their fathers. Sometimes Diego felt like a coward for not practicing his religion openly, but had no desire to be tortured to death. He was descended from generations of Marranos, and deception had been their last resource against the hostile Christian world.

After long and sometimes heated deliberations, Diego and Maria Dolores's mother had decided not to tell their daughter about her Jewish ancestry. What Maria Dolores didn't know couldn't hurt her, they figured. Why perpetuate a potentially dangerous creed, and who could promise that an Inquisition would never return?

He put on his skullcap, then kissed the collar of his prayer shawl, which he wrapped around his shoulders. He picked up his Bible, bowed, and prayed softly in Spanish-accented Hebrew: *"Hear O Israel the Lord our God the Lord is One."*

"Lieutenant Nathanial Barrington reporting for duty, sir!" Nathanial snapped out the salute as he stood at attention before the man who'd dominate his life for the foreseeable future.

Deeply tanned, in his late fifties, Brevet Major James Harding wore a full gray beard, the hair atop his head was cut short, and his pate was smooth and shiny. "Have a seat, Barrington," said the major. "How was your trip?"

"Uneventful, I'm pleased to say, sir."

"Well, your life won't be uneventful here. You're replacing a good man who was killed in action against the Apache. We've got our hands full of the redskinned devils, and they're getting worse, not better, as more gold-diggers are passing through the territory."

"Everywhere I went," replied Nathanial, "people were talking about California gold, sir. Some say it's all a big humbug, and there isn't as much as everybody thinks. The Indians must feel like they're being invaded."

"Feel, hell," said the major, "they *are* being invaded, and there's some that says gold can be found right here in New Mexico. My advice to you, since you've never fought Apaches before, is to listen to your first sergeant wherever possible, because he's been fighting Indians all his life. Another good one to learn from is the scout assigned to your company." The major paused and looked both ways, as if a spy might be in the vicinity. "If you have any difficulty, feel free to come to me. I'm an old friend of your father's, but it might not be smart to let the word get out, for obvious reasons."

Now Nathanial understood why he'd been assigned to Camp Marcy, of all possible outposts in the West. "Yes, sir." Then he waited for the ax to fall.

"Your father's told me all about you," continued Major Harding. "You're supposed to be quite a hellion, but if you give me any trouble, I personally will rip those shoulder straps off you and drum you out of the army. The Apache is a deadly foe, and I can't accept anything less than your best effort. You've caused your father a lot of heartache, and if it'd been me, I would've shot you long ago."

"Do you have any children left, sir?" Nathanial asked before he could seal his lips together.

Major Harding stared at him coldly. "My personal life is none of your business. I wish you all the best in your new assignment, Lieutenant Barrington, and you may be interested to know that I consider the firing squad an excellent solution for insubordinate officers. That is all. You're dismissed."

* * *

Elena perched on her hands and knees and scooped dirt atop mescal roots roasting in the pit below. She worked among the other women in her clan, and the cabbagelike vegetables would take several hours to cook. Then a great feast would be held.

Elena's stomach carried the child of a chief, and now at last she was treated almost equally with his real wives, without insults, kicks, and the worst chores. She enjoyed her new status, could speak their language fairly well, and considered White Painted Woman the Apache version of the Virgin Mary.

The People moved in harmony with the seasons, lived beneath open skies, and ate what grew in their midst. When the pit was covered, the women stepped back and smelled fragrant aromas streaming through the earth.

Ten warriors adorned with feathers, war paint, and Killer of Enemies Bandoliers rode war ponies out of the encampment, led by the great chief Mangus Coloradas. Elena shivered uncontrollably, because that's how he'd looked when he'd killed her husband and friends. Sometimes she considered herself wicked, for she had made love with the murderer of Father Alfonso, but the bad times had occurred long ago, and she tried not to think of them. She entered her wickiup and placed her hands on the tiny creature growing within her. It changed position, and she smiled in contentment. I am no longer a *Nakai-yes*, she thought happily. Now I am of the People.

In the Officers' Mess, Beau introduced Nathanial to the men with whom he'd be living and working for the foreseeable future. Two had been his upperclassmen in West Point, and he'd met one in General Taylor's army, but most were strangers, some Regular Army, others volunteers. Nathanial decided to keep his mouth shut and listen carefully, so he could gauge their characters carefully.

The Officers' Mess consisted of six tables, and

adobe walls were adorned with regimental and American flags. The principal topic of conversation was the presidential campaign, and all the officers seemed to be for Old Rough and Ready, regardless of whether they were Whigs or Democrats.

They all seemed decent enough, not too different from the bachelor officers Nathanial had met previously during his military career. One officer was missing three fingers of his left hand, and another wore a patch over his eye. The newest had been one of Nathanial's underclassmen at West Point, Franklin Dorsey from New Hampshire, butt of all the jokes, but the New Englander bided his time until the next lowest-ranking officer came along, and then he'd moved up the pecking order.

Nathanial was considered a veteran of the Mexican War, but felt like a virgin compared to Captain Morgan, who'd held the line at Buena Vista, or Lieutenant Cassidy, who'd stormed the parapets of Chapultepec.

And then there was Captain Simmons, who'd fought in the Black Hawk War, and Major Briggs, who'd battled the Seminoles in Florida. These weren't staff officers who sat behind desks and fought the battle of the pencils, but men who'd climbed obstacles with the enemy firing down at them point-blank. As far as Nathanial was concerned, these were the soldiers who'd laid their asses on the line, instead of writing endless letters concerning the most ridiculous and petty regulations.

He'd been in the army long enough to know that every officers' mess would contain the same types of officers. For instance, there was the abstemious Bible-basher, and at Fort Marcy he was represented by Captain Sturgis, who sat rigidly upright in his chair, reading his King James, moving food to his mouth in precise moves, the only officer drinking water.

No officers' club would be complete without at least one serious drunkard, and that was Captain Farnsworth, who wore muttonchop whiskers and appeared

ready to pass out at any moment. And then there
was the fellow who knew everything, the regimental
quartermaster, Major Todd.

"Where are you from, Barrington?" asked Todd.

"New York City, sir. Ever been there?"

"No, nor would I want to go there. Cities are the
abominations of mankind, as far as I'm concerned. I
was in St. Louis once, and I never saw so much muck
in all my days."

Captain Sturgis jabbed his finger into the air.
"Sodom and Gomorrah were cities," he reminded
his congregation.

Whiskey flowed, and Nathanial felt more at ease
with them than with his family back in New York
City. What is it about army life that I love so? he
asked himself. He couldn't deceive himself that they
were all staunch patriots, because some probably were
there for their pensions, and others because they
couldn't or wouldn't do anything productive in civilian
life, like himself.

Nathanial basked in the camaraderie of the officers'
club, although Captain Farnsworth's face now rested
on the tablecloth as he snored loudly. Nathanial's most
important test would come tomorrow, when he assumed command of his company. After apple pie and
coffee, he pushed back his chair and placed his napkin
on the table. "I hope you gentlemen will excuse me."

He felt their eyes upon him as he walked toward
the door, and knew they were evaluating him as he
was them. Their main concern was how he'd hold up
under fire, and he didn't know himself. He headed for
his room, reflecting on his brief and mostly uneventful
military career. I was wounded in the first minutes of
my only battle, and they've rewarded me with my own
company of dragoons.

He was determined to make good at Camp Marcy,
with no more bad decisions or erratic behavior to mar
his career. That meant going to bed early, getting up

early, and facing his men with a clear conscience and full determination, his uniform neatly pressed.

He hung his hat on the peg and prepared to remove his boots, when he heard the faint strains of guitars in Santa Fe. Then he undressed, washed, retired to his narrow lumpy cot, and it sounded like a carnival through his open window. Searching for a comfortable spot, he tried to fall asleep. He felt anxious because he had to admit, in the privacy of his room, that Camp Marcy was a most uninspiring post, and some of his fellow officers were the bottom of the barrel. He wondered why he'd been so anxious to leave actresses and dancing girls, but he always wanted to be someplace else, never felt comfortable in his own skin, and frequently caught himself acting according to the expectations of others. Who am I and what do I really want? he asked himself as he lit a cigar in the darkness. I've traveled halfway across this continent, for what?

There was no point trying to sleep, so he rolled out of bed and dressed himself. I'll have a drink, get the lay of the land, and return to bed in about an hour. A strange restlessness spurred him out the door.

Lamps burned brightly in the barracks across the way as the men prepared for tattoo. He came to the gate, and the dragoons on duty presented arms. "Good evening, sir!"

"Evening," he muttered, returning their salute. They appeared well trained, their uniforms proper, and it gave Nathanial satisfaction to be living in his regulated and rational military world. He walked across the square, saw the spire of a church in the distance, and beyond were the ever-present mountains sleeping peacefully in the night.

Drawn to music, he crossed the square, turned a corner, and saw a squat adobe cantina a few doors down, with a sign above the entrance that said: EL SOMBRERO BLANCO.

A group of dragoons stood outside passing bottles, talking loudly, and they stiffened as he approached, but he paid them no attention, lowering his head and entering the cantina.

It was a small, squarish room packed with dragoons, and the guitarist strummed the melodies of Andalusia in the corner. Something told Nathanial to get the hell out of there, but the only thing to do was order his drink and make the best of the clumsy situation. A stained Apache blanket decorated one wall, while a wrinkled American flag adorned another, illuminated by candles, with illustrations of seminude women nailed into adobe. Two soldiers made way for him as he bellied up to the bar, and the bartender approached, wiping his dirty hands on his dirty apron. "Senor?"

"Whiskey."

"No wheesky, senor. Only mescal and beer."

"Mescal."

The bartender poured a half glass of clear white liquid, and Nathanial tossed him a few coins. Nathanial had never drunk mescal before, so he raised it to his lips and took a cautious sip. It tasted sharp, fiery, yet smooth and warm as it trickled down his throat. Then he accepted a more copious swallow and placed his back to the bar. All eyes were on him, as though he were an oddity, and he supposed that officers weren't supposed to frequent such oases, but didn't think he was breaking regulations.

Two soldiers vacated a table against the far wall, and Nathanial headed for it, threading among uniformed gamblers, drinkers, readers, and the usual debating teams. A corporal and private advanced toward the same table and arrived simultaneously with Nathanial. When they saw the silver bars on his gold shoulder straps, they smiled nervously and stepped back.

Nathanial sat at the table and blew out the candle in its center. A wisp of acrid smoke curled toward the ceiling as a medium-sized black mongrel dog walked past, chewing a bone. Nathanial took another gulp of mescal while observing two private playing cards at the next table, their eyes half-closed.

Nathanial scanned their faces, because he wanted to remember them. The good soldiers were on post preparing for the next day's assignments, whereas these were cantina rats, malingerers, liars, and potential deserters. And I am their officer, he realized with a start, spilling a few drops of alcohol onto his tunic. I should leave immediately, but I haven't finished my drink yet.

The one thing soldiers don't like is an odd officer, he lectured himself. They can handle a disciplinarian, or the officer who couldn't think his way out of a bowl of corn mush, or even an officer who wouldn't know a bull's ass from a banjo, but the odd officer was the one who worried them most, because they could never figure out what useless mission he'll send them on next.

At the bar, a big, burly, bearded corporal turned around and said, "Who the hell d'ya think yer a-pushin'!"

Across from him, a tall, skinny private with a long nose and black goatee replied with a lopsided grin, "It's crowded in here."

"Yer goddamned right it's crowded in here, 'cause horse's asses like you can't see where they're a-goin'."

It fell silent in the saloon, because the gauntlet clearly had been thrown down. All eyes turned to the private, who measured the broad shoulders of the corporal. According to the unwritten code of the barracks, you can't let anybody insult you, so the recruit drew himself erect, squared his shoulders, and said, "Somebody pushed me, and I ran into you. It wasn't my fault, and I got nothing to apologize for."

He was a wharf rat from Baltimore wanted for a certain string of robberies, but the Baltimore police would never come to Camp Marcy, and he had gutter pride running in his veins.

"Izzat so?" asked the corporal, a leer on his face.

Then he reared back his arm and launched it in the
direction of the wharf rat's face. It landed on his nose,
cracking it out of shape. The wharf rat's eyes rolled
up into his head, and he went sprawling backward,
where he fell over a card table, tipped a cuspidor, and
landed in a puddle of spit, vomit, cigarette butts, and
dead *cucarachas*.

The corporal smiled. "Who's next?"

There was silence as everyone made space around
the bull-like corporal. Then a voice came from the far
side of the cantina. "I am."

All eyes turned to the singular personage arising
from his chair. He was a big, young first lieutenant
with a scarred cheek and a white wide-brimmed vaquero hat. The corporal was confused, because he was
still in the First Dragoons, although he was off post
and no other officers were around. "Take them straps
off'n yer shoulders, sir, and I'll kick yer ass all over
this cantina."

"You're under arrest," replied Nathanial. "Turn
around and walk out the door, or I'll carry you out."

"You'll carry me out?" the corporal asked. "You're
talkin' awful rough, 'cause yer a-hidin' behind yer
rank."

Nathanial looked him in the eye as he unbuttoned
his tunic. He knew that he should never have come
to the cantina, but he might as well resign his commission if he showed hesitation in front of the men. He
draped his tunic over the back of a chair as the corporal also stripped to his waist.

Nathanial had been itching for a fight ever since his
father had smashed him in the mouth. An inarticulate
rage boiled within him, because nothing ever turned
out to his advantage. Bare-chested, no rank showing,
the adversaries faced each other in front of the bar.
The corporal was bearlike, with thick hairy arms and
chest. He bent his knees, reared back his right hand,
and heaved it without ceremony directly at Nathanial's
nose, the same tactic that had worked so dramatically

with the private. But Nathanial leaned to the left, avoided the blow, then buried his right fist to the wrist into the belly of the corporal, who expelled air from all his orifices. The corporal bent over, then Nathanial hit him with an uppercut, and the corporal snapped to attention, leaned backward, and fell like a ponderosa pine to the floor, where he lay on his back, chest heaving, eyes closed.

Calmly, Nathanial thrust his arm into his tunic as they all stared at him. He buttoned up, placed his hat on his head, and spotted three stripes at the edge of the crowd. "Your name?"

The sergeant drew himself to attention and saluted. "Sergeant Hazelton reporting, sir."

"Escort this soldier to the stockade."

Nathanial left the cantina and slammed the door behind him, leaving soldiers surrounding the corporal out cold on the floor.

"Who the hell's that officer?" somebody asked.

"West Pointer," one of them replied. "Got shot up in the Mexican War."

"He's a-gonna git shot worse here, he keeps on like that."

Sergeant Hazelton selected four men, and everybody grabbed an arm or leg belonging to the corporal. They carried him out the door as the wharf rat picked himself up off the floor, his nose shattered and blood dripping onto his tunic. He removed his bandanna and wiped his wound of honor as the bartender poured a fresh glass of mescal. "Be happy you are alive, my friend. That officer is one bad hombre, no?"

He was answered by an old battle-hardened sergeant sitting at the end of the bar, licking beer foam from his mustache. "We'll see how he does against the Apaches."

The six White Eyes had no notion they were being observed as they sat in their campsite next to a laughing stream. No guards had been posted, although each man maintained weapons close at hand as they roasted meat over a bright fire, drank whiskey, and smoked cigarettes in the firelight.

The People's warriors lay in the darkness, admiring weapons, clothing, whiskey, and cooking utensils. They could not understand the lack of caution. Didn't the White Eyes know they were trespassing on the People's homeland?

"If'n I strikes it rich!" one of the White Eyes hollered, motioning with his fork, "I'm a-gonna build a palace, and fill it with nineteen-year-old dancing girls."

"They'll make you more loco than you are already, you old turd," guffawed another would-be miner. "If I find any of them gold nuggets, I'll give half to my mother, because she worked so hard fer me all my life."

"Horseshit," said a compadre. "You'll keep it all fer yerself, 'cause yer the cheapest son of a bitch I ever see'd."

The great chief Mangus Coloradas lay on his belly behind a chokecherry tree. He wondered why they were so stupid, careless, noisy, and always quarreling with each other. *Yet these filthy dogs are swarming over our land, always talking about yellow metal,* he concluded. He gave the signal, and the warriors withdrew into the shadows, leaving the miners alone on the last night of their lives.

Nathanial made his way across the parade ground, heading for Officers' Row. The more he thought about it, the more pleased he was by his performance at El Sombrero Blanco. *I knocked him out with one punch, and if he pulled a knife on me, I would've shot him. It's the only way to treat hooligan soldiers, otherwise they'll infect the whole camp.*

He came to Officers' Row and reflected upon the incongruity of domestic life on an army post. Prostitutes plied their trade not far away, and the warlike Apache nation wasn't far beyond that, while here dwelled tiny children and doting mothers. They were in as much danger as the men, for children and women were valuable property to the Apaches, who believed in the time-honored tradition of chattel slavery.

While engaged in these lofty thoughts, Nathanial heard the front door of a house open. "Good night, Mrs. Grimes," said the voice of a woman. "Thank you so much for inviting me."

Nathanial slowed his pace as a green shawl and sky-blue dress cut into his line of vision. It was a woman hurrying toward Nathanial, apparently an officer's wife or daughter. She drew closer, her features came into sharper focus, and he realized that she was fairly pretty, blond, not very tall, and not a New York actress by any means. She must be the major's daughter, he surmised.

"Good evening, miss." He tipped his hat, searching for something interesting or exciting to say, to capture her heart forever, but all he could think of was a confused, "Am I on the right path to the Bachelor Officers' Quarters?"

She wore no cosmetics, and her blond hair was a few shades darker than Layne Satterfield's. "You arrived at Camp Marcy early this afternoon, Lieutenant Barrington, and I suspect you know very well where the Bachelor Officers' Quarters are." Then her nose wrinkled. "My God, you have been drinking, sir."

Even he could smell the mescal on his tunic. "I only had one, but I'm afraid I spilled it when someone jostled me."

She looked at him disapprovingly. "We're shorthanded in every department, and you're replacing a man who will be greatly missed. If you don't take your duties seriously, my father will not hesitate to throw you out of the army."

"You're quite right—I should've turned in early. But I was curious about Santa Fe. What do you think of it?"

"It's a rathole," she replied. "I much preferred the Jefferson Barracks."

"I've always believed that it's the people who make a place enjoyable, and size has nothing to do with the friendliness of a town. Do you have any friends, Miss Harding, or is everybody afraid of you because you're the major's daughter?"

She stared at him thoughtfully. "To tell you the truth, most people *are* afraid of me. There isn't much to do here, but at least you'll be able to go on scouts and see some scenery. And don't worry about the Apaches, because they seldom attack soldiers unless the soldiers are lax, and you won't be, will you?"

"Certainly not, but perhaps we can take a walk some evening. I get tired of being around men, because they're always drinking and fighting, and always drawing me into it. Women have a benevolent effect on me."

She couldn't suppress a smile. "Did you really pass out in the dining room of the Emory Hotel?"

Nathanial was shocked that she knew, but evidently her father had told her. "It taught me the most valuable lesson of my life."

"Which you promptly forgot, evidently."

"You're too smart and pretty for this godforsaken army post," he told her. "Why don't you and I take a walk to Santa Fe sometime, and I'll be we'll find something interesting to do."

She raised an eyebrow. "I'll have to ask my father."

"How old are you?"

"Almost eighteen." She placed a finger on her chin. "At least you're not boring. If my father says yes, I'll permit you to escort me to Santa Fe. Good night, it was very nice meeting you. I think we'll be friends."

They shook hands, then she hurried along Officers' Row. Nathanial waited until she was safe indoors, then continued toward the Bachelor Officers' Quarters, where he entered his room, sat on the bed, and stared at the dark wall.

Maybe I should marry Miss Harding, he thought. She's all-army just like me, the ideal wife for an officer. As he pulled off his left boot, there was a knock on the door. He drew his Walker Colt and pressed his back against the wall. "Who's thee?"

"I want to speak with the lieutenant, if it ain't too late. I been comin' all day, but kept missin' you."

Nathanial opened the door on a big hulking jet-black Negro dressed in rags, the whites of his eyes vivid in the darkness. "My name's Otis Jackson, and I was Captain Dellinger's slave, suh. I was a-wonderin' if'n you might need an orderly, 'cause you sure look like you can use a bath right now, and you spilled somethin' on yer jacket. I can take care of that, you just give it to me, sir."

"Who owns you now?"

"Captain Dellinger's estate, suh. I'm a-gonna have to go back to the plantation, unless somebody buys me." The slave looked both ways, to make sure no one was about. "I heard you was from the North, and you might he'p me. It ain't no good on that old plantation, sir."

Nathanial had read about mistreated slaves on good old Southern plantations, and he'd intended to hire an orderly anyway. "All right—what the hell," he replied. "Just tell me where to send the money. I'd like a bath about an hour before reveille, and please press a fresh uniform. Do you know how to shave a man without cutting his head off?"

"Captain Dellinger said I was the best barber he'd ever met."

Nathanial reached into his pocket and threw him a few coins. "Get some new clothes."

"Don't go worryin' 'bout me. Good night, sir. And thank you, sir."

Otis said "thank you" eight times before he was out the door, and he showed a slight limp. Then Nathanial lay on his lumpy cot and stared at the ceiling. It looks like I've become a damned slaver, he realized. But it's better than that poor Negro going back to his old plantation.

As Nathanial reviewed the day's events, they appeared imbued with supernatural force, for what else was his star-crossed meeting with Rebecca Harding? Has Fate sent me all the way to this lonely army post to marry the major's daughter? He wondered.

Covered to her neck with soap suds, Rebecca Harding lay in her hot tub, blond hair piled high on her head. She gazed at herself in a hand mirror, not overly pleased by what she saw. She considered her nose too broad, lips too full, and jaw too wide. Everything about her was overdone, in her opinion, and she wished she were more elegantly beautiful.

She knew that men liked frail women, but food was her greatest pleasure at the remote army camp. She felt isolated, had no close companions, was sick of reading, and had been hoping for something, anything, to happen.

But now apparently it had occurred in the person of Lieutenant Barrington. She'd always had a weakness for well-bred rascals, and Lieutenant Barrington was a fine example of the breed. She liked the twinkle in his eye, his insolent manner, his northeast accent. Such an officer could go a long way in the army, especially with a father in the War Department and the daughter of a major at his side. Rebecca smiled in the darkness as she closed her eyes. Suddenly life seemed filled with enticing possibilities.

TWELVE

The miners' camp was still, except for the guard leaning his back against a wagon wheel and smoking a
cigarette. His name was Murphy, he hailed from
Worcester, Massachusetts, a poor farmer who'd sold
everything in a gamble to win his own pot of gold.

He knew about Indians, but most miners got
through to the gold fields of California, according to
what he'd heard. Murphy hoped he'd reach Sacra-
mento before it filled with fools tripping over each
other, but fortunately most Americans didn't believe
the gold news—yet. Until then, an intrepid miner had
a chance to become dirty filthy rotten stinking rich!

Murphy's vision filled with mounds of gold blinding
him with radiance. He saw himself living in a castle
such as were drawn on the pages of fairy-tale books,
but with naked women in all the parapets, and he
running among them, a glass of whiskey in his hand,
availing himself of their delights.

It was his fondest dream, and he died with its image
on his eyelids as the arrow pierced his heart. In seconds he was flat on his back, his eyes open and staring
sightlessly at the Apache war party passing over him.
The People's warriors came to the edge of the camp,
pulled back their bowstrings, and let fly a hail of
arrows into the four tents. Screams of pain erupted
within, there was a terrible commotion, and then the
warriors advanced, knives in their fists, blades aimed
upward.

Within seconds, the campsite belonged to the People. They said not a word, as one group collected booty and another mutilated the White Eyes. The great chief Mangus Coloradas took an ax and smashed open a wooden trunk, which was filled with shovels and pickaxes. They dig in the dirt for yellow metal, which they trade for money to buy whiskey, he reasoned.

Mangus Coloradas knew many canyons and rivers where the yellow metal could be found in abundance, but the People believed that it belonged to the mountain spirits and must be left alone. The White Eyes are vain and arrogant, he reflected, much given to ordering others about, but too stupid to guard their lives.

The warriors loaded rifles, ammunition, knives, and axes into one wagon, then set fire to the campsite. They mounted their war ponies and herded the six mules onto the open plateau, heading toward their encampment in the mountains.

An hour before reveille, Nathanial slipped into his new orderly room. The Charge of Quarters slept on a cot in back and jumped to his feet, reaching for his percussion pistol. "Who goes there?"

"As you were," replied Nathanial, lighting the desk lamp.

The Charge of Quarters saw the gold shoulder straps. "Corporal Daniels reporting, sir!"

"Tell the men that they'll meet their new commanding officer at reveille, so they'd better be on their toes. And that goes for you too, Corporal Daniels. Have you ever thought of trimming that mustache?"

"What the hell for, sir?"

"Because you look like a polecat, not a dragoon in the United States Army, or do you think you're in some other army, Corporal Daniels?"

"This is sure the American Army, sir, but we're on this godforsaken outpost, and the officers don't generally mind if we give up some of the old parade ground spit and polish."

"We can't let ourselves fall apart just because there are no generals around. From now on, facial hair will be neatly trimmed in Company B. I wouldn't be surprised if you carried half of your last meal in that rag mop above your upper lip. You might as well start getting ready for reveille."

"Yes, sir!"

Nathanial saw the sign upon a door: COMMANDING OFFICER.

He entered the tiny office, and it had a window behind the desk, illuminating a popular poster of Zachary Taylor nailed to the opposite adobe wall. Nathanial had seen it before, thousands had been printed and sold, and it showed old Rough and Ready at the crucial moment in the Battle of Buena Vista, when the Mexicans had been about to overrun his position. He'd stood in the thick of flying projectiles, his arms crossed imperiously, and issued his now-famous command to his commander of artillery, Captain Braxton Bragg of North Carolina. The command was the caption to the poster: "A little more grape, Bragg."

Old Rough and Ready had captured the heart of America, he was running for the presidency, and the poster evidently had been put there by the late Captain Dellinger. Nathanial sat behind his desk and thought about meeting his men in a few short minutes.

The first notes of reveille shattered the silence, and candles were lit across the camp. Nathanial arose, looked at himself in the mirror nailed to the wall, and adjusted his wide-brimmed hat at the appropriate jaunty angle. Then he strode outside, for the first fateful meeting of the day.

Soldiers poured from their adobe barracks, buttoning tunics as they ran helter-skelter to their assigned positions. It looked like chaos, but then suddenly they were standing in ranks, the formation came together, dressed right and covered down.

"Company at-ten-SHUN!"

The sixty-two men of Company B snapped their

heels together and held their arms rigidly down their sides. Before them stood Sergeant Duffy, and behind him a tall beefy officer with blond hair showing beneath his wide-brimmed white hat, their new commanding officer. A few had seen him knock out Corporal Dunleavy with one solid punch in El Sombrero Blanco.

The bandy-legged sergeant had a face like a leprechaun. He performed an about-face, then saluted the new commanding officer, "All present and accounted for, sir!"

Nathanial saluted back. "Please step aside, Sergeant."

"Yes, sir!"

Now Nathanial could see his first command more clearly, and recognized the habitués of El Sombrero Blanco. "I am Lieutenant Nathanial Barrington, your new commanding officer," he began. "We're going to spend a lot of time together, and the nature of our association will be up to you. Sooner or later, and it may be sooner, you and I will face the Apaches. I don't want to lose any of you, and especially I don't want to lose myself."

There were snickers in the ranks, and Nathanial let them pass before continuing. "In the days to come, you and I will train to fight the Apaches. I want expert horsemen, and each of you must be a dead shot with pistol or rifle, plus able to fight with a knife, broken bottle, or anything else that may be lying around. Always remember that preparation is nine tenths of any battle, and if you give an Apache the slightest advantage, he'll cut your throat. I suspect that you've had a nice vacation without a commanding officer, but the party is over. There will be a full field inspection at ten o'clock tomorrow morning. First Sergeant?"

Sergeant Duffy marched in front of Nathanial and saluted. "Sir?"

"Dismiss the men, and I'd like to see you in my office immediately after this formation."

Ramrod straight, Sergeant Duffy spun around, faced his men, and hollered, "Dismissed!"

Nathanial sauntered back to the orderly room, to prepare for the all-important second meeting of the day. He hung his hat on the peg, sat behind his new desk, which was rough-hewn local wood, with drawers fitting loosely. There are limitless opportunities for a capable officer, Nathanial thought as he looked at the poster of Old Rough and Ready. But it all begins in Company B.

There was a knock on the door, then the first sergeant stopped in front of the desk and saluted. "Sergeant Duffy reporting, sir."

"Have a seat, Sergeant, and relax."

The sergeant accepted a cheroot and scratched a match on his boot heel. He lit Nathanial's first, then his own, and soon they were immersed in thick clouds of blue smoke.

"I don't like the way the men look," Nathanial began in a friendly and engaging tone. "They seem to think that because we're not at the Jefferson Barracks, they can do as they please." He leaned forward and peered into the sergeant's eyes. "I know what you're thinking—that I'm a young shavetail, you're an old soldier, and you know better than I about how to run this company. Well, maybe you're right, but there's just one thing." Nathanial tapped his shoulder strap. "You may not respect me, but you'd better respect my rank. Any questions so far?"

"What're you so mad about?" asked Sergeant Duffy. "I ain't even done nothin' wrong yet."

"You whip these men into shape—you'll have no trouble with me. Everybody knows that first sergeants *really* run the army. You have much experience with Apaches?"

Sergeant Duffy blew a ring of smoke into the air. "Been in a few skirmishes with 'em."

"Where are you from?"

"Kentucky, sir. I been a-fightin' Injuns all my god-damned life."

There was a knock on the door, and a private burst into the room, shot to attention, and said, "Major Harding would like to speak with you immediately, sir."

"Tell him I'll be right there."

The private saluted, then ran out of the office. Nathanial arose from his desk and put on his hat. "Looks like the old man's going to cut me to shreds. I got into a little fracas last night in one of the cantinas."

"So I heard," replied Duffy, arising from the chair with a grin. "Good luck."

Nathanial marched across the parade ground as men filed into mess halls around him. Frying bacon filled the air and he was starving, but first had to face his third ordeal of the morning. The only thing to do is brazen it out, he figured. If he court-martials me, I'll go back to New York and chase actresses around Union Square.

Determined not to let a major intimidate him, he entered the headquarters orderly room. "In there," said the sergeant major grumpily.

Major Harding sat behind his desk, fidgeting with a report. He glanced up at Nathanial and said, "So there you are."

Nathanial saluted, reported, and stood at attention. The major arose slowly from his chair and looked into Nathanial's eyes. "What in the hell is wrong with you?"

"I stopped for one drink, but a corporal started a fight, and I took him into custody. I'm sure the incident was blown out of proportion by the time it reached your ears, sir."

The major scowled at Nathanial. "I've been around the parade ground a few times, and you're not putting anything over on me, young lieutenant. Surely you know that an officer doesn't go to low drinking establishments frequented by the men. You're not a *total* madman, are you?"

"I've been in worse places, and I'm sure you have too, sir. But it won't happen again, sir."

"You're damned right it won't, because you're going on a little journey. I've always believed that the best way to train an officer is send him on a scout with a more experienced commander. That means you're leaving with Captain Grimes after breakfast. I've already ordered the supply sergeant to arrange for your rations and equipment, but I'm sure you have other preparations to make, so you're dismissed."

A half hour later, Rebecca knocked on the door to her father's office. "Daddy?"

"Come in, dear." He arose behind his desk to greet her.

"I hope you're not busy," she said as she kissed his proffered cheek. "But there's something I want to ask you. I'd like to take another tour of Santa Fe, and I've found a gentleman to escort me—Lieutenant Barrington."

His face turned purple, and she thought his collar had become too tight. "How do you know Lieutenant Barrington?" he inquired.

"I met him last night. He was returning from town, and said he'd just arrested someone."

"Who introduced you to him?"

"He asked directions, as I recall."

That hound, reflected Major Harding. Treating my daughter like a common streetwalker. "Lieutenant Barrington is not the sort of man I want you to pass time with. According to his own father, he's been a hellion practically from the time he could walk, and he's caused his mother to go gray before her time."

"People probably don't appreciate how funny he is."

"Do you think it's funny to be a drunkard? No, he's definitely not the right companion for you. How about nice Lieutenant Dorsey?"

"Father, I'm nearly nineteen years old, but you're treating me like a child."

"You *are* a child, and Lieutenant Barrington is not a man of honor where women are concerned."

"He's just lonely, and he's looking for a friend."

"I really ought to challenge him to a duel."

"Why can't I select my own friends?"

"Lieutenant Barrington is going on a scout this morning, and won't be back for approximately a month. You're too old to spank, and I can't lock you in the stockade, unfortunately, but if, after he returns, you still want to walk with him, you may do so during daylight hours out-of-doors where everyone can see you."

Beau strolled into Nathanial's room, dropped onto a chair, lit a match across the floor, and brought the flame to his cigar. "You appear to be getting off to a spectacular start at Camp Marcy. I've just heard the news about El Sombrero Blanco."

"I punched a corporal and I suspect it was the best thing that ever happened to him. I'm going on a scout with Captain Grimes—what can you tell me about him?"

"Grew up in Indiana, son of a farmer, married, two children, very popular with the men. Try to memorize as many landmarks as you can, in case you break your compass. Most scouts are uneventful, but we have to show the savages that we're active in the area. Get ready for long hours in the saddle, but you probably won't see any Apaches."

"What about Rebecca Harding?"

"Spoiled rotten."

"She's prettier than I expected. I'm surprised you haven't snapped her up."

"I don't like nice girls, especially when their fathers rank me."

There was a knock on the door. "Captain Grimes is waiting for Lieutenant Barrington, sir."

Nathanial closed the clasp on his saddlebags and turned toward his friend. "I guess it's adios, Beau. See you in a few weeks."

They shook hands, and wondered if they'd see each other again, like that long ago morning at Palo Alto. Then Nathanial threw the saddlebags over his shoulder and was out the door. A detachment had formed in front of the command post, and Otis was waiting with Nathanial's horse, a saddled chestnut sorrel stallion selected hastily by Nathanial earlier in the morning. "I'll throw your trunk in the wagon," said Otis.

The West Pointer climbed into the saddle, wheeled his horse around, and faced the twenty dragoons arrayed before him with a sergeant and a scout in front. Nathanial didn't know any of them, and figured they hated him because of what he wore on his shoulders.

He sat in the sun for what seemed an interminable period, waiting for Captain Grimes to emerge from the command post. Events were moving too quickly for Nathanial, and he wished he knew the characteristics of the men on the scout, not to mention the capacities of his animal. This is the worst preparation for a scout that I could imagine. He hoped his new horse wouldn't buck him off a ledge.

The door to the orderly room opened, then Captain Grimes stomped out, dressed for the field in blue tunic and tan wide-brimmed hat. He was short, heavyset, with a full but short black beard and a beak like an eagle. He climbed onto his horse, angled it toward the sergeant, and said, "Move the detachment out."

The sergeant issued commands as Captain Grimes, Nathanial, and the scout trotted to the head of the column. Then they slowed and formed into a triangle, the captain in front, and the scout beside Nathanial in the rear. The dragoons advanced in a column of twos, and there were cheers, hoots, and slaps on knees from dragoons remaining behind.

Nathanial sat straighter in his saddle, held his elbows into his sides, maintained an erect posture, and was carried forward by his new horse toward a woman with blond hair standing anxiously at the edge of the crowd. It was Rebecca Harding in a long pink dress, and he couldn't believe his eyes as she touched her fingers to her lips and blew him a kiss.

Nathanial raised his right hand, extended his fingers stiffly, and performed a smart West Point salute. Their eyes met, and at that moment Lieutenant Nathanial Barrington of the First Dragoons realized that he had something to live for.

Her lips formed the words "Be careful." He winked back confidently, and then it was time to face forward.

The detachment of blue dragoons proceeded onto the sagebrush plain, with the Sangre de Cristo Mountains gleaming in sunlight ahead. Nathanial felt like a knight of the round table, while his lady waited anxiously in her castle at Camp Marcy. His heart swelled with storybook romance and knightly pride. I'll return carrying my shield or being carried upon it, he swore as the detachment of fools invaded the Apache homeland.

The great chief Mangus Coloradas sat in front of his first wife's wickiup, biting the shank of an arrow-in-the-making. Then he held it to the morning sun to scrutinize its fine line. Not enough, so he held the aberrant section in the fire a few seconds, then brought it between his strong teeth again, biting more firmly.

Every child of the People was expected to add to his family's food supply, and Mangus Coloradas had been crafting arrows since he was four years old. A warrior utilized his spare time for the manufacture of weapons, while his woman collected firewood, mended or made clothes, worked skins, cooked, cleaned, gathered vegetables and fruits, and so on.

Apaches made two kinds of arrows, one for light game, the other for heavy animals like deer, antelope, and enemies. The light arrows had a reed shank and a sharpened hardwood tip, but the sturdier ones were constructed entirely of hardwood, and it was this latter variety that Mangus Coloradas was crafting.

First, the slender branches were peeled, straightened, and dried. Then they were painted in distinctive colors, so that every warrior would know his own. Next they were given three fletches, usually of buzzard, eagle, or hawk feathers, and Mangus Coloradas liked to add fluting, to make the projectile spin as it flew to its target, thereby increasing penetration. The final step was carefully sharpening the point.

Some warriors added special power to their arrows by dipping them in poison made from putrefied gallbladders of deer bitten by rattlesnakes, or from decomposed animal blood mixed with prickly pear spines. Mangus Coloradas had learned a third method during a visit to the Chiricahua People. They mixed spit, deer spleen, and nettles, let them rot, and then painted the foul-smelling result onto their arrow tips. A small tan clay pot of this evil-looking poison was being warmed by the fire, and Mangus Coloradas dipped into it a brush made of horsehair. Carefully he applied the concoction called *Eh-ehstlus* to arrowheads ready for the final touch.

Other warriors across the rancheria also worked on bows, shields, lances, clubs, and knives. But for every White Eyes they killed, a hundred more arrived. Mangus Coloradas knew the legends of his people, that they'd been pushed south by larger tribes until they ended in rugged inhospitable regions that no one else wanted. This was the homeland that Yusn had given them after their many long years of fighting and wandering, but Mangus Coloradas feared the god of the White Eyes was stronger than Yusn. Would Yusn cease to exist when there were no longer People to revere Him?

He glanced at his newest son sleeping in a cradleboard suspended from the branch of a tree. Mangus Coloradas wanted peace for the children, but the very

land itself was crying in outrage against the White
Eyes. There were fewer birds and animals, while
plants were dying in places.

None of his strategies had worked against the White
Eyes, and he almost wished that a younger warrior
would challenge him for leadership, but none had
stepped forward. *I must find a new way*, he said to
himself as a painful twinge in his stomach caught his
attention.

He'd been experiencing gut aches during the past
moons and feared that he was becoming ill. Sometimes
he was unable to sleep, so worried was he about the
future of the People. Every day brought more news
about the activities of White Eyes. *Is this the end of
the People?* he asked himself. *Will my children grow
up in a world dominated by the wicked* Pindahlickoyee?

The sun rose in the sky as the lone detachment
rode steadily across a vast basin covered with grass,
sagebrush, and several varieties of cacti. In the distance were the usual mountains, mesas, and spires, but
Nathanial never tired of gazing at them. They caused
him to think of lost civilizations, the eons of the
earth's history, and the mountains of the moon. *At
last I'm doing what I've been born for*, he said to
himself. *The soldier's life is the life for me.*

He felt no need for whiskey, for the very land itself
was making him hallucinate ghost Apaches in the sky.
He turned in his saddle and observed the dusty column of twos behind him, the dragoons wearing bandannas over their noses, so they could breathe fresh
air. Somehow he had to prove himself worthy to
lead them.

There was one characteristic about the army that
had always bothered him: its resistance to efficient op-
eration. No officer should be sent into danger with
strange soldiers, but Major Harding was of the school
that taught a child to swim by throwing him into the

river, and he'd learn or die. When I become a general, I'll change everything, Nathanial said confidently to himself, although he knew, deep in his heart, that he was too peculiar, rebellious, and cranky ever to advance that far.

The most curious member of the expedition, in Nathanial's opinion, was the scout, who rode about a mile ahead of the formation, accompanied by two soldiers, looking for water holes, game, and Apaches. His name was Potter, another former mountain man forced to work for the army due to the precipitous decline of beaver hat sales.

But Nathanial was confident he'd marry Rebecca Harding within the year, and soon his worries would be over. When I return from this scout, I'll take her on that tour of Santa Fe, and if I'm lucky, she'll let me kiss her. No officer can expect to be happy in the army unless he's married, and it looks like Rebecca Harding is destined to become my bride.

That night after dinner, Diego Carbajal lit a cigar, blew smoke into the air, and said, "There is something I must take with you about, my dear Maria Dolores."

The dutiful daughter looked up from her chili, because her father's voice carried a serious tone. "What is wrong?"

"I have been thinking it is time to move again. We must go where the competition is not so entrenched."

"What about Indians?"

"We will do business with them too, and they will protect us."

"Father, I do not think this is one of your better ideas."

"We will be starved out in a few years at the rate we are going now. You do not seem to understand—we are not big enough for Santa Fe."

"But in Las Vegas you said we were too small!"

"I am new to the store business, but am learning as

I go along. There is nothing else for me to do, or do you expect me to join the American Army?"

"Maybe, when the Americans conquer the Indians, we can have our own ranch again."

"That will not be for a long time, my dear daughter, and maybe never, because I do not believe the Americans will make any more headway against the Apaches than we. But if you are afraid, I can leave you here in Santa Fe, and perhaps you can find employment sewing other people's clothes or scrubbing floors."

"I have a question for you, Father, and I hope you will not be upset, but ..." She glanced around, to make sure no one was listening, although they lived alone. "If Jews are supposed to be good at business, why are you always losing money?"

He looked at her sternly. "Sometimes you are a very foolish child, but to answer your question, it was the Apaches that put me out of the ranching business, not my own errors. However"—he raised his forefinger in the air—"next time I will know how to treat Apaches. *You can catch more flies with honey,* your dear mother used to say. I will learn their language and even practice their religion, because God does not want us fighting each other, and one religion is as good as another once you understand that God loves us all. We must live and prosper together, and that is the message I will carry to the Apaches."

"Supposing they smear your face with honey and stake you to an anthill? What God will you pray to, the Jewish one or the Christian?"

"There is only one God, but unfortunately he made quarrelsome daughters such as you. Start packing, and if I ever hear you use that word," he whispered, "*Jew,* again, I will strangle you, and I do not care whose daughter you are."

The army horses were picketed, guards posted, and antelope steaks sizzled over open fires. It was night on the open sage southeast of Santa Fe, and two saddle-weary officers sat to supper beneath the sparkling Milky Way.

Captain Grimes looked like an overfed wolf in an army uniform as he removed a loin of antelope from the fire. "First of all," said he, "there's no point in talking politics, since I'm from the South, you're from the North, and we wouldn't agree." He sliced into the meat, blood seeped out of the wound, so he returned it to the forked sticks that kept it suspended in proper succulent relation to the coals. "And we can't talk about women, because soon we'll be lying to each other. We're here in the middle of nowhere, Barrington, and I suppose the biggest question in my mind is why the hell you ever joined the army. On your first day at Camp Marcy, you walked into a cantina full of drunken enlisted men, none of whom knew you, and it's a wonder you weren't killed. Now that's reckless, and I hope it doesn't carry over onto this scout. An officer must be extremely prudent in the field, because the Apaches will be all over you if they detect the least weakness."

"Major Harding gave me a good talking-to," replied Nathanial, "and I'm sure I won't forget in the future."

"The men can spot stupidity in an officer unerringly, and they'll deteriorate into a band of uniformed ruffians. Then the officer will be relieved of command." Captain Grimes stabbed his forefinger into Nathanial's shirt. "Don't let it happen to you." He reached for the spit, removed it from the fire, submitted the meat to the nostril test, and said, "It's done."

Grimes sliced thick slabs of tender antelope loin, placed a few on a tin plate, and handed it to Nathanial. Another plate between them contained bread baked by one of the men, and potatoes roasted in the fire, while coffee brewed in a battered tin kettle.

Crickets sang fugues, firelight flickered on the officers' faces, and a horse whinnied on the picket line as a bucket of water was placed before him. Nathanial thought of how magnificent New Mexico was at night, with moonlight carpeting distant mountains with silver tinsel. "I'm not surprised that the Apaches won't give up this country," he said. "It's so spectacular."

"They don't have to give it up—they just have to stop raiding, but they won't because we can't stop them. The only thing an Apache understands is brute strength, otherwise they'll steal the eyeballs right out of your head. Unfortunately, army appropriations have been cut to the bone, now that the war is over, and we'll never get enough to really do the job."

"The territory's too big," said Nathanial, "and we don't even have decent maps."

"The problem isn't maps. A dragoon carries seventy pounds of equipment, but an Apache carries a bow and his arrows. An Apache warrior can travel a hundred miles in a day, whereas we're lucky if we make twenty. It looks like the Apaches will raid pretty much at will until enough citizens are murdered, and then maybe Washington'll get up off its ass and do something."

Rebecca Harding sat in the living room of her home, reading *The Lady of the Lake* by Sir Walter Scott, while her mother leaned over the desk and wrote a letter to her sister, Rebecca's Aunt Barbara in Savannah. The front door opened as her father returned from a staff meeting, a vexed expression on his face. "What's this I heard about you blowing a kiss to Lieutenant Barrington today as he was leaving on his scout—young lady. If you're not careful, you'll not only destroy your own reputation, but also make me the laughingstock of the camp."

"It was only a harmless gesture," she replied lightly. "He's the first friend I've had since the Jefferson Barracks."

"How can you be friends if you only met him last night? Don't you think you should get to know each other first?"

"That's what we're doing, but you forbade me to take a walk with him."

Mrs. Harding raised her eyebrows as she spoke for the first time. "How do you expect them to find out about each other if they don't take walks? Isn't that what we did?" Before Major Harding could answer, she turned toward her daughter. "Who is he?"

"A West Point officer, but Daddy doesn't like him."

The camp commander cleared his throat. "It's Stephen Barrington's son, the disgrace of his family, but Rebecca thinks he's oh-so-charming."

Margaret Harding smiled. "You don't think *anybody's* good enough for your daughter, Major Harding, but a West Pointer is nothing to sneeze at these days, and quite often we see that wastrels are just lonely men who need a good woman, like you when I met you."

"True," the colonel agreed, anxious as always to mollify his wife, the true commander of Camp Marcy. "I was headed straight for the gutter, and I'd still be there if it weren't for you."

"I'd like to meet him," said Mrs. Harding. "Rebecca—tell him that he'll need my permission before you can go anywhere. He can call on me tomorrow evening."

"But he's gone, Mother. Father has sent him on a scout!"

"If he's as clever as you say, he'll be back."

"I've been wonderin' how long it'd take fer you to come over here," said Potter, the scout, as Nathanial approached. "I've seen you a-lookin' at me all day. Wa'al, pull up some grass and have a seat. I'll bet I know what you want. Yer a-gonna ask me to teach you how to be an Injun, but an Injun takes a lifetime to larn what he knows, and I can't teach it to you in two weeks."

Nathanial sat opposite him. "They say you're part Pawnee."

"That's right—my mother was full-blooded Pawnee," replied dark-complexioned Potter as he stroked his thin black beard. "She couldn't speak a word of English."

"How come you speak so well?"

"I was raised among the Americans, where I went to school. But my mother taught me some of the old Pawnee ways, and after I grew up, I returned to my relatives for a spell. I can track as good as any Injun, and made a good livin' trappin' beaver, but then the bottom fell out of the market."

"This is my first scout," confided Nathanial, "and I was wondering what you can tell me about Apaches."

"Stay alert, because sometimes they sneak up at night."

"Have you ever fought them?"

"Sure, and they bleed just like any other man, so don't be afraid of 'em. But if yer careful, you won't have no trouble. They don't want to die neither, but if you ever get into a fight with them . . ."

Nathanial interrupted. "Save the last cartridge for myself?"

"That too, but the only way to kill an Apache is to be even wilder than him, and don't give him no chances, 'cause he'll cut yer throat afore you know what hit you."

Rebecca undressed in front of her oval full-length mirror as steam arose from the tub of hot water prepared by her Negro slave maid. The major's daughter smiled saucily at herself, her body tingling with pleasure, because she was in love with a rather attractive officer, and her lonely nights probably would be over within a decent interval of time.

She hung her garments on the chair, placed her hands on her hips, and raised herself on her toes, looking at herself from all the angles. Am I pretty? she wondered, wrinkling her nose. But it didn't matter, as long as *he* thought so. What if he really is just another drunkard and seducer as my father says?

She slid into the warm water, and admitted that she wanted to seduce him too. Mother will like him, and he could go a long way in the army, if he stops drinking. I can make him a general, but if I ever catch him in a lie, I'll boot him right out the door.

The warm soapy water flooded over her, warming her firm young breasts. She closed her eyes and smiled in anticipation of her possible wedding night. "Oh, Nathanial," she whispered into the soap suds, "we can be so much for each other."

THIRTEEN

Around noon, the dragoons spotted buzzards circling in the sky, their piercing calls echoing across the sage. "Looks like trouble," said Captain Grimes, puffing his briar pipe.

Nathanial felt eerie after a week in the saddle, surrounded by colossal perspectives. He'd almost forgotten the army's business, when the buzzards appeared straight ahead. Probably an Indian massacre, he figured gloomily, reaching for his canteen. He took a swig of tepid water, scratched his growing beard, and glanced at his traveling companion, Captain Grimes.

Nathanial admired Captain Grimes's military demeanor, his firm command of the dragoons, and his efforts to be helpful to a junior officer. "Apaches prefer to attack at dawn, while everybody's asleep," explained Grimes. "They hit wagon trains like wildfire, and it's usually over in a few minutes. Every caravan should have a military escort, but folks would rather get killed than pay taxes." Captain Grimes laughed sardonically. "There's one big flaw with democracy, Nathanial. It presupposes an intelligent citizenry, but that's the biggest joke of all. There's never been such a thing and never will be. I don't know what the solution is, because I don't believe in the hereditary rights of kings, but it's too bad that men have to risk their lives for the sake of cheap politicians."

The scout's horse appeared on the orange horizon, trotting toward the column, and Grimes turned down the corners of his mouth. The air filled with the rustle of weapons being drawn as the half-breed Pawnee arrived at the head of the column. "Massacre ahead, sir. Pretty bad. About a day or two ago."

A faint whiff of rotting flesh touched Nathanial's nostrils. Swallowing hard, he held himself erectly, shoulders squared, so the men couldn't see his revulsion. Black-winged vultures dropped out of the blue sky, eager to fill their bellies before the dragoons arrived. Nathanial, Grimes, and the scout came to the crest of a hill, and saw next to a stream the remnants of burned wagons, with ominous shapes lying upon the ground.

The stench became overpowering as the dragoons advanced. Semi-eaten corpses were scattered about, portions of white bones gleamed in the sun, while rats scurried in the opposite direction. Captain Grimes, bandanna over his nose, climbed down from his horse, walked among the bodies, and shook his head at a length of black jelly that once had been somebody's arm. Then he climbed back on his horse and rode toward the wagons as the dragoons gazed meditatively at the victims. "Goddamned savages," said one of them, spitting at the ground.

"Kill 'em all," agreed another.

Nathanial feared he'd spit his breakfast all over his horse. Overhead, buzzards squawked in complaint, and now Nathanial appreciated their role in God's creation, because they cleaned up the mess.

Captain Grimes poked his saber inside a wagon as Potter rode toward him. "I've found their trail." He pointed in a southerly direction.

Sergeant Boylan Moynihan re-formed the men into their marching column of twos, and nobody dawdled, so great was the stench. Captain Grimes, Nathanial, and Potter cantered to the head of the column, which then rumbled away from the ghastly slaughter.

Grimes snorted angrily. "Apaches aren't human, and the moral code that all men live by is alien to their nature. Folks say that a good Indian is a dead Indian, and I warmly embrace that view."

It was windy that afternoon as Mangus Coloradas climbed a mountain near the encampment. He was restless, his stomach had kept him up most of the night, and he recalled vague snatches of dreams about burning wickiups and shrieking children. He wanted to do something, anything, to halt the inevitable bloodshed, but felt powerless before the numbers and weapons of the White Eyes.

He recalled the night when immense armies had been poised for battle, and he could imagine the outcome if such numbers ever invaded the homeland. The great chief Mangus Coloradas lowered his head and prayed, when he noticed terrifying objects on the ground.

The wind had kept the smell away, but they were bear turds, and the chief leapt backward. The People believed that bears were the ghosts of criminals, and bear sickness could be contracted by merely smelling them. A musty whiff passed Mangus Coloradas's nose as he turned and ran in the opposite direction. He'd seen the effects of bear sickness before: malformed limbs, fainting spells, constant tiredness, loss of memory. When he was sufficiently far away, he threw himself to the ground and rolled over the dirt and grass, hoping to rub emanations of bear turds off his body.

But the horrible stink lingered in his nostrils.

After supper that night, Nathanial meandered toward Potter as the scout sat before his little fire, smoking his corncob pipe. "What can I do fer you, sir?" asked Potter, an ironic tone in his voice, as if he really didn't respect Nathanial much.

Nathanial knelt beside him, tossed a twig in the fire, and said, "I've been thinking about you, Potter. You're part Indian, but you lead us against your own people. I can't help wondering why?"

Potter scowled, taken by surprise. "I have no people." Then he recovered quickly, and spat tobacco juice into the fire. "Besides, yer not gonna see any Indians on this scout, unless they're far away. If they ever git close up"—Potter winked—"you'll be deader'n this rock I'm a-sittin' on."

"Why don't they join together into armies, and then they could take on a column like this?"

"Maybe they will someday. It might even be tomorrow. You ain't afraid to die, are you, Lieutenant? Maybe death isn't as bad as people think. You go with the Great Spirit, that's all." The scout smiled. "Time to go to sleep, Lieutenant. See you in the mornin'."

Nathanial returned to his tent, thumbs hooked in the front pockets of his blue regulation trousers, unaware that he was under observation by the People's warriors. They nestled in thick bushes at the edge of darkness, studying the location of horses, number of guards, disposition of tents, and crates of ammunition.

Plunder glittered in the firelight, but guards had been posted and the bluecoat soldiers also kept their weapons close at hand. The White Eyes are learning, thought the prominent subchief Cuchillo Negro, leader of the raid.

The encampment was too strong to attack, but that didn't mean the White Eyes could pass through the Apache homeland unmolested. Cuchillo Negro believed that White Eyes should be killed at every opportunity, to show that they had never conquered the People. The warrior subchief inserted the end of an arrow into his bowstring as he made the sound of a desert swallow.

Headed toward his tent, Nathanial heard many bird calls in the symphony of a New Mexico night as he weighed his conversation with Potter. The man is part Indian and part white, and that's why he doesn't feel part of anything. The only thing he's loyal to is his next payday, and such a man must be watched at all times.

Nathanial neared the tent that he shared with Captain Grimes, when that officer emerged on his way to the latrine. "Beautiful night, sir."

Grimes looked up at the sky. "Yes, it really makes one feel humble to live in the midst of all this glory, doesn't it?"

Nathanial heard a strange *sssssttttt* sound, and surprise came over Grimes's face. He stared at Nathanial, his eyes glazing over, and blood burbling out of his mouth and nose. Nathanial stared at him in disbelief as Grimes fell into Nathanial's arms.

Shouts erupted across the camp. "Injuns!"

Nathanial was frozen with astonishment as shots fired around him. Then he dived toward the ground, yanked out his Walker Colt, thumbed back the hammer, and glanced about excitedly. Captain Grimes lay motionless a few feet away, his eyes wide open and staring, the arrow sticking out of his back, and Nathanial hadn't the slightest idea of what to do.

"Take cover, men!" he ordered, and then regretted it because they'd all taken cover long ago. Calm down, he said to himself. You've been trained to handle situations like this, haven't you?

He wondered if the Indians were still there.

"Mr. Potter—may I speak with you please?"

"He's daid," said a dragoon not far from the scout's camp. "One arrow through the haid, the other through his chest."

"What about Sergeant Moynihan?"

"Present, sir."

"Please tell me how many men are fit for duty, and double the guard on the horses."

It was pitch black beyond the perimeter of the fires. Nathanial wondered whether to douse them, so the Apaches couldn't see the dragoons so easily. But then the dragoons wouldn't see either, and might shoot each other by mistake. Nathanial crawled toward Captain Grimes, felt his pulse, but there was nothing. One moment the captain had admired the scenery, next he was extinguished forever.

The voice of the sergeant came to him from across the campsite. "Three dead, five wounded, and twelve fit fer duty, sir."

"Be on your guard," advised Nathanial. "Captain Grimes has been killed, and I'm in command."

Nathanial lay on his belly and held his Walker Colt ready to fire as the sergeant crawled toward him. Meanwhile, dragoons scanned the terrain around their campsite, ready to shoot any unusual movement. A rifle discharged nearby, its report echoing off distant mountains.

"What's there?" asked Nathanial.

"Thought I saw something, sir."

"Keep your eyes peeled—all of you."

"I think they're gone," said the sergeant, his forage cap turned around on his head, as he came abreast of the new commanding officer.

Nathanial hadn't spoken much with heavyset red-faced Sergeant Moynihan, because he'd been more interested in the scout's opinions, although the detachment wouldn't move one step without the noncommissioned officer. Nathanial studied the campsite as he spoke: "I know you're much more experienced at Indian fighting then I, and I'd like to know what you think we should do."

The burly sergeant shrugged. "Nothing to do, sir, 'cept let half the men sleep, while the other half stand guard. I'll work out the roster so's nobody'll get cheated."

He sounded efficient, the opposite of what Nathanial had expected. What kind of dragoon rises above the others and becomes a sergeant? he wondered as he crawled into the command post tent. It was just as Grimes had left it, with a half-written report on the desk. Nathanial found Grimes's document pouch and withdrew the maps and orders.

Their mission had been to follow a route laid out

on the maps, but Nathanial wondered whether to continue or return to Camp Marcy. We'll bury our dead here, Nathanial concluded, and continue the scout. Orders are orders, and we've got to show the damned Apaches that they can't stop us.

Grimes had been married, the father of two children, and Nathanial felt enraged at the murder of a decent man, although Grimes had been a Southerner and perhaps a slave owner. Nathanial sat behind the desk, opened the drawer, and a flask of whiskey was there, Captain Grimes's private stock that he nipped when no one else was around. A secret drinker, mused Nathanial as he absentmindedly unscrewed the cap.

His hand froze. "This is no time to be a drunkard," he said to himself as he emerged from the tent. He walked several steps, up-ended the flask, and let the whiskey drip to the ground. Then, peering into the lethal night, he wondered if he were a target for an Apache bow. He dropped to one knee, yanked out his Walker Colt, and noticed that he was beginning to hate the Apaches personally. "Stay alert, men!" he shouted. "They might attack, but we'll be ready for them!"

The great chief Mangus Coloradas didn't mention bear sickness when he returned to the camp. If he visited a *di-yin* medicine man, soon everyone would know, and the hotheads would question his ability to lead. Fighting among clans would follow, as in the old time, and fragmentation of the People would begin. Mangus Coloradas had worked all his life to wield the Mimbrenos together, and couldn't let his work be destroyed.

The camp was peaceful, firepits filled with white ash, and everyone had gone to bed. He wanted to make love with his concubine, but Apache law forbade it until she had weaned the baby. Yet it was her wickiup he tended to visit, because all his three wives were angry with him.

He entered their wickiup, and she stirred. "Who is it?"

"Me," he replied, wrapping his arms around her.

The baby slept next to her, wrapped in skins and odd lengths of cloth. Perhaps someone will kill him because he is the son of Mangus Coloradas, the chief mused as he nuzzled her heavy breasts, trying to draw life and sustenance from her body. A drop of her milk squeezed out, smearing his cheek.

"Be careful of the baby," she said.

I need you too, thought he, but I can never tell you, because I am Mangus Coloradas. He raised himself off her, rolled to the far side of the wickiup, and covered himself with skins. Exhausted, rattled, fearful of the future, the great chief fell off to troubled slumber. In his dreams floated the snout of a bear with golden fangs, sparks flying out of its eyes.

FOURTEEN

Nathanial rode at the head of his detachment as they passed cattle grazing on both sides of the trail. A few miles in the distance, Santa Fe gleamed in the autumn sun, while a wagon train rolled toward him, furling clouds of dust. More miners headed for California, guessed Nathanial, his soul seared by the massacre of travelers and the death of Captain Grimes. Nathanial thought he'd seen everything at Palo Alto, but that was before he'd met the Apaches.

The remainder of the scout had been uneventful, but nobody had slept during the long dark nights; they'd been especially tense at dawn. Now the detachment commander wanted a meal, bath, and bed. The wagon train drew closer, and he decided that the taxpayer had the right of way. "Sergeant Moynihan— move the men to the right of the road!"

The West Pointer angled his horse onto open sage as the sergeant shouted the command. "Oblique right—hooooo!"

Nathanial turned in his saddle, to make certain that no dragoons were breaking their necks in the maneuver, but Sergeant Moynihan was flawless in his execution, leaving his commanding officer free to contemplate abstractions.

Nathanial understood why many officers drank, while others became Bible-bashers. The war against the Apaches can't be won the way it's being fought, he realized, and good men will die because the damned taxpayer wants a bargain.

Nathanial felt annoyed at the approaching civilians in their wagon train, for they demanded protection on their jaunts into Indian territory, while other civilians in distant parts of the country refused to foot the bill. This nation is a good idea gone awry, speculated Nathanial. Perhaps a mad king with venal advisers was better than a mad electorate making its own rules.

The wagon train drew closer. It consisted of men with their women beside them, and everyone was heavily armed.

Goddamned gold-grubbing fools, though Nathanial. Did I go through four years of West Point just to protect them?

"Hey, Lieutenant!" shouted one of the bullwhackers. "Yer a-goin' the wrong way."

Nathanial smiled and touched his forefinger to the brim of his hat, as his detachment followed him toward Camp Marcy. The well-scrubbed travelers gazed at the dust-covered officer, and couldn't tell whether he was twenty-six or fifty-six. On the buckboard of the fifth wagon, seated next to her father, Maria Dolores didn't conceal a twinge of distaste as the dragoons passed, for she considered American soldiers thieves and louts, despite her involuntary change of citizenship.

But she wished they'd escort her wagon train into Indian territory. It was fifteen wagons of armed men and women, and she hoped the Apaches would leave them alone. She peered around the canvas covering of the wagon at Santa Fe receding in the distance, and fancied herself a rootless waif, always traveling from one place to another, a lost wandering Jewess.

At that moment the officer turned around. Their eyes ricocheted for a moment, then she pulled back and faced forward again as teams of horses and mules hauled the *conducta* onto the Apache homeland. The officer vanished from her mind as she contemplated the hazardous journey that lay ahead, thanks to her father's latest farfetched plans.

Meanwhile, Nathanial reached the last wagon, then angled his horse back to the yellow dirt road. He recalled the Mexican he'd just seen, the one with that smoldering beauty for which Mexican women were justly praised. Then he returned to the mental letter he was drafting to his father, detailing his recommendations for further operations against the Apaches. The War Department is too far off to understand New Mexico, he thought, and it looks like I'll have to tell them the truth.

The guards at the Camp Marcy entrance presented arms, and Nathanial saluted them as he led the detachment through the gate. He headed straight for Major Harding's headquarters, while dragoons poured out of the barracks and mess hall to see the detachment that had lost its commanding officer.

Sergeant Moynihan led the men to the stable, while Nathanial pulled his horse to a halt in front of the command post headquarters. He tied the reins to the rail, and Sergeant Ferguson came out to greet him. "He's expecting you, sir."

Nathanial squared his shoulders, straightened his backbone, and reported to the major.

"Have a seat, Lieutenant."

Nathanial dropped to a chair, but his legs felt bowed from so many hours in the saddle. "It was a night attack," he explained, "and the guards didn't see anything until too late."

The major examined Nathanial carefully for clues to the young man's mental capacities. Occasionally officers became unhinged by casualties, and some blamed themselves unduly. But Lieutenant Barrington appeared in command, if weary, bearded, and covered with the trail. "Why'd you continue the scout after losing Potter and the company commander?"

"I believed that I should follow Lieutenant Grimes's orders, sir."

"I wouldn't've faulted you for returning, but you made the right decision. I'll expect your report on my desk by noon tomorrow, Barrington. You may return to your quarters. That is all."

Nathanial departed the major's office, and was about to untie his horse, when a blond woman in a purple gingham dress appeared on Officers' Row, walking toward him quickly. He removed his hat and tried to smile.

"Are you all right?" asked Rebecca as she slowed her gait.

"Yes, but I'm afraid Captain Grimes wasn't so lucky."

"Mrs. Grimes has been in bed since she received the news. I've been so worried about you."

He held his hands about twelve inches apart. "If I'd been standing this far to my right, the arrow would've hit me."

Nathanial had the stunned look that she'd seen in soldiers after skirmishes with Indians. "I hope you're not going to get drunk."

"So do I."

"I'll keep you company. To tell you the truth, I've thought of nothing but you since you've been gone."

He led his horse toward the stable as Rebecca walked beside him, their coupling noticed across the camp. The two gazed into each other's eyes, and the remote army camp vanished around them, to be replaced by grand pavilions and sweeping vistas of mountain flowers, as the New York Philharmonic played a crescendo by Mozart.

She waited outside the stable, while he escorted his horse inside. Then he returned, and she boldly hooked her arm in his. "Shall I escort you back to the Bachelor Officers' Quarters, sir?"

"Let's go to town," he said.

It would violate etiquette, but he'd been in a fight with Indians, his commanding officer had been killed, and the iron obligations of command had been clamped upon him when he was least prepared. She decided to stand by her newly acquired man.

They walked arm in arm across the parade ground, observed by, among others, her parents standing behind the window of their home. "Look at her," growled the major. "She appears to have fallen head over heels in love with this young rogue, and now she's making a spectacle of herself."

"Leave her alone," said her mother. "She's not a little girl, and stop trying to protect her."

"But he's up to no good."

"So are all men, but I'm sure she can handle him."

"The way you handled me?"

She smiled, her eyes closed to slits, and he realized that his daughter had studied at the knee of a skilled persuader. "Perhaps you're right," he replied.

She held his hand. "She's a high-spirited girl, and will get into mischief if she's not married soon."

"But he's worthless, and even his father says so."

"His father was the worst hell-raiser of all, even when he was married, but we shouldn't interfere until we give the young man a chance. Let's invite him to dinner and see what he's made of."

The squat adobe church had a steeple of white-painted wood, with a bell hanging in the belfry, as the Romeo and Juliet of Santa Fe observed it from the far side of the plaza.

"Some of these peons don't get enough to eat," complained Rebecca, "and they live in tiny crowded huts, but the church keeps squeezing money out of them anyway. I've always thought the Catholic religion is for people who don't like to think for themselves."

Nathanial weighed her words as he compared the edifice to Grace and Trinity churches in New York City. One could call San Francisco Iglesia crude, with no Byzantine arches or soaring Gothic columns, but it appeared a functional fortress of God in the wilderness. "The people need to pray somewhere," he replied.

"Why do you need a special place to pray? And the priests tell everyone to be celibate, while half of them keep women on the side."

There was something strident about her, but he appreciated her gold hair, upthrust breasts, and shapely hips. "Let's go inside."

"Oh—do we have to, Nathanial?"

"Some of these little Mexican churches can be quite interesting."

"Well . . ."

She let him pull her toward the door. No two people are exactly alike, she told herself. We've got to make compromises, but I'll be damned if I'll do this all the time.

Burning incense made her gag as peasants prayed in pews and flickering candles illuminated painted saints. One old lady with eyes closed rubbed the toe of a life-size Jesus crucified on a wall. Catholicism seemed pagan and grotesque to the major's daughter, a prostitution of faith with old men in Rome pulling the strings.

"Have you ever read Ralph Waldo Emerson?" she asked Nathanial. "He said that organized religion brings out the worst in people, and who'd know better than he, because he'd been a Unitarian minister, and quit."

He wished she'd stop talking as he stood in the shadows, observing Catholics in prayer. He'd just returned from blood and death on the open range and felt the need for spiritual nourishment. "I'd like to say a prayer," he said.

"In here?"

"If you don't mind."

They entered a pew, she sat on a chair and watched with dismay as he dropped to his knees, clasped his hands together, and bowed his head like a damned Catholic. What kind of man is this? she wondered. The last thing she wanted was a Catholic for a husband. I hardly know him, she realized.

Nathanial closed his eyes and saw contorted corpses covered with dried blood and gaping buzzard beak holes, not to mention burrows of rats and mice. The hale and hearty Captain Grimes had gasped his last in Nathanial's arms, and the young West Pointer felt dizzy, nauseous, and haunted by nameless terrors. My God, forgive me my sins, he prayed silently.

He became aware of the young blonde beside him, and could feel her emanations. "Are you finished?" she asked, a tone of impatience in her voice. "I don't like it here."

"Let's go," he replied.

They threaded among worshipers, and Nathanial turned for one last look at the altar. It seemed to be calling him, but then he was out the door, arm in arm with his wife-to-be, and they headed back toward the camp.

"I hope you're not thinking about becoming a Catholic," she said with a faint whine in her voice.

"Of course not. But don't you believe in God?"

"Not like the Catholics. Religion should be personal, and you know what they say about priests."

Nathanial was familiar with anti-Catholic arguments, because he'd been hearing them all his life, and in fact agreed with most of them, although he'd always felt attracted to the mystical symbols and rituals of the Catholic Church, which weren't so different from the Episcopalian faith. But more than Catholicism, he was drawn to the ravishing maid beside him. "Why don't we get married, Rebecca?" he asked.

It was the question she'd been awaiting all her life, but she had to be coy. "We hardly know each other, Nathanial."

"What's the point of waiting a year?"

"Are you asking me to elope?"

"Well ... yes."

"My father might very well shoot you. No—we'll have to get engaged, and then wait a decent interval.

I don't want to start my one and only marriage with a scandal."

Both knew how scandals could undermine otherwise promising military careers, but the street was dark and semideserted, so he leaned closer, smelled the clean fragrance of her healthy hair, and touched his lips to her cheek.

"Don't . . ." she whispered.

Their bodies touched, and he felt the power of those firm breasts shielded by numerous layers of fabric. She gazed up at him, fear on her quivering lips, as he bent his knees in order to kiss her. "I love you," he whispered as he placed one hand on her haunch.

She wanted to push him away, but this was her first kiss, and she savored it like fine champagne. Her skin felt itchy, a hunger gnawed within her, and she opened her mouth to his inquisitive tongue. Something happened, she wasn't sure what it was, but it felt as though the top of her head had blown off. She'd never dreamed that kisses could be so . . . it frightened her, she was losing control, and frantically pushed him away. "Stop," she whispered, her skin mottled by emotion.

They looked into each other's eyes and realized that they'd been far over the line. "I'm sorry," he said, reluctantly letting her go.

She breathed deeply, her breast rising and falling. "We have to wait."

"Why?" he asked with a wicked smile.

"Just think of how wonderful it'll be when we're married. A year isn't so long and might be worth it." She laughed nervously. "I know. I sound like a silly goose. But it sure will be one helluva wedding night, if we can last that long."

Swathed in blankets beneath her wagon, Maria Dolores dreamed of crucified Jesus toppling through the sky, starlight flashing upon his strained features, with a gaping gash in his side. She reached out to touch him, when something hard and cold jutted her forehead.

"Get up," said a voice above her.

Maria Dolores opened her eyes. Ramsay, a member of the wagon train, was aiming his pistol at her, a fiendish smile on his face.

"What's this all about?" asked her father indignantly from his cot next to hers.

"Put yer clothes on, Pablo," said Harry, another fellow traveler. "This is a real pistol in me hand, and it's got a real chunk of lead inside."

Maria Dolores awakened to the possibilities of robbery, rape, and murder. Shivering uncontrollably, she wrapped the wool blanket around her cotton nightgown as the robbers stood in the darkness. She'd been afraid of the single travelers since they'd departed Santa Fe, and now realized that her intuition had been correct. Her father's hands trembled as he pulled on his pants underneath his nightshirt. "You can do anything you like to me, but please leave my daughter alone."

Ramsay looked at Maria Dolores and licked his thin lips. "How'd an ugly son-of-a-bitch greaser make such a purty daughter? Lookit the tits on her, Harry."

"Forget her tits, you fool," replied the leader of the robbers. "Outside, you two."

"Are you all right, dear?" asked Diego as he reached to comfort her.

Ramsay smacked him in the face with the pistol and sent him flying against the wall of the tent. "The man said go outside, peahaid."

Diego's cheek was torn open, and his eyes were wider than Maria Dolores had ever seen. She took his hand and helped him to his feet. "Do as they say, Daddy."

"You can say that again," replied Ramsay, poking her hindquarters with the gun. "Git movin'."

She crawled through the opening of the tent and saw the other pioneers gathered in the center of the clearing. Several men, the ones who'd been traveling alone, held the rest under the threat of pistols, muskets, shotguns, and knives. Maria Dolores and her father joined the weaponless majority, and were surrounded by the robbers. She could make out their faces, and wondered if this was her last night on earth. *Hail Mary, full of grace, the Lord is with the* . . .

"We're lookin fer cash, coins, gold, jools, watches, and anythin' else of value," said Harry. "When we pass the bag, throw all yer belongin's inside. If we catch you holdin' out, we'll kill you, and if you don't think we're serious, go ahead and test us out."

One group of robbers moved among them, holding out a big gunnysack, while the victims reluctantly tossed in money and jewelry. Everyone was searched roughly, while a pair of robber cohorts scoured tents and wagons for more. "Look at this!" one of them shouted, holding up a wood box full of paper money and coins, somebody's grubstake about to disappear.

A bearded ruffian held the burlap bag in front of Maria Dolores. "Let's go, missy. We ain't got all night."

"I have nothing except my rosary." She pulled it out of her nightdress. "It is just wooden beads—not worth much."

The ruffian appeared uncertain. "Take it," said Harry. "Any Injun'd give five rabbit skins fer beads like that."

Maria Dolores removed her blessed beads, dropped them into the sack, and saw the eyes of the robber assess her body. She blushed as the bag moved in front of her father. Then another robber stepped before her and he gave her left breast a pinch. "You're not bad fer a greaser gal," he murmured.

Without thinking, she reared back her hand to slap him. Then, out of the night, came a battering ram fist, catching her on the mouth. Everything went dark, and when she opened her eyes, she was lying on her back.

A robber held the sack in front of her father. "Hurry up, Pablo. We ain't got all night."

Maria Dolores had never been punched, and now understood the full ramifications of the word *desperation*. Her father usually slept with a money belt beneath his nightshirt, and she wondered if he was going to give it up. Trying to smile, he dropped the contents of his pockets into the bag. "That's all," he said cheerily.

The searched stepped forward as Diego retreated. "My ribs are very sensitive today, and if you don't mind ..."

Two robbers held his arms, while the searcher's hands unerringly sought the money belt. With a chortle, he yanked out his knife, ripped open Diego's shirt and trousers, and cut the belt off his body. "This old fart must be rich!" he said, holding the trophy in the air.

"Hurry up," said Harry impatiently.

The sack was thrust in front of the next man, an old flinty-eyed farmer from Vermont, with a gray goatee and suspicious eyes. "I'm not givin' you a goddamned thing," he said, "and if you don't like it, go ahead and shoot me."

Harry stepped forward, then placed the point of his gun against the man's forehead. "Yer life don't mean shit to me, old man. Hand it over."

The farmer looked into those eyes, felt the gun barrel press into his skull, and obeyed orders.

Maria Dolores pulled the blankets around her nightdress and rose to her feet as birds chirped in her ears, her head inundated with pain. She'd seen men fight before, but never appreciated the purifying power of a solid left hook. It was as though she'd been transported to another plane of existence.

Three robbers held the travelers under guard, while Harry led the others in the systematic plunder of the campsite. "Don't leave 'em nawthin'," he ordered.

A selection of jewelry, coins, clothing, and arms

were loaded onto one of the wagons, while other robbers rounded up cattle and horses. "You'll never get away with this," said the Vermont farmer.

"You talk too much, mister," said Harry, raising his pistol.

It fired, the campsite filled with acrid smoke, and the farmer appeared shocked by the sudden turn of events. "But . . ." he said as his knees began to wobble and his eyes stared into the middle distance.

Maria Dolores sucked wind as the farmer fell to the ground. His wife screamed, dropping to her knees beside him, as his son gazed angrily at Harry. "Mister," he said through clenched teeth, "if I had a gun right now, I'd kill you."

"But you ain't," said Harry. He thumbed back the hammer, closed one eye, aimed, and tightened his finger around the trigger. The younger man's eyes bulged as he learned the lesson of false pride. Then Harry grinned. "I guess you think I ain't really a-gonna shoot you."

The boy tried to smile, wondering if he was missing the joke.

"Come on," said Harry. "Tell the truth. I wouldn't shoot you fer talkin' back, would I?"

"I . . . don't know," said the young man, his face sickly green.

Harry's finger tightened around the trigger, then he smiled viciously. "I don't much give a damn how many people I kill today. You been warned."

Harry loosened his finger around the trigger, but continued to aim at the frightened travelers. Maria Dolores stood by her father, who placed his arm around her shoulders. She gazed in wonderment at the dead man on the ground, for she'd never seen anyone killed before. One moment he'd been on his feet, defying the outlaw band, and now was dead meat.

Her father smiled at Harry. "Surely you are not going to take all our weapons. Why, we will be defenseless against the Indians."

Harry shrugged. "That's the way she goes, greaser."

Maria Dolores wanted to inquire why they were godless fiends, but the next lead ball might be headed in her direction. Shuddering with fear, she ground her teeth together and forced herself to stand steady. The wagonload of booty was ready, as the robbers climbed onto their horses. Removing his hat, Harry announced, "*Hasta la vista,* ladies and gentlemen. My deepest thanks fer yer contribution to my favorite charity—me!"

With a laugh, he pulled on his hat and kicked the ribs of his horse. The animal stepped forward, and the robbers followed him out of the camp, pulling their purloined wagons, driving cattle and horses, leaving behind anxious victims defenseless in the Apache homeland.

Rebecca walked down Officers' Row, feeling doubts and misgivings about her just concluded farewell with Lieutenant Nathanial Barrington. She feared that she'd been too forward with him, and even let him kiss her in that tantalizingly personal way. Her ship steered an uncertain new course, and she wondered if she'd crash on the rocks.

I let him touch me as if I were his wife, she realized, but I'll bet there are wives who wouldn't tolerate such disrespectful behavior. She remembered that humiliating moment when she'd been ready to give herself totally, in a doorway of all places! Anyone could've come upon them, and she'd let him place ill-behaved hands wherever they wanted to explore.

She imagined herself writhing in the gutter with him like two screeching alley cats, and felt weird, as if melting into a puddle of fried butter. You don't feel this way about a man unless there's a reason, she surmised. It came from our hearts, and all we can do is follow our deep feelings no matter where they lead.

She approached her home, and the door opened in

front of her. "Where have you been, young lady?" asked her mother.

The tone said *trouble ahead,* but Rebecca had been raised among soldiers and absorbed their rough ways. "I took a walk," she replied casually as she continued into her home, not slackening her pace.

Her mother got out of the way, and Rebecca landed in the vestibule, where her father stood in front of her, unyielding as Camp Marcy itself. She was forced to stop as he inspected her carefully, looking for signs of disarray in her uniform. "Well?" he asked. "What happened?"

"Nothing."

There was silence, and her father didn't appear ready to move. "I hope you haven't made a fool of yourself, young lady," he said coldly.

"Certainly not as much as the fool you're making of yourself, my dear father. I was only taking a walk with an officer who needed someone to talk with after undergoing a difficult trial."

Her mother raised an eyebrow. "We have no quarrel with talk, but gentlemen frequently take advantage of inexperienced young women."

Her father nodded firmly. "I can tell you from personal observation that men cannot be trusted with women, and especially not this particular man."

Rebecca replied, "He took me to the church."

Her father narrowed an eye. "The *Catholic* church?"

"Nathanial is quite amazingly religious, you know."

"If there's anything I can't tolerate," replied her father, "it's a Bible-basher. They're always the first to steal your wallet or your wife."

Rebecca scowled. "If I were to tell you that he sprouted wings and ascended into heaven, you'd find something wrong with that too. The plain fact is you don't like him because of rumor and hearsay."

Her mother sighed. "He has a terrible reputation, and even his father admits it's true."

"You have to look at the man himself, not his reputation," replied Rebecca staunchly. "It is entirely possible that I shall marry Lieutenant Barrington one day, and perhaps you should start accustoming yourself to the notion."

Wind whistled over the roof of the adobe residence as the major and his wife stared at each other in alarm. "Marry?" asked her father. "Surely you can't be serious. Has the scoundrel actually proposed?"

"Let's just say we've been having certain discussions, and don't think you're going to stop me."

"But you hardly know him," stuttered her mother.

"I have the rest of my life to know him better."

The major stepped to the side as Rebecca continued down the corridor to her bedroom, where she sat on the bed, removed her boots, and stared out the window. *What did I just say?* she asked herself.

Why shouldn't I marry her? Nathanial inquired silently as he walked back to the Bachelor Officers' Quarters. *So what if she's a freethinker, and probably an atheist?*

He liked the way she'd felt in his arms, and he'd sleep with her every night for the rest of his life, placing his hands wherever he wanted. *No two people are ideally mated,* he reminded himself. *There'll always be disagreements, but the important thing is we love each other, don't we?*

Nathanial wasn't sure, but how could anyone forecast the future? He recalled what his father had said about marrying the daughter of an officer. *It would be a sensible marriage,* realized Nathanial. *I'd become a legitimate man, instead of everybody's embarrassment.*

He noticed a light in Beau's window, knocked on the door, and it was opened moments later by his old chum, who held a glass of mescal in his hand and appeared to've drunk prodigious amounts that evening.

"Come on in," Beau said in a thick voice. "Have a seat."

Beau tossed the bottle to Nathanial, who was tempted to pull the cork and follow through like a good American officer, but Beau was unsteady, bleary-eyed, his flesh hanging loosely on his face. Nathanial passed the bottle back. "No thanks."

Beau sat heavily in a chair, sucked on the neck of the bottle, and hiccuped. "Grimes was a pretty good friend of mine," he allowed.

"If it's any comfort, he died quick and clean."

"For what?" snarled Beau. "Do you think anybody cares besides the people in this camp? What the hell are we supposed to be doing here? We're not protecting people, because there aren't enough of us. But we pretend as if we are, and occasionally some of us get killed, while the big money boys back east just keep raking it in, because it's no skin off their backs. So what if there are a few more widows and orphans, right?" Beau balled his right fist and bared his teeth. "You may consider me bloodthirsty, but I think that every Apache should be shot like the dangerous vermin that they are. We should pay the same bounty as the Mexicans, and station a few more regiments of dragoons here. Instead of reacting to Apache outrages, we ought to seek them out."

"It could take a million dragoons, and even that might not be enough."

Beau's eyes were bloodshot, and he was working himself into a rage. "The loudmouthed fools in Washington don't have the courage to face the Indian problem, or anything else. There's a goddamned war going on, but no one wants to admit it. It's the war against the Apaches, and it started on the day General Kearny captured this territory. I don't know what the end will be, but we just lost a fine officer today. We ... we ..."

Beau's eyes became glassy, he leaned forward in his chair and went crashing to the floor. Nathanial stared at him thoughtfully, realizing that he, Nathanial Bar-

rington, had performed the identical trick in front of
his father in a prominent Washington hotel. Now, in
the cold light of sobriety, he could see what a madman
he'd been, ranting and puffing about everything under
the sun, until collapsing from overindulgence in drink.

He knelt beside one of Charleston's most eligible
bachelors, who presented the same slack-jawed expression as all slumbering drunkards. Nathanial placed
one arm under his friend's head, another beneath his
knees, then carried Beau to his bunk, removed his
boots, and covered him with a blanket.

Am I really getting married? Nathanial wondered
as he continued toward his quarters. Did I really pro-
pose to Rebecca Harding? It seemed preposterous,
but why not? he asked himself. I might as well have
some fun, because where would I be if that arrow had
struck me?

FIFTEEN

Nathanial loathed the necessity of acting, but the time had come to meet his prospective in-laws. He was stone-cold sober, bathed, cleanly shaven by his slave, and wore a clean uniform, with black boots highly polished. I have nothing to be ashamed of, he said to himself as he traversed Officers' Row. Just because I've been obnoxious in the past, it doesn't mean I have to be obnoxious tonight.

He knocked on the chosen door, and after an interval, where he felt himself dropping through space, the portal was opened by Francine, one of the Hardings' Negro slave maids. "I'm Lieutenant Barrington," he said.

"So I see," she replied with a twinkle. She was about thirty years old, another beautiful Negress, and Nathanial wondered if he should buy one like her, but he'd probably end up as *her* slave. The Negress ushered him into the empty living room, where a reproduction of a painting of George Washington crossing the Delaware hung above the fireplace. "May I get you something to drink, sir?"

"A glass of plain water, if you don't mind."

She narrowed her eyes as if to say: *Who do you think you're trying to fool, you drunkard!* Then she departed, leaving him alone.

He felt uneasy in the strange parlor, and thought he heard urgent whispering in another part of the house. He knew that Major and Mrs. Harding weren't eager to see him, but they had to be civil to a fellow officer, especially one from a distinguished old New York family involved in politics.

He heard footsteps, expected the maid to return, but instead Mrs. Harding entered the room, wearing a maroon wool dress with a gray sweater. "Ah, Lieutenant Harrington, I mean Barrington," she said nervously. "So good to meet you."

He arose and bowed, then Francine arrived with his glass of water.

"That's all you're drinking?" asked Mrs. Harding.

His hand shook barely perceptibly as he swallowed the tasteless pallid liquid. "I've always believed water the most refreshing beverage in the world."

"I prefer tea myself. Won't you have a cup?"

"The water is fine, thank you."

The room fell silent, for neither knew what to say. Nathanial wanted to jump out the window and run screaming across the parade ground. Shall I talk about the weather, or is that too banal? he asked himself. What possible statement should I make to this woman, who appears ready to faint. He felt warm beneath his tunic as pinheads of sweat appeared on his brow.

At that awkward moment, Major Harding bounded into the room, holding his hand out stiffly. It appeared that either his shoes were too tight or he was suffering from constipation. "Good evening, Lieutenant," he said. "I trust that you've recovered from any ill effects of the scout?"

Nathanial shook the proffered paw. "I feel fine, sir. Has anyone seen Mrs. Grimes?"

Mrs. Harding replied, "She's deeply shaken by the news, but is up and around, I understand."

They sat in the small room, with Nathanial facing George Washington standing bravely in the prow of the boat. Since a babe, Nathanial had been told that his grandfather Joshua Barrington had paddled one of those small rowboats on Christmas Eve, 1776, when the American colonials surprised the Hessian mercenaries at Trenton, and routed them. Why am I intimidated by this major and his wife? Nathanial asked himself. For God's sake, my people *made* this damned country.

Nathanial sat straighter as he looked at them from a higher elevation. "I think I'll have a talk with Mrs. Grimes. Perhaps I can give her some comfort, since I was with her husband when he died."

Mrs. Harding smiled for the first time. "I think that would be very kind."

Major Harding said, "The trouble with this country is the goddamned Indians. If we could build enough forts, we'd stop them."

"But how would the Indians exist if we stopped them?"

"The Apaches must adapt to America, not the other way around. And if they can't comprehend democracy, they will perish like everything else that stands in the way of progress. General Taylor knows how to treat Indians, and after he becomes President, I'm sure we'll have changes for the better in the army."

Nathanial realized that he'd lost track of time. "When's the election?"

"Three weeks. It's hard to imagine, but big political rallies and marches are going on right now back east. This country needs a good cool-headed man of the people, instead of the usual thieving politicians. I served with the general in the Black Hawk War, and he was the steadiest man I've ever known."

A vision of loveliness appeared in the doorway, the delectable Rebecca Harding, attired in a white faille dress imprinted with pink flowers and green leaves. Nathanial rose to his feet as she floated toward him and extended her hand. "What are you discussing so earnestly?"

"The election," said her father. "And I don't think Cass has got a prayer." He turned to Nathanial. "Did you know that when Cass was governor of Michigan, he charged the government for an office and a clerk that he didn't have? I read it in this newspaper." Ill at ease, uncertain how to behave before a man of whom he disapproved, Major Harding waved an old copy of the *Washington Globe* in the air. "It's from a speech by a congressman named Lincoln, and what a funny fellow he must be. I'll read part of it to you. *'At eating, General Cass's capacities are shown to be wonderful. From October 1821 to May 1822, he ate ten rations a day in Michigan, ten rations a day here in Washington, and nearly $5 worth a day on the road between the two places.'*"

Major Harding continued reading compulsively while Nathanial and Rebecca gazed at each other longingly. They didn't care about Congressman Lincoln's speech, or how Lew Cass had bilked the government.

Their mutual interest didn't go unnoticed by Mrs. Harding. They look well together, the lady thought. His manners are good, he's clean, and no one could accuse him of being unattractive. Maybe this isn't such a bad match after all.

Meanwhile, her husband was rambling through the newspaper, too ill-tempered to engage in genuine conversation. "The Democrats are trying to make Cass into an American war hero, and the equal of Zachary Taylor, but listen to what Lincoln said about Cass's war record: *'... all his (Cass's) biographers have him in hand, tying him to a military tail like so many mischievous boys tying a dog to a bladder of beans. True, the material they have is very limited, but they drive at it with might and main. Mr. Speaker, if ever our Democratic friends ... take me up as their candidate for the presidency, I protest they shall not make fun of me, as they have of poor Senator Cass, by attempting to write me into a military hero.'*"

Major Harding laughed uproariously, clutched his stomach, and rolled his eyes. He was attempting fellowship with his daughter's chosen gentleman, even if it meant making a fool of himself.

Nathanial tried to smile, although he'd barely been listening. "I've never heard of this Lincoln before."

"At least he's trying to bring comedy to Washington." Major Harding laid down the newspaper and tried to figure out what else to say.

It grew silent in the parlor, because no one dared speak what was really in his or her mind. It reminded Nathanial of home, and he wondered for the first time if he really wanted to marry into this family. But then Rebecca filled his eyes, and he experienced the usual disreputable desires. I'm not marrying her parents, and I can be as empty a conversationalist as anyone. Nathanial wanted to think of an insightful political analysis, but distrusted political analysis. The only jokes that came to mind were ones he'd heard in barracks and taverns, inappropriate for the occasion. The room became still as Rebecca sat opposite Nathanial, and they continued looking at each other with more than passing interest.

Major Harding felt like a stranger in his home, and knew that his daughter was slipping through his fingers. He was just the old fuddy-duddy daddy, while the dashing lieutenant evidently had captured her heart. The major felt tired and old, as if the younger man were defeating him. The silence became oppressive, and the camp commander realized that he was turning red with discomfort.

The Negress appeared in the doorway. "Dinner is served," she said.

Nathanial followed his host and hostess to the dining room, with a window overlooking a red and gold sunset. A mirror with wood trim hung above the mantel, spreading rays of light in all directions. In the corner was exhibited a framed reproduction of a painting of General Washington riding a horse into the Battle of Yorktown.

Nathanial held a chair for Rebecca, and watched her bottom sink into it. Someday we'll dine alone in our own home, he thought. He imagined himself rolling around on the floor with her. She smiled reassuringly, as if to say: *You're doing just fine*.

The Negress was herself a beauty, carrying the tureen of soup to the table. Even Mrs. Harding wasn't unappealing, because sometimes age gave a woman a patina that Nathanial found fetching.

It was clear chicken broth with a few slices of carrots and potatoes, not the greasy glue of the Officers' Mess. Again, deadly silence pervaded the gathering. Nathanial searched for a witty topic, but Captain Grimes's death cast a pall over the table. It was Mrs. Harding who spoke next. "I understand that you visited the Catholic church with Rebecca."

"Yes, I like churches," replied Nathanial. "I find them peaceful."

"You don't have to go to church to have peace," declared Rebecca sarcastically.

Major Harding appeared annoyed by her remark. "My daughter is an admirer of that old drunkard Thomas Paine, and considers herself a deist. I've always believed that a deist is an atheist who's afraid to admit it."

Nathanial wondered how to extricate himself from the delicate situation that was emerging. "You can't apply logic to religion," he explained, and wondered if he was making sense as he groped for the truth himself. "It's not a science like mathematics and chemistry."

The Hardings stared at him as he sipped chicken broth. "I swear, I don't know where my daughter gets her ideas," said Mrs. Harding. "Certainly not from me or my husband."

Her husband growled. "It's those damned books that she's always reading."

Nathanial was glad that attention had shifted from him to books. *I could dine with these boring people every night for a year, if that's what it takes to marry Rebecca.*

He leaned back and waited patiently for the next

course when suddenly the maid entered the room. "Sergeant Ferguson would like to speak with you, sir. It's important."

The atmosphere in the dining room became electrified, because the major would never be disturbed at dinner unless something significant had occurred. "Send him in."

The maid departed, and seconds later Sergeant Ferguson marched into the dining room, saluted, and said, "Sir, a wagon train has been robbed by white men, and the survivors have just arrived at the camp. What should I do with 'em?"

"Tell them I'll be right there."

The sergeant performed an about-face as the major dabbed his lips with the napkin. "I have to talk with them," he explained to his family. "If it's not the damned Indians, it's the damned outlaws."

He pulled on his forage cap as he headed for the door. Nathanial followed him outside, where a crowd had formed in front of the orderly room. A tall distinguished-looking Mexican in a black sombrero stepped forward. "I am Diego Carbajal, and we were on our way to California when the very people we hired to protect us robbed us. And they killed Mr. Pelletier from Vermont."

Senor Carbajal described the fearful deed, and Nathanial found his eyes drawn to a buxom Mexican woman standing near the speaker. Is it his wife or daughter? wondered Nathanial. Dust covered her clothes and face, but her eyes drilled into him. He smiled, but she was either too tired or indifferent to return the favor.

Meanwhile, Senor Carbajal was coming to the end of his narration. "I was in Las Vegas on the day that General Kearny promised to restore law and order, and I foolishly believed that the trails had become safe. Well, Major—what are you going to do?"

Major Harding wondered whether to send a detachment to pursue the thieves. The trail would be old, but at least the citizenry would know that the army wasn't completely indifferent to their suffering.

"I'll go, sir," said Nathanial. "Just give me Sergeant Duffy, a good scout, and about ten men." He was aware of the beautiful Mexican woman's eyes upon him.

"It's not your turn. Sergeant Ferguson, make certain that everyone here gets a hot meal, and tell Captain Sturgis that I want to speak with him in my office."

Sergeant Ferguson barked orders to men in the vicinity as the robbery victims were escorted to the mess hall. Major Harding headed for the orderly room, while Nathanial drifted back toward the Harding residence. Francine led him to the dining room, where the Harding women were looking out the window. "What happened?" asked Mrs. Harding.

Nathanial explained the bloody crimes. "The major is organizing the pursuit, and I don't think he'll be back for a while."

"We'll dine without him, and I'll direct the maid to bring him something at his office. Excuse me."

The matriarch left for the kitchen, while Nathanial and Rebecca stood alone by the window, watching travelers streaming into the mess hall. "I hope I haven't made a complete fool of myself," he said.

"Not at all."

She placed her palm on the small of his back, and he turned toward her. "I don't think I can last a year," he said.

"You must," she replied as she raised her pouty lips.

He kissed her lightly and felt her small breasts against his tunic, while the fragrance of flowers radiated from her hair. Their legs touched, their bodies were separated only by a few layers of fabric, but her mother was in the kitchen, the maid in the vicinity, and the major himself might return at any moment. They heard approaching footsteps, separated quickly, and the maid entered, carrying a silver platter covered with meat, potatoes, and carrots swimming in gravy. "Mrs. Harding will be with you in a few minutes."

Nathanial and Rebecca sat opposite each other, with the steaming haunch of meat between them. "This is the way it'll be when we're married," he told her. "But a year is such a long time."

"If we really love each other, we can do anything," she replied.

Maria Dolores sat with the other robbery victims in the mess hall, gulping down spoonfuls of beef stew and bites of bread, as cooks and mess attendants waited on her and the others. Her father was in the major's office, explaining the robbery, while she sat alone with her thoughts, safe at last from the dangers and pitfalls of the wilderness.

Events had taken on the petrifying aspect of nightmare. She'd been robbed, punched, and made to walk through Apache territory to Santa Fe, without any weapon except a dinner knife. Many times she'd expected Indians to appear with lances and hatchets, and she'd barely slept at night.

Her father had bounced right back after the disaster, and was chattering away with the major, always making friends, everybody loved her dear old father, but unfortunately he'd made too many unwise decisions, in her opinion.

Since the robbery, Maria Dolores viewed the world in an entirely new perspective. She comprehended more acutely the pressing need for armies and police forces, but everyone, even demure young Mexican ladies, had to look out for themselves.

There'd been moments when she'd thought she and the others would never survive. Water holes had been few, they couldn't carry much food, and the constant threat of Apaches nearly drove her mad. Many times she'd felt like dropping to her knees and shrieking with sheer terror, but that might've attracted Apaches.

She'd died a thousand times in her imagination, ripped to shreds by charging Apache hordes.

I will never leave Santa Fe again without a full military escort, she swore, and I'm going to run a successful business here if it's the last thing I do. My father is a wonderful man, but he doesn't know anything about business. From now on, I'm making the decisions in this family. Fortunately, her father left a small sum in a Santa Fe bank for emergencies.

She finished her meal, pushed the dishes away, and lay her head in her arms as others ate hungrily around her. She fell asleep amid clanking forks and knives, and dreamed again of young Jesus crucified in the sky, surrounded by angels and choruses.

On the way back to his room, Nathanial noticed a light in the window of the Grimes residence. The West Pointer had promised to offer his consolation to the grieving widow, since he'd been last to see her husband alive. But what'll I say to her? he asked himself.

An officer can't know every detail of battle in advance, and Zachary Taylor had taught him the art and science of tactical improvisation. So he strode toward the door, his wide-brimmed hat slanted low over his eyes, and rapped his knuckles three times.

No one responded immediately, so he waited patiently, glancing from side to side, in case an Apache might be creeping up on him. He even inspected the roof, to make sure an Apache wasn't lurking with an old blunderbuss. The habits he'd acquired on the scout had stayed with him, and no Apache would ever catch him unawares again, he hoped.

The door opened and a stout brunette woman stood before him, a handkerchief in her hand. Nathanial removed his hat. "I'm sorry to bother you, Mrs. Grimes. I'm Lieutenant Barrington, and I was with your husband when he was . . . killed."

The brave woman held out her hand and tried to smile. "I've heard your name mentioned many times in connection with my husband's last hours, and thank you so much for coming. I was just sitting with my children, and we were remembering all the good times we had together with the captain. Won't you come in and have a cup of tea?"

What am I doing here? Nathanial asked himself as he followed her into the parlor. On chairs angled around the fireplace, a boy and girl sat, eyes red from crying, but trying to hold it in before the stranger.

"Lieutenant Barrington was with your father when he died," said the widow. "I've invited him to tea. Have a seat, Lieutenant. I'll take your hat."

It flew out of his hand, and he dropped to a chair in front of the boy and girl, who peered at him as if he contained the key to their father's existence. Do I tell them Captain Grimes was killed on the way to the latrine? he wondered.

Mrs. Grimes poured another cup of tea, then perched opposite him. He realized that he was sitting in the chair that the captain must've occupied on the evenings that he spent with his family. They looked at him expectantly, and now the time had come to face the consequence of his rash act. What would Zachary Taylor do? he asked himself. Zachary Taylor would tell the truth.

"Well," Nathanial said, bowing his head before their grief, "your father spoke of you often during the days I rode with him, and he tried to convince me that I should marry, because he was so happy with his family. Now I can see why."

His mind went blank, so he smiled politely and reached for his cup of tea. The children continued to study him carefully, while the widow appraised his profile.

The boy was twelve, round-faced like his father. "I'd like to know how the captain died," he said.

"We were under attack, and your father led the defense. He was the kind of officer who got out in front, so he was in the most exposed position, fearless about his own personal safety. We were getting the better of the Apaches, when the arrow struck him. As far as I'm concerned, your father died a hero.''

A tear rolled down the boy's cheek, while the little girl sobbed audibly, then covered her mouth with her hand and ran from the room. "Excuse me," said Mrs. Grimes as she followed her daughter, leaving Nathanial alone with the boy, who looked Nathanial in the eye and said through quivering lips, "I miss my father so very much.''

"He was a fine soldier," Nathanial said as he placed his hand on the boy's shoulder. "The best gift you can give him is to be just like him. He'd want you to take good care of your mother and sister, and to be brave, honest, and good.''

Later, on the way back to his room, Nathanial speculated on the half-truths and untruths he'd told the Grimes family. That's how I'll write my report, he thought, and it'll be the official version. Captain Grimes died a hero, and maybe his widow will get a medal to hang on the wall. Perhaps someday an old professor in a dusty college will read my report and think it's true. Is history a matter of opinion, inference, and well-intentioned lies?

Maria Dolores felt somebody shaking her shoulder and opened her eyes to her father smiling above her. "Let us go to the hotel," he said.

They joined a group of other robbery victims, with soldiers to escort them to town. They were led by Lieutenant Beauregard Hargreaves, who appeared surprised to see her.

"Maria Dolores—don't tell me you were robbed too!''

"I am afraid it is true," she admitted.

Diego Carbajal said, "We could have used you a few days ago, young man.''

"The army can't be everywhere, sir. We've got some

wagons coming, so you don't have to walk. You look plumb tuckered out."

Beau was surprised to see Nathanial approaching out of the night, apparently deep in thought. "Here comes a friend of mine," Beau told Diego. "He came back from a scout a few days ago, but his commanding officer was killed by Apaches."

Nathanial noticed Beau amid the crowd in front of the mess hall, talking with the Mexican woman he'd seen earlier. Beau beckoned to him. "These poor people have been robbed."

Beau made introductions, then Nathanial realized that he was staring at the Mexican woman. She was tall, full-bodied, but perfectly proportioned all the way down, just as he. Then suddenly she appeared surprised.

"What's wrong?" he asked.

"Just a moment of dizziness," she replied. "I need a good night's sleep."

"Here come the wagons," somebody said.

Diego excused himself, to talk with the bullwhackers, while Beau had duties to perform. Nathanial found himself alone with the gorgeous Mexican woman, who was startled by his resemblance to the crucified Jesus of her dreams. She told herself not to make startling revelations until she was sure it wasn't just a random coincidence.

He wanted to make a ringing remark that would herald him as an exceptional human being, but his mind never failed to disappoint him in the presence of beautiful women. "It must have been quite an ordeal," he said, trying to be sympathetic.

She crossed herself. "Thank God I am here."

She's Catholic, he realized, and somehow it gave her already acknowledged beauty celestial dimensions. He saw her as an angel in white, with a halo behind her head, although she was wearing a dirty serape. The wagons drew closer, and he had to talk quickly. "Where are you staying?"

"A hotel where they are taking us."

"Do you think I might see you again?"

She looked into his eyes. "If you like."

"I'll find you—don't worry. Do you have any money left?"

"My father saved some, but I do not know what we are going to do. We used to own a store."

"If I were going into business, I'd open a real American-style saloon. You'll have more money than you know what to do with."

The wagons came to a stop in front of the mess hall, and Senor Carbajal returned. Maria Dolores and her father boarded one of the wagons, to be joined by other robbery victims. Maria Dolores looked down at Nathanial from her seat. They didn't have to say a word, but a powerful communication passed between them. Nathanial wondered what it would be like to hold such a magnificent woman.

She waved to him as the wagon began to move, and he waved back. Then the wagon rolled away, grinding wheels sending up clouds of dust. Nathanial knew that something profound had just happened, but had no idea what it meant. As matters stood, he was practically engaged to his commanding officer's daughter.

Nathanial returned to his room and thought about Maria Dolores Carbajal. Am I no better than a tomcat prowling the back alleys, ready to jump on every female who has the misfortune to happen along? he asked himself.

There was a knock on the door, then his big hulking slave limped into the small room. "Can I git you somethin' fore you goes to bed, suh?"

"No thank you, Otis."

Otis turned down the bed and fluffed up his pillow, while Nathanial felt embarrassed before his slave. It seemed a violation of the moral law to own another man. What in the hell can be done with these people? he wondered.

Otis raised an eyebrow. "You ain't lookin' so good, suh."

"Tell me something, Otis—we've known each other a long time now, and I was wondering what you think of the slavery situation."

Otis blinked. "Yer foolin' with me, suh."

"Everybody's always talking about slavery, but I've never spoken with a Negro about it. I'm truly interested in your opinion."

"You ain't gonna git me in trouble, is you, suh?"

"I swear that I won't say a word to anyone, but some folks argue that slaves are mistreated terribly, while others say slaves live better than workers in Northern factories. You've been on a plantation, and presumably you know the truth. Can you give me an objective answer?"

Otis stared at him, then shrugged and unbuttoned his shirt. When he was bare from the belt up, he turned around. His back was covered with whip scars so deep that a pencil or a finger could be placed into them.

Otis buttoned his shirt. "Anythin' else you want me to do in the mornin', suh?"

SIXTEEN

Mangus Coloradas sat in a remote canyon, playing with a lump of gold. He was accompanied by a three-year-old grandson, and gold nuggets were strewn all around them, while a fat yellow vein gleamed across the mountain straight ahead.

It was morning, and the little boy had no name because he hadn't yet performed anything significant. He walked around unsteadily in his tiny moccasin boots, kicking gold nuggets around. Occasionally he stopped, held one to the sun, and cooed like a little bird.

The canyon of gold was well known to the Apaches, along with a few other spots where the yellow metal could be found in abundance. Mangus Coloradas studied the rock systematically and could appreciate its lustrous beauty, but why did it drive the White Eyes loco?

Why not some other substance? wondered Mangus Coloradas as he sought to penetrate the mind of the White Eyes. Water is far more valuable, and safety best of all. Why do the White Eyes come to desolate places to dig this stuff?

He bit a lump of gold, and made a scant dent into the soft metal. Then he touched his tongue to it, and it tingled his taste buds. The White Eyes wore the yellow metal, but it made them conspicuous from long distances. What honor is there in digging like a rat, and why should anyone pay for pieces of the ground?

* * *

Next day, Diego Carbajal and his daughter lunched in the dining room of their hotel. On the other side of the window, a wagon of goods rolled past, while a stagecoach approached from the opposite direction.

"I looked at an empty store on the way back from the bank," said Diego. "It is a little run-down, but I'm sure we can fix it up."

"I hope you have not signed the lease," she said.

"As a matter of fact I did. I can buy merchandise on credit this afternoon, and we can be in business in a few days."

Normally, Maria Dolores would say *yes, papa,* but she'd seen a man get shot in cold blood. "Father, I think it is time we had a talk."

He waved his hand impatiently for the waiter. "About what?"

"We probably will not be any more successful with this store than the last one." She looked him in the eye. "I think we should open an authentic American saloon."

He appeared shocked as the waiter placed two mugs of coffee and a menu before them. Before Diego could respond, his daughter was ordering breakfast for two. Sometimes the shopkeeper thought his daughter far too presumptuous, as if she knew his likes and dislikes better than he.

The waiter departed, and Diego said, "Did you say a *saloon*?"

"If we are going to be in business, we might as well be in the most lucrative business there is."

"But people get killed in saloons, which I consider a major drawback."

"There is nothing worse than a business that is not making money, *like every other store we have had.*"

Her father wagged his long bony finger from side to side. "Business is mostly luck, and I think I have found the right location this time."

"That is what you always say, but I am not going to sit meekly and let you throw all our remaining money away. By rights, half of what we have is mine. You take your half and start a store, but give me my half, and I will show you how to make money."

"But who will manage the saloon?" he asked. "I do not know anything about that business."

Or any other business, she wanted to say, but instead, "I will do it, and you can be the cook."

"What if somebody starts shooting at me?"

"Stay out of arguments, but if you do not want to cook, I will hire somebody. I shall be the bartender, and I am not afraid."

He scrutinized his daughter in the afternoon light. "I do believe you are serious about this."

"I am not going broke with you, my dear father. Do you know what happens to women who do not have money?"

Mangus Coloradas lay beneath an aromatic squaw-bush, while only fifty feet away, five miners were digging and scratching the earth like prairie dogs with furry faces and tiny beady eyes aglitter with madness.

No matter how hard Mangus Coloradas tried, he couldn't fathom the White Eyes. What kind of man would dig day after day with only the vaguest hopes that the yellow metal would be found? In fact, the metal was quite rare in the full breadth of the land.

Mangus Coloradas was accompanied by six warriors, and they noted the locations of rifles, pistols, powder, lead, and percussion caps. The features of the camp became engraved on their minds as they awaited the signal to attack.

The goal was lethal speed, and the warriors wondered what their chief was waiting for. But Mangus Coloradas was watching a miner fill a pan with dirt, pour in water, and then shake the pan, searching the mud for minute particles of yellow metal.

Another miner walked about aimlessly, while consulting an object in his palm. A third expended great effort digging a hole, and it seemed to the chief the most absurd activity imaginable.

Yet the White Eyes knew how to make deadly weapons, and no one would dare confront their armies. But they didn't understand how to live in harmony with the world.

Another White Eyes fool was building something of logs, and he too perspired heavily, working in his red shirtsleeves. Mangus Coloradas smiled, for surely it was a sign from the mountain spirits, and perhaps it meant that his bear sickness was gone. The chief's name, *Mangus Coloradas,* meant *red sleeves.*

Why are they always building things? he asked himself. What is their infatuation with staying in one place? Their structures will fall one day, but the earth will abide forever. Why don't they see the way I do?

He heard a horned lark nearby, but it was really Cuchillo Negro reminding him of the task at hand. Mangus Coloradas replied with the call of the black phoebe, the signal to attack. Suddenly armed Apaches rushed miners preoccupied with handfuls of dirt swishing in water. The miners glanced up and were dead before they could think about defending themselves.

Father Paolo Zuniga sat in his office behind the church and tried to compose a suitable homily. It was for the fourth Sunday in Ordinary time, not the birthday of a famous saint, and he thought he might try the theme of morality versus self-indulgence, when there was a knock on his door.

He sat straighter in his chair as Maria Dolores entered his office. "May I speak with you, Father?"

"But of course, my dear," replied the cleric, for Diego Carbajal was a generous supporter of the church. "Do you wish to make a confession?"

"I want to ask you a favor," she replied, sitting opposite him, "but I hope you will not be angry."

Only a few years older than Maria Dolores, Father

Paolo was reminded beneath his priestly garb, he was still a man. "I'd be happy to help in any way I can."

Maria Dolores paused as she gathered her courage. "I wonder if you can give me the name of someone who knows how to make mescal."

The priest shrugged. "Just find any old *boracho*. Are you going into the mescal business?"

She bowed her head. "I am afraid so, Father."

"Can't you find something better to do?"

"I need money, Father."

He nodded sympathetically. "I have heard about the robbery. Well, as Christ said, we are made holy not by what we put into our mouths, but what comes out of our mouths. And you are right, holiness can be anywhere, even in a cantina. You are a good woman, Maria Dolores, and you will bring the light of God wherever you go. There is a man called Vargas, who is part Yaqui Indian. He is very old, but they say he makes excellent mescal, and in fact, even I myself have sampled his wares. The beverage was quite smooth, without the burn that you run into so often."

Maria Dolores bought a new rosary from the priest, dropped a coin into the poor box on the way out, and headed for the jacale where the mescal maker lived. She glanced into cantinas as she passed, and they were dark cheerless places full of hideous-appearing men. A shudder passed through her as she wondered how she could ever stand up to them. If only I were a man, she thought. Then she saw a sign: J. CRATCHETT, Gunsmith.

It was a small, well-lit shop, with an Americano in his thirties behind the counter, wearing a white shirt, string tie, and black leather vest. "Help you, ma'am?"

"I'd like to buy a pistol."

He smiled, and there was something wicked about him, with his long black side-whiskers and roving eyes. "Have you ever fired one before?"

"A few times, but I don't know how to load and take care of them."

"You buy a gun from me, missy, I'll show you anything you want." He winked.

She decided to behave as if she didn't know what lecherous suggestion he'd just made. "What kind of gun do you recommend?"

"The best pistol manufactured in the world today is the Colt Dragoon. It's the same model that the army is buying, and I have one right here." Cratchett dropped a heavy iron weapon onto the counter. "Go ahead. See how it feels in yer hand."

"What is so special about it?"

"You don't have to worry about it falling apart if you drop it, and if you hit an Injun in the head with the barrel, so much the better. I've seen you around before, but you don't look like the type who'd carry a gun."

"Can you sell me a holster."

"I can sell you anthing you want, senorita, and there's a couple of things you can have for free."

He winked, but again she ignored him. "I'd like a gunbelt and holster."

"What size?"

"My size."

He grinned like a dog. "I'll have to measure you."

"Guess," she replied. "I'm sure you won't be far off. And how do I load it?"

The door to the gun shop opened, interrupting the sale. Maria Dolores spun around, and was surprised to see Lieutenant Barrington entering the store. "Is it you, Miss Carbajal, beneath those clean clothes?" he asked with a grin.

"What are you doing here?" was all she could say.

"I need to buy ammunition."

She picked up the Colt Dragoon. "I am about to get this. Is yours the same?"

He picked up the gun and turned it in his hands. "No, this is the latest Colt, and it's supposed to be better than mine. I'd say you couldn't go wrong with it."

"Mr. Cratchett said he'd teach me how to use it."

"I'm sure he has better things to do, but I don't. I'll teach you if you like. We can ride a short ways out of town and I'll give you some target practice. How about Saturday afternoon?"

Cratchett coldly accepted her money. The first looie had stolen the Mexican woman when she was practically in his grasp.

Nathanial checked out the gun, to make sure it wasn't damaged merchandise. He snapped out the chamber, spun the cylinders, thumbed back the hammer, and squeezed the trigger. *Click.* "Music to my ears," said Nathanial.

"By the way, I am taking your advice and going into the saloon business. In fact, I am on my way to talk with somebody who knows how to make mescal."

"I'll walk with you, if you don't mind."

She strapped on her gunbelt, dropped the new Colt into the holster, and covered everything with her serape. A heavy weight lay against her leg, and she realized that she felt happy. If I were a soldier, this is the kind of officer I'd want, she figured. He looks so strong.

He packed his purchases into his saddlebags, chucked them over his shoulder, and opened the door. They stepped onto the busy street, and he took the outside position to protect her from muck flying off wheels and horse's hooves.

"There's something I want to tell you," he said out of the corner of his mouth. "I didn't want to say it in front of the gunsmith, but if you seriously want to go into the saloon business, you should think about whiskey, not mescal, because Americans prefer whiskey."

"Do you know how to make it?"

"It's a skill I've never learned, but I'm sure there's a soldier in camp who knows how to do it. I'll see if I can find somebody, but do you think you can manage the kind of people who go to saloons?"

"That's what I bought the gun for, but why would anyone want to harm me?"

"For the money in the cash box."

"I will give them the cash box, but I will not hesitate to shoot if necessary. Nobody is going to make a poor woman of me."

He glanced at the position of the sun. "I've got to get back to the camp. See you on Saturday?"

Maria Dolores was tempted to watch him walk away, but if he caught her, it would tell him of an interest that she didn't want to reveal, yet. A man like that must have many girlfriends, she speculated. How strange that we have met again. She recalled her Catholic dreams, and felt an uncanny link with Lieutenant Barrington. Can this be the man I have been waiting for? she wondered.

She returned to the vacant store her father had rented. Chunks of adobe were missing from the ceiling and walls, the windowsill was crooked, and a few floorboards were missing in action, but she tried to see the possibilities.

She plotted where to place the bar and tables. An outhouse would have to be constructed in back, and she'd need a big tub to wash all the glasses, or maybe she could have tin cups to cut down the inevitable breakage. She had no idea what to call the saloon, but it would have to be an English name.

She knew that Americans were the growing population in Santa Fe, and she definitely had to appeal to them if she wanted the business to be successful. I'll even hang an American flag on the wall, and maybe I can find a picture of an old moth-eaten American general to hang behind the bar. And I can nail some crossed American swords to the opposite wall. If a Mexican woman expects to prosper in Santa Fe, she must be flexible in her politics, she told herself.

The saloon materialized in her imagination, and she saw it full of happy Americans drinking and falling all over themselves as she raked in the cabbage behind the bar. There would be the occasional shooting, but she didn't care so long as no one shot her. Fist and knife fights could be expected, but she'd keep her distance and wait patiently until they ended. If I behave like a lady, I'm sure they'll treat me like one, she hoped.

The door opened, then her strange Mexican-Jewish father appeared in one of his dark suits, his sombrero crooked atop his head. "I have spoken to several friends," he said, "and they have all discouraged me from the cantina business. It is more trouble than it is worth, according to them. I think we should go ahead with our plans for a store. Perhaps this time we can sell fresh baked goods."

She placed her hands on her hips and blew a strand of hair out of her eye. "There are plenty of places to buy bread, but the men of Santa Fe need somewhere to relax, and this saloon will be their second home. We are going to have the prettiest girls in town serving the best whiskey and food available."

"But we do not know anything about those things!" he protested.

"We will learn, but we do not have time to waste. Let us go to the lumber yard."

"I am afraid we will lose our shirts."

"It will not be the first time," she reminded him.

He elongated his neck and looked like a giraffe with a mustache. "Are you defying me, young lady?"

She leaned forward and peered into his eyes. "Yes."

Nathanial found Sergeant Duffy on the parade ground, leading the company in close order drill. "Halt!" the sergeant bellowed as he saw his commanding officer approach. "At ease!" Then he turned toward Nathanial and saluted. "They're doin' just fine, sir."

Nathanial glanced around, to make sure no officer was listening. "Sergeant Duffy, is there any man in this company who might know how to make whiskey?

And I'm talking about the good stuff, not the usual rotgut variety."

Sergeant Duffy didn't have to think long. "That's Private Warfield, sir. He's from Tennessee, where they make the best sour mash whiskey in the world."

Nathanial scratched his cheek as a big bald eagle flew over the parade ground. "Would you tell Private Warfield that I'd like to speak with him?"

The recently appointed civil and military governor of New Mexico was Colonel John Macrae Washington, a distant descendant of George Washington and a graduate of West Point, 1817. He'd served under General Winfield Scott during the removal of the Cherokees, and helped pacify the Maine-New Brunswick border dispute in 1839, but his crowning achievement was at Buena Vista, where his artillery battery had helped hold the critical La Angostura heights against repeated assaults from Santa Anna's army, thus saving the day for Old Rough and Ready.

Now Colonel Washington commanded one thousand soldiers scattered throughout New Mexico. His mission was to protect the citizens from Indians, and prevent Indians from raiding into Mexico. Unfortunately, he lacked the resources to accomplish these objectives.

A day seldom passed when a herd of sheep wasn't stolen, a village burned to the ground, or miners slaughtered indiscriminately. Colonel Washington could contend with an enemy he could see, but Apaches disappeared into the mountains after finishing their bloody work, and no one knew how to catch them.

All he could do was hope the federal government would send more troops to New Mexico, and methodically root out every Apache from the lost canyons and hidden gorges of the territory. We've got to take the initiative against them, he told himself, and demonstrate that they can't steal and kill whenever they feel like it. The time has come to get tough with these savages. It's the only language they understand.

High in the Pinos Altos Mountains, the *di-yin* medicine man sang:

> *"The home of the long-life dwelling ceremony*
> *Is the home of White Painted Woman*
> *Of long life the home of White Painted Woman is made*
> *For Killer of enemies has made it so*
> *Killer of enemies has made it so"*

The *di-yin*'s voice pierced the silence as the People gathered around. A maiden in a new deerskin dress was brought forward, and her name was Morning Cloud. This was the greatest moment of her life, because she would become White Painted Woman for four full days.

It was the *Nah-ih-es* puberty ceremony, the most sacred and important liturgy of the Apaches. Masked dancers cavorted in the background, portraying the mountain spirits, while the *di-yin* continued his song before the assembled clan.

Chief Mangus Coloradas graced the ceremony with his attendance, because Morning Cloud was a granddaughter of one of his brothers. The girl had been covered with sacred pollen, and stood in front of her new ceremonial wickiup especially constructed for the occasion. She had been bathed and then clothed in a special dress dyed yellow and decorated with beads, studs, drawings of the crescent moon, morning star, rainbows, and sunbeams.

The ceremony, celebrating her first menstruation, had been organized by her parents at great expense. Her attendant was an old woman with magical powers, who escorted the candidate to the southeast of the structure, where the skin of a four-year-old black-tailed deer lay on the ground. The girl knelt upon the skin, while the attendant placed before her a coiled tray made of the unicorn plant, and covered with bags of sacred pollen, an elf-hoof rattle, a bundle of grama grass, and an eagle feather.

The attendant offered pollen to the four sacred directions, then painted a line of pollen across the bridge of Morning Cloud's nose. Morning Cloud reciprocated by marking her attendant the same way, then a line of children accompanied by their mothers lined up to the south of Morning Cloud, who proceeded to paint them with pollen, insuring long lives and freedom from illness.

Morning Cloud lay facedown on the buckskin as dancers leapt over her and the singer continued his mournful wail. The attendant administered a deep muscle massage, so that Morning Cloud would have a good disposition and be kind to others for the rest of her life.

> *"May this girl be good in morals*
> *May she grow up, live long,*
> *and be a fine woman."*

Mangus Coloradas bowed his head to his niece, for he believed with the others that she was becoming White Painted Woman incarnate. The girl arose after the massage, and the attendant outlined four prints in pollen. Morning Cloud stepped into them, right foot first. Then the attendant pushed her, and the girl trotted clockwise around the basket. She picked up the buckskin and shook it to each direction clockwise, beginning with the south, to banish any disease that might afflict her womanhood.

Dancers pranced gleefully, shaking their fantastical headdresses, as the girl's family brought baskets of fruit and nuts, which they dumped onto the black deerskin rug. A great rush ensued as members of the clan advanced to accept the presents, and thus the great feast began, celebrating the fructuous power of the universe.

White Painted Woman retired to her sacred bower as members of the tribe filed past her to receive her blessing. The little goddess felt herself pulsating with golden pollen light, so overwhelmed was she by the significance of the ceremony. Famous warriors and virtuous women bowed before her as she performed the ancient blessing over their heads. Her eyes widened with the solemnity of the occasion as the great chief Mangus Coloradas knelt before her and closed his eyes. "I absolve you from all illness, great chief," she intoned. "May your life be free from care."

Mangus Coloradas felt drenched with fire as he backed away from White Painted Woman. Only yesterday she'd been another child beneath his feet, but today she carried the power of Yusn in her tiny body. The chief clasped his hands together as the singer continued the hymn.

> *"In the middle of Holy Mountain*
> *In the middle of its body stands a hut*
> *built by the mountain spirits*
> *brilliant lightning illuminates the shadows*
> *as White Painted Woman lives among us*
> *purifying us with her blessing."*

Camp Marcy's officers assembled in Major Harding's office, and Nathanial sat on a wooden chair in the back row. The major stood behind his desk, hands clasped behind his back.

"Due to increased Apache marauding," the major began, "Colonel Washington has decided that it's time to take the field. A skeleton force will be left here, and everybody else will be divided into ten detachments, which will sweep the territory beginning tomorrow morning and search for Apache raiders. If you find any trace of the devils, you are to pursue vigorously and kill or capture as many as possible. Let me remind you, gentlemen, that you're here to halt the depredations of Indians, and your vacation is over.

Besides, I think it's time we avenged the death of Captain Grimes, don't you?"

The bar consisted of a two-by-ten-inch plank resting atop three empty barrels. Maria Dolores had bought a few mismatched tables and creaky chairs. No crossed cavalry swords adorned the wall, and the washtub leaked. Maria Dolores's money hadn't stretched as far as she'd anticipated.

Her father paced back and forth in the light of two candles burning on the shelf behind the bar. "This is the most idiotic thing I have ever done," he complained. "The moment you open those doors, those gringo soldiers will tear this place apart, and that will be the end of us."

"I wish you would stop worrying so much," she said. "Cannot you be optimistic for once in your life?"

"Optimistic about what?"

She left him sputtering by the stove, where he tested his cooking skills. They'd bought two cast-iron frying pans, a side of beef, a bag of potatoes, and some flour. She entered the back room, where the dragoon named Warfield was brewing whiskey. He'd been plucked from obscurity by Nathanial, and sent to teach Maria Dolores how to make fine Tennessee whiskey.

Maria Dolores frowned at the network of brass piping, kettles, and barrels atop her second stove. A pile of wood decorated the backyard, and she estimated that fuel would become a major expense in the days to come.

Her office was a corner of the back room, just a few feet from the still, and consisted of another plank suspended over two barrels, with no wall for privacy. She sat and studied the ledgers once more, as Warfield fiddled with the still. If her saloon didn't break even in a month, she imagined herself destitute on the streets of Santa Fe, sleeping outdoors beneath eaves, begging for crusts of bread, or selling her body to the highest bidder.

She rubbed her tired eyes with her knuckles. At least they wouldn't have to pay hotel bills anymore, because the saloon had become their bedroom, living room, and source of sustenance. Somehow their establishment would have to attract customers from all the others in town. And she couldn't hire waitresses, because she didn't have money to pay them.

She wondered if she were losing her mind, and maybe her father was right. The door to the back room opened, and she was gratified to see Lieutenant Nathanial Barrington. Then Warfield startled her by jumping to his feet and saluting him. Nathanial grinned at him. "How's the whiskey coming?"

Private Warfield pointed proudly to the steaming kettle. "You give me another two days, and you'll be drinking the best aged Tennessee whiskey you ever tasted in yer life."

"Unfortunately, you're not going to have two days. We're going on a scout first thing in the morning. So you'll have to make sure Maria Dolores knows how to operate that damned thing."

"But . . ."

Nathanial ignored him, turning instead toward Maria Dolores. "Can we have a talk . . . alone?"

He opened the back door, where clouds cast a pall over the alley. "I'm afraid I can't teach you how to shoot on Saturday," he said as they headed for the street. "But I don't think you have anything to worry about. You give the men a good pour and act glad to see 'em, and you won't have any trouble."

"But why will they come to my place instead of another saloon?"

"Because their first drink will be free, and the men remaining behind at Camp Marcy will spread the word. Also, you need a sign. Have you figured out what to name the place?"

"I was hoping you could tell me a name, since you understand these matters better than I."

"Saloons all have the same kind of dumb names,

the more pretentious, the better. How about the Silver Palace? And underneath it you should write BEST WHISKEY IN TOWN. That way everyone can see that they won't be getting the usual mescal."

"You seem to know a lot about saloons."

"I wonder why," he replied with an amused smile. Then he reached into his pocket and took out a roll of paper money. "I should be back in about a month, but if something happens to me, consider it a gift."

They gazed into each other's eyes as Santa Fe's night denizens, most of them male, passed on the sidewalk. She examined Nathanial's tanned cheekbones, and it was hard to imagine a buzzard gnawing on his nose. "Please take care of yourself," she said.

He shrugged nonchalantly. "I probably won't see any Apaches, but it looks like it's going to rain."

She placed her palm against his stubbled cheek. "Don't be a hero."

He placed his hand on hers, and a jag of electricity passed between them. "I'll be careful."

It seemed the most normal act as he drew her closer. This was not a slim woman like Layne Satterfield, or even a healthy but short one such as Rebecca Harding, but a big tawny Mexican woman, and he felt enlivened as her ample bosom crushed into his tunic. Their lips touched lightly, and then suddenly the enormity of their act struck them; both drew back at the same time.

The sidewalk lizards watched jealously as the young lovers cut into an alley.

A dragoon turned to his bunkie and said, "Wasn't that Lieutenant Barrington?"

"Looks like he's a-havin' better luck than us."

Other soldiers had taken note of the romantic interlude, for romance was the principle frustration of their virile lives. Meanwhile, Nathanial and Maria Dolores circled back toward the Silver Palace Saloon. "You're not going to believe this," she admitted, "but I have dreamed about you before I ever saw you."

"You're the mirror of myself," he replied. "Perhaps we are meant for each other."

They came to the back door of the Silver Palace, and she realized that he might be killed by Apaches in the days ahead. "Please be careful."

"Nothing can keep me from you, *muchacha*."

Their lips touched, he felt her sumptuous formation again, but then, in the depths of Christian love, the door flew open and an irate father stood before them, wearing his sombrero and a stained white apron and waving his butcher knife threateningly. "What's this?" he asked, his eyes bulging out of his head. "Young lady, you may go inside. I'll speak with you later."

"Father," she replied, "I was saying good night to Lieutenant Barrington, who is leaving in the morning on a campaign against the Indians."

"*That* is the way you say good-bye? Please do as I say."

She decided not to fight her father in front of Nathanial, so she gave Nathanial a long look that said *I love you,* then entered the back of the saloon.

Diego stood before Nathanial, the knife tight in his hand. "I should challenge you to a duel, but you would kill me. I should forbid you to speak with my daughter, but unfortunately I cannot control her. Therefore, I must ask you to please respect her, because she is a good girl and deserves a decent chance in life, which she will not have once it becomes known that she is the cast-off former concubine of an American soldier. Young men have no conscience, and I know because, believe it or not, I was young once myself." Then he threw up his hands in despair. "Oh, it is no use!"

Diego entered the back room of the saloon, where his daughter stood beside the still. "I am ashamed of you," he told her. "If your mother were alive right now, she would slap your face."

Maria Dolores ignored him as she examined mash bubbling in kettles and transparent liquid dripping into the copper vat. Not only was she making her own whiskey, thus saving the cost of buying, but it wasn't much different from preparing soup or stew.

Her father left for the chop counter as she sat at her desk. Her head was spinning with Lieutenant Barrington, her father's insult, and the saloon business. She'd led a fairly tranquil life until a gun had been stuck in her face, and since then events had been moving too quickly for her to assimilate.

She reached into her pocket and took out the roll of money. It amounted to nearly two hundred dollars, a small fortune. And he just gave it to me, she pondered, but that's how it would be if he were the one foretold.

The door opened, and her father appeared, carrying a steak platter. "I am sorry," he said as he placed the steak before her. "I have made a fool of myself yet again, but soldiers have the worst reputations in the world, as I am sure you know."

"No one will ever take advantage of me," she replied.

"But American officers do not marry Mexican girls, especially the kind who work in saloons."

"We shall see about that," replied Maria Dolores as she sliced into her steak.

Rebecca Harding paced back and forth in her parlor, becoming more distressed with every turn. Where is he? she wondered. Her mother crocheted a sweater at the end of the sofa, while her father had gone back to his office.

"You're distracting me," said her mother. "Why don't you sit down?"

"I can't." Rebecca rubbed her arms and scowled, because she'd been looking forward to seeing Nathanial, and perhaps she could receive more of those wonderful kisses. But he'd yet to show his face, and it was after supper.

"I'm sure he's busy," said her mother. "He'll be gone for a long time."

"It only takes a few minutes to say good-bye."

She heard boots scraping the mat outside the door, and her heart leapt. The door opened, but it was only her father returning from the office. "I'm exhausted," he said. "If you'll excuse me, I'm going directly to bed."

"Have you seen Lieutenant Barrington?" asked Rebecca.

"No, but I imagine he's with his men."

The major entered the master bedroom, leaving Rebecca stewing in jealousy and resentment. How could he touch me that way, and then forget me? she wondered. Is he the seducer that everyone says, or am I taking counsel of my fears?

"Perhaps you should have a glass of warm milk before you go to bed," said her mother.

"I hate warm milk."

"It'll help you sleep."

"I don't want to sleep."

Rebecca resumed pacing the floor. Why am I so upset? she asked herself. I'm not in love with him, am I? Why, we barely know each other, and I may never see him again. How poignant it would be if the Apaches burned him at the stake.

There was a knock on the door, and she jumped two inches into the air. "I'll get it," said her mother.

Rebecca hovered in the corner as her mother opened the door. Lieutenant Barrington stood in the darkness, hat in hand. "I realize it's late, ma'am, but I was wondering if Miss Rebecca was still awake."

"She was just about to make a cup of hot milk, prior to going to bed. Won't you come in?"

He stepped into the parlor as Rebecca appeared out of the shadows. "I'd like to go for a walk, Nathanial."

He could hear annoyance in her voice, her lips pinched with anger, and Nathanial had passed sufficient time with women to know when they were ready to explode. He helped her with her coat, then followed her out the door as a cool breeze blew in from the sage, carrying the spice of decayed leaves and lost dreams. They walked along Officers' Row as she fastened her top button. Here it comes, he thought.

"Where have you been?" she asked crossly.

"With the men," he lied. "We're going on a scout tomorrow."

"Seems as though you could've stopped by sooner, just to set my mind at ease."

"I thought you'd understand, since you're in the army yourself."

"Nathanial, it's only a short walk across the parade ground."

"I'm sorry."

"Sometimes I wonder if you're the rat that everyone says you are."

"I'm not the most considerate person in the world, I admit."

"I hope I'm not wasting your precious time," she said.

"I've set aside this evening for you, Rebecca." He didn't want to offend her, and she looked exceptionally adorable in the starlight. He recalled their passion the previous night, and then remembered the plush configuration of Maria Dolores Carbajal. Nathanial felt confused and oppressed by his own urges on the night of the big campaign.

"You seem different," she said, "as if you don't care about me anymore."

He maneuvered her into the shadows of the provost marshal's office. "I've got lots to be concerned about, because tomorrow at this time I may be up to my eyeballs in Apaches."

"Perhaps I'm selfish," she sighed, "but those things I've done with you—do you think they happened with others? We were talking about getting married, after all. You haven't changed you mind, have you?"

"Not at all," he replied as he lied himself deeper into the hole.

"Perhaps when you come back from the scout, we can announce our engagement?"

"Perhaps."

"You don't sound very enthusiastic."

"I might not come back at all. Let's not forget the example of Captain Grimes."

"If you think you won't come back, then you surely won't. Much of our fate is in our own hands."

"I fail to see how Captain Grimes's fate was in his hands when that arrow came out of nowhere."

He sought to bury the bloody memory in the fragrant golden hair before him. There wasn't so much of her, and he felt bones here and there, but that didn't mean she wasn't soft, warm, and oh-so-inviting. Their tongues engaged in soft combat as he leaned her against the wall and brought the full weight of his body against her.

"Oh, Nathanial," she whispered as she rubbed against him.

The seducer of women glanced around, but no one was in the vicinity. You might be dead within the next few days, and perhaps you should take this pleasure while you have the chance, whispered the devil into his ear. Nathanial touched his forefinger to her nipple.

"Oh . . . Nathanial . . ." she whispered as she placed her hand on a portion of his anatomy which no decent unmarried woman was permitted to touch.

Nathanial figured they could do it against the wall, for he'd engaged in vile acts on a variety of surfaces in the past. But if they got caught, there'd be hell to pay. She was panting in his ear, squirming against him, and he'd want to possess her from the moment he'd first set eyes on her. He was ready to pull down her underpants, but something said she was the major's virgin daughter, and there came a time when a man had to be responsible, no matter how desirable irresponsibility might be.

"Somebody's coming," he muttered into her lips.

She snapped erect and began examining her clothing, while he was amazed at how quickly her mood had changed. He peered onto the walkway, but no one was there. "Guess I'm hearing things," he said. Perhaps, he conjectured, she wasn't as out of control as she'd seemed, and she knew *exactly* what she was doing.

Rebecca blushed as she struggled to make sense of what had happened. Was that me? she asked herself. "I'd better get back home."

He walked beside her down Officers' Row. They were still recovering from their fleeting moments of young lust, and the flagpole rope slapped in the wind, as the first note of taps could be heard across the parade ground. Finally they came to a halt in front of Major Harding's adobe hacienda. They turned toward each other in the darkness as the first drops of rain began to fall.

"Good luck, Nathanial," she said. "I hope you won't forget me, because I surely won't forget you."

"I'm sorry if I was disrespectful, but I'm not myself tonight."

"I love you, Nathanial."

"And I love you," he felt compelled to say, although he wasn't sure who he loved at that point, certainly not himself. He tossed her an affectionate salute, then turned and walked away as swiftly as his legs would take him, and he didn't look back.

He needed somebody to talk with, but could trust no one, not even Beau. So he visited the quartermaster, to check his supplies, and then the stable, to look at the condition of the horses his men would ride. Finally he made his way back to the Bachelor Officers' Quarters. I'm in love with two women, he acknowledged, and if another pretty one happened by, I'll probably chase her too. I'm no better than a yard dog, and I'll be in serious trouble if I don't settle down.

The bugle would blow reveille in a few hours, and

tomorrow he'd sleep beneath the stars. Bewildered passion combined with fatigue, while the prospect of sudden death provided a philosophical turn of mind. He wondered about his Apache foe coming down from the mountains to kill, maim, and take slaves. He'd heard many stories about Mexican and white women captured by the Apaches, and the strangest part was, given the choice, the captured women often had elected to remain among the Apaches!

Maybe those bucks are fabulous lovers, Nathanial considered with a wry grin as he opened the door of his hut. To his surprise, lying on his pillow was a rosary and an envelope. On it was written in a feminine scrawl: *It was made by nuns, and we shall pray for you.*

It wasn't signed, but he knew who'd sent it. Has Maria Dolores been here? he wondered as he sniffed for traces of her perfume. He held the wooden beads on a string, with a crude crucifix carved out of wood. Some beads were large, others small, and they were spaced in a particular pattern. He had no idea how it was used, but decided to wear it on the scout for good luck.

He hung it on the bedpost, then unstrapped his holster, yanked out the Colt, and lined the sights on himself in the mirror, but didn't thumb back the hammer. He imagined an arrow piercing his skull and erupting out the other side as blood squirted from his ears. A bolt of fear shot through him, but he stuffed it down. I won't let those son-of-a-bitch savage bastards scare me, he swore. I'll kill as many as I can, before I'd let them get near me.

There was a knock on the door, and he aimed his gun at whoever was there. "Come in."

It was Otis, eyes widened at the gun. "I heered yer goin' to war tomorrow, and I was wonderin' if you needed me fer somethin'."

Nathanial looked at the man whom he owned lock, stock, and barrel and again felt like a snake in Otis's presence. It wasn't because Nathanial was a raving abolitionist, but he couldn't manage the transaction anymore. "Have a seat, Otis. I want to talk with you."

"Has I done somethin' wrong, boss?" asked Otis, a worried expression on his face.

"I'm going on a scout tomorrow, and I've decided to set you free." Otis looked astonished, but Nathanial kept talking. "I'm going to give you some money and the address of my mother in New York. I want you to go to her, and she'll take care of you."

Otis stared at him as if struck by an earthquake. "Free?" he asked, as if unsure of whether he'd heard correctly. "If I goes to New York, I'll git picked up fer a runaway afore I gits ten miles."

"I'll give you an affidavit signed by me and another officer. If there are difficulties, get in touch with me, or if I don't come back, my mother."

Otis appeared speechless as Nathanial sat at his desk and laid a blank sheet of paper before him. Then he wrote:

> *I hereby certify that this slave, Otis Jackson, belongs to me, and I have sent him to New York City to take care of my mother. He is a good slave and please do not delay him.*

He signed at the bottom, then said, "Stay here."

Nathanial walked down Officers' Row and knocked on Beau's door. Beau opened up, and Nathanial was surprised to see him completely sober, his equipment laid out on his bed, as he packed saddlebags. Nathanial held out the paper. "Do me a favor and sign this."

Beau held it to the candlelight. "He'll probably run away, and you'll never see him again. But it's your money, not mine." He signed and handed the affidavit back. "Well, Nathanial old boy, it looks like we're going to war again. The odds are that you and I won't see any Apaches, but if I never see you again, it's been good to know you."

They shook hands, then Nathanial returned to his room, where Otis waited on the chair, an expression of distress on his face. Nathanial handed him the affidavit, then a handful of money. "You might as well leave first thing in the morning."

Otis arose, unbuttoned his shirt, and folded the paper against his skin. "I don't know if yer plumb loco, but thank you, suh."

"Say hello to my mother for me."

Now Nathanial no longer felt rotten before Otis. Mumbling thanks, the big black man shuffled uncertainly from the room. After he departed, Nathanial stuffed the Colt beneath his pillow, then undressed in the darkness, crawled beneath the blankets, and tried to fall asleep, but his mind boiled with images of screaming Apaches, seductive Rebecca, Otis running from bloodhounds, magnificent Maria Dolores, his warring parents, unhappy little brother, the women he'd known in the biblical sense, the ones he hadn't, and so on into the night, as rain fell lightly upon the sage and tiny creatures scurried for shelter.

I wonder if I'll kill somebody during this scout? mused Nathanial. Or maybe I'll be the one who won't come back, but at least I won't have to worry about women anymore.

SEVENTEEN

No bands, parades, or stirring speeches attended Nathanial and his detachment when they departed Camp Marcy next morning. A drizzle fell, but mere water couldn't stop the First Dragoons.

Only a few scattered ponchoed wives and kids were on hand, and Nathanial expected Rebecca among them as he led his men toward the gate. His hat was low over his eyes, and drops of water pelted his face as he rocked back and forth in his saddle. He heard muffled hoofbeats behind him, turned around in the saddle, and saw the dragoons hunched in their ponchos, utterly miserable, sorry they had ever joined the army. He faced front, as women and children drew near. Rebecca didn't rush forward to clasp his hand in one last thrilling gesture, and he wondered what had happened to her, although he wore another woman's rosary beads around his neck.

He reached beneath his poncho and touched the crucifix as he passed through the gate. His detachment followed onto the open sage, no mountains were visible, and the gray day encompassed them like a cloak, mercifully concealing them from the watchful eyes of the Apaches. Rain hissed as it fell on foliage as a pungent vegetative fragrance filled Nathanial's nostrils. If we run into the savages, I'll give them a fight they'll never forget, he swore, and if they don't kill me, maybe I'll marry Maria Dolores Carbajal.

Sergeant Major Ferguson approached Major Har-

ding's desk cautiously, looked both ways, and said,
"A man should mind his own business, but somethin's
happened that I think you should know about. I hope
you won't think I'm oversteppin' my bounds."

"Out with it, Sergeant."

"I've noticed Lieutenant Barrington a-payin' court
to Rebecca as of late, but I thought you might want
to know that he was seen in town last night with a
Mexican whore."

Major Harding was deeply shaken. "Are you sure?"

"I heard the men a-talkin' in the stable. A few of
'em seem 'im and the whore last evening. The lieutenant kissed her in full view of everybody!"

Did he visit my daughter after leaving a prostitute?
The question stung Major Harding. "Thank you for
the information, Sergeant Major. If you learn any
other interesting facts about Lieutenant Barrington,
I'd be grateful if you'd let me know."

The Silver Palace Saloon opened for business with
no great fanfare or line of dancing girls on the bar.
Instead, Maria Dolores merely placed a sign that said
OPEN in the one front window and unlatched the door.
Outside, the street was a rainy swamp, not a soul in
sight. It wasn't a very propitious beginning.

She returned to the saloon, where the walls had
been whitewashed, and her new helper, a hunch-
backed dwarf named Miguelito, had hung a painting
of Zachary Taylor, conqueror of her nation, above the
bar. Maria Dolores had hired Miguelito with the
money that Nathanial gave her, for a woman had to
be flexible in her politics if she wanted to survive in
the United States of America.

Her father sat on a stool beside the stove, reading
an old newspaper. "Try to smile," he said to her.
"Otherwise you will scare customers away." He wore
a white canvas apron, his sombrero tilted atop his
head. He'd owned a ranch, been a storekeeper, and
now was a cook. How low my poor father has sunk,

she thought, but at least he's trying his best to make this venture successful.

She opened the door to the back room, where Miguelito knelt before the still. He placed the tip of his forefinger into the vat, touched it to his tongue, and announced, *"Mas bueno."*

"I hope the customers will think so," she said.

"Do not worry about that, senorita. This is even better than the Jew sells."

He was referring to Martin Seligman, the sutler at Camp Marcy. She wondered why the Americans had elevated Seligman to such a high position, and whether he still prayed in Hebrew like her father. Then the door opened, and he stood there. "First customers," he announced.

Maria Dolores returned to the bar, where two Americanos lurked with their thumbs hooked in the front pockets of their trousers, looking around and sniffing. "Not a bad place," one said.

"At least they've got Old Rough and Ready on the wall."

Maria Dolores wore her most captivating smile. "Whiskey, gentlemen?"

One customer, who wore a black wide-brimmed hat, declared like a lawyer in a courtroom, "The sign in the window says it's free."

Maria Dolores grabbed the first bottle on the right behind the bar. "Here you go," she said, filling two dented mismatched tin cups. "On the house."

The other customer, who wore a red and white checkered shirt, grabbed his free drink, sipped it like a connoisseur, and pronounced, "Not bad."

"As a matter of fact, it's pretty good," replied his cohort. "Where you git this stuff?" he asked Maria Dolores.

"Made it myself," she replied proudly. "It is aged as least two days."

The Americanos laughed heartily, then the checkered shirt leaned closer. "You know, you ai'nt bad-lookin'. How's about a little ..."

She smiled. "Sorry, but I am not a prostitute."

"Then what the hell're you doin' here?"

"Selling the best whiskey in Santa Fe, and do not forget to tell your friends."

Rebecca read books not because she was thirsty for knowledge, or even because she liked reading, but only because there was nothing else to do. Day after day she perused history, poetry, biographies, and philosophy, but her current favorite was *Recollections of a Southern Matron* by a famous Eastern writer named Caroline Gilman.

It told the fictional story of Cornelia Wilton, only daughter of a South Carolina slave owner, who lived on a large plantation not far from Charleston. Unlike most of her silly belle friends, Cornelia prepared herself thoroughly for the august responsibilities of managing the plantation when her parents grew old. In a few short chapters, she protested the cruel treatment of slaves, celebrated the Sabbath, prevented a duel, and convinced a depraved gentleman to repent his wicked, wicked ways. In addition, Cornelia hunted, fished, rode horses, and danced expertly. In short, she was everything Rebecca Harding wanted to be.

Unfortunately, Rebecca Harding's parents owned no plantation for her to inherit, and their influence in the army would be of help to a son, but not her. She didn't want to become one of those old maid aunts who take care of other people's children, the butt of everybody's dirty jokes.

Her father entered the parlor, and Rebecca arose from the sofa where she'd been reading, as her mother emerged from the kitchen. "What are you doing home?" asked the lady of the house.

"I have news for Rebecca," he said, "but I'm afraid she's not going to like it." He looked at his daughter. "Perhaps you'd better sit down."

"I'm not afraid," she replied, trying to stop her hands from jittering. "What happened?"

"It's not pretty, but I'll give it to you straight from the shoulder. Lieutenant Barrington was seen in town last night, when he said he was preparing for the scout. He was with a Mexican prostitute, according to reliable eyewitnesses. Evidently he called on you after he was finished with her."

It felt like a dagger, she gasped and took a step backward. It's so! she thought. Her beautiful domestic tale, as penned by Rebecca Harding, cracked before her eyes. She was speechless, paralyzed, dazed, lost, as her mother placed a chair beneath her.

"I'm sorry to hurt you," said the major, "but you scoffed at my previous warnings. Rebecca, even his *own mother* threw him onto the street on Christmas Day. This is a man who knows no moral boundaries, and his every act is calculated to ffff ... ah ... satiate his bestial lusts. Thank God the truth has revealed itself before something terrible happened." He gazed at his daughter coldly. "You're not *with child* are you?"

"Of course I'm not with child," she replied, trying to catch her breath. "Are you absolutely sure it was Nathanial, and not some other officer?"

"I have it on the best authority, and I'm going to transfer him to the worst duty I can find, while his efficiency report will include certain incisive comments regarding his revolting character. We don't need men like Nathanial Barrington in the army. When I finish with him, he'll wish he never heard of the army. He's the kind of officer who gives us all a bad name."

In a pouring rain, Nathanial sat on a boulder and smoked a cigar as his detachment fumbled with tents. Water streamed down their hats, onto their ponchos, and seeped through their shirts, while boots had become waterlogged long ago.

It had rained all day, providing no dry areas for the

tents. A miserable wet night of little sleep was next, but that didn't mean the Apaches wouldn't attack, and perhaps they were hiding in the mists a hundred yards away. Nathanial's eyes tried to penetrate gray fog lifting off the sage, but the whole Apache nation could be there and he wouldn't know.

Water dripped from the end of his nose as he arose from the boulder, his hand on the butt of his Walker Colt, well protected beneath his poncho. Four guards had been posted, and all his other men maintained their weapons close at hand, their eyes continuously raking the soaking terrain, as the mud sprouted tents like mammoth mushrooms.

If Rebecca Harding possessed a weapon, and if Lieutenant Barrington had been standing in front of her, the temptation would be very great to shoot him. She paced back and forth in her room, caged like a tigress, unable to go outside due to inclement weather.

She couldn't believe Nathanial could be callous and cruel, yet the evidence was incontrovertible, according to her father. He had his way with one woman for money, and then tried to take me for nothing, fulminated the major's daughter. That man is a pig rutting after every sow, except a pig is a slave of his instincts, and a man, especially an officer, must make the decision to be wicked.

It horrified her to think that she'd nearly surrendered to him with her dress hiked up around her waist, like a common gutter slut. So that's what he thinks of me, she calculated. I'm just another piece of fluff to play with, and the more the merrier. I'll bet there are little boys and girls who look like him in the vicinity of every camp where he's been stationed.

He has humiliated me, she deduced as she remembered where he'd placed his terribly soothing hands. He didn't even take a bath when he came to me, and he lied in front of my parents. "My father is a powerful man," she said in a quavering voice as the devil cackled beneath the windowsill. "I'm going to get even with Nathanial Barrington if it's the last thing I do."

Maria Dolores hustled behind the bar, pouring whiskey amid a roar of conversations, arguments, speeches, and the drunken ravings of her customers. She collected money as fast as possible, but it was spilling out of the pockets of her apron. Miguelito, assistant bartender, clumped beside her, while a cloud of smoke arose from the stove where her father flipped a steak into the air.

Perspiring, her feet aching, Maria Dolores was propelled onward by the incredible success of her first business venture. She'd already taken in more money that day than the average two weeks of her father's old store, and she hadn't even fixed the place up yet.

"This is the best goddamned whiskey I've tasted since St. Louis!" shouted a man with a hole in his pants, holding his glass in the air. He poured the remaining ounce into his throat, his eyes went white, and he collapsed onto the floor.

Miguelito came out from behind the bar and dragged the drunkard into a corner where no one would step on him. Men stood three deep in front of Maria Dolores, waving empty tin cups in the air, while others sat on the floor, and card games were under way on the two tables. A man spit at a cuspidor, missed, and a brown stain appeared on the boots of a stagecoach driver just in from Albuquerque, who was fondling a young woman, evidently a prostitute.

Maria Dolores didn't ask the young lady what her profession was, and a few other doves had also found the establishment, but the proprietor tolerated them as long as they didn't shoot anybody. It's supposed to be a free country, thought the recently converted American.

At least half the customers were dragoons who'd heard of the free whiskey and stayed for more. A few sat at the bar, staring at her hungrily, and she knew

precisely what was in their minds, but she smiled politely as she poured the next glass of whiskey.

Incredible wealth poured into her coffers, and she
was so happy she clapped her hands and performed a
little fandango dance behind the bar. A roar went up
from the crowd, and a private shouted, "More!" Maria
Dolores laughed as she collected additional coins.

At the end of the bar, one soldier looked her over,
then turned to his friend and said, "Ain't that the one
we seen with Lieutenant Barrington t'other night?"

The rain stopped before dawn, and the sun rose on
a partially cloudy sky. The detachment continued its
probe to the south, and in days to come saw ranches
and towns depopulated by Apaches, with the inevitable bones stripped clean by scavengers.

Nathanial had read reports of Apache devastation,
but the scope of their plundering was astonishing
when actually encountered. It appeared that they were
trying to force whites out of New Mexico, while folks
back east didn't give a damn about the embattled
settlers.

If he and his detachment were killed by Apaches,
the War Department would send another detachment,
but never enough to really do the job. Nathanial
placed his gloved hand over his eyes and gazed at
hazy orange mountains in the distance. How many
men would it take to search every cave and lost canyon in this land? he wondered. Would it be feasible
to even attempt such a thing?

Every day he and his men rode constantly, but covered little ground relative to the immensity of the
West. He could see hundreds of miles through clear
brilliant atmosphere, with steep-walled mesas like unimaginable Spanish castles, and spires resembling zig-
gurats of lost Arab civilizations. He'd read that long
ago the region had lain beneath an ocean, the home
of prehistoric fish. It made Nathanial feel like a speck
in the panorama of time, and sometimes, in bright

afternoon sun, the mountains were brown heads saying, *We were here long before you arrived, dragoon,
and we will be here long after you depart.*

An ideal spot for a cattle ranch, he evaluated as he
examined the carpet of grama grass over which he
rode. He imagined himself living in his own hacienda,
with his wife and crew of cowboys, a hardy, satisfying
life without army regulations, and a man could get
rich if he was willing to apply himself. Nathanial considered himself a forward-thinking gentleman, and had
no doubt that railroads would serve the region
someday.

He felt invigorated by the colossal spaciousness of
the land, so alien to his Eastern eye. A stone eminence
in the distance looked like a pharaoh's palace or perhaps a minaret in Damascus, with pious Muslim priests
calling the faithful to prayer.

Two scouts rode ahead, searching for Apaches,
while more guards watched his flanks, and another
two riders brought up the rear. Nathanial rode with
his weapons primed, for his reveries never interfered
with his relentless scanning of bushes and trees.

He recalled when he'd been a boy, canoeing on Cor-
tlandt Lake, north of New York City. He'd admired
a flock of beautiful and elegant white swans, but when
he'd glided closer, they raised their wings, lowered
their long curving necks, and charged. At first he'd
been too astonished to react, because the nastiness of
the majestic creatures was unexpected. Then he paddled out of harm's way, having learned a new lesson.
Everything has a dark side, even white swans, and in
the same way, the golden paradise before him was
Apache hell.

Maria Dolores stood in the yard behind her saloon,
watching workmen stacking sunbaked adobe bricks for
a new wall of her expanded establishment. When complete, it would feature another bar, a small dance

floor, and a stage for the orchestra she intended to hire, plus many more tables.

The Silver Palace Saloon was the place for dragoons to go in Santa Fe, and she'd noticed how delighted the men had been whenever she sang and danced behind the bar. They were starved for entertainment, and that's what she'd give them next.

She'd taken a loan to expand the saloon, and hired real bartenders, plus a cook and the prettiest waitresses she could find. Now she was free to make plans, while her father passed his time at the home she'd bought a few blocks away, probably performing Jewish rituals he feared to acknowledge.

Maria Dolores had learned that volume was the most important characteristic of business, and now realized how pathetic their former stores had been. Maybe I should open another saloon on the far side of town, she dared think. If I'm not careful, I'm liable to become the richest woman in Santa Fe.

Otis Jackson traveled east with the baggage atop a stagecoach as the white passengers below drank whiskey and played cards. Rain lashed down, there was an extra seat in the cab, but no one invited poor Otis inside. So he hunkered beneath his torn wool coat, which sucked water thirstily.

Otis feared he'd never reach New York City, because any white man had the right to ask Negroes personal questions, and whites weren't prosecuted for killing uppity niggers. Otis had been whipped and beaten many times during his slavery career, because he found it difficult to swallow his masculine pride. He'd tried to escape the dear old plantation, but the bloodhounds tracked him down every time, and one nearly had taken his leg off, causing his limp. Then kindly Captain Dellinger brought him to New Mexico, and effectively saved his life. They'd grown up together, and been friends across the slavery line, sort of.

Otis shivered in the rain as he reflected upon Lieutenant Barrington. Out of the blue, the hard-drinking officer had freed him, given him money, and sent him on his way, although Otis was worth one thousand dollars on the New Orleans slave market.

Otis despised white people, and if his scarred back wasn't enough, they'd sold his wife, two sons, and one daughter down the river, separating a family for dirty dollars. But he couldn't hate Lieutenant Barrington, because Barrington didn't give a damn about dirty dollars. He saw me man-to-man, figured Otis.

In Austin, the ex-slave shuffled respectfully before every white man he saw, and never let his eyes linger on white women too long. He caught a stagecoach for Vicksburg, and in that great metropolis disappeared into shacks occupied by brothers and sisters at the edge of town. He didn't resurface until three days later, when he bought a steamboat ticket for the *Henry Clay* headed north to the Promised Land.

There was trouble almost from the moment he set foot aboard the *Henry Clay*. The ticket seller had looked at him suspiciously and whispered something to another white man. Otis walked meekly toward the rear of the boat, where he assumed the brothers and sisters would be. But he was wrong, evidently the slaves lived below decks, and he was going to stick out like a big black thumb.

He reached to his inner jacket pocket, to make sure his paper was there. He could lose his hat, pants, or even his mind, but he didn't dare lose that paper. A darkie on his lonesome was sure to attract attention, and he expected the worst. He turned a corner, where he found five army officers playing cards around a table, and they all looked drunk.

Otis sat upon a nearby chair, for lack of anything better to do. It was late afternoon, the *Henry Clay* scheduled to leave in the morning, and slaves were loading cargo, fuel, sides of beef, and crates of whiskey. Otis wondered how to avoid whitey, when a fourteen-year-old slave girl turned the bend, walked by him, looked at him curiously, paused, glanced at him over her shoulder once more, and then stepped toward him cautiously. "Who're you?"

He smiled, showing white teeth. "Otis Jackson, missy."

She glanced both ways. "You ain't a runaway, is you?"

"No—I'm a slave like you. My massa is sending me to New York."

"What you goin' to do there?"

"Damned if I know."

Her name was Michelle, and her expression of honest curiosity became terror as she spotted a man with a badge heading toward her. Without a good-bye, she headed in the opposite direction, like a good dutiful little slave.

The constable was accompanied by two brawny white men, and Otis realized with a sinking heart that they were coming for him. He smiled nervously as he rose to his feet.

The constable and his deputies looked at him coldly. "Keep yer hands where we can see 'em, nigra. Wha't're you doin' here?"

Otis reached into his shirt, but the constable's hand clamped his wrist. Their eyes met, and Otis wanted to punch him through the bulkhead, but instead smiled foolishly. "I was goin' to show you some paper, suh. It 'splains who I is."

"Put your hands in the air. I'll git it myself."

The constable withdrew the document, read thoughtfully, and turned to his deputies. "It says his owner is sendin' him to New York."

A deputy cocked an eye. "How do you know he din't write it hisself?"

"Can you write, nigra?"

"Not *that* good, suh."

The constable pondered his next move. The nigra could be a runaway, but no runaway would board the

Henry Clay unless extremely stupid, which Otis didn't seem to be. Then the constable's eyes fell on the officers playing cards at the nearby table. He shambled toward them and said, "Excuse me, gentlemen, but maybe you can he'p. Has any of you ever heard of a Lieutenant Nathanial Barrington or Lieutenant Beauregard Hargreaves, both from the First Dragoons?"

The soldiers at the table looked at each other with droopy eyelids, for they'd been trying to remember who'd dealt the last hand. Then a young lieutenant sitting on the far side of the table said, "I went to West Point with both of them. What's wrong?"

"Does this look right to you?"

The constable realized that the officer's left arm had been amputated, with the empty sleeve hanging loose. The officer focused on the document, then smiled. "Looks fine to me. I met Lieutenant Barrington's mother once."

The constable thanked the officers, then returned the passport to Otis. "It's a long way to New York," he growled. "Don't git any ideas 'bout runnin', 'cause we'll track you with dogs, and they'll rip yer damned nigra head off."

The herd was a huge sullen being spread across the valley, masticating and digesting grama grass. No coyotes skulked nearby, to pick off the young and old, and the cattle were at peace that afternoon, listening to the rhythms of the earth ... when figures appeared on the horizon.

The animals at the edge of the herd cocked their eyes at the newcomers. Then, suddenly, the two-leggeds on horses charged. The cattle stared at them in curiosity, until it appeared that the intruders were going to run right into them! Bovines snorted, mooed, and tried to get out of the way, their dismay echoing across the valley. Suddenly the rest of the herd was alert, and then it sprang into action.

As if one body, the terrified bovines galloped away

from their attackers, a raiding party led by Chief Mangus Coloradas, cracking his rawhide whip and aiming his galloping horse into the herd. The cattle fought to escape, while Mangus Coloradas and his warriors penetrated their perimeter, lashing haunches of steers and cows, trying to separate two hundred head. The warriors shouted and a few fired army pistols as they drove their human wedge farther into the squirming beasts.

The mounted People's warriors worked the cattle as skillfully as vaqueros, and soon succeeded in gathering the number they wanted. The stolen herd was diverted from the main body, then pointed south toward the encampment in the Pinos Altos Mountains.

The cattle sped over the grass, their interrupted meal forgotten, simple minds befuddled, as the People's warriors raced alongside them, terrifying them further. Mangus Coloradas rode on the right side of the herd, not surprised by the ease of the harvest. The *Nakai-yes* were afraid to encounter the People, and the White Eyes soldiers could never find them.

Mangus Coloradas raised his eyes to a rock formation thrusting into the sky like a man's fist at the far edge of the herd. He was pleased to note that no warrior had been hurt in the raid, and it was almost like the old time, when the land belonged to the People. Tonight we will feast on beef, and then sell the rest to the Comancheros, he decided. The *Nakai-yes* have taken our scalps, so why should we not steal their cattle? Are the People to starve?

His eagle eyes scanned hundreds of miles, but no Mexican vaqueros or White Eyes soldiers were in sight. The People had been raiding with impunity for several moons, and Mangus Coloradas laughed with pleasure as the wind ran its fingers through his long hair. No enemy can stop the living force of the People, he thought confidently. This homeland is ours.

EIGHTEEN

At three o'clock in the morning, President James Knox Polk gazed down Pennsylvania Avenue from the window of his darkened office in the White House. He wore his white nightshirt, a blue velvet robe, and a grim expression as he contemplated the future of America.

The election was tomorrow, and aides had indicated that General Zachary Taylor would win. If so, President Polk expected a catastrophe for the nation, and possibly the end of the noble experiment in republican government known as America.

President Polk considered Zachary Taylor ignorant, stubborn, and narrow-minded, without the intellectual vigor required of the presidency. But Americans loved war heroes, and General Taylor was latest in a line that had begun with George Washington. Old Rough and Ready had prevailed in countless battles against impossible odds, and President Polk appreciated his fighting qualities, but believed the soldier would be hopelessly outclassed in the rough game known as Washington politics.

The slavery issue became more intractable every day, with neither side willing to compromise, and it was only a matter of time before the fuse blew. A great man was required to pilot the ship of state through the coming explosion, not a simpleminded old soldier with a penchant for successful brawling, like Zachary Taylor.

President Polk didn't arrive at the White House on

a white charger, but through political sophistication.
He'd been speaker of the House, governor of Tennessee, and President Andrew Jackson's foremost pro-
tégé. He'd learned from the master that victory meant
maneuvering behind closed doors, the unsaid bribe,
the handshake that sealed the double-cross. James
Polk had wielded those weapons so well, he'd come
from behind to defeat Martin Van Buren, Lewis Cass,
and James Buchanan for the Democratic nomination,
and then went on to defeat the fabled Henry Clay,
the Star of the West, the Great Pacificator, and the
most outstanding orator in America, in the general
election. It hadn't happened because James Knox Polk
was ignorant about the character of the American
people.

He knew that Americans were brawlers, just like
old Zack Taylor. And like brawlers, neither Northerners nor Southerners were willing to take a step backward. Since the birth of the republic, the slavery issue
had become a bottomless pit of constitutional, economic, and moral issues. President Polk would never
dream of freeing slaves by presidential decree, because
it would guarantee civil insurrection and probably the
end of America. Like most decent-thinking middle-of-
the-road citizens, he hoped the practice would die due
to its own inherent contradictions.

But the slavery issue had become more virulent as
the result of the Mexican War, and President Polk had
proven inadequate for the task of reconciliation. If he,
the most winning politician in America, couldn't heal
those gaping wounds, he doubted that anybody else
could either.

Northerners hated him because he'd annexed Texas,
which they feared as a new slavocracy. Southerners
considered him weak and vacillating, because he
couldn't guarantee slavery until the end of time. He'd
heard that Varina Davis, wife of Senator Jeff Davis of
Louisiana, had called him "a small, insignificant man."
It stuck in his craw, because he'd been a sickly child

looked down upon by older boys, but then became the dark horse candidate who'd captured the highest prize in the land. He knew that people would say anything in Washington politics, the more scurrilous the better, and if they wounded you, they scored a victory.

The responsibilities of the office had broken James Polk's health, and now he realized that the sickly child had never really gone away. Sometimes his hands shook, and often he had to take long naps. He had lost weight, slept poorly, his skin had taken a yellowish pallor, and his stomach was a pit of gas. Doctors had prescribed rest, and now America was destined to receive Zachary Taylor as President.

The nation was barely sixty years old, and President Polk wondered if it was destined to disappear. The United States of America was a land of rebels descended from rebels, the kinds of cranks who usually ended up before firing squads, but they believed in freedom and justice for all, even outcasts and adventurers such as themselves. Perhaps, Polk hoped, that spirit will save them from themselves, and they'll stop listening to their most extreme elements, or maybe those stubborn bastards will give this continent a bloodbath such as civilization has never seen.

Sometimes, during long hours in the saddle, Nathanial found himself thinking of his mother, brother, and Tobey back in New York City. He felt guilty for not writing one letter since he'd been at Camp Marcy, but it was considered bad form to introduce disagreeable subjects into his home.

He could imagine Tobey and Jeffrey playing on the parlor floor, while Mother read a book and Shirley Rooney delivered hot drinks and delicacies. But nostalgia for home and hearth didn't prevent Nathanial from searching cholla cactus, hackberry bushes, and grama grass for Apache bushwhacks.

In the near distance leaned an off-center column of stratified rock, possible concealment for the devils.

Nathanial decided that he didn't want to go anywhere near it, so he steered his horse to the right, and the detachment followed dutifully, the First Dragoon guidon flapping in the wind.

Sergeant Duffy pointed straight ahead. "Looks like the scout's found somethin', sir."

Nathanial pulled his brass spyglass out of a saddlebag and focused on the scout, who had stopped his horse. "I hope it's not more dead miners."

Sergeant Duffy spat a stream of tobacco juice at a rat snake perched on a rock and caught the hapless creature between the eyes. "Anybody loco enough to roam around out here deserves to die."

"Nobody deserves to die just for digging in the ground, Sergeant Duffy."

"They die fer their stupidity, sir. You know what I think we should do? We should start pizenin' the Apaches' water, like the Mexicans used to."

The men had been increasingly ornery in past days as the discomfort of the scout wore on. It was they, not Lieutenant Barrington, who dug the latrines, set up tents, and performed myriads of other unpleasant chores under primitive conditions. In addition, Nathanial sensed that they hadn't fully recovered from the killing of Captain Grimes and were anxious to even the score. They received little money, the citizenry considered them lazy oafs, and all they had was loyalty to each other.

The scout was a former Texas Ranger named Nichols, a rangy man with a pockmarked face, and he was crawling around on his hands and knees. As Nathanial drew closer, it looked like a herd of something had passed within the past several hours.

Nathanial climbed down from the saddle. "Cattle or horses?" he asked.

"Stolen cattle," replied Nichols, wiping his hands on his pants.

"How do you know they're stolen?"

"Because they're bein' run by Apaches, and how do

I know they're Apaches?" He pointed to the ground. "Unshod ponies."

Nathanial dropped to his knees to examine the tracks. He wanted to learn as much as he could about reading sign, but his men were disconcerted to see their commanding officer peer at the dirt from a distance of six inches.

Nichols pointed in a westerly direction. "They're headed thataway, and I reckon they're about one to two hours ahead of us."

Nathanial's orders were to pursue Apache raiders, and this time the savages couldn't move quickly due to the herd. "It looks like we might see action today, gentlemen," Nathanial declared. "Nichols—ride ahead and find out where they are, but don't let them see you. We'll follow as quietly as possible, and once we get within striking range, we'll attack. After that, you can make all the noise you want. Are you with me, boys?"

He looked into their eyes, not a man flinched. Captain Grimes had been a popular officer, almost a father to them, and they were rough quarrelsome sons of bitches to begin with, otherwise they wouldn't have joined the First Dragoons. "We're with you, sir," said Sergeant Duffy.

"Let's move it out," replied the commanding officer.

In the stable, Rebecca petted her palomino mare, Ophelia. Rebecca couldn't help feeling sorry for her, penned up on a sunny afternoon. But they couldn't go riding without a military escort, due to the Apaches.

Rebecca sat on a barrel near Ophelia and watched the animal munch corn. From other parts of the stable, she heard soldiers cleaning out the stalls, stacking hay, repairing the roof, and so on. Rebecca was utterly miserable and found the boredom of Camp Marcy beyond endurance.

She'd fallen into melancholy since her unhappy ex-

perience with Lieutenant Barrington, had no outlet for
her energies, and it didn't appear that she'd be marrying soon. Nathanial had awakened a thirst that she
needed to quench, except there was no socially accept-
able way. Damn, she thought, and wrinkled her nose.

She didn't want to leave her mother and father, but
might have to in order to find a husband. She could
travel to Savannah, where her Aunt Barbara lived, but
it would involve an expensive and dangerous journey.
She thought she'd go mad if she had to spend another
year at Fort Marcy.

She heard soldiers talking several stalls away. "Sergeant, can I talk with you?" asked the voice of a
dragoon.

"What's on your so-called mind," replied a brogue
that could only belong to Sergeant Moynihan.

"I ain't feelin so good, sir, and I was a-wonderin' if
I could lie down fer a spell. Otherwise I'm a-gonna
throw up on the floor."

"It's not my fault that you stayed out all night, you
drunkard. But nobody listens to old Sergeant
Moynihan."

A new voice asked, "Din't I see you at the Silver
Palace t'other night, Sarge?"

"But I wasn't flat on my ass, like you."

Another voice added, "Did you ever see a better-
looking Mexican woman than Maria Dolores?"

The sergeant chortled. "If I ever put my hands on
that filly, it'd be the end of me."

"Too late, Sartch," said the German accent of Private Schultz. "Loit'nant Barrington has already got
her."

"Shaddup and do yer work!" shouted Sergeant
Moynihan as he took command of the detail. "This
ain't the conversation hour."

The stable fell silent, except for the scraping of
shovels and grunts of men as they worked. Rebecca
sat rigid as a flagpole, her mouth hanging open. Who
the hell is Maria Dolores?

* * *

Nathanial lay on his belly and peered at the Apaches through his spyglass. They'd gathered their stolen cattle for the night, and now were preparing roast meat for supper, the fragrance wafting over the sage. Nathanial's stomach felt cavernous, because he hadn't eaten since that morning.

But for once he was the fox, not the lost little rabbit. The Apaches appeared satisfied that they owned New Mexico, and no one could ever bother them. It comforted Nathanial to know they were human, with the same heedless vanity, but the sun was setting and he didn't have much time.

He retreated silently two hundred yards on his stomach, then Sergeant Duffy's face loomed out of the sagebrush as the setting sun produced a bronze sheen on the noncom's cheeks. Their clothes were dirty, ragged, and they looked like a bunch of derelicts in their wide-brimmed hats. "They're straight ahead, men," reported Nathanial, "and they're not expecting anything. Mount up, and let's give 'em hell."

They climbed onto their horses, then formed a skirmish line. Nathanial took his position in front, drew his Walker Colt, and thumbed back the hammer. Then he turned in the saddle and made certain that the line was dressed right. Forage caps were tight on the heads of his dragoons, all pistols pointing straight up in the air, their horses pawing the ground; it was time to even the score.

This is it, thought Nathanial as he put the spurs to his horse. The animal bounded forward, and then the other beasts stretched their long muscles behind him, pushing against the wind, working themselves into a trot, then a canter, and finally an all-out full-tilt hell-bent-for-leather cavalry charge. Wind whistled in the beards of the bold dragoons, and a terrible clamor was on the sage as they reached full momentum.

With Nathanial far in front, they streaked across grama grass, or leapt over cacti and sagebrush. All maintained their pistols straight up in the air, and some dragoons were experiencing their first charge, while others were old battle-scarred veterans. They all remembered Captain Grimes, as if he were cheering them on from the big officers' club in the sky.

The dragoons kept glancing about them, because they had to remain dressed right. The tactic had been drummed into their heads on parade grounds practically from their first day of enlistment, and now at last they were earning their pay. Some were confident, others terrified, and a few messed their pants. Their hearts beat wildly as they emerged from the last rays of the setting sun and bore down inexorably on the Apache raiders, who were fleeing desperately toward their horses.

Nathanial worked with his animal's musculature, urging him to greater effort. The wind blew Nathanial's hat off, but it remained fastened to his neck via a leather thong; his long blond hair trailed in the wind. He ducked low beneath the mane of his powerful horse, aimed his Colt pistol straight ahead, and screamed at the top of his lungs, "Follow me!"

Before him Apaches readied weapons, cattle stampeded, and bareback war ponies raised their front hooves in the air. *I have achieved surprise,* thought Nathanial as he took aim for his first shot of the engagement. A cluster of Apaches ran toward their horses, but the First Dragoons descended upon them like the wrath of God.

Holding his saddle tightly with his legs, Nathanial fired at the back of the Apache on horseback in front of him. A red dot appeared on the Indian's brown flesh, and he slid out of the saddle as Nathanial's horse leapt over him, and Nathanial saw the back of another mounted Apache trying to get away. Nathanial came up behind him, aimed, and triggered. The Apache turned around at the last moment, his eyes wide with horror as the bullet rammed into his breastbone. The

Apache pitched backward and rolled around the mane
of his horse as Nathanial's horse rampaged onward.

It appeared that Nathanial had ridden through the
Apaches, and was on his way into the herd, as gunfire
sounded behind him. He found himself surrounded by
bovines hooting and braying, and then a hunk of lead
whistled over his head. All was confusion, gunsmoke,
and deadly projectiles. He wheeled his horse, but his
men had followed him, evidently they'd overrun the
Apaches too, and had to re-form for another charge.
Nathanial coughed and spat as he steered back toward
where the Apaches had been. "Skirmish line!" he hollered. "Quickly!"

Nathanial realized that he'd just committed a tactical error that could prove fatal to his command, but
he'd learned from Old Rough and Ready that when
in doubt, attack. "Ho—First Dragoon!" he bellowed.
"At them!"

The remaining Apaches were leaping onto their
horses as the stolen herd rumbled away from the awful
commotion. Nathanial was surprised to notice the
Apaches turning to face their attackers, instead of retreating. They were singing war songs, preparing to
counterattack, but General Taylor's dictum rang true
in all military situations. "Onward you dragoons!" Nathanial yelled as the excitement of sudden death carried him away.

Nathanial glanced behind him, to make sure that
his men were there, but reliable Sergeant Duffy rode
beside the guidon flag streaking across the blue sky,
and the others charged forward like the horsemen of
the apocalypse. Nathanial's steed reached speed once
more as Nathanial aimed him directly into the center
of the Apaches.

A barrage of arrows flew toward him, he ducked
his head, his horse broke his stride, and then, sickenin-
gly, began to go down. Oh, no, thought Nathanial as
a dragoon's worst nightmare came upon him. He tried
to throw himself clear, the horse whinnied terribly,

Nathanial landed on his left shoulder, rolled frantically, dust filled his eyes, all was hellish madness, and
then his forward motion stopped.

He jumped to his feet in time to see an Apache
racing toward him on foot, holding a war club poised
to crash his skull. The Apache was taller than Nathanial, covered with slabs of muscle, with an oversize
head and long black hair streaked with gray. Nathanial
fired at this singular individual without aiming, missed,
the club came down, and Nathanial managed to catch
the Apache's wrist with both his hands, while bringing
up his knee for the coup de grace.

But the Apache wasn't there, he'd twisted out of
Nathanial's grasp and took a sideways swing at the
kidney of the hapless young officer. Nathanial dodged
backward, and the Apache dived for the shiny pistol
that Nathanial had dropped, but Nathanial kicked him
in the face, then grabbed the pistol himself, positioned
it in both his hands, and was rocked off his feet by
the Apache, who had dived wildly onto him, clawing
at his eyes.

Nathanial backpedaled, tried to get off a clear shot,
and heard a sickening *click*. The Colt had jammed at
the crucial moment, and then suddenly the Apache
grabbed his throat with one hand and drove him backward toward the ground. Nathanial punched the
Apache in the mouth and twisted sharply to avoid a
knee to the groin. He and the Apache rolled over in
the dirt, kicking, biting, and trying to gouge out each
other's eyeballs. Nathanial felt as if he were wrestling
a giant cougar as he fought frantically for his life. His
hand fell onto a rock, he tried to smash it through the
Apache's skull, but the Apache dodged and rolled
over the dead body of one of the dragoons as shots
and screams reverberated across the campsite.

Nathanial had no idea how the skirmish was pro-
ceeding as he dived onto a pistol lying on the ground.
He picked it up and swung it around, catching the
giant Apache on the jaw, laying it open to the bone.

The Apache fell backward, Nathanial went after him, when suddenly a riderless horse appeared, forcing Nathanial to hold his fire. After the horse passed, Nathanial aimed where the Apache had been, but his target had flown the coop.

Nathanial spun around, expecting a war club to come whizzing at his head, but it appeared the encounter was just about over. Thirteen dead Apaches littered the ground, with three dragoons among them. The breeze blew gunsmoke and dust away, and the rustled herd could be seen in the distance, running frenziedly into the nether regions of New Mexico.

Nathanial found his horse lying on its side, blood bubbling through its nostrils. The detachment commander took aim, looked away, and pulled the trigger. The shot echoed off mesas and rolled across great basins. He reloaded the chambers, made sure no Apaches were creeping up on him, and said, "Sergeant Duffy—bury the dead. And please direct the scout to find us a campsite for the night. Cookie—see if you can round up a steer. I'm in the mood for a steak."

Blood thudding in his ears, Nathanial rolled a cigarette. He felt light-headed, white dots appeared before his eyes, and nearby lay a dead Apache, the first that Nathanial had shot.

Nathanial dropped to one knee beside the Apache, who was about eighteen, with a line of ochre paint across the bridge of his nose. There was nothing demonic about him; he appeared sleeping. Nathanial felt guilty about killing him, but then remembered Captain Grimes's grieving widow and children.

He recalled the Apache Hercules whom he'd fought hand-to-hand, and wondered who he was. Nathanial admitted to himself that the Apache had nearly killed him numerous times during the struggle. I've got to stop drinking, he warned himself, and next time I'll attack in two separate waves. But I've learned one important lesson: *Apaches can be defeated*.

Nathanial raised his eyes, and in the cloud formations swirling above him, he saw Captain Grimes sitting erectly in his saddle, his campaign hat at a jaunty angle, and throwing a regulation salute as he rode across Valhalla's golden range.

In downtown Santa Fe, across the street from the Silver Palace Saloon, Rebecca Harding tried to stand nonchalantly as she examined the establishment belonging to the woman who had stolen her man. She'd never been alone in this part of town, but it didn't seem dangerous in the daylight. The Silver Palace Saloon was no different from any other drinking establishment on the street, and she wondered what foul deeds transpired behind the white-curtained window.

Naturally, she wanted to get a closer look, but purely in the interests of science, and not because she was curious about the Mexican prostitute. Rebecca walked daintily to the corner, looked both ways, and then prepared to place her foot into the street when she noticed a dead creature, either a cat or small dog, in the middle of the thoroughfare, near a pile of horse manure and other substances that she didn't care to name. She realized that she'd go in up to her ankles, but had worn riding boots beneath her long skirt, so all she had to do was lift it to her knees.

"Wanna cross the street?" asked a voice beside her.

She turned toward a big burly fellow with his stovepipe hat caved in on the side and a belly like an unwanted pregnancy. "Yes ... I do," she replied hesitantly.

He picked her up and carried her in his arms before she knew what hit her. A wave of tobacco and alcohol reeked from his person, and he was missing three teeth. Never had a total stranger handled her so familiarly, but nobody seemed to pay attention, so she sailed over the dead creature and was lowered gently to the sidewalk on the far side of the street.

Her benefactor tipped his hat, winked, and headed

for the Silver Palace Saloon. He opened the front door, and she caught a glimpse of men's hats in the murky interior. Someone played "The Yellow Rose of Texas" on the piano, and a few voices sang off-key. Why do men like places like this? Rebecca asked herself, pinching her lips. It looks absolutely disgusting.

The door opened again, this time disgorging a man in worn jeans, a dusty coat, and a bright red misshapen nose laced with prominent blue veins. Rebecca studied this personage as he approached unsteadily on the sidewalk, the front brim of his vaquero hat pinned to his crown. She moved out of his way, for she feared that he'd fall on top of her, but he stopped, removed his hat, and bowed low.

"Good afternoon, Maria Dolores," he said.

"Good afternoon," replied a Mexican woman coming from the opposite direction, carrying a satchel on a leather belt crossways over her shoulders, and it appeared that she was sporting a gunbelt beneath her serape.

Rebecca stared in fascination at the woman. This was no namby-pamby diaphanous creature, but a tall sturdy woman, and Rebecca felt intimidated by her sheer physicality. The woman was probably stronger than many men, yet graceful and even somewhat aristocratic in her bearing.

Maria Dolores entered the Silver Palace Saloon, leaving Rebecca standing pigeon-toed on the sidewalk. The major's daughter felt defeated and demoralized as she trudged back to Camp Marcy. Evidently Nathanial's taste runs to big bosoms, she figured glumly. He doesn't appreciate my subtle charms, but perhaps they're so subtle, he didn't even notice them.

But one day he'll leave her too, because that's the kind of man he is. He's a liar, he has no honor, and he should be punished for his misdeeds. But how?

* * *

It was night in the Manzano Mountains, and Nathanial lay in his tent, reliving the fear and frenzy of mortal combat. When his Colt refused to fire, he'd thought he'd lost the game. He was disappointed by his performance, yet proud of his victory. It wasn't every day that the First Dragoons defeated Apaches.

His mouth went dry as he recalled rolling, fighting, scratching, and kicking the mighty Apache warrior. A vicious madness had come over Nathanial, and he wondered who was that fellow who shot Indians in the back or tried to gouge out their eyes. *That big damned Indian nearly bludgeoned me to death, and even a stray bullet from someone I couldn't see might've finished me off. Life is the most fragile commodity in the world, and I should enjoy it as much as possible. To hell with what people think of me.*

No clouds shielded the blazing heavens, and a half-moon illuminated scraggly foliage surrounding the campsite. He crawled out of the tent, opened the flap of his holster, yanked out his Colt, and carried it cocked and loaded in his right hand.

His men lay in their tents, and three of their number had been killed, and he'd preside at the funeral in the morning. They'd kicked the asses of the Apaches for a change, and everyone felt proud.

"Halt—who goes there!" cried a voice in the night.

"Lieutenant Barrington."

"Advance, sir, to be recognized."

The sentry wore a bandage like a turban around his head, with his forage cap askew on top. It was Private Baldridge, who hailed from the great state of Wisconsin. "Friends of those Apaches might pay us a visit tonight," said Nathanial. "Keep your eyes peeled for them."

"Yes, sir!" said Baldridge, standing at attention.

"How's your wound?"

"There ain't nothin' wrong with me that a good drink of whiskey wouldn't cure."

*   *   *

He was a tall, gangly fellow, and his face looked as though life had handled him roughly. "My name's Cochrane, and I hee'rd yer a-lookin' fer a guard."

Maria Dolores sat behind the desk in her new enclosed office, wearing a long brown dress with a high white collar. "Have a seat."

He dropped to the chair, and she could smell him across the room. His shirt looked as though it had been soaked in axle grease, wrung out, and put on. He might be the bravest man west of the Pecos, but she didn't want someone like that in her establishment.

"What's the pay?" he asked.

"Twenty dollars a month, and your meals."

"I can start right now."

"I'll let you know. Can you write down your address?"

She pushed a pen and pad toward him, and turned her inkwell around. He pulled back as if he'd just seen a rattlesnake. "You mean I come all the way over here, and I ain't gonna git the job?"

"A lot of people have applied," said Maria Dolores. "I have not made my decision."

He leaned forward, pointed his thumb at his chest, and squinched up one eye. "You think there's somethin' wrong with me, like I'm not purty enuf or somethin'?"

He was trying to menace her, and she touched her fingers to the gun in her holster. "I do not have time to argue with you. I think you should leave."

"Oh, yeah?" He arose, leaned over the desk, and snarled, "Fuck you, you greaser bitch! Now what're you going to do about that?"

"This," she replied as she drew the Colt Dragoon, simultaneously thumbing back the hammer.

He stared down the barrel, then took a step backward. "Whoa—point that thing in another direction."

She held it tightly in both hands and sighted on the center of his chest. "Get out of here."

He tried to stare her down, but it didn't work. Then he forced an arrogant laugh. "You ain't got the sand to shoot a man."

"If you like."

Her knuckle went white around the trigger, and he was out the door. Maria Dolores waited a few moments, took a deep breath, then eased forward the hammer. Could I have shot him? she wondered as she holstered the gun.

Yes.

Thirteen warriors had been killed in the raid, and one died of wounds after returning to the camp. His name had been Yanoza, and inside his wickiup, his scarred body was being prepared for his journey to the land of shadow spirits.

His wife and two brothers bathed his corpse and combed his hair, then dressed him in his best clothes. Meanwhile, outside the wickiup, friends and relatives had gathered to recall Yanoza's great deeds and drink *tizwin*. One of these was the great chief Mangus Coloradas, a distant cousin of the departed warrior and leader of the disastrous raid.

The dead warriors had been friends and relatives whom the chief had known all his life. Their families had become paupers, and he felt deeply ashamed. He'd arrogantly thought himself safe, but then the White Eyes attacked out of the sunset. The People's warriors fought back as best they could, and a handful had managed to get away, carrying some of their dead with them.

Mangus Coloradas couldn't forget the White Eyes with sunny hair who'd nearly defeated him. If the horse had not come between us, I could not have lasted much longer. A strong young warrior can always defeat a strong older warrior in time, he realized.

Other days could be devoted to the soldier with sunny hair, but the funeral came first. The bereaved families would be supported by the rest of the tribe, an economic hardship for all, but one dutifully accepted. Yanoza's corpse, wrapped in a white deerskin robe, was carried to a pit that had been dug at the edge of the campsite. Yanoza's favorite horse stood beside the pit, next to his bow, arrow, stolen musket, and a new pair of moccasin boots.

Yanoza was lowered into the hole, with his feet to the east, then his belongings were dropped on top of him as family and friends wailed in grief. Dirt was shoveled over him, then a layer of boulders, and finally everything topped by another two feet of dirt. Coletto Amarillo, a friend of Yanoza's, held the reins of Yanoza's horse beside the burial mound as Chief Mangus Coloradas stepped forward and slashed the horse's throat. The animal died in seconds and collapsed onto the grave.

The People broke camp and loaded their few belongings onto horses. They never returned to that place again.

White men commanded the *Henry Clay*, but slaves kept the engines running, cooked the food, and so on. They lived below decks in the hottest part of the hold, but the paddle wheeler was docked in Memphis for the night, portholes were open, and a cool breeze drifted through hammocks in the slave quarters.

In candlelight, slaves sang hymns about baby Jesus, as above their heads well-dressed men and fashionable ladies strolled about moonlit decks, or in spacious chandeliered parlors men in ruffled shirts played cards and discussed the upcoming election campaign. The two worlds floated on the great muddy Mississippi, as different as two worlds could be.

Otis Jackson meditated upon the contrasts as he sat near a porthole and sang along with the slaves. He was on his way to New York City, and never in his

wildest dreams could he have imagined such good luck
would be his.

> *"Go down, Moses*
> *Go down to Egypt's land*
> *and tell old Pharaoh*
> *to let my people go."*

He hummed the harmony in his deep basso voice,
for he'd been raised in the Christian religion like the
other slaves. But his mother had taught him an older
religion, where a God named Amma took a handful
of clay, squeezed it in his fist, and threw it away from
him, thus creating the world.

She'd explained that before they were slaves, their
ancestors had belonged to a nation called Dogon, and
their forebears had been free farmers and traders.
Their history went back to the beginnings of time,
and the Dogon were guided in all they did by the
Nummo spirits.

His mother had regaled him with legends about sacred tortoises, *dougué* stones, and the sun lizard. Once
she told him an old Dogon expression that he'd never
forgotten: *The jackal was alone from birth, and because of this he did more things than can be told.*

The door to the slave quarters was flung open, and
the captain's voice said, "These is where the nigras
live."

He led ladies and gentlemen into the hold, where
they wrinkled their noses at crowded living conditions.
"How quaint," said a matron, pointing to one of the
empty hammocks.

"Keep on singing!" ordered the captain. "Don't let
us stop you."

The darkies resumed their hymn:

> *"Swing low, sweet chariot*
> *comin' for to carry me home ..."*

The distinguished guests treated the Negroes like zoo exhibits, but the sweetness of the hymn captivated them. The white masters and mistresses smiled indulgently as they tried to convince themselves that darkies were happy people, and slavery the best thing in the world for the poor dumb brutes, for did it not teach them religion?

NINETEEN

Nathanial and his dragoons returned to Fort Marcy bedraggled, half-starved, bearded, and smelling to high heaven. At the front gate, guards snapped to attention, and Nathanial returned their salute smartly. "How're you doing, boys?" he asked out of the corner of his mouth, like a seasoned old campaigner. "Who won the election?"

"General Taylor, sir."

A cheer went up from the dragoons, because one of their own, Old Rough and Ready himself, was headed for the White House. Everyone on the post ran toward the last detachment as it proceeded toward the stables, while its commanding officer peeled off toward the orderly room. Nathanial rode with his spine erect, and felt like Caesar returning to Rome, except Roman generals rode in chariots accompanied by an ordinary soldier saying over and over: "Remember—thou art but a man."

Nathanial could understand how vanity could be inspired as soldiers applauded and hooted all around them. The last detachment had hammered an Apache raiding party, a rare occurrence in the New Mexico Territory. Nathanial steered his mount toward the command post headquarters, climbed down from the saddle, and threw the reins over the rail. Then he swaggered into the orderly room, expecting the first sergeant to welcome him back, but that old soldier glanced up dourly. "What can I do fer you, Lieutenant?"

"I'd like to have a word with the major."

"He's busy."

"I want to give him my report."

"Put it in writing, and he'll read it in the morning."

Nathanial thought it odd that the major wouldn't see him. He rode toward the stables, where his men were removing saddles and blankets from their mounts. Nathanial handed his reins to a stable hand, then made his way to his little room in the Bachelor Officers' Quarters, where he sat on the chair, lit a cigarette, and gave thanks that he was still alive. It was his first time alone since he'd ridden out the gate, and he didn't have to worry about Apaches anymore.

Maybe next time the damned savages will think twice before they steal cattle, he figured. *What makes them think this is their land—just because they've been here longer than us? By that standard, it belongs to the snakes and coyotes.*

There was a knock on the door as Beau arrived with a bottle. "Want a snort?" He threw the bottle, and Nathanial caught it in midair. "I heard you killed some Apaches."

Amid sips of whiskey, Nathanial explained his semisuccessful tactics, and told how he'd felt when his horse had been going down. He omitted the gory details of his hand-to-hand fighting, and then said, "We killed about a dozen of them, and they got three of us, but by Jesus, they know they can't take the First Dragoons for granted anymore."

"Your detachment was the only one that made contact with them," replied Beau. "You were lucky, or maybe unlucky, depending upon one's point of view."

"Have you ever gone hand-to-hand with 'em."

"Not yet."

"Carry two pistols, because that's what I'm going to do from now on. Sometimes, at the worst moments, these Colts jam. I heard that General Taylor won the election."

"He beat Cass by about one hundred and forty

thousand votes. I'm for General Taylor, but America is two countries, the North and the South. I think we should try to be good neighbors, instead of living together under the same government."

"The best part of my scout," replied Nathanial, "was that I didn't have to think about politics. It's just a lot of liars hollering at each other and striking poses that they hope will get votes. They all want to save America, but what they really want is to line their own pockets. They always make everything worse no matter who's in the White House."

Beau shook his head in disgust. "You can bury your head in the sand if you like, Nathanial my friend, but one day history will catch up with you. And by the way, do you know who's suffered most from the damned slavery debate? The darkies themselves. The great myth of abolition is that we Southerners are always whipping, killing, and raping our slaves, but one of my father's darkies is the overseer, and my father built them a school, a church, and they have their own little garden, where they can grow whatever they want and sell it. Daddy even goes to the fields and picks cotton alongside them, so it's not as simple as you damned Yankee think. The problem with America is the sanctimonious Yankees who can't stop haranguing us. They need something to tear down and have settled on the South."

Nathanial had seen Otis's shredded back, but hated arguments with his old West Point comrade. "Slavery began a long time ago," Nathanial explained, "and nobody's hands are clean, not even the Negroes themselves, because some of them sold Negro captives to the Yankee captains. Maybe America will break apart someday, but I just came back from a scout, and I'm tired." Nathanial yawned. "What's going on with the major? He wouldn't see me today."

"That's because you've been a-courtin' Miss Rebecca, and you've also been seen with Maria Dolores Carbajal. Since Rebecca is the apple of her daddy's eye,

I'd say that your next efficiency report will be a great disappointment to you. This is why men of common sense never go near the major's daughter. You may be a Yankee first lieutenant for the rest of your life, but if I ever make general, perhaps I'll appoint you as my aide-de-camp."

Maria Dolores stood on the sidewalk in front of the Silver Palace Saloon, observing workmen nailing a sign above the door.

WELCOME HOME, DRAGOONS
FIRST DRINK FREE

She'd heard that Lieutenant Barrington had returned, and the man himself could be expected to stop at the Silver Palace Saloon that evening. Sometimes Maria Dolores thought her silly romantic nature was preparing her for disappointment, and Nathanial was just another lonely, lying soldier, but she'd dreamed of him crucified, there seemed to be a connection between them, and she felt as if he were the brother she'd never had. Maybe I should throw a big fandango, with free drinks for everybody, she thought. She'd learned that if you wanted a successful business, you had to give customers something free once in a while. Maria Dolores loved to dance and felt in a festive mood. With a happy heart, she returned to her office, to decide which musicians to hire.

Rebecca sat in the parlor, listening to knocks on the door. Her mother held her hand, while her father sat in his easy chair, scowling. They heard the door opened by Francine. "Oh—good evening, Lieutenant Barrington."

"Is Rebecca home?"

"I'm sorry, but she's indisposed."

"Would you tell her that I called?"

The door closed and the footsteps faded away. Francine returned to the kitchen, where she'd been cleaning up after supper. Rebecca raised her handkerchief and dabbed her cheek. "I hate him," she whispered.

An orchestra had been set up on the sidewalk, while couples danced in the middle of the street, surrounded by a conglomeration of Americans and Mexicans of all ages, types, and stages of intoxication. The dwarf Miguelito dressed as a clown was cavorting at the edge of the mob, performing back flips and giving candy to children.

The fandango was in full swing when Nathanial arrived, attired in a clean, pressed blue uniform, but retaining his silverbelly wide-brimmed hat. Paper lanterns were strung across the street, and standing on the sidewalk was Maria Dolores, wearing a red patterned skirt and white blouse buttoned to her neck, with a matching red ribbon holding her thick mane of black hair. Nathanial made his way past the clown, some beggars, and a couple kissing. The beat of Aztec and Toltec drums pounded in his ears as he landed on the sidewalk in front of her.

They examined each other's faces, sparks flew off their eyes, and then she said, "Welcome home, Nathanial."

"Let's take a walk," he replied.

They steered away from the bright lights, and silently advanced toward the edge of Santa Fe. Their fingers touched, wrapped around each other, and came to rest entwined. He felt her womanly loveliness pass into his arm, and a wave of bottomless desire came over him, weakening him when he needed strength most.

"I have heard that you were in a big fight with the Apaches," she said.

"It's true," he replied, but how could he explain hand-to-hand fighting with a naked, squirming savage? His long ordeal was over, and the moment he'd awaited had arrived. They came to the edge of the wilderness, and the half-moon floated like a ship across the blazing sky.

"I've thought about you many times during the scout, Maria Dolores," he began. "I've decided that I want to marry you, but before you answer, I want to tell you the truth about myself. I'm afraid I've been a fool for most of my life, and have disgraced my family on countless occasions. There are those who say I'm bad to the bone."

She burst into laughter, covering her mouth with her hand. "Why are you saying all these things about yourself, Nathanial?" she asked as she placed her arms around his neck.

He felt her strong body against him as he settled his callused hands on her waist. "I don't want to misrepresent myself, but if you were my wife, I could accomplish anything, because you make me so ..."

Their lips touched lightly, and it felt as if her energy were radiating into his body. She was warm and supple beneath her garments, causing an artery to throb in his throat. She touched her lips to his ear. "Will you marry me in the Catholic Church?"

"Sure."

"Where will we live?"

"Wherever you want."

She peered into his eyes. "If we marry in the Church, it means that we must be married forever. Will you be faithful to me, Nathanial?"

"Certainly. I want you to be the mother of my children because we're so similar, and we're both God-fearing people."

"At last He has sent you," she sighed.

He panicked, as if falling into a bottomless chasm, and realized there was much about her that he didn't know. But her warm flesh and bones pressed against him, her nipples like punctuation marks on his chest, and he heard fandango music floating in the air.

He felt the mad urge to ravish her, but this time he didn't want to be a scoundrel. With a monumental effort nearly beyond his capacity, he drew back from her. "When will you speak to the priest?" he asked.

"Tomorrow."

They returned to the Silver Palace Saloon and joined fandango dancers whirling in the street. The accordionist perspired as he pumped his instrument enthusiastically, while the fiddler played tunes of Seville. Children laughed, and gentlemen wearing sombreros and mustaches partnered raven-tressed ladies in gypsy dances.

Nathanial moved his hands behind his back as Maria Dolores pirouetted before him. Couples embraced in alleyways as the fandango cast its magic web. Children clapped their hands, the night filled with fast-paced melodies, and Maria Dolores's shapely hips moved with the rhythm. I don't care how many relatives write me out of their wills, Nathanial said to himself. There comes a time when a man must listen to the song of his blood.

"Madam, there is a *Negro* to see you. He claims that he belongs to Nathanial!"

Amalia Barrington hadn't heard from her son since he'd departed New York, but nothing surprised her where Nathanial was concerned. She placed her book on the coffee table, followed Shirley down the stairs, and opened the front door.

A giant Negro male dressed in rags shivered on her stoop, his lips blue. Amalia Harding didn't know whether he was a murderer or thief, but said, "Come in."

The Negro entered the vestibule, teeth chattering, and handed her a wrinkled sheet of paper. She read that he indeed had been her son's slave and wondered what to do with him. "How's Nathanial?"

"Just fine, ma'am," lied Otis.

"He isn't in any trouble?"

"No, ma'am."

She realized that she was being rude, because the

Negro hadn't eaten, and he surely needed a bath. She directed the grumbling Shirley to provide his needs and make a bed for him in the servants' quarters.

Otis followed Shirley into the kitchen, where he consumed three ham sandwiches and a bowl of left-over chicken and noodle soup. Then he lay in a tub of hot water and recalled the unimaginable bright lights of Broadway that he'd just seen. He was given articles of Nathanial's clothing, and that night, the son of a Dogon high priestess slept on clean cotton sheets in a mansion on Washington Square.

After Mass, Maria Dolores approached Father Paolo as he was returning to the rectory. "May I speak with you, Father?"

"Of course, my dear," the padre replied, although he had much to do. "Right this way."

He led her to the vestry, where he removed his priestly garb that covered the black trousers and black shirt of his trade he wore beneath them. They sat in his office, and he offered a cup of black coffee.

"What can I do for you?" he asked with jolly familiarity.

"I want to get married, Father."

He appeared surprised, but recovered quickly. "Who's the lucky man?"

"His name is Nathanial Barrington, and he is an American Army officer. But unfortunately, he is not Catholic."

"He will have to become one, of course. Does he have objections?"

"No, but I hope we will not need to wait long."

The priest raised his finger in the air. "Marriage is a step not to be taken lightly. How long have you known this man?"

"Nearly two months," she said with slight exaggeration.

"I've always thought it unwise for people of dissimilar backgrounds to marry."

"Nathanial and I are very similar, and we love each other."

He leaned toward her and smiled cynically. "But what is love?"

"When you want to be with somebody."

"Then dogs would be the best lovers of all."

"Maybe they are."

No matter how he preached, they never listened. Who has ever made a sensible marriage? he wondered. His own parents had quarreled incessantly, and when the pious youth recognized certain sinful desires for other males, he surrendered to God and became a priest.

"You are a fine women, Maria Dolores. I know what you think of me, that all I want is your money, but a person's contributions to Holy Mother Church are an indication of her dedication, and you have always been most generous. I must speak with the gentleman, and he may require study in our religion."

"He's an Episcopalian, Father. That's not so different from us."

"We shall see," replied the priest.

Nathanial was strolling across the parade ground, lost in reveries of Maria Dolores, when he realized that Major Harding was headed straight for him. Nathanial wanted to hide, but there was no cave to dive into. All he could do was raise his arm and throw a salute.

Their eyes met, and Nathanial saw glimmers of rage. Major Harding returned the salute perfunctorily and walked past as if Nathanial were beneath contempt. I've insulted him profoundly, Nathanial realized. I should've stayed away from Rebecca, but my flaw is that I think the laws of nature don't apply to me, when in fact I'm the biggest imbecile of all, just as my father said.

He wondered if he was making a new mistake with Maria Dolores, because his mother would be horrified when she learned that he'd converted to the Catholic religion. New York gentlemen of his class simply didn't marry Mexican senoritas, but he was in love, whatever that meant, and was tired of his lonely cell in the Bachelor Officers' Quarters.

Maria Dolores wouldn't belittle his inclinations to prayer, but most of all, he had to confess, he was in lust with her. She was big and strong like he was, not petite like a doll or skinny as a scarecrow. Perhaps I've inherited my taste for dark-skinned women from my father, he mused.

His fondest dream was to wrestle naked with Maria Dolores, although he considered lust the most superficial reason for getting married. Yet, like most officers of his acquaintance, he secretly believed lust the finest, purest love of all and refused to deny himself paradise when life could end so suddenly.

If the major tries anything cute, I'll resign my commission, determined Nathanial. I don't need the army, but I need this woman. She's dreamed about me, and I've been waiting for her all my life. We're meant for each other, and nothing can stop me now.

Mangus Coloradas sat alone in a cave, listening to the murmurings of the mountain spirits. He had killed many enemies during his career, including Mexicans, Navahos, Comanches, Kiowa, and the White Eyes, and considered himself superior to any warrior in the world, yet his long reign had nearly ended with the pasty-faced White Eyes soldier with sunny hair.

Never had the great chief encountered such strength, not even when he'd wrestled famous warriors such as Ponce, Cuchillo Negro, Delgadito, Coleto Amarillo, and even young Lucero rising star of the People.

Mangus Coloradas had believed that the White Eyes were weaklings compared to Apaches, but now he had something new to chew upon. The experienced warrior had required all his much vaunted speed and

skill merely to stay alive against the soldier with
sunny hair.

"That White Eyes possessed strong medicine,"
Mangus Coloradas acknowledged to the mouth of the
cave, which framed an endless plain covered with
snow. "But if ever I meet him again, I shall be ready."

On the basalt floor lay a wooden handle, a roundish
rock the size of three fists, and a square of rawhide.
Mangus Coloradas placed the rock into the rawhide
pouch and tied it to one end of the wooden handle,
leaving enough slack for flexibility, the better to frac-
ture an enemy's skull. Then he fashioned buckskin
around the handle, so it wouldn't slip out of his hand,
with a length of rawhide to loop around his wrist, as
a final safety measure.

When finished, he held the war club in his right
hand, stood, and brandished it as if an enemy were
standing before him. "Sunny Hair is a great chief of
the White Eyes," he intoned, "but ..." He brought
the club down swiftly, crushing the skull of the gold-
haired phantom standing before him.

Maria Dolores Carbajal had made another substantial contribution to Holy Mother Church, and Father
Paolo sat at his desk, trying to figure if he could afford
a school. A knock on the door disturbed his calcula-
tions, and he recalled that Maria Dolores's paramour
had made an appointment.

Father Paolo distrusted deathbed conversions, not
to mention those converting to the faith so they
could marry.

"Come in," he said.

The door opened, and a giant in uniform stood
stiffly in front of him. "Are you Father Paolo?"

"Indeed I am. Have a seat, Lieutenant Barrington."

The pastoral side of his profession had given Father
Paolo experience with many kinds of people, and this
officer appeared a big friendly boy, except for those

calm, determined eyes. "I want to talk with you about marrying Maria Dolores Carbajal, sir."

Father Paolo leaned forward, for a closer look into those steely orbs. "Do you really love her?"

"Definitely."

"Are you aware that Catholic marriage is forever, in good times and bad times, till death do you part? Because, my friend, the bloom is not on the rose forever."

"Father," replied Nathanial, "I saw three of my men get killed two weeks ago, and I'm lucky I'm alive. I've known a few women in my life, but Maria Dolores is the one I want to make a family with. She and I are more similar than is apparent from the outside. I can't explain it, but that's how it is."

"How do you feel about becoming a Catholic?"

"Fine with me."

"I imagine you'd become a Ubangi for Maria Dolores. But the Church isn't just a place where people get married. It is the body of Christ. Will you raise your children as Catholics?"

Now it was Nathanial's turn to lean forward, and his nose was four inches from Father Paolo's. "I can't live without Maria Dolores, and I'll do anything for her, even if it means kissing the Pope's ring."

"Mother, may I speak with you alone?"

Mrs. Harding was supervising slaves in the kitchen as she noticed her daughter in the doorway. "Of course, dear."

Rebecca was twitching, and her face looked lopsided, with her eyes red from crying. She had been eating like a bird, and her cheekbones showed starkly on her pallid face. "Mother, I want to leave this place. Can you and Father lend me some money?"

"Where will you go?"

"To Savannah, where I'll live with Aunt Barbara. I mean no insult to you and Father, but I need to return to civilization as quickly as possible. This horrid little camp is making me sick, I'm afraid."

Mrs. Harding knew what was making her daughter sick. "It's a dangerous journey for a woman traveling alone that distance. We'll have to wait until soldiers head in that direction, and it might be months."

"I'm willing to go by stagecoach, and I don't need an escort. The worst Indians are south of here, not in the direction I'm going."

There was a knock, then Francine dried her hands on her apron. She opened the front door, and Rebecca heard a slow Southern drawl say, "Is Miss Harding available?"

"Who shall I say is calling."

"Lieutenant Beauregard Hargreaves."

Francine closed the door in his face, then walked to the parlor, where mother and daughter were arguing quietly. "I don't want to talk with anybody," hissed Rebecca.

"But it's unhealthy to spend so much time alone, dear," said her mother. "Why don't you go for a walk with him? Might do you good."

"Mother, everybody knows that Lieutenant Hargreaves is the worst drunkard in the camp, even worse than someone else whose name I won't mention."

"I've always considered Lieutenant Hargreaves a delightful conversationalist, and it's only a walk."

"But it's too embarrassing!"

"Only because you make it so. You should talk to people your own age, like Lieutenant Hargreaves. His father is supposed to be quite wealthy, by the way. The Hargreaves family owns a big plantation in South Carolina."

"But I look so ugly."

"Are you going to hide for the rest of your life, just because of a man?"

Maybe she's right about that, Rebecca thought. She looked in the mirror, pinched her cheeks, and smoothed down her hair. Then she threw a shawl over her shoulders and opened the front door. Lieutenant Hargreaves stood on the stoop casually, puffing a cigarette, his wide-brimmed hat low over his eyes. "Howdy, Rebecca," he said, a self-confident smirk on his roundish face. "Care to take a walk?"

"Where?" she asked.

"Anywhere you want."

Side by side, they passed down Officers' Row, headed toward the main gate. "I was afraid you wouldn't come with me," he admitted, the cigarette in his teeth.

"This is quite a surprise," she replied. "It's been my impression that you've always avoided me like the plague, Lieutenant Hargreaves."

"I've always been afraid of offending you, Miss Harding, but I've wanted to talk with you about Nathanial."

She froze at the sound of his name. "Please don't ever mention him to me again."

"He feels terrible that you're angry, because he really likes you, Rebecca."

"He's a brute." She stopped in the middle of the parade ground. "I don't think I want to go anywhere with you."

"Don't hold a grudge, because a grudge is a worm that eats you from within," pleaded Beau.

"It may interest you to know that Lieutenant Barrington pretended that he was going to marry me, and then ran off with that ... woman."

"I'm not surprised," chortled Beau. "Even I was mad about Maria Dolores at one time, but all the ladies are in love with Nathanial wherever he goes. I don't understand it, except he's the kindest man I've ever known, and when it comes to courage under fire, Nathanial is incredible. You should have seen him at Palo Alto."

"I detest him and everything he stands for," replied Rebecca.

"They say that hate and love are sides of the same

coin, but I have another reason for calling on you tonight, my dear Rebecca. If you want to marry somebody, why don't you marry me?"

Diego Carbajal sat in his office, wearing skullcap and prayer shawl, studying Torah. The door was locked, drapes covered the window, and he was ready to toss everything into the open drawer at the first threatening sound. Nobody was going to pull out his fingernails, if he could help it.

The religious background bequeathed by his father had been heavily spiced by the Zohar, the so-called Book of Radiance written by the Cabalists of Old Spain, and it lay before him on the desk.

Rabbi Simeon then rose and spoke: In prayer, I have envisioned that when G-d was prepared to create man, then in the upper and lower worlds, all beings trembled with fear.

Every word had infinite possibilities, according to the Holy Cabala, for they had been written by His Holy Name through the minds and hands of the patriarchs and prophets. There were layers beneath layers, like an onion that had no boundaries.

Diego burped, for he'd been overeating as of late. His daughter had become rich, and he often found himself overindulging in food, an evil impulse that he needed to defeat. Sometimes, in states of deep meditation, he suspected that G-d had made them prosperous so Diego could study Torah. According to the Tradition, studying the word of God was the most significant thing a man could do. He opened a black tome at random, and his eyes fell on:

And this is the law which Moses delivered to the children of Israel, after they came up out of the land of the Egyptians.

The twists and turns on the paper were not mere words written by men, but eternal expressions of the Almighty written in fire on Mount Sinai, thought Diego deliriously, for he'd polished off a bottle of wine with lunch.

He heard footsteps in the corridor, and suddenly prayer shawl, skullcap, mighty Torah, and glorious Book of Radiance were flying into the drawer. It slammed shut, then he leapt to his feet and unlocked the door. It was their maid, Luisa, looking at him curiously. "Are you all right, sir? You look strange."

"What is wrong?"

"Time for supper, Senor Carbajal."

He often lost track of time when studying Torah. "I'll be right down."

She wrinkled her brown nose as she peered around the room. "What do you do here, sir?"

"I read books."

"You should get some fresh air and move around a little."

She looked at him askance, then closed the door. His heart beat rapidly and he gasped for breath, for the transformation of the Talmudic scholar to Senor Carbajal and back again had made him confused. He reopened the drawer, folded his religious articles carefully, and was returning them when there was another knock on the door.

"Who is it?" he asked, slamming the drawer shut.

"Me," said his daughter as she entered the room. "There's something I want to tell you. Guess what? I'm getting married to Lieutenant Barrington. The ceremony is the last Sunday of the month, so you will have plenty of time to buy a new suit. And you are going to give me away, Daddy."

"Me?"

"Are you not my father?"

"Are you in love with him?"

"I wouldn't marry a man I did not love."

Diego narrowed one eye and looked at her for a

few moments. Then he stepped behind her and latched
the door. Finally he stood before her again. "You may
marry whomever you want, but you must promise that
you will never mention . . ."

"Father—this is America, and nobody cares about
those things anymore."

"If you do not promise, I will not give you away."

"But my husband has a right to know what I am!"

"My rights are greater than his, because I am your
father. Besides, you are a Mexican Catholic, and so
am I." The old Talmudic scholar wrapped her in his
arms and kissed her forehead warmly. "Do not look
for trouble, my dear girl. Be satisfied with what you
are. I am sure he is a decent young man—congratulations. Is he going to ask for your hand?"

"Not unless you want him to."

Diego dropped into his chair, propped his chin in
his hand, and thought for a few moments. "If your
husband ever asks about me, just tell him that your
father is a demented old recluse and he should be
left alone."

"Must we lie about *everything*, Father?"

He looked into her eyes and replied vehemently,
"Yes!"

Delicate crystals of snow fell on Washington Square
as Amalia Barrington sat in the dining room of her
home, sipping coffee and reading the *New York Daily
Times*. Before her sat a half-eaten corn muffin as Shirley Rooney entered with the mail. "A letter from Nathanial, ma'am."

Amalia faltered, because she wondered how much
money he needed this time. "Please leave me alone."

Shirley cleared away the dirty dishes, poured a fresh
cup of coffee, and meekly retreated from the room,
mumbling something unintelligible, for she'd been
going slightly daft lately. Fortunately Otis had shown
up at the right time, and now was butler, footman,

assistant cook, and all around workman at the mansion on Washington Square.

Amalia waited for the door to close, then transformed into an eager little vixen as she tore the letter open. She narrowed her eyes, read feverishly, stopped suddenly, went back and read again, then stared into space, dropping the letter to the floor. I've always known that Nathanial was outrageous, she said to herself, but never dreamed he'd marry a ... Mexican. Then she recalled that Mexicans were Roman Catholics!

Tobey opened the door and saw his adoptive mother sprawled on the floor, out cold. He yelled for help, touched his hand to her white cheek, and watched her eyes open, as Jeffrey, Shirley, and Otis rushed into the dining room.

"What happened?" asked Jeffrey.

Amalia tried to smile. "Your brother is getting married, and we must all rejoice."

"But why are you on the floor, Mother?"

"I must've fallen asleep."

Jeffrey and Tobey exchanged meaningful glances as they helped her to her feet. Then Tobey asked, "Who'd he marry?"

"Why ... a beautiful Mexican girl from a lovely family. I'm sure they'll be very happy together, and now, if you'll excuse me, I'd like to be alone."

She walked unsteadily out of the dining room, the letter in her hand, and everybody expected her to collapse again at any moment, but she made it to the stairs, and they heard her climbing to her sitting room.

Nobody ever dared enter her sanctuary without precise instructions. She closed the door behind her, dropped onto the nearest chair, and gazed out the window at Washington Square blanketed with snow.

It was here that she brooded, cried, and slammed her fists on the table. That ungrateful no-good brat, she stewed. Naturally he married the kind of woman of whom I would disapprove, a woman not of our class, background, religion, or anything. It's as if he wants to punish his father and me by disgracing himself thoroughly.

She wondered how it could be that a piece of her own flesh, nurtured inside her womb, could behave in such an opposite manner. It was as though she were at war with herself, but Nathanial had been a difficult child since birth, and never liked any of the maids hired to raise him, no matter how hard they tried to please him. He'd been spoiled all his life, Amalia decided, and soon he'll bring half-breed children into the world. Amalia shook her head and sighed wearily. He'd been her first child, the son she'd always dreamed of having, and she would love him forever, but had to confess, in the privacy of her sitting room, that he'd ruptured her fragile little world yet again.

He cares only about his own selfish desires, she concluded. One day I'll have to meet this ... creature that he has taken to his bosom, his wife, or whatever she's supposed to be, or maybe he'll divorce her and marry an Eskimo, because anything is possible with Nathanial, and the more bizarre, the more likely he'll do it. It's as though he's pushing at the edges of the world, to see how far he can go.

TWENTY

On March 1, 1849, President-elect Zachary Taylor arrived in Washington, D.C., for his inauguration. Rockets shot into the air, bonfires blazed alongside the railroad tracks, and a reporter from the *Intelligencer* wrote that Old Rough and Ready had been met by the largest gathering ever seen in the nation's capital.

The short, stout general stood on the railroad platform next to his bags and bowed his hoary gray head as waves of applause rolled over him. He was a simple soldier from the wild frontier, and the outpouring of affection moved him deeply. When the cheering diminished, he addressed the people briefly in his booming parade-ground voice, the one that had ordered Lieutenant Ker's dragoons to counterattack at Palo Alto less than three years ago. "Heaven bless you, citizens!" he declared. "Peace be with you!"

A middle-aged woman rushed from the crowd, and his aides thought she was a demented assassin, but instead she clasped his hands warmly. "I hope you can bring America together, sir," she said sincerely, peering into his eyes.

"I am your humble servant, ma'am," he replied.

Zachary Taylor's sharp soldier's eyes spotted an elderly workman in the swarms of citizens and made his way toward him to shake his hand. "It does my heart good to see you, sir," the general confided. "Like myself, you are an old man, and it seems that everybody else around us is in the prime of life."

The crowd thundered approval as the President-elect and his entourage proceeded to the Willard Hotel. His first duty call was to President Polk at the White House, but it was a cold official encounter, and General Taylor had the distinct impression that Polk was in ill health. Then, back at the hotel, General Taylor met Senator Cass, whom he'd defeated in the election. Both men were exceedingly polite, although the campaign had been bitterly fought, filled with personal invective, and both sides had played cavalierly with facts, as befits any American presidential campaign.

It was cloudy on March 5, 1849, and church bells pealed across Washington, D.C., as military bands played patriotic tunes. One hundred mounted marshals escorted General Taylor's carriage to the Irving Hotel, where stony-faced President Polk boarded. They were accompanied by Robert Charles Winthrop of Massachusetts, speaker of the House, and General Taylor waved warmly to masses of boisterous Americans as the carriage rolled down Pennsylvania Avenue. "Ain't he a hoss?" a Virginia shopkeeper cried. Some had traveled hundreds of miles to see the hero of Palo Alto, Monterrey, and Buena Vista.

President Polk felt dispirited, for the cheers were not aimed at him. He was the despised President, although he'd given America vast territory that the people had coveted. The unforeseen consequence was the annexation of Texas had opened a new snakepit of national divisiveness over the slavery issue, and finally driven him from office. Meanwhile, paradoxically, General Taylor was considered a savior for winning the identical controversial war! President Polk observed General Taylor receiving accolades from the crowd, and thought, *He is a well-meaning old man, but is uneducated, exceedingly ignorant of public affairs, and, I should judge, of very ordinary capacity. He will be in the hands of others, forced to rely wholly upon his cabinet to administer the government.*

The procession stopped in front of the Capitol, and

the President-elect, surrounded by family, friends, supporters, and reporters, proceeded to a specially erected platform in front of the east portico. Thirty thousand citizens had gathered at the spot, and the old soldier gave thanks to the Almighty for offering the highest honor of all to a Kentucky farmer's son.

Well-wishers crowded and jostled him, his gnarled hand was shaken again and again, and he saw smiles of falsehood, gallons of flattery, and tons of deceit, because everyone had a son or brother needing a job in the government, or a business deal, an angle, or possessed a scheme to improve the world.

Speaker of the House Winthrop introduced the President-elect with glowing praise, and finally the time had come for Old Rough and Ready to speak to America, prior to being inaugurated.

The audience became quiet as the old soldier with the face of a kindly bulldog mounted the podium. No one had ever called him a great orator, like Daniel Webster, Henry Clay, or James C. Calhoun, all in attendance that day, but he spoke simply, in a low voice, and first expressed gratitude for the confidence that the people had shown in him. He acknowledged the "fearful responsibilities" of the presidency. He promised to bring the most qualified people into his administration, and then Zachary Taylor said, "With such aides, and an honest purpose to do what is right, I hope to execute diligently and impartially, and for the best interests of the country, the manifold duties devolving upon me. In the discharge of these duties, my guide will be the Constitution I this day swear to preserve, protect, and defend."

Later in the speech, touching on foreign policy, Zachary Taylor said, "We are warned by the admonition of history, and the voice of our own beloved George Washington, to abstain from entangling alliances with foreign nations on all disputes between conflicting governments. It is our interest, no less our duty, to remain strictly neutral."

Regarding slavery, Zachary Taylor said, "I shall look to the enlightened patriotism of the Congress to adopt such measures of conciliation as may harmonize conflicting interests, and tend to perpetuate the Union, which should be the paramount objection of our hopes and affections."

Standing at the edge of that great assembly, recently defeated Whig Congressman Abe Lincoln nodded sagely. A crescendo of applause erupted from the crowd, which he joined optimistically. But Honest Abe knew that mere words couldn't save the Union, and much difficult legislation lay ahead. A conflagration of hatred and animosity was engulfing the land, and the self-taught Illinois lawyer wondered if any leader, no matter how honorable or talented, could quell it.

Next day, the Richmond *Whig* reported that the speech had been "short, pithy, and to the purpose." Enthusiastically, it predicted a return to an era "of Presidents who were great even when there were giants in the land."

In the remote New Mexico Territory, far from the tumult of national politics, Nathanial and Maria Dolores Barrington resided in an adobe home midway between Camp Marcy and the Silver Palace Saloon. In the evenings, after supper, they usually repaired to their office, to complete final tasks for the day.

It was their favorite room, though one of the smallest in their modest home. Their desks were jammed side by side, illuminated by two candles, and they sat only inches apart as they pursued their varying interests.

Maria Dolores still managed the Silver Palace Saloon, always adding new wings, plus investing in Santa Fe real estate, betting her growing fortune that it would remain an important commercial center. She was learning to love the freedom of America, because it didn't matter who your parents were or where they were born. Zachary Taylor, who'd grown up among wild Indians, had become not only a great general but President of the United States.

But most of all, she had to admit to herself, the greatest advantage was Nathanial himself, always so amenable to her wishes, attentive in every way, except for about one major fight per month, when chinaware would be broken, and each would sulk for a few days.

Maria Dolores glanced at him bent over books and maps, always studying, searching for meanings, trying to understand purposes. It wasn't difficult to visualize the West Point cadet studying for the big examination, yet he was unpretentious, with a mischievous choirboy lurking barely beneath the surface. I have never been so happy in my life, she knew. No matter what happens, I will always have these evenings with Nathanial.

An arm's length away, paging through history tomes, Nathanial believed that the key to the nineteenth century could be found in the carefully examined career of Napoleon Bonaparte, whom the West Pointer considered the single most important personage of the century thus far. How is it, wondered Nathanial, that a Corsican nonentity could become first Emperor of France, and then end imprisoned on St. Helena Island, where he'd died only twenty-eight years ago.

Nathanial thought that Napoleon could be best understood through study of his 1812 invasion of Russia, where he and his Grand Armée not only had been defeated, but effectively destroyed. Nathanial wondered whether the flaw had been bad strategy, wrong tactics, poor intelligence, or one man's overweening pride? Some historians whom he studied considered Napoleon a fiend from hell, while others spoke of him in the same breath as Julius Caesar and Alexander the Great. How could the greatest military genius of the century make such a horrendous decision? pondered Nathanial. Why didn't he understand the logistical nightmare of Russia, the vast spaces to be crossed, the loyalty of the people to the tsar, and the ferocity of the Russian winter?

Nathanial believed that the lessons of Napoleon's 1812 campaign could be applied to New Mexico Territory, 1849. As in Russia, immense distances comprised the main obstacle, and then came vicious climate, plus constant guerrilla warfare. Like the Russians in initial stages of the invasion, the Apaches also avoided costly battles, in the hope of wearing their opponents down and catching them unawares.

Nathanial planned to utilize stirring examples from history in a letter he was writing to President Zachary Taylor, his former commanding officer. He suspected that Old Rough and Ready would never read it, but wanted to remind the general of their happy times together, and then the ambitious first lieutenant intended to present his thoughts on how to solve the Indian problem. If the newly elected President decided to appoint Nathanial as Secretary of Indian Affairs, so much the better. He held up the sheet of paper, examining the draft once more, when he heard the voice of his beloved wife.

"I'm tired," she said.

It was the same every night, but Nathanial never complained. He enjoyed retiring early for many complex reasons, not least of which was appearing alert and sober when reporting for duty in the morning. He blew out the candles, as his wife headed for the bedroom.

It was located at the rear of the house, and consisted of a bed, two dressers, and a closet, with a three-foot crucifix nailed to the wall above the headboard. They washed in the basin, undressed in the darkness, and he joined her in the bed.

Their naked bodies touched, just as they had so many other times, but Nathanial still couldn't get enough of her. It gave him great pleasure to know that she'd be there every night, and for once, he'd made the right decision.

He nibbled her ear as he recalled their wedding day. Diego gave the bride away, Beauregard was best man, and the matron of honor was a Mexican woman whom Nathanial never had met before and never had seen since. Nathanial had taken a snort of whiskey prior to the ceremony, and felt as if God Almighty were in attendance, sanctifying Nathanial's formerly meaningless life.

But now the wedding was over, and the newly marrieds were snug in their little bed, authorized by God to perform acts forbidden to single folk. He placed his big right hand atop her melonlike left breast and nearly fainted with joy. This was a main course of a woman, not a dainty hors d'oeuvres or frothy dessert. Since their wedding, he'd made love with her at all hours of days and nights, engaging in every intimate act imaginable, and he still wanted more.

He chewed his way up her thigh as she gripped his hair in her fingers and thrashed her head from side to side. She was healthy and energetic, yet soft and wonderfully pliable, and he didn't have to worry about smashing her to pieces, like the little women he'd slept with previously.

The crowning glory was that she seemed to really love him. Somehow, through the grace of God, the vestal virgin had given herself to the scoundrel Nathanial Barrington, but sometimes he regretted that he himself had not been pure. He often wondered what Elysian heights they might have reached if he had possessed the virtue of his wife.

What he lacked in religion, he made up with experience, as he maneuvered her into positions that shattered him with their sheer perversity. Sometimes he thought he was flying with the angels, as he rocked her gently, and sometimes not-so-gently, into the night.

Three days later, he completed the letter to President Taylor. The missive was duly mailed by him at the camp next morning and journeyed in a bag via stagecoach, riverboat, and railroad, appearing at the post office in Washington, D.C., approximately one month later.

A special White House clerk picked up the mail for the President, carried it in an army carriage to the White House, dumped it on a desk in the basement, and began to sort the huge pile.

Correspondents requested jobs, demanded results, scrawled mean threats, made inquiries, complained about roads, and every other conceivable subject. The clerk wasn't an evil man, or even especially political, but he had to glean the wheat from the chaff.

Near the bottom of the pile, he came to a letter postmarked Fort Marcy, New Mexico Territory. It was stained, wrinkled, with a dried coffee drop blurring the return address. The clerk opened the letter, and it sounded like another crackpot military scheme, with a not-so-subtle request for a job, and the writer had taken great pains to show his great erudition, whereas Old Rough and Ready, with his failing eyesight and heavy workload, couldn't be expected to read each scrap of paper. I guess every officer was a close personal friend of the general's, the clerk thought wryly as he dropped the letter into the wastebasket.

Following the presidential honeymoon, the press attacked General Taylor for giving too many government jobs to Whig cronies and not to the cronies of the opposition. Then the most critical issue became the national exercise in maintaining parity in the Senate between North and South, or in other words the slavery issue.

If California was admitted as a free state, as seemed likely, the Senate would become unbalanced against the South. The greatest orators of the day, including Stephen A. Douglas of Illinois, Salmon P. Chase of Ohio, and Jefferson Davis of Louisiana, fenced with words in the halls of the Capitol as they tried to determine a just solution. The debate became so acrimonious that Senator Davis confided to his wife that the current session of Congress might well be the last. One day, John C. Calhoun of South Carolina stood on the floor of the Senate and declared angrily, "We have borne the wrongs and insults long enough!"

The sectional crisis that threatened America frustrated newly elected President Taylor's efforts to seek a just solution. Sixty-five years old, battered by a lifetime of arduous frontier campaigning, he couldn't conceive how to reconcile warring factions, and neither could anybody else.

He had bought a plantation in Louisiana, owned three hundred slaves, but believed slavery shouldn't be extended to new territories. On the other hand, he felt no compelling need to overthrow basic institutions, because national catastrophe would doubtlessly result. Like James Knox Polk, the new President had become hopelessly entangled in the slavery trap.

On March 7, 1850, in a speech before abolitionists, he infuriated them by requesting that they try to compromise with slave owners. Meanwhile, Southerners worried that he'd sell out their interests, although old Rough and Ready had never betrayed anybody in his life.

Plagued with illness, racked by the responsibilities of the presidency, Zachary Taylor's last great battle was called the Compromise of 1850. It provided that California would become a free state, to balance Texas, the new slave state. Texas would relinquish claims to New Mexico, while the slave trade would be abolished in Washington, D.C. In addition, a tough new fugitive slave law was written to appease Southerners.

The great crisis had passed for the time being, although neither North nor South was satisfied with the new arrangement. The press had to find something new to sell papers, and it wasn't long before news of financial improprieties surfaced among Zachary Taylor's circle of advisers. Then another boundary dispute between Texas and Mexico erupted, with both sides expressing willingness to go to war again, and Zachary Taylor was blamed by some Americans, because he'd followed orders and whupped Santa Anna's army. There was talk of impeachment, and Senator Cass accused President Taylor of military usurpation of the United States Government.

Old Rough and Ready felt more embattled than at Buena Vista, but no longer could he throw Captain Braxton Bragg's artillery battery into the breach, with the First Mississippi Rifles providing cover. His conscience was clear, he had shown no special favors, but the drumbeat of criticism continued unrelentingly. He felt ancient, fatigued, surrounded by the yapping dogs of the press, and feared that American was becoming a failed dream.

On the Fourth of July, 1850, President Zachary Taylor was featured at the celebration in front of the Washington Monument then under construction in the Mall. He felt feverish in the sunbaked stands, listening to innumerable speeches. That night, after supper, he complained of cramps.

Dr. Robert Charles Wood, his son-in-law and the White House physician, advised him to go to bed. Upon retiring, President Zachary Taylor told his male nurse, "I did not expect to encounter what has come to me in this office. God knows, I have tried to do my honest duty. But I have made mistakes, my motives have been misconstrued, and my feelings have been outraged."

On the ninth of July, as Andrew Pickens Butler of South Carolina was delivering a tirade in defense of slavery on the floor of the Senate, several presidential aides entered the chamber in a great hurry. A hush fell over the gathering as Senator Butler halted his histrionics. The aides made their way to Senator Daniel Webster of Massachusetts, whose craggy visage scowled at the receipt of a message. Then he raised his massive forehead, walked forthrightly to the podium, and Senator Butler stepped backward, because it was clear that something extraordinary had happened.

Senator Webster took his place before the august body and peered gravely at his fellow statesmen. "I have a sorrowful message to deliver to the Senate," he said in the ringing voice that had earned him international acclaim. "A great misfortune threatens this nation. The President of the United States is dying, and may not survive this day."

The next morning the great bell tolled in the dome of the State Department and was answered by every belfry in Washington. Zachary Taylor had succumbed during the night, and the nation mourned the man they had attacked so strenuously the day before.

On the thirteenth, the funeral cortege left the White House, and at its head, on a spirited horse, rode General Winfield Scott, attired in an immaculate blue uniform, with yellow plumes sprouting from his tall helmet. Detachments of soldiers, sailors, and marines followed him, plus formations of civil and fraternal organizations. Along the procession's route, cannon were fired from nearby parks, saluting the nation's great soldier. Multitudes wept along the side of the road, as the hero of Buena Vista rolled unswervingly toward the Congressional Cemetery.

The funeral carriage was drawn by eight white horses, each led by a Negro in a white suit. In the bier, the coffin was sheltered by a canopy of white satin, held aloft by poles topped with golden eagles. And tethered to the bier, walking behind slowly with his head low, was Old Whitey, carrying an empty saddle, with his master's boots reversed in the stirrups.

Certain ironies weren't lost on General Scott that day, for he'd competed against General Taylor during their rise in the private club of the officers' corps. But General Scott had seen much action too, and knew that Old Rough and Ready had been a fine soldier. Rocking back and forth in his saddle, General Scott was reminded of the line from Shakespeare, when

Marc Antony declaimed about just-assassinated Caesar. *From whence comes such another?* the old warrior
asked himself as he rode the last mile with his former adversary.

Vice President Millard Fillmore of New York ascended to the presidency and swore to follow the poli-
cies of Zachary Taylor. One of the ongoing foreign
policy issues was the border dispute with Mexico, and
in the spring of 1850, a special commission was organized to visit New Mexico and study the situation
firsthand.

The Boundary Commission would be headed by
John Bartlett, a New York businessman and antiquar-
ian. Since Apaches were active in the area, naturally
he'd require a military escort. Major Harding still
hadn't forgiven Nathanial for spurning his daughter,
now married to Lieutenant Hargreaves, and decided
the time had come to get even. Shortly thereafter Nathanial received orders posting him to Bartlett's staff.

The Commission's camp was scheduled for establishment at the Santa Rita Copper Mines, site of the
bloodiest massacre in Apache history. Twelve hundred
warriors were said to reside in the vicinity, led by the
great chief Mangus Coloradas, so Nathanial couldn't
bring his pregnant wife with him. As the time drew
closer to the date of his departure, he sought ways to
spend time with her, and she remained home more,
to comfort him in the best way she knew how.

On the intermittently sunny Sunday before he left,
a group of Camp Marcy officers, wives, and children,
plus armed guards, rode to the top of a nearby peak
in the Sangre de Cristo Mountains, for a last picnic
together. Nathanial was depressed about separation
from his wife, but tried to smile as he spread the blanket a distance away from the others, so he could be
alone with her.

Maria Dolores was troubled and great with child,
needing him more than usual. "You can always resign

your commission," she said softly, so others wouldn't hear.

"Soldiering is all I know," he replied, "and I can't conceive of doing anything else. Besides, don't you think this land is worth fighting for?"

"You have fought enough for this land. It is time to let someone else do the killing for a change."

He loved her logical mind, and frequently could think of no rejoinder to her arguments. At those times he had to content himself with merely observing her maternal magnificence. No longer was she the shy vestal virgin of Santa Fe, but had transmogrified into the Madonna of the Sangre de Cristo Mountains. He placed his hand on her stomach bursting with life, wondering if it would be a boy or girl, and whether there'd be a United States of America by then.

Maria Dolores placed her palm on the back of his hand, pressing him against her belly, and he felt the outline of his child sleeping in her womb. Meanwhile, the sun peeked through clouds, illuminating stupendous vistas of purple and gold. The Barringtons were so high, they could look down on hawks riding updrafts, searching for wayward mice and lizards. In the distance, rain clouds drifted across the sky, drenching great expanses that lay in their path, as the couple sat in bright sunlight.

"Look!" he said.

She glanced up at a red-tailed hawk hovering above them, studying the aliens with great interest, wondering if they were food. The West Point officer and Mexican lady of secret origins arose with their arms around each other's waists, viewing stunning perspectives in all directions. They saw towns, farms, and on the horizon Nathanial thought he spotted a raiding party of Apaches, but they might've been a flock of swallows, for he was disoriented by the sheer magnitude of the land.

Rays of sunshine beamed down on the great panorama of the Southwest, a rich kingdom for which

Nathanial had already spilled his blood. The power of the land surged through him as the arm of his wife encircled him. He felt oddly exalted, realizing that his direction had been fundamentally sound, regardless of low tendencies he'd developed as a single man. But his quest was finally over, and demons no longer afflicted him as persistently. Although Boston and Charleston clamored for war, and twelve hundred Apaches were waiting for him at the Santa Rita Copper Mines, led by the great chief Mangus Coloradas, he found joy with his growing family, and it would sustain him in the difficult trials that lay ahead.

"God, I love this land," he whispered. "Don't you, Maria Dolores?"

The child within her stirred. "I will never forget this day," she replied. "No matter where we live, we shall always be together in our hearts."

Hawks sang melodiously above them as Nathanial and Maria Dolores stood for a long time, arms entwined, gazing in awe at the splendor of America.
